A WITCH

is a powerful work of magic dark and bright brewed up for you in this volume are potent enough to sweep you out of the everyday world into the realms of the truly fantastic. So if you dare, sample such enchanting fare as:

"Dealing in Futures"—When a Nexus is bound to Earth, even the greatest enchantresses of all time may lose their grip on the past, present, and future. . . .

"The Witch's Cat"—Will a bargain made between wizard and witch determine who ascends to England's throne?

"Birds of a Feather"—When technology and witchcraft combine, an untimely computer glitch could prove a warlock's undoing. . . .

"Threefold to You"—Forced to cast a spell at the king's bidding, she could not be responsible for the consequences. . . .

WITCH FANTASTIC

Other FANTASTIC Anthologies
from DAW Books:

CATFANTASTIC I, II, and III *Edited by Andre Norton and Martin H. Greenberg.* For cat lovers everywhere, three delightful collections of fantastical cat tales, some set in the distant future on as yet unknown worlds, some set in our own world but not quite our own dimension, some recounting what happens when creatures out of myth collide with modern-day felines.

DINOSAUR FANTASTIC *Edited by Mike Resnick and Martin H. Greenberg.* From their native Jurassic landscape to your own backyard, from their ancient mastery of the planet to modern-day curiosities trapped in an age not their own, here are unforgettable, all-original tales, some poignant, some humorous, some offering answers to the greatest puzzle of prehistory, but all certain to capture the hearts and imaginations of dinosaur lovers of all ages.

DRAGON FANTASTIC *Edited by Rosalind M. Greenberg and Martin H. Greenberg. With an Introduction by Tad Williams.* From a virtual reality watch dragon to a once-a-century get-together of the world's winged destroyers, here are swift-winging fantasies by such talents as Alan Dean Foster, Mickey Zucker Reichert, Esther Friesner, and Dennis McKiernan.

HORSE FANTASTIC *Edited by Rosalind M. Greenberg and Martin H. Greenberg. With an Introduction by Jennifer Roberson.* From a racer death couldn't keep from the finish line to a horse with the devil in him, here are magical tales by such top writers as Jennifer Roberson, Mercedes Lackey, Mickey Zucker Reichert, Judith Tarr, and Mike Resnick.

WITCH FANTASTIC

Edited by
Mike Resnick and
Martin H. Greenberg

DAW BOOKS, INC.

DONALD A. WOLLHEIM, FOUNDER

375 Hudson Street, New York, NY 10014

ELIZABETH R. WOLLHEIM
SHEILA E. GILBERT
PUBLISHERS

First Printing, January 1995

1 2 3 4 5 6 7 8 9

DAW TRADEMARK REGISTERED
U.S. PAT. OFF. AND FOREIGN COUNTRIES
—MARCA REGISTRADA
HECHO EN U.S.A.

PRINTED IN THE U.S.A.

ACKNOWLEDGMENTS

Introduction © 1995 by Mike Resnick.
Clotilde La Bruja © 1995 by James Stevens-Arce.
Our Lady of the Toads © 1995 by Deborah Wheeler.
Dealing in Futures © 1995 by Judith Tarr.
Circles © 1995 by Jane Yolen.
In a Yellow Dress © 1995 by Jo Clayton.
The Witch's Cat © 1995 by Byron Tetrick.
The Swineherd © 1995 by Lois Tilton.
Miracle at Devil's Crick © 1995 by Jeffry Dwight.
Giant Trouble © 1995 by Katharine Kerr.
Spell Check © 1995 by Terry McGarry.
Birds of a Feather © 1995 by Charles von Rospach.
Lose Weight Like Magic © 1995 by Linda J. Dunn.
Witch Doctor © 1995 by Kate Daniel.
The Trouble with Big Brothers © 1995 by Nina Kiriki Hoffman.
Witch-Horse © 1995 by Josepha Sherman.
Glamour Profession © 1995 by Beth Meacham.
Witch War © 1995 by L. Emerson Wolfe.
Till Death Do Us Part © 1995 by Sandra Rector and P. M. F. Johnson.
Threefold to You © 1995 by Deborah Millitello.
Taking Back the Night © 1995 by ElizaBeth Gilligan.
Witch Garden © 1995 by James D. Macdonald and Debra Doyle.
An Eye for Acquisitions © 1995 by Bruce Holland Rogers.
Diddling with Grandmother's Iron Maiden © 1995 by Nicholas A. DiChario.
The Three Tears © 1995 by Byron Tetrick.
That Old Black Magic © 1995 by Deborah J. Wunder.
The Journal of #3 Honeysuckle Lane © 1995 by Lea Hernandez.
Wooden Characters © 1995 by Roland J. Green.
The Witches of Delight © 1995 by Kathe Koja and Barry N. Malzberg.
Stock Answer © 1995 by Leah A. Zeldes.
The Hidden Grove © 1995 by Michelle Sagara.
An Un-Familiar Magic © 1995 by Mel. White.
The Spell © 1995 by David Gerrold.

CONTENTS

Introduction

Some themes are ephemeral. Like, for example, espionage stories in which Russia is the Bad Guy. Their time has passed, never to return.

Some themes are topical. Such as stories about dinosaurs, which have been given a temporary boost in the public consciousness by Steven Spielberg.

Some themes are recurring. Like cowboys. They've been popular before; we're just finishing up a decade in which you couldn't *give* a cowboy story away if your name wasn't Louis L'Amour; and now they seem to be making a comeback.

And a very few themes have such power over the human imagination that they are eternal.

Like witches.

They come in all shapes, sizes, and flavors. They can be horrifying or hilarious, beautiful or ugly, well-intentioned or fiendish, objects of fear or objects of sympathy. The one thing they all have in common is that they represent the supernatural, that secret side of the world that we claim to disdain, but from which we hide under the covers when we find ourselves alone.

And just as witches come in all flavors, so do those who write about them. This anthology features brand new writers such as ElizaBeth Gilligan, Byron Tetrick, and Leah A. Zeldes; rising stars like Nicholas A. DiChario, Michelle Sagara, and Deborah Wheeler; and journeyman pros like Judith Tarr, David Gerrold, Katharine Kerr, Barry Malzberg, and Jane Yolen. (And if you'll just step over to the Table of Contents, you'll find 23 *additional* authors waiting for you.)

They all have one thing in common: they were willing to suspend their disbelief in witches long enough to write these stories—which are intended, in turn, to make you suspend your own.

—Mike Resnick

CLOTILDE LA BRUJA

by James Stevens-Arce

The witch woman's skin was black as tar, and the flickering lantern light gouged such fearsome shadows into her crushed eye socket and shattered features as to render her more grotesque than any *bruja* Don Ignacio could have imagined. Worse, her one good eye fixed him with so rancid a glare as to fill his already queasy belly with dread.

"What is it you wish of me?" the gruesome apparition grunted.

Breath thick with the dark rum he had drunk for courage, the overseer confided his need of a love philter that would make him irresistible to Magdalena Vega.

The African appraised him silently. Her missing teeth and horribly broken face testified to a vicious beating in her youth. The overseer wondered who had done it, and why. But the baleful look in the woman's remaining eye kept him from asking. Instead, he took the phial she pressed into his cold hand, and shoved it deep into his trouser pocket.

"Drink this before the setting of the moon," the witch woman said, "and when next you approach her, she will welcome you."

"What is your price?" the Spaniard mumbled.

The witch woman considered. "To have served as an instrument in the attainment of true love is payment enough."

Did a hint of irony shade that hoarse voice? The woman's single eye gave no clue.

"You are certain she will desire me, old woman?" The overseer fingered the phial in his pocket. "It will go badly for you should you make a fool of me."

The woman's thick lips hooked back in a jagged grin. Ironically, two nights earlier Magdalena Vega had also come here, demanding a *fufú* to make this aloof Asturian desire her most among women. As tradition dictated, the witch woman had lighted tapers in the room's four corners while she prayed to San Antonio, patron saint of marriage, then sacrificed a chicken and invoked the sacred name of Changó, high lord of *santería,* to hedge her bet.

"Will it be as I desire?" Magdalena Vega had asked in a hushed voice.

A half century of practicing the dark profession had taught the witch woman magic was nothing if not unpredictable. A stock answer fended the girl off: "If your faith is strong." Apparently it had been, for now the object of the girl's desire was here declaring the girl the object of *his* desire.

Well, that was what kept the making of magic interesting. Sometimes it worked. And sometimes it didn't. And sometimes a little inside knowledge made all the difference. Such as now.

"The magic will not fail," the witch woman told the overseer. How could it, under the circumstances? Still, mindful to guarantee nothing, she quickly added, "Unless *you* should fail the magic."

Don Ignacio uncorked the phial and raised it to his lips, only to stop, nose crinkled in disgust. "This concoction smells as vile as rotting fish!"

"Proof of its powerful *fufú,*" the witch woman growled.

The overseer turned his face away, fastidiously holding the container at arm's length. "I cannot drink this."

The problem, the old woman suspected, lay in the ripe, finely chopped shark fin she had stirred into the potion for texture as well as stench. Long ago she had learned that her clients equated how evil a draught smelled and tasted with how effective they imagined it would be. Clearly, though, Don Ignacio was an exception.

"Wait." The witch woman wanted this to work. Taking the phial back, she mixed in a powder that lent the liquor a more appetizing bouquet.

"Drink now," she purred, "and Magdalena Vega will be yours."

Her name was Clotilde Molina. But in the town of Aguirre on the south coast of Puerto Rico, people called her la Bruja—though they dared name her witch only when they thought her out of earshot. Her ears were sharper than they supposed, though, and overhearing those dark syllables—*brew*-ha, *brew*-ha, *brew*-ha—would twist her lips into a grim smile. To her face they called her la Comadrona, because she was also the town midwife.

A breeze ruffled the red calico curtains of Clotilde's kitchen window, but did nothing to lessen the afternoon heat inside her weathered wooden shack, a tiny hut cobbled together from bits of salvaged scrap lumber and discarded sheets of corrugated zinc. The old woman studied her reflection in the faded mirror over the sink. Disfigured. Grotesque. Not like when she had still been white man's property. Over those features which could frighten even grown men, memory superimposed the face of a striking young Yoruban woman. High cheekbones. Straight nose. Strong white teeth. An elegant jawline. Ships had still carried sails then, and the scarlet-and-gold flag of Spain had still fluttered over the mayor's office in place of the bestarred red-white-and-blue standard that flew there now.

The witch woman sighed. Despite seventy-five autumns of accumulated wisdom, she still made mistakes. She had fashioned the magic Don Ignacio desired because it coincided with Magdalena's wishes and the girl had owned a special corner of her heart since the sad morning of her birth. There was nothing Clotilde could have done to prevent the tragedy of that day, but a *comadrona's* soul suffers a scar each time she loses the mother, even if the child survives. By helping join Magdalena and the haughty Spaniard, she had thought to bring a bit of happiness into the girl's life. Besides, the man had seemed oddly familiar; a stranger, yet not entirely so.

That had been six months ago. Now Clotilde detested Ignacio Cienfuegos. The wretch had seduced her granddaughter. Taking advantage of Alfonsina's desperate need, he had enticed her with promises of steady work in the fields for her husband, José Juan.

"We needed the money for Carmencita's medicine," Alfonsina had confessed tearfully. "I did it for her."

Clotilde had felt a pang of guilt that none of her potions or spells had been able to help Carmencita. Mind you, she did not for a moment believe Alfonsina's motivations had been purely altruistic, for her granddaughter had always suffered from too roving an eye. But neither did she doubt Carmencita's plight had played its part in Alfonsina's unfaithfulness.

Had she known of this before his first visit, Clotilde thought angrily, Don Ignacio's love philter would have contained worse than rotting sharkfin. Now Alfonsina's belly bulged with that Spanish son of a whore's unborn bastard, while Carmencita still coughed up phlegm spotted with blood into a dirty rag. And Alfonsina's sacrifice had gone for naught. The overseer had reneged on his promise. Each sunrise at the sugar mill's offices when the names of the *peones* lucky enough to be included on Don Ignacio's work roll were read, José Juan's was no longer among them. Men with weaker backs and less experience rode away in the huge trucks that returned at sunset piled high with the sweet harvest, while José Juan was forced to creep back to the shack he shared with Alfonsina and Carmencita, face hot with the humiliation of being helpless to provide for his family or save his daughter.

Overseers. Pah! Clotilde loathed them. Before the Spanish Abolition in 1873, she had suffered the cruelty of one, deeply. In this first quarter of the new century there were no longer slaves, at least not officially. But there were still men like Don Ignacio to control the lives of the poor, the weak, the humble.

Clotilde recalled her overseer, Victoriano Lozada. A *blanco*, a white man, a pure Castilian. How flattering his attentions had been. Hot breath in her ear, he had whispered his need for her, how he wished to make her his wife and a free woman. She had distrusted his words, but only at first. He was the man with the whip, and had no need to lie to her. So Clotilde had finally believed.

Soon she was eagerly anticipating his nightly visits. And the quiet talks after with the only *blanco* who had ever treated her as something more than property. Her heart filled with real affection for him. So the night she confided the good news that she was pregnant with his child, his reaction had more than stunned her. She had expected him to smile and say, "We must wait no longer, then. We must marry now, this month, this *week*." She had not expected him to call her a black whoring bitch. She had not expected his fists to crush her nose and splinter her cheekbones. She had not expected to lie curled up screaming while the steel-tipped toe of his boot burst her left eye, shattered her lips and teeth, fractured her jaw, and sank deep into her belly again, and again, and again.

Oh, the baby! The memory still haunted her. When she lost the child, with it went her trust in the words of white men. She had gained something else in its place, though—a lifelong thirst for revenge.

A year later she became a free woman after all. Not as the beloved wife of Victoriano Lozada, but as a beneficiary of the Spanish Abolition. Victoriano Lozada, that wretched son of a whore, had booked passage on a schooner bound for Mariel to seek better fortune in Cuba. Though countless times since she had worked and reworked the spell that should have brought him back—scorpion's sting and mongoose piss, salamander's tongue and sea slug flesh—Clotilde Molina had never seen him again. Perhaps the obsession had made her a little crazy, but never had she given up hope.

Don Erasto Vega's new 1925 black Cadillac touring sedan glided majestically past Clotilde's shack along the dirt road that bordered Barrio Miseria, the cane cutters' shantytown. The chauffeur sat stiffly behind the wheel, while Don Erasto's daughter Magdalena rode alone in the

rear seat, trying to read a novel she had purchased in
Ponce—*Women in Love,* by a Britisher named Lawrence.
She had heard its racy passages had caused it to be
banned in Boston. Unfortunately, it was in English, not
her strongest subject at school, and the convoluted sen-
tences made little sense to her.

While the car's white sidewall tires bounced over the
ruts and rocks in the road, its heavy-duty Detroit-
manufactured suspension provided its passenger with the
illusion of riding a magic carpet. Magdalena had no idea
that this luxurious experience embodied the very essence
of her lover's greatest desire. To her it was one trivial detail of a monied birthright she had always taken for
granted. As Don Erasto's only child, Magdalena would
one day inherit the old man's vast canefields, his sprawl-
ing sugar mill, his enormous fortune, and his Cadillac,
one of only six such magnificent vehicles on the entire island.

Sighing impatiently, the girl put her book aside. Even
with all the car windows cranked down, Magdalena sim-
mered in a bath of warm sweat, and the leather seat stuck
to her pale skin, putting her in a foul mood despite her father's generous birthday gift of a shopping trip to Ponce.
In an orgy of spending, she had crammed the car's ample
trunk with dresses of Spanish linen, shoes of fine English
leather, bracelets of Moroccan gold, seductive French per-
fumes, and a wardrobe of silk lingerie from Paris that
looked utterly sinful on her.

Her mood improved as she recalled the wicked pleasures she had discovered in Ignacio 'Cienfuegos' bed.
Since first she saw him, she had found the overseer so
arousing she could barely look at him. His black hair and
mustache, aquiline nose and dark eyes made him
heartstoppingly desirable. His twisted foot and clumsy
limp only rendered him all the more endearing. How she
had yearned to feel his slim, almost dainty, fingers tracing
the contours of her flesh, probing the recesses of her frustrated innocence.

Yet even as she lusted for the sensual touch of a hand
not her own, she had found herself dreading Ignacio's ca-

ress and increasingly fearful of her own stirrings. That way lay death. She knew how the creature a man puts in a woman's belly may grow there for nine joyful months, then kill her to get out. Had not she done that to her own mother seventeen years ago this day?

Prompted by this anxiety, Magdalena had paid the witch woman a second visit shortly after giving herself to the overseer.

"Only one week late?" Clotilde had said. "Surely this is no cause for concern."

Magdalena kneaded her fingers nervously. True, her *regla* tended to be erratic, but now she was *eight days* overdue. And while her father valued Ignacio Cienfuegos so highly she doubted he would object to a marriage because the overseer had made her pregnant, a terrible fear haunted her.

"If it lives, it will kill me."

Anguish lined her face. Her fingers kneaded her belly. "How can I rid myself of this monster? I know you care for me. Can you do nothing to help me?"

The old woman was certain the girl was overreacting. But she feigned deep thought, then rummaged among the bottles on her shelves for a purple elixir that stank of dank earth. "Drink and your moonblood will resume its normal flow." The brew was harmless, intended only to ease the girl's distress until her normal menses returned, which, Clotilde calculated, should be no longer than another day or so.

The violet concoction tasted as evil as it smelled. Though it brought tears to her eyes, Magdalena downed it in a single gulp. Two fretful days later, she awoke joyfully to the fullness of her *regla*. Now she swallowed a dose every twenty-eight days lest the flow should falter again.

The Cadillac jounced around a stand of palm trees, bringing the main house into view. Built of thick pine painted dark green with white trim, its three stories contained twelve bedchambers, six baths with indoor plumbing, and a half dozen other rooms beneath its enormous roof of corrugated zinc sheets. Villa Marina, Don Erasto had named it, after Magdalena's mother, the only woman he had ever loved. She had been sixteen when they met, seventeen when they wed, eighteen when she made him a widower. He was fifty and had never remarried. He had never found another woman with the same sweetness of spirit.

Everyone said Marina Saavedra had been the prettiest girl in Aguirre. Everone agreed her daughter looked exactly like her. Yet no one thought Magdalena Vega the prettiest girl of anyplace—perhaps because she lacked her mother's inner light—except Ignacio Cienfuegos, who now limped heavily toward Villa Marina to make his daily report to her father. At the crunch of gravel beneath the Cadillac's wire-spoked tires, he turned, and his eyes chanced to look directly into Magdalena's. The girl's breath caught in her throat. The sweat slithering down her back and between her thighs seemed to grow as slow and thick as sweet cane molasses. Fearful the driver might notice her reaction, she looked away.

See how she still turns from the sight of me, Don Ignacio noted bitterly. Now, she did so to hide their secret from her father. But before Ignacio sought the witch woman's assistance, he had known Magdalena averted her gaze because she found him repulsive. Who could blame her? Ever since he could remember, his clubfoot had been a source of misery and shame. Only his mother had ever touched it with anything resembling love, only she had ever pressed her lips to it and called him beautiful. Physicians had prodded and examined it, but offered no help beyond a corrective shoe. While the thick-soled black monstrosity indeed made his limp less pronounced, it also drew even greater attention to the twisted limb.

To survive, Ignacio developed a thick skin and a hard heart. His resolve to make himself a man of wealth and power none could look down upon had fetched him to Puerto Rico. Once Mother Spain's poorest child in the Caribbean, the island was now a stepdaughter of America and, he believed, rich in opportunity. While his affliction appeared a handicap to some, it had made him tougher than the so-called able-bodied men who labored under his iron hand. It had invested him with dreams more ambitious. And it had given him the strength to will those dreams into reality.

In Don Erasto's daughter, Ignacio saw his salvation. Engineer a marriage, and all he had ever desired would be his—wealth, position, power, beauty. And a Cadillac. That most marvelous machine, that peerless jewel of the automaker's art and ultimate trapping of success *americano* style.

To ride in a Cadillac. . . .

Ah, what a grand and glorious thing that would be, proclaiming to the world that Ignacio Cienfuegos, the despised crippled lad from Asturias, was finally a man of position, and to be reckoned with!

That alone seemed worth any sacrifice.

And he would possess Magdalena Vega, a lovely girl with an arousing face and figure. He had tried to imagine how it might feel to be the object of such a woman's tender affections, freely given. Surely much different from his liaison with the black girl Alfonsina, which had so quickly soured. That had been a mistake. Scarcely three months of clandestine meetings, and she tried to blackmail him with claims that his seed had blossomed within her. Well, the child in her belly might be other than her husband's, but it could never be his. Not content to visit him with a twisted limb, his Creator had made Ignacio Cienfuegos as sterile as a mule as well. Enraged by the black girl's perfidy, the overseer had stricken her husband's name from his work rolls. Permanently.

But, ah, Magdalena Vega. Don Ignacio visualized her as an unexplored continent—untouched, unspoiled, pure—though sometimes he thought he detected something . . . quirky behind those innocent eyes that sent a little frisson of fear squirming down his spine. But then she would turn away and he could never be certain he had seen that queer spark at all.

What *was* certain was that a man such as he could never hope to win a woman such as she. Not without some wile that would blind her to his flaw and make her fall in love with him utterly, despite herself. To that end, he had sought out a crone from Barrio Miseria said to be a mistress of the dark arts. An African woman. A brewer of potions, worker of hexes, teller of fortunes, caster of spells. Clotilde Molina. La Bruja Negra.

And the Black Witch had proved herself genuine.

Don Erasto's Cadillac glided to a stop before the veranda steps. Exquisite machine. Don Ignacio made clumsy haste to open Magdalena's door. As he offered his arm, he thought he detected that quirkiness in her eyes again. Then she lowered her gaze demurely, as though nothing existed between them. But her fingers on his forearm sent an almost unbearable tingle through his flesh.

Curious, Clotilde reflected, how if one waited long enough, life would find a way to set itself right. Last night, Don Ignacio had come again, out of sorts with Magdalena's secrecy and eager to bring matters into the open.

"The question," the overseer had muttered, "is how?"

Clotilde eyed him as a teacher might regard an especially slow pupil. "Fill her belly with your child."

She had meant to sting his conscience with a reminder of his sin against Alfonsina, but saw the barb had missed. She could well imagine what selfish thoughts danced inside that handsome head instead: *Of course! Confront Don Erasto's paternal instincts and unbending sense of propriety with a pregnancy out of wedlock, and a grand wedding at the Cathedral of Our Lady of Mercy in Ponce's main plaza would surely follow.*

"Brilliant, old woman." The overseer sighed. "But impossible."

In a haughty tone, he confessed his secret: though Magdalena might be ready to flower with life, he could never make her blossom.

Clotilde could scarcely believe her ears. Did the Spaniard think to refute Alfonsina's accusation thus? Her good eye glittered with rage. Was she expected to swallow a lie so crass? Did the son of a whore think her *simple?* No matter. Feigning to credit his words would provide the opportunity she needed to avenge her granddaughter.

"I will brew for you a *noche de gloria*," la Bruja Negra said slowly, plotting as she spoke, "a potion so powerful that once you lie with Magdalena Vega again, her belly will bloat with new life in less than a month."

"Is this possible?" the overseer asked, eager to believe, but still dubious.

Equivocation, evasion, misdirection had always been a part of the magic. "Did my artifice fail you before?" Clotilde's single eye burned into him.

Don Ignacio shook his head, any doubts vaporized by the heat in that fiery orb. *Noche de gloria,* he thought admiringly as he departed. Night of glory!

The battered black kettle burbled on the ancient woodburning stove. Flames flickered. Yellow. Orange. Blue. Shadows jittered on the walls. Clotilde smelled the fraudulent potion. Pah. The poison needed masking. The overseer was far too finicky to allow anything so vile past his pure Iberian lips.

Inspiration struck. With the sugar harvest in full swing under Don Ignacio's stern eye, there was an abundance of sweet cane molasses to cloak her treachery. The witch woman grinned. The overseer would smack his lips at the taste of his own death. And pay well for the pleasure.

A harsh knock at the door made her jump, shattering her visions of revenge. The overseer. This stranger, yet not entirely so.

In that moment of. *Dislocation.* Between fantasy and reality. A whirlwind. Seemed suddenly to. *ROAR.* Through her. Mind. Sowing *madness* and. Lucidity. *Ripping loose* the scales. From her. Eyes. *Revelation!*

The man at the door was really . . .

. . . *had* to be . . .

. . . Victoriano Lozada . . .

—*returned in the guise of Ignacio Cienfuegos!*

Of course! How could she not have known? Her perseverance *had* borne fruit! Through more than five decades her thirst for revenge had remained unquenched. Now quenched it would be—and by the same enticing brew she had fashioned to avenge Alfonsina.

As the unsuspecting overseer departed with his fatal draught, leaving her fifty cents richer, the witch woman chuckled deep in her throat. How fitting that Don Ignacio's "night of glory" should prove the instrument that finally precipitated her own day of vengeance.

A weak breeze fluttered the curtains against Clotilde's kitchen window. Outside, the funeral procession advanced slowly on foot toward the curve in the dirt road. The professional mourners hired by Don Erasto to keep emotions at a proper pitch preceded the crowd of cane cutters and their families, none of whom appeared especially saddened by the loss. In the lead, resplendent in his trademark funeral suit of sugar white linen, came the head mourner, Elpidio Santana. Short, fat, bald, and squeaky-voiced he was. But no one could move a crowd—or himself—to tears more quickly.

Magdalena's father must have harbored a great appreciation for the overseer to have lavished such expense on his final farewell, Clotilde thought. Besides Elpidio Santana, la Madama Guevara and Jacinta la Negra were here, fierce mourners each in their own right—and none of the three came cheap. A carriage followed, laden with wreaths enough to have emptied every florist's shop between Aguirre and Ponce. Then the hearse. And bringing up the rear, Don Erasto's Cadillac. The driver sat behind the wheel in his black suit; Don Erasto and his dry-eyed daughter, in opposite corners of the back seat.

Yes, sometimes the magic worked, reflected Clotilde. Though maybe not as people expected. So often they didn't know what they really wanted. Take Magdalena Vega and Ignacio Cienfuegos. Each had come to her seeking the other's love. But though both got what they asked for, neither was happy with the results. No matter. In the end, though Magdalena lost the lover she had thought she wanted, she *did* get her most important wish—not to be pregnant by Don Ignacio. And if Don Ignacio had never achieved his desires, well, he and Victoriano Lozada could rot in hell together for all Clotilde cared. The magic had finally worked for *her*.

Outside the witch woman's window, Elpidio Santana's sweet tenor sailed into *"Alabanza al Sēnor,"* buoyed up by la Madama Guevara's husky contralto and la Negra Jacinta's rumbling bass. The witch woman's thick lips hooked back in a jagged grin as dozens of happy voices joined in praising the Lord and the car bearing Don Ignacio slowly rounded the curve, white sidewall tires gleaming in the sun. Hired at great expense from Ponce's finest funeral parlor, the stately black Cadillac hearse glided majestically along the dirt road that bordered Barrio Miseria, its heavy-duty Detroit-manufactured suspension providing its passenger the illusion of riding a magic carpet on this, his final trip anywhere.

This story is dedicated to my father, James Herbert Stevens, who gave me the capper for it thirty-three years ago. I just didn't know it was about a witch until now.

OUR LADY OF THE TOADS

by Deborah Wheeler

In Gideon's dream, the walls of the steamer trunk pressed in on him. The velvet lining had a pungent, musty smell. His ears echoed with the sound of the lock clicking shut and footsteps retreating, fainter and fainter until he was alone in the airless dark, alone with the beating of his heart.

Then came the first clammy touch on his hand, hesitant, as he knew it would be, only this time he couldn't move away, couldn't scream, couldn't breathe. Could only lie there under the tiny paws, the soft amphibian belly, one lurching step and then another, up his arm and over his sleeve. In their wake, he felt the faint tingling where warts would soon begin, then only a lingering pressure through the fabric of his shirt.

Breath seeped from his lungs. It wasn't over yet, he tried to tell his dream-self, his child-self. But his body was already melting into relief as he thought of the bar of lye soap his mother kept underneath the kitchen sink. In a little while it would be morning, safe sweet morning.

Plop! A squirming mass landed on his face, then another low on his throat where the collar gaped. Raw, unfocused sound poured from his mouth. His body bucked, thrashed, elbows and feet pummeling the bitter hardness of the walls. Fingers scrabbled against the arching lid and bits of lining shredded away, powdering his face.

His throat swelled shut with aching and his nose ran watery snot down the sides of his cheeks and still the screams kept coming. He clamped one hand over his mouth, screaming silently now, screaming inside—

Gideon Eldridge sat bolt upright in bed, a sweat-drenched sheet twisted around his legs. Despite the sultry Ohio summer heat, goose bumps peppered his bare arms. He ran his hands over his stubbled cheeks, raked back his hair.

Jesus! He hadn't had that dream in years, not since he was a kid. It had felt so real, so like a memory.

He wasn't seven years old any longer, Gideon told himself as he disentangled the sheet. He was thirty-seven, he'd been through State college, Army Reserves, two divorces and a decade in New York City. By rights, nothing should have the power to frighten him any longer.

Why this dream, why now? He'd returned to the house on Maple Street after his father had finally drunk himself to death, and then only long enough to sell it.

Wearing only his briefs, Gideon padded to the window of the second-story bedroom, the guest room, not the one he'd had as a boy. Below, the drowsing town shimmered in the light of a moon gone watery and green. The houses, each with its square of lawn and fungus-shaped clumps of hydrangea and lilac, had faded to gray. Nothing moved except the rippling shadow of a cat.

Twelve o'clock and all's well, he thought and turned back to bed. But his eyes, gliding over the motionless streets, caught a flash of light, a bar of yellow where none should be, quickly snuffed as if someone had jerked a curtain closed.

He strained to make out the house it had come from, elevated above the rest. His sweat turned cold as he recognized it—the house on the hill. The house his friends had taunted him to enter alone after dark when he was seven years old, although he could never quite remember what he'd seen there. The house reputed to have its own garden of nightshade and hemlock, as well as its own basement cemetery, its own pond of piranhas. The house on the hill was vacant no longer.

* * *

The phone rang as he was finishing his third cup of coffee and looking over the latest pile of manuscripts. It was the real estate agent handling his father's house.

"I've got a prospective buyer coming by to look at the property at one o'clock," she said, meaning he should make himself absent.

"Okay." His father's house had been for sale for three weeks without an offer. Why now? he thought again, and felt a sudden electrifying *zing!* in his guts. "Listen," he said suddenly, "do you know who bought the house on the hill, the one that's been empty so long?"

"The old Newbury house? Why, were you interested in it?"

"Just curious." He forced a laugh.

Papers rustled over the phone lines. "Here it is. Hmmm, it was never for sale, only lease. The owner—a Miss Lily Newbury—has been out of the country. Seems she's changed her mind and decided to live in it herself."

Gideon shivered as he replaced the receiver. The thought came to him that the owner's reappearance was no coincidence. The house on the hill, dormant for all these years, had only been waiting for him to return.

The house looked much as he remembered it, with its brooding cobwebbed gables and paint bleached to a pale fungus color. It stood by itself, surrounded by a weathered board fence, with streets on three sides and a vacant lot on the fourth. Gideon circled around to the lot and squinted through a gap between the planks. He couldn't make out anything like his father's yard, with its close-shaven lawn, kettle barbecue and sagging plastic lawn chairs. Weeds rioted in every corner and something splashed in the depths of the pond at the far end.

"If you find my garden so interesting," said a low-pitched female voice at his shoulder, "why don't you come in for a closer look?"

Startled, he spun around. The woman behind him was thin and tall, horse-faced. She wore a billowy black dress with red and yellow embroidery at the neck.

"Well, I—"

"You can tell the others all about me, so they don't have to go peeking through the fence, too." Slipping one hand through the crook of his elbow, she led him around to the gate.

Gideon's muscles obeyed her, as if by meeting her gaze for that single moment he had allowed her to gain some kind of preternatural control over him. He started sweating.

"People are naturally curious," he stammered. "Where you come from, what you do."

"If I'm married, they mean. Who my friends are."

She led him around the yard, point out the various plants, *Matricaria, Symphytum, Cycades, Equisetum, Artemisia.* He didn't recognize the Latin names; they all looked like overgrown weeds to him, vines and bushes and plants which were part fern and part palm. Unseen creatures rustled in the flower-tipped grasses and leaves rippled in the breeze like flirting dancers, showing their silvery undersides. The longer he stayed, the deeper his sense of unease. The place had a pungent, untamed smell. A dangerous smell, it stirred uncomfortable memories.

"Well," he said, "I'll see you around."

He felt her eyes on him until he was almost through the gate, and only then did he turn back for a last fleeting glance. He saw her crouch in the tangled grass, black skirts spread around her, whispering to something small and brown which she held in her hands, cradled as if it were precious.

Gideon's nerve broke and he rushed down the hill. He knew that warted hide, those bulging eyes. And to hold it so close, almost tenderly, to remember—

—mountains of jade and onyx, whales singing in the depths of crystalline oceans, forests of deepest green, mammoths trumpeting as they danced beneath the moon, a circle of standing stones—

Yowl! Gideon tripped over a cat, scrambled to catch his balance on the sloping street. The cat hissed at him, tail twitching, and bounded toward the house on the hill, a ripple of sleek black fur. Heart hammering in his chest,

he watched it go. He could not have remembered those
things. He must have been bewitched.

Black cat—unmarried woman—hard unfeeling bitch of
a woman—a toad for, what was it called? a familiar. . . .

Gideon thought of running back to the relative safety
of New York City. But he knew instantly he would not,
could not. The witch, like the dream itself, had come to
him for a reason.

Weeks crept on. Gideon took the house on Maple Street
off the market and made arrangements to do his
copyediting from there. He spent hours in the public library, looking up everything he could find about witches
and their powers and weaknesses. The books didn't agree,
being part history and the rest superstition, but he was
able to sift out the most potent-sounding weapons and
protections.

As the harvest season approached and the first tinge of
frost crept into the evening air, the children returned to
school and the town made ready for its annual Pumpkin
Festival. Gideon noticed the Newbury woman's first visitors. Two women arrived in a taxi from the airport in
New Athens.

Gideon couldn't work, couldn't sleep. He drank too
much and wrote snide remarks on the manuscripts he was
editing. He forced himself to clean out the attic, but
found no trunks among the bags of old clothes, the broken furniture, the boxes of yellowed photographs.

Then a fourth arrived, and a fifth. *More will come,* he
realized with sickening certainty. *Thirteen in all to make
a coven.* And Halloween was drawing near, the night
when their powers would be at their greatest.

He stopped counting and started gathering the supplies
he would need.

Gideon waited in the shadows at the base of the hill,
watching the last of the trick-or-treaters make their way
down the sidewalk. He clicked his pencil flashlight on
and checked the time. Ten o'clock. Two hours left. The

night around him lay still and shivery as the voices of the children faded into silence.

He patted the pockets of his fisherman's vest, where he'd hidden his supplies—a cross, a blue bead on a string, a bag of salt which had been consecrated on Palm Sunday, a vial of holy water and an automatic pistol loaded with the silver-plated bullets he'd gone all the way back to New York to find, although he wasn't positive they'd work on witches.

Gideon crept up the hill and around to the side of the house, his ears straining for any sound. Lights flickered through the cracks of the board fence. He caught the sound of women's voices in some sort of chanting. His hackles rose and his mouth went dry. He took out the cross.

There, perched in front of the gate as if on sentry duty, was the largest, ugliest toad Gideon had ever laid eyes on, truly worthy of being a witch's familiar. In the flashlight's glare, its unblinking eyes gleamed like polished obsidian. Eyes, he thought, which had watched the empires of men and dinosaurs rise and then crumble into dust. Eyes which beheld the slow circling dance of galaxies and the most insignificant microbe. Eyes which looked right through him. Then, in an instant, the creature was gone.

Gideon's hand shook as he took hold of the latch. The gate creaked on its hinges, but the muted singing did not waver. With a silent prayer, he clutched the cross, put his shoulder to the gate, and shoved.

He stumbled into a clearing aglow in the brilliance of a bonfire. Surely, he thought dazedly, the blaze should have been visible from outside. And surely the yard could not be so big. The fence had disappeared behind waving grasses and silver-boled trees, wild and arching under the sweep of stars. Shadowy figures stood in a circle, thirteen in all.

The singing stopped. Gideon thrust the cross in the direction of the nearest witch. "Stop!"

The figure turned, a plain, gray-haired woman in an old-fashioned costume. She was sopping wet. Something moved at the corner of his vision and he turned to see a young girl, hair cropped short and wearing the charred tatters of some white garment over armor. She reached up, touched the cross, and gently brought it to her lips. The cross burst into light, casting an unearthly radiance across the girl's face. She murmured something in French and the light subsided to a clear glow.

"What dis mon doin' here? Here, where we work deep magic?" A black woman, tall and strong-looking, stepped forward. She wore a homespun dress, a rag wrapped around her head.

"He has come seeking witches, though he knows not what they are," another woman said in a heavy accent. Her dark hair was caught up in shining ringlets, her dress a glimmer in the shadows. Gold encircled her neck and bare arms. "Shall we show him what *real* witches do?"

Gideon's heart hammered against his ribs. He fumbled in his pockets. His fingers met the cold steel of the automatic. He drew it out. "Stay back!"

The Newbury woman stepped into the light. She wore a long robe that seemed one moment to be flowing water, the next, a cascade of petals or the milky tails of comets. "This man has come into our midst uninvited, that much is true. He may be ignorant and frightened, but I do not think him evil."

"You always were too generous, Lilith," said a plump, English-accented woman who would have looked grandmotherly except for the livid bruises around her throat. "Consider the harm he has already done, intruding here. The juncture cannot hold much longer and we have work yet to do."

"I'm not afraid of you!" Gideon cried, but his voice came out in a terrified squeak.

"No?" said the Greek woman, moving closer. "Perhaps you should be."

"Turning him into a pig is too good for him!" A dark-eyed girl stepped forward. She wore full, tiered skirts, a patterned shawl over her shoulders. When she pointed an accusing finger, Gideon noticed the numbers tattooed along her forearm. "An eye for an eye, that's what his book says. Let us have justice!"

"Silence!" Lilith held up one ivory hand and the clearing fell silent. Shadows stirred behind her eyes, waking Gideon's memory. The black terror of the steamer trunk, no longer securely anchored in the past, flooded through him. His fingers tightened on the trigger of the automatic, but nothing happened. The safety catch had somehow been left on. He hurled the gun away and pulled out the pouch of consecrated salt. When he threw it in her face, she laughed and the crystals drifted glittering to the earth.

"You have followed those who sinned against us," Lilith said, "those who tried, in their ignorance, to rend the very magic with which we bind the fragile threads of time."

"I don't believe you! I don't believe any of you!"

"Why think you we gather here?" the drowned woman said in a kindly voice. "Why think you we died?"

Slowly, Gideon lowered the cross. How could he fight them, these witches who were already dead? In the back of his mind, a child's voice pleaded, *"Please don't—"*

Gideon felt his body shrivel around him. His vision went bleary and the room receded to a blur. When he raised his hands to his face, he felt the huge, hairy warts. They had always been there, all those years, but had never been visible before.

Gently Lilith took his hands and placed the toad in them. His fingers curled around the fragile body. He felt the intricate pattern of the creature's hide, a silken tent over the miniature cathedral of its bones, the jewellike glands along its throat. For a moment, he felt himself falling into the fertile darkness of its eyes. Then he blinked and the eyes turned into mirrors, only it was not his own face he saw reflected there.

Gideon's flesh turned cold. He knew now who had locked him in the steamer trunk. He knew why.

On a dare, a seven-year-old boy had penetrated into the center of a magical garden, had seen places which no longer existed and things which might never come to be. A warted toad had been his guide to wonders beyond reason. And a terrified, drunken father had locked him all

night in a steamer trunk with half a dozen of the creatures
to cure him of such nonsense.

Gideon understood why witches were seen as evil,
these women caught forever in fragments of time, pursu-
ing their own mysterious goals. They were as dangerous
to the world of human cruelty as the unblinking stare of
the toad in his hands.

"Talk to her." Lilith's voice came in a sweet, silvery
whisper. "Tell her your fears and your dreams. Let her
wisdom cleanse your memories."

Around him, Gideon heard murmurs of approval, even
though he could no longer see the other witches. The
clearing had gone misty, replaced by the outlines of his
own garden. But a garden changed, the manicured beds
sprouting into a tangle of exuberant growth. A gap
opened in the middle of the tight-clipped lawn and a
spring bubbled forth. The toad gave a convulsive kick and
jumped to the ground, heading for the burgeoning grass.
Gideon hurried after the toad as if his soul depended upon
it.

DEALING IN FUTURES

by Judith Tarr

"**R**ight," says Lachesis. "So where were we?"

"Pigs," says Circe, who crashed the meeting on a technicality. "Pork futures. Swine plague in—was it Gondwanaland?"

"Botswana," says Orgoch, who wants a vacation. "Along with bubonic plague in Santa Fe, tobacco mosaic in South Carolina, and a plague of dental plaque in Stockholm. For this particular sub-era."

In honor of the sub-era, everybody's in dress-for-success superwoman mode, in your basic boardroom, with pads and pencils logoed *Futures, Incorporated: Que sera, sera.* They're also, because this is that kind of continuum, in a cave lit by flickering lamps, wearing robes and sniffing fumes from the vent in the floor, and on a withered heath around a cauldron (which gets crowded when they've got a quorum), and in an environmental module jacked into a neural net, not to mention the completely indescribable not-place in the not-there that makes even Orgoch—who keeps the minutes—stop and think before she comes up with an era-reference. Somewhere a long way down the line. She gets a break after that, and somebody else gets to be Orgoch.

Anyway, they've covered Disease and are into Disaster, and Lachesis is running through the rest of the list. "Right, so," she says. "Is that enough trouble for Sarajevo? How about Berlin?"

"We already did Berlin," says Tyche, also present on a technicality.

In Orgoch's opinion, since Lachesis put herself in charge, there are an awful lot of Greek types getting in on technicalities. Or were. Or will be. Time slips in this continuum. Makes it hard for even a Fate to keep up. She tends to get things confused herself—runs together Genghis Khan, Gog and Magog, and George Bush, or thinks about hitting Ur of the Chaldees with a nice blast of the Black Death.

While Orgoch thinks about rats in Ur, Lachesis makes a note. "Berlin, normal complement of disasters, check. Who'll take care of Belfast? It's due another bombing."

"No way," says Mary Ann.

Mary Ann doesn't know she's just uttered words that resonate through the continuum and stop Lachesis cold. Mary Ann thinks she's riding Leroy the gift Thoroughbred up in the woods behind the barn, and Leroy wants to jump a four-foot deadfall. She hauls him back down to a reasonably slow gallop from a flat run, and swerves him in between the deadfall and a tree. Quite a bit farther on, he actually slows down.

Mary Ann starts breathing again. She hates it when Leroy gets it into his head to jump anything and everything that's even halfway in his path. Leroy thinks that he was born to leap tall buildings at a single bound. As a matter of fact he was, but something happened and that particular twist of fate got sidetracked, and the essence that should have headed right at the second star from the left, took a left at the second star from the right instead and landed at a crossroads in the dark of the moon. A mare happened to have stopped there after breaking out of her barn, and was going about having the foal she was six weeks and six days and six hours and six minutes late with. The essence, being too curious for its own good, got sucked in. By the time it realized what was happening, it found itself in the body of a then very gangly burnt-sugar-colored Thoroughbred with a mark on its forehead like a five-pointed star.

Now, five years later, having had a completely lackluster career on the track thanks to his habit of trying to jump out of the gate before it sprang open, not to mention the time he did a mile and a quarter like a steeplechase, hurdling every shadow that hit the track, Leroy belongs to Mary Ann, who thinks he should learn to be a dressage horse. What Leroy is, in fact, is an Accident of Fate. Which makes him a Nexus, and a Critical Point. He doesn't know that. He just wants to jump.

Mary Ann just wants him to learn how to go around a circle at less than thirty miles per hour, and maybe stop once in a while on command. Mary Ann really wants a Lipizzaner, but Lipizzaners not being easy to come by, she takes what she can get. She's beginning to think that she should have looked this gift horse in the mouth, or at least in the eye, and pegged him for a grasshopper in a Thoroughbred suit.

Whatever, she thinks, when he finally comes jolting to a halt. He snorts and does a little bit of a happy-horse dance—he sees another deadfall, and it's even higher than the last one. He's going to jump this one, his whole body says, no matter what.

"—what?" Lachesis looks around. Nobody moves. The boardroom is looking wan around the edges—there's a touch of cave wall showing through, and a suggestion of glasteel dome. The echoes are still ringing. "Who said that?"

Blank faces. Circe's suit has a distinctly classical—as opposed to classic—look. Sleek, well-groomed Third Witch is looking quite a bit ruffled, as if she's been standing in the wind.

Orgoch shakes herself out of a dizzy spell. She's been seeing things she wasn't supposed to see for another two sub-eras according to the agenda. That war on Ceti Five—

"Well," says Lachesis, straightening her wimple. "Just an interruption in the flow. We were on the Black Death, weren't we? Third round, the score gets better for the human faction. What say we make it worse for round four? Add a little more pneumonic to the mix?"

* * *

"Not bloody likely," says Mary Ann, cranking in rein before Leroy can head for his dream jump. She has no idea she just saved Belfast from a bomb that would kill twenty and injure thirty-four. Or that, just now, back a sub-era or three, round four of the Black Death didn't up the ante and wipe out most of northern Europe.

She rides Leroy at a walk past the deadfall—he's sulking, dragging his feet and making sure he stumbles at least twice as they go around the obstacle. After that it's pretty well a clear ride down to the road and home. Mary Ann can't really stay mad at Leroy. She pats his neck and tells him he's all right for a Thoroughbred. He hears the "all right" part and snorts. Sure it's all right. He didn't get to jump, did he?

He'll jump the pasture fence later and head for Mackey's-down-the-road, which has a field full of jumps all set up, and usually a pretty white mare grazing in it. The mare, being a mare, believes in putting geldings in their place, but Leroy's not proud. He knows his place as well as her princesshood does.

"—and then they end the interregnum on Ceti Five," says Lachesis, in the environmental module, linked to the rest of the Fates and Fortunes through the neural net. "Give the CEOship to Princess Marjo-Sixteen, send the king into exile, polish it off with a nice short space war."

Nods around the net. Except for Orgoch, whose headache is getting worse. She can't remember the shift from sub-era to sub-era. Weren't they doing the Black Death? Or the Early Computer Age? Or are they still in the Ur-era, and have the mammoths died?

She starts to say something, but gives up. Circe is at it again. "Men are such pigs. Let's zap the patriarchy on Gehenna and roust out the Retro-Feminists."

"Oh, no, you won't," says Mary Ann. She had a feeling Leroy would get up to something once she put him out to run off his frustration. Sure enough, there he is, ready for takeoff over the pasture fence.

He's gone before she gets there, with a little flick of his

heels. She says something not very nice and starts trudging. No use running. She knows where he'll go.

And to be honest, she doesn't much mind heading over to Mackey's. They've got a Lipizzaner. All right, just a mare, and all the books say the mares aren't any good, but she looks pretty good to Mary Ann. Mary Ann thinks the books are just a little bit sexist, you know?

Right, and there's Leroy in the jumping field, but he's barely paused to say a polite horse-hello and get his due squeal-and-strike from the mare, before heading for the jumps.

"I think he's trying to tell you something," says Mackey's kid, the one who's a year behind Mary Ann in school, what's his name, she can't remember. Doesn't matter anyway. They lean on the fence and watch Leroy jump a nice clean round, then go back and do it again, just to show everybody how he did it. The mare isn't paying any attention. She's got priorities, and those start with the clover in the south corner.

"I think," says Mary Ann, "I've got the wrong horse. All he ever wants to do is jump."

"You don't jump?" asks Mackey's kid. Mary Ann hopes he isn't sneering, because she'll pop him one if he is.

"Of course I jump!" she says. "Just not every spare minute. When he's not jumping, he's running his feet off."

Mackey's kid looks sympathetic, for a boy-type. "All Belladonna wants to do is levades. And caprioles. She doesn't see why she has to do the other stuff, too."

"Oh," says Mary Ann with a bit of a sigh, "but she's a Lipizzaner."

"And your guy's a Thoroughbred. They run. And jump."

Mary Ann hates it when people are logical. "I'd rather have a horse who did levades."

Mackey's kid shrugs. "She jumps, too. Just not all the time."

* * *

"Time," says Lachesis, "is getting short. Are we done with Disaster? Do we add a few, or keep them for the next session?"

"I don't think . . ." says Tyche. She's looking puzzled. "Did we do the early late empire yet? I can't recall."

"Why, of course we—" Third Witch stops. "By Hecate, I can't remember, either."

They all look at one another. Getting confused is one thing. Even a Fate is subject to that, what with everything she has to look after. But forgetting—that's not in the specs. Fate remembers everything. Every fall of a sparrow. Every vibration of that damned butterfly's wing in Venezuela, and if you think it's easy getting that to resonate just right so it makes a president trip over his feet on the golf course, you should try it yourself.

"Check the records," says a voice so old it's barely a whisper, but it throbs in every corner of the continuum. Everybody starts and stares at the One who always sits alone, who never changes, who doesn't even have a name. When she swam out of the dark, nothing was named; everything just was. She never talks—can't, Orgoch would have said, except that obviously she can.

Lachesis doesn't argue. Doesn't ask questions. Just does what she's told. That's power, Orgoch thinks. She's interested to see how strong it is, especially coming from that tiny, wizened, naked figure like a mangy monkey, with its heavy forehead and its moist brown eyes.

It's a long while, reckoning in shifts of the continuum, while Lachesis goes from record to record. Stone tablet, clay, papyrus, parchment, paper, phosphor, neural induction, pure mind-to-mind, she runs through them all. The others wait. Nobody says anything. They all look as headachy as Orgoch feels.

Finally Lachesis sits up straight. Her face is grim. "Something," she says, "has been meddling with our continuum."

Orgoch mentally applauds her. *Brilliant* deduction. It only took Orgoch half a millisecond to reach the same conclusion.

But Lachesis can prove it, which helps with the skeptics, such as Circe, whose obsession with pigs keeps her from seeing much of anything else. Lachesis calls up an image of the continuum—it comes through to Orgoch as a flow chart inside a crystal ball—and points with a long bony finger.

"There," she says. "There, and there. Disruptions. Shifts of fate from one line to another."

Third Witch, known in polite circles as Dame Fortune, considers the scrying-bowl in front of her and nods. "Somebody's turning the wheel out of turn."

"That's not possible," says Tyche. "Fate rules even the gods."

Lachesis casts her a quelling look, but not before Orgoch observes, "It's possible if someone's done it. Does anyone have a spell for migraine?"

"Moly," says Circe promptly.

"Willow bark," says Third Witch with a sharp glance at Circe, "gathered in the dark of the moon, steeped in water from a virgin's bath, drunk three times standing and three times sitting, while intoning a Paternoster."

"What nonsense," says Lachesis. "Take two aspirin and call your broker in the morning."

Orgoch sighs. Her headache is worse, or maybe better. It's hard to tell. "So who's twisting fate? That poet isn't loose in Baghdad again, is he?"

Lachesis shudders delicately. "Spacetime forbid. This is something different. Something that—"

"*Stop* it!" Mary Ann whacks Leroy on the nose. He's objecting to coming home after his visit with the pretty lady mare, not to mention the hunt course with its lovely, lovely jumps. So of course he tries to jump the shadow of a telephone pole in the road, and nearly pulls Mary Ann off her feet.

"I'll sell you down the river," she threatens him. "I'll chop you up for dogmeat."

He picks up the irritation but not the threat, seeing as how Mary Ann would never sell any horse to a cannery, even Leroy the grasshopper horse. He's just a little bit contrite. He likes Mary Ann, she sits light on his back

even when she won't let him run, and except for not letting him jump enough, she's a nicely trained human. She
feeds him fine grain and sweet hay, and grooms him
when he itches, and talks to him in that long pleasant
water-flow of speech that humans are so inexplicably
fond of.

So he doesn't jump the next few shadows, and walks
quietly into his stall, where there's plenty of hay and
fresh water and—oh joy joy joy, a carrot in his special-
sweet-things bucket. Carrots are almost as good as jumps.
He eats it with loud appreciation, dribbling orange bits in
thanks-offering to the human who's leaning over the stall
door.

Mary Ann shakes her head. "I don't know what I'm
going to do with you," she says. "I'm *not* about to take
you on the Grand Prix jumping circuit. Couldn't you just,
like, be a little bit inclined to do exercises on the flat once
in a while?"

Leroy, nose down in his hay, swishes his tail and
stamps at a fly. He's thinking about leaping things. Tall
buildings, why stop there? Mountains. The moon.

Leroy thinks big. And Leroy, not being entirely a
horse, thinks in the future tense once in a while, which is
part of what being a Nexus means.

"—means trouble," says Lachesis jerkily. They all felt
the continuum shift that time. Being aware of it means
they can feel it, but it doesn't stop the shift. Orgoch no-
tices that the room's edges are blurry. Bits are starting to
fade out altogether.

"*What* can cause a thing like this?" Circe demands.

"You should know," says Tyche.

"There, there," says Third Witch. She looks at Circe
with something resembling kindness. It comes across as
condescension. "Witchcraft could do it, yes. It would
have to be a very strong witch, or a coven of witches.
And they would need a very strong will."

"We would know of such," says Lachesis.

"But why would they do it?" Circe wants to know.

"Why do witches do anything?" asks Tyche. "For the fun of it. For power."

Orgoch is fascinated. She's not paying much attention to the catfight, she's seen enough of those through the aeons to leave her yawning unless the blood flies. She's found something else to fix her eye on. The robe that Lachesis is wearing at the moment seems to be all white, but it's subtly and intricately figured. And it's unraveling around the hem. As she watches, bringing her eye a bit closer to be sure, the thread slips another handspan.

Lachesis doesn't seem to notice, but then anyone can see how the walls are turning transparent. What's beyond doesn't bear looking at, even if you're a Fate and inured to anything. She says, "Get to work, ladies. Find the coven."

"And then?" asks Third Witch. She has a gleam in her eye, and Circe and Tyche in either hand, spitting at one another.

"Then," says Lachesis, "we do what we have to do."

"No," says Mary Ann, pushing Leroy's nose away. He's hunting for another carrot. She isn't carrying any. He's death to her carrot budget as it is, and he hasn't done much to earn one carrot today, let alone two.

He goes back to his hay. She thinks for a while, then heads into his stall with brushes and currycomb, and starts grooming him. She doesn't have to. She just feels like it.

His mane is in knots. His tail is even worse. She starts working out tangles. While she works, she hums to herself. Nothing particular. She hates Top Forty. She likes to make up her own songs anyway.

This one has words to it, sort of. *Tangle in, tangle out, tangle back and round about.*

"*Got* it!"

Orgoch's howl wouldn't shame a wolf. The whole continuum by now is swimming like an underwater extravaganza. Her voice brings the others homing in on her like fish to a blood trail. They're losing shape. Circe's profile has a remarkably porcine cast. Third Witch's cloak looks like a bat's wings. The others have a shadowy look to them.

They're solid enough close up, crowding around Orgoch's scrying-bowl. "What's that?" Lachesis snaps. She sounds waspish—Orgoch can almost see the stinger.

They all stare at the image in the bowl. It's a big brown horse, eating hay, and a smallish brown girl, grooming the horse. She's singing to herself. The horse is in horse bliss.

"*Look* at it," says Orgoch. "Really look."

It's Circe who says, "Great Father Zeus. Look inside the horse."

A slow sigh goes round the circle. "A Nexus," Third Witch says. "How in the world? None of us approved that!"

"Who rules the Fates?" says the voice they've all forgotten, the old, old voice, the One who alone stays solid and substantial no matter where she is, no matter how the continuum frays. "We deal in futures—we make them, we like to think. Who balances us?"

"Why," says Lachesis, "no one. We are past and present and to come, all that was and is and will be."

The Old One shakes her head.

"Chance," says Orgoch suddenly. "Chance balances Fate."

"But *I* am Chance," says Tyche, "and I had nothing to do with this."

The Old One shakes her head again. Tyche looks mulish. Or pigheaded, Orgoch thinks, not very kindly.

"You are Chance given coherence and substance," Orgoch says. "Raw Chance, essence of chaos—that's something different. Look, there's a seed of it in the horse. And every time she touches him—"

"Stand still," says Mary Ann, working away at Leroy's mane. The horse stands still. So does all the rest of the continuum, Fates and Chance and all.

"All right," she says, smoothing the last of the mane, moving back toward the tail.

And the continuum can move again.

"Lightning," says Tyche. "A thunderbolt."

"A spell," says Circe. "If she were a pig, could she touch the horse and affect the continuum?"

"Cast her from the wheel," says Third Witch with blood in her eye.

Lachesis frowns, thinking about it.

"Obviously," says Orgoch, wondering why the others can't see it—her eye is good, but she never thought it was that good—"this child is a little something more than a slave to her fortune. Or, for that matter, to her horse."

"Coincidence," says Tyche. "Chance. Every time she touches him, she says just the right thing."

"But how could she," Orgoch points out, "if she weren't something else in her own right?"

"There are no witches in her sub-era," says Lachesis. "We removed them. You seconded the motion, as I recall."

Orgoch shakes her head. "This is raw Chance, ladies. Anything can happen. Anything at all."

"And," says Third Witch, "if she says the right thing—or the wrong one—"

She breaks off. They all freeze. But the girl is still brushing out the horse's tail, and she's not even singing. She's working at a knot full of burrs, scowling with concentration.

"I wish," she says suddenly, "that you could keep it all straight."

The continuum quivers. Are the walls more solid? Orgoch doesn't dare hope.

It's a rare spectacle. The on-line committee of Fate, Chance, and the Future Imperfect, huddled around a scrying-bowl, praying as hard as even gods can pray. They can't do direct intervention. That's against the rules. All they can do is wait.

It's beastly like being human.

"I wish," says the girl behind the horse, "that you could be reasonable about things."

The continuum is making a noise somewhere between a groan and a purr. The horse, to Orgoch's eye, is starting to glow from inside, like a very large clay lamp. The girl doesn't seem to notice.

"I wish," she says, and it rings like gongs under the sea, "that you could be, like, normal, you know?"

There's a seed of fire in the horse, so bright it turns the big horse-body to air and shadow. It's not sentient, not exactly, but it has purpose. That purpose has been asleep. It's remembering stars. And mornings. And leaping over the moon.

"There," whispers the Old One. Her voice somehow sounds the way the fire-seed looks. "There, out yonder. Second on the left."

The spark wobbles a bit. It wavers to the right. It hesitates. Then all at once, so fast it leaves a trail like a meteor, it heads where the Old One is pointing.

In the cave that's a heath that's a boardroom that's an environmental module that's a nexus of not-space, there's an immense and awful quiet. The walls are solid. So is the floor. Circe has her Greek-vase profile back, above a Halston twinset. Third Witch straightens her blazer and smooths her impeccably coiffed hair.

Lachesis takes a deep breath. "Right. Then. Orgoch, the minutes, please? You can leave out the ... disturbances. We were on Belgrade, I believe."

Belfast, Orgoch thinks, but she doesn't say it. It's business as usual again, and vacation not much closer than it was before. She sighs. She's going to be glad to hand over that eye and head for Club Med Elysium. Meanwhile, there are futures to deal, fates and chance and all the rest of it, just one more aeon in the old continuum.

Mary Ann finishes brushing Leroy's tail, gives him the horse cookie she finds in her pocket, and adds a hug to it. "Oh, well," she says. "You may not be perfect, but you're my horse. I guess I'll keep you."

Leroy sighs contentedly and nibbles her hair. He has a vague sense of something missing, and a lot more of something asking for a way in. He thinks about jumping mountains. No, maybe not that. Maybe outrunning the wind. Yes. He'll show his human tomorrow. Grand fun, a grand run, and carrots joy joy joy.

Leroy is a happy horse. Leroy is also a Nexus. There's a whole continuum full of essences, and a crowd of them right here, all begging for a turn. What's a horse for, after all, if you can't ride him?

CIRCLES

by Jane Yolen

Peter Terwilliger drew a circle in the dirt, the circumference larger than his head. He drew an X in the center.

"There," he said. "Spit in it and make a wish. It'll come true."

I didn't believe him, of course. I may have been only seven years old, but I knew a thing or two. Spit didn't make wishes any more than it made polish. But I was sweet on Peter Terwilliger, who sat next to me in first grade, though I never showed it.

I spit and said, "I wish Old Man Johannson would die."

"Not out loud, stupid," Peter Terwilliger said, by which I knew he liked me.

Old Man Johannson didn't die, or at least not all at once. But he had a stroke that very night and spent the better part of a month drooling and staring at the wall. Enough time, in fact, for my father to get the money we needed to save our farm—Mama never dared ask him from where—and to pay Old Man Johannson's heirs off. They were just as mean as their father, tying the rest of the estate up in the courts for years. But Dad managed to sell our farm, poor as it was, for more than it was worth and moved us to the city.

I never saw Peter Terwilliger again.

In the city, Dad drank up all of the farm money and took to abusing Mama, first in small and then in big ways. He started by cursing her out, calling her down for her cooking or her mending or the dust under the bed. It progressed from there to pulling her hair and pinching her arm. One time he tripped her as she went by with a plate of mashed potatoes and she fell, breaking her arm. "It was an accident," she swore and I believed her.

The night he beat her, however, was when I stopped believing. I could hear her trying to keep his voice and her cries low enough so as not to wake me or the neighbors. I got out of bed and trundled downstairs, not even bothering to put on my shoes or coat, though it was colder than a mineshaft outside.

I drew a circle in the dirt of an empty lot next door, as big around as Peter Terwilliger's head, or what I remembered of it. Then I drew an X in the center.

"Make Dad leave Mama alone," I said, and spit.

He left her the next night for a blowsy waitress at the bar he frequented. It wasn't quite what I had in mind.

Mama never recovered from his desertion and she never remarried. She raised me up alone.

It took a third wish to make me understand that my spit wishes worked, but they sure didn't go in circles. More like ellipses. Of course at seven and then at eight I didn't even know the word, much less its meaning. But I understood enough so I didn't make any more spit wishes for years.

It was when I was sixteen and mad at the world, but at Mama in particular who was stricter than anyone else's mother, that a spit wish I made when I was drunk with friends at a school dance led me to the understanding of this odd witching power I had.

Between Jemmy Sanders and Stephen Gallagher and Curtis Bast and me, we had downed a fifth of vodka. Jemmy and Curtis had gotten sick and Stephen had more or less passed out, making us wonder how we were going to get home since he was the only one old enough for a license or a car. The vodka had just made me extraordinarily happy and loose.

"Car?" I said. "We don't need no stinking car. I'm a witch. I've got magic."

"Pumpkins?" mumbled Jemmy in between bouts of puking. "You gonna turn a pumpkin into a coach?"

"Even better," I said. "Just you watch." I drew a circle bigger than Peter Terwilliger's head. Bigger even than his head would have been at sixteen. I drew an *X* in the center. Okay—it was a bit wobbly. So was I. But it was a recognizable *X*. Then I leaned over and spit on it.

"Cool," said Curtis.

"Gross," said Jemmy and she promptly threw up again, well outside the circumference of the circle.

I laughed. "I wish we had a ride," I said.

At that very moment a police car pulled up next to us. In it was Haps Parker, the town constable, and Stephen's stepfather. He waited until Jemmy and Curtis were through being sick. He waited until I stopped giggling. He slapped Stephen two or three times to wake him, then took us to the clinic for coffee and a thorough evaluation.

"I can't let your mother see you like this," he said several times to Stephen. Haps was actually a nice guy; Stephen's dad had been a falling-down drunk.

That's how we spent half the night in the clinic and that's where I first met Polly Bangs, a nurse and a *real* witch. And that's where I learned how to control my circles of magic. Quite a ride indeed.

Polly said the trick was in the spit, not the circle. All bodily fluids, actually, contained magic. As a nurse she had access to the lot of them: spit, blood, urine, etc. Of course not everyone could just spit or pee and wish, or we'd be neck-deep in wishes. That was Polly's line, not mine. You had to be born with the talent, like me.

After she told me—cleaned up Jemmy and Curtis and Stephen and told me—a lot of things became clear. Like my not getting drunk. Like my good grades in school, even though I never studied. Like Stephen, the most popular and best-looking guy in the class falling for me. I had wished those things and they had happened. Not wishes with a circle, but wishes nonetheless. I remembered the evening I had discovered how much I wanted Stephen and I sat in the bathroom and alternately cried and had the runs. And wished he liked me. Wished as hard as I could. And he had.

"You mean," I whispered to Polly, "that I can have *anything* I want just by wishing?"

She shook her head. "You can get anything you wish for, but it won't ever be exactly what you expect. You are untrained. Wishes don't go in easy circles. They go in ellipses."

"We studied those in algebra," I said, remembering suddenly that I hadn't studied very hard. "Made graphs and everything." I had gotten an A and learned nothing. "Besides, I do, too, get exactly what I want. I got Stephen." I looked fondly over at him. He was sitting at the table with Jemmy and Curtis and drinking coffee. The little lock of blond hair fell down over his forehead. I loved that lock. I really did. Even if he was a funny color, kind of green, at the moment.

Polly touched my hand gently and mumbled something and Stephen seemed to age thirty years. It was as if I was sitting across a kitchen table from him and he was that same funny color, apologizing to me—once again—for getting drunk and promising it wouldn't happen again. I looked down. My hands, folded on the table, were shaking. My wrists and arms were bruised. I shook my head and everything was the same as before. Only it wasn't. I suddenly didn't want Stephen any more. Not even a little.

"Ellipses," I whispered, sort of like underlining a word in a textbook to aid in remembering it. "Ellipses."

I went back to the clinic every weekend after that. My mom thought I was interested in becoming a nurse. Actually I was studying witchcraft with Polly. We borrowed slides of blood samples from patients which I studied under the microscope and learned about identifying witches. Witch's blood makes more white cells. Taken to the hospital, we are thought to be leukemic. Treated, we get sicker. Unless we are treated by a witch doctor.

Okay—I laughed the first time I heard that, too. But Polly made sure I got to know the names of those doctors who were witches themselves, and who worked locally.

She made sure my name got on the master list so they would know me as well.

And then, after I understood all the background, she taught me how to work on my wishes.

I would never be able to make them less elliptical. That's the nature of wishes. But I did learn how to anticipate the worst of the results. That way I could change the actual wording of the wish, or decide not to make the wish at all.

I got good and I got older.

I studied with Polly all the way through high school and then decided to study medicine in college. I became a doctor and used my talent to help good folks get well. Bad folks—well, I just left them to their bodies own devices.

And then one day—it was June 17th—a man was brought into the emergency room where I was working. He was pretty badly torn up, his color and general state of wear and tear made me recognize him as a drunk. He had been a big man once, but age and other stuff had shrunk him down like one of those apples off the tree.

But I knew him. Hadn't seen him since I was a kid, but I knew him. A witch knows her own.

"Hello, Dad," I whispered. His eyes widened, but he was much too sick to answer back. I took his vital signs. They weren't good at all. My guess was he had next to no liver function left. I patched him up and stitched him up. I did everything that medicine could do, which wasn't enough.

He had just enough strength to grab my wrist. "Want a drink . . ." he murmured.

I closed the white curtains around us, cocooning us from the rest of the world. I stared down at him for a long while.

"Do it for me," he begged.

I drew a circle around his head on the gurney with my finger. I put a little cross on the right side, just by his ear. Not necessary, I knew, but the memories of that child in the cold empty lot were suddenly quite strong.

"Dad," I said slowly, "I wish you wouldn't die." Then,

knowing no one could see us with the white curtains closed, I spit—very accurately—onto his forehead.

He cried out once and closed his eyes. He didn't even have the strength to wipe away the spit, but lay there still as death. I watched as my spit dried on his skin, as his skin turned cool, then cold.

I opened the white curtains at last and went to the next patient, a child who had broken her arm. It was a quick and easy fix and we traded knock-knock jokes all the while I was plastering the thing.

Dad lingered for fifteen years that way, floating in and out of consciousness, full of needles, full of pain, not alive, not dead.

Mama visited him once out of memory and once out of mercy, and never again.

At the hospital he was a kind of mascot and a kind of teaching tool. He lasted the entire time I was there. When I retired, I let him go, pulling the witching plug. I was the only mourner at his funeral.

At night I dream of him, large and still and cold and not quite dead. I expect I always will.

Ellipses.

IN A YELLOW DRESS

by Jo Clayton

Ashfar put on her yellow silk dress and had her daughter braid her long black hair into cornrows, sliding the end of each tiny braid through four yellow beads.

Six-year-old Sygny brushed her hands over the beads spread across her mother's back, laughing at the ticktack clickclack they made. "All done," she said. "Is it time yet?" She spoke with gravity and care; a missing front tooth made esses exacting.

"Ticca-tacca," Ashfar sang as she rose from the braided rug. "Sygny, sweetie, swing with me." She held out her hands, pulled Sygny from the hassock and into a little whirldance that took them across the room and out the back door into the garden, the fly imps buzzing along behind.

"Time time time," she chanted and lifted the latch on the back-fence gate, pushing it open.

"Time time time," Sygny chanted, giggling as her mother swung her up and set her down on the circle of white sand way behind the house.

"Round the spiral Ashfar goes, step by step young Sygny follows." Ashfar tapped Sygny on the head, turned, and raised her arms, the moonlight yellow on her skin, soft as the silk of her dress. "The Due has been paid, the Balance is true."

Braiding strands of moonlight into a rope, dropping the rope beside her feet, she danced inward on a tightly wound spiral, Sygny like a small white shadow stepping where she stepped, mouthing her words, miming her gestures. "Tari ber-tari," she sang, "cast down the pale plait/ Pintu tup-pilin pry open the gate/Buka bu-berlan on the moon coil we dance/Ranga ter-ranga by the moonglow advance. . . . "

Round and round they went, round and round till they stepped into mist and out on a braided rag rug.

Sygny whooped when she saw the portrait waiting on the easel. "Mum, it's you."

Ashfar looked at it and clicked her tongue. "Indu Mulia, his memory's gone bad." The woman in the yellow dress, her black hair hanging loose, was prettier than she'd ever been.

Beside the easel there was a table with three chairs, a boxed hamburger at each place, and twin round cupcakes on a plate, chocolate with chocolate icing and three pink candles on each, the candles pushed down into white icing roses. Harlach had pulled the spotlight on the overhead rail directly above the rug and it was the only light turned on, leaving the rest of the loft dark and echoing. "Look, Sygny, your father's got a party ready for your birthday."

"Burgersz," Sygny said, her grin so wide it threatened her ears. She loved hamburgers and only got them when her father bought them for her. "Daddy?"

Ashfar heard a faint sound from the darkness, felt a wash of pain. "Sygny, sweetie, go put the shades up. Har, it's Ashfar, where are you? What's wrong?" She edged round the easel and began groping through the dark. "Har, if you can hear me. . . ."

The first shade snapped up, rattling in its hangers.

Ashfar glanced toward the window, shivered when she saw a powersink rising like windblown smoke behind the roofs across the alley, Little Moon's tiny crescent rocking atop it. *I shouldn't have listened to Sygny,* she thought. *We shouldn't have come so early.*

Another shade rattled up, its pull dancing against the glass.

A row of cabinets ran along the end of the loft, the place where Harlach kept rolls of canvas, paint jars, brushes, and other supplies. There was a dark blotch in the angle where the cabinets met the wall. Ashfar ran toward it, flung herself onto her knees, and snapped a flash of light between thumb and finger.

Harlach was lying on his back. His face was cut to bone and dotted with small round burns, there was a sucking wound in his chest and his life burned so low she could hardly feel it.

Another shade went rattling up.

A muffled squeal.

Ashfar swung round on her knees and saw a dark figure pulling her daughter through the window onto the fire escape outside. Another stood beside him. "No!" She leaped to her feet and started toward them, hands reaching to gather moonpower.

The second figure shot at her. There was a burning at the top of her arm where the bullet creased her before it buried itself in the wall. She ignored the pain, flicked a hand that sent the next shot wide.

Behind her life fluttered lower in Harlach.

She groaned and began clawing moonlight into a ragged sphere, filled with terror because it came partly from Little Moon and might make everything worse. She had no time to think, no edges to play in. If she went after them, Harlach died.

The man fired again, clipped one of her braids and sent it flying, the beads clattering as it hit the wooden floor. She flung the Power sphere at her daughter and cried out in triumph as she saw Sygny absorb it. "Hang on, Signy," she cried. "Remember what I taught you. I'll come. I promise I'll come."

A second later the window was empty. Ashfar could hear feet on the metal steps, then the creak as the tilt ladder lowered to the ground.

She opened her mouth as wide as it would go, her jaw hinges cracking as she gulped moonlight until her body glowed with it. With a cry that burst up from her heels, she spat a gout of that swallowed light at Harlach. It hardened into a crystal seal that would hold him as he was till she could get him through the Gate.

She carried him to the braided rug, laid him down, and

sang the Gate again. When the plaited spiral was glowing white, she rolled him into the mist.

A moment later she was standing on the round of white sand, Harlach at her feet, the seal melting, Little Moon's curse that was, his life ebbing with it.

"Indu Mulia!" She ran into the house, found her ointment jar, her scissors, a needle and thread, and ran back.

Forcing herself to work with meticulous care, she cut his shirt away, sewed symbolic knots in each wound, then ran her thumb along them, sealing edge to edge. She spread ointment over the fine red lines, over the blackened burns, and dragged him onto the grass, breaking the spiral and sending bits of trapped moonlight floating off like dandelion fluff.

She straightened, wiped her hands down her sides, and began humming, a deep burr that started soft as a whisper, then grew louder and louder. Compelled by the sound, the fly imps came to buzz round her body, their coldfire flickering yellow and green.

She lifted a foot, set it down, lifted it again, moved her right arm in an angular arc, drew it back, moved her left arm in the mirror arc, drew it back. Then she was dancing round and round Harlach, the two note drone filling the night's silence, the yellow silk dress belling out from her body. Round and round till the healing spell was wound up, the fly imps caught in it, power points to feed it.

She opened her arms, no laughter left in her, no joy this time, only desperation. "I acknowledge the Balance," she cried. "For what I take and what I do, I will pay a price, a year and a day of not-being, not-thinking, add a year and a day of service and abstinence. Help me get my daughter back." Heart beating in her throat, she waited—and cried out with relief as the Gate Mist formed about her.

When she stepped onto the braided rug, she heard a pounding at the door, a shout. "Police. Open up."

She spun a glamour about herself that would hide her from ordinary eyes—if it held, if Little Moon didn't tweak it and melt it on her, then she knelt by the easel and waited.

A key turned in the lock.

The door slammed open.

A policeman jumped into the doorway, gun braced.

He straightened, twisted his head around. "Nothing there. Take a look round, I'll cover you."

The second policeman pulled a long, heavy flashlight from loops on his belt, and walked into the loft. He waved the light around, crossed to the corner where Harlach had been. "Blood. Lots. Still wet."

"Right. Hey, you."

The building superintendent came into the light on the landing, stood with shoulders hunched, hands in the pockets of his ancient jeans. He was a skinny small man with a neat brush of gray hair running from ear to ear. If he had more than three words of Anglish, Ashfar had never heard them. Half hidden in the shadows behind him she saw another face she recognized. Ratworm, Harlach had called him in a savage moment when he'd been interrupted once too often.

"Not you, Beanhead, the other one. Who you? What you doing here?"

"Heard you coming up the stairs, wondered what was going on. Name's Voelks, I live in 2A." Ratworm twisted his head round and looked back down the stairs as if he were sorry he'd walked up them.

The policeman pointed at the easel and the table with the party setup. "You know what that's about?"

"Yeah. The painter, he was expecting his ex-wife and his kid. It's the girl's birthday."

"Ex-wife, hm. That her in the painting?"

"Yeah. Except she's taller than she looks there, near six feet. Thinner, too. And the little girl's a lot like her except she's a towhead."

"They fight?"

"Yeah. Couple of times I thought they were going to off each other."

Ashfar ground her teeth together and almost lost con-

trol of the glamour. Liar. Her eyes narrowed. Why lie?
You protecting someone?

"You hear the shots?"

Voclks' eyes slid away again, then he shrugged.
"Yeah."

"And you didn't call in a report."

"Sounded like they came from out in the alley. Lot of
stuff like that round here. Didn't want to get involved."

The second policeman pulled the door shut on the lav-
atory, joined his partner. "No one in the place, alive or
dead. Nothing to say the man didn't just cut himself and
go running to emergency. And like the guy said, the shots
could've been out in the alley."

They left. In a short while the only sounds in the loft
were the faint buzzing of flies gathered round the pools of
drying blood.

Ashfar let the glamour fall away and walked slowly to
the window. She rubbed at her eyes, then breathed a
Blessing. Little Moon had dropped behind the sink veils,
its power for mischief near gone.

This world was filled with powersinks and other traps
and the two moons interacted in ways that made every
call on them a chancy thing. Little Moon was a trickster,
plucking the strings of spells spun to Big Moon's tropes
so that nothing was exactly what the spinner expected.
Everything here scared her and made her skin itch. That
was why she came across so seldom though her love for
Harlach was strong in her—only when Big Moon was full
and Little Moon dropping early past the horizon. That
was why she refused to let Sygny spend half the year
with her father. That was why finding Sygny would either
be quick or impossible.

Ashfar shook off the darkness that settled over her at
the thought of failing, crawled through the window, and
sat on the fire escape with her legs drawn up, her eyes
closed, Big Moon's light melting into her, pooling at the
bottom of her belly.

When she was ready, she tapped her palms lightly on
her knees and sang into the rhythm, "Sygny. Manan
kemana. Sygny. Daja jawaba. Sygny. Mana kemana.

Sygny. . . ." Over and over the summoning call, over and over and never an answer, as if Sygny were erased from this world.

Someone was fiddling with the lock.

Ashfar let the useless chant fade, knelt by the window, and watched Voelks come creeping in. After he pushed an odd device into the lock, there was a snick-snicking sound, then the bolt clunked home. He dragged a stool along the cabinets till he found the one he was looking for, climbed onto the stool, pulled the top door open, reached inside, his arm going in up to the shoulder.

Ashfar slid over the sill, drew on a cat face, and changed her fingernails to cat claws.

"Ah! Come to papa, horsey baby." He pulled out a plastic bag filled with coarse white powder. "Didn't get it, the. . . ." He yelped as Ashfar's shoulder slammed into his legs and sent him crashing off the stool. He ended on his face with her knees in the middle of his back.

She used her claws to jerk his head around.

When he glimpsed what was hanging over him, he squealed, tried to buck her off, then lay shuddering, his breath hot and wet against her palm. "What are you?" he muttered.

"Who were those men and where did they take the girl?"

"I don't know anything. Let me up."

She hated the feel of his breath on her, the brush of his lips against her palm, but she didn't move. "No. You know them. Who are they?"

"All right. All right. It's like this. I don't know their names, but I seen them somewhere . . . yes, yes, I remember, they were talking to Harlach in a place down the street. Gingerpot, it's called. Vegetarian. Why I noticed them. Thugs like that in there. . . ." He screamed as she slapped her free hand against the back of his head.

"You lie," she said. "I can smell it on you. What was in the cupboard?"

His fear was a stink that sickened her, but her daughter's life hung on his answers and nothing was going to stop her finding out what he knew. She shoved the claw on her little finger through his cheek, scraped the tip against the roots of his teeth. He screamed again, coughed out a gout of blood. "Heroin. My stash."

"They were hired men. Who owns them?"

He wriggled like a snake trying to escape the forked stick that pinned it to the ground.

"You pointed them at Har somehow. You're the reason they cut him. Don't bother denying it. I don't have time to care about that. The name," she said. "Tell me the name."

"He'll kill me."

"You'll wish he did if you pull a lie." She spoke slowly as if she were tasting the words before letting them out of her mouth. "I'll cut your hamstrings so you crawl like the worm you are and play with your face until you'd scare a gorilla. You better believe me. I want my daughter back."

"Roland Markey, penthouse C, Angla Towers." He shuddered and started crying.

She pulled her claws free and got to her feet. "We'll call a cab from your place. You're coming with me." She smiled. "You'll pay the fare."

Voelks slammed the door to the cab and edged away from Ashfar, eyes flicking along the street, back to her and away again.

She put her hand on his arm and felt it twitch. "Let's move."

"You're killing me," he muttered. His nose was running and he kept blinking. "Let me go. I brought you here. Let me go."

"When I know where my daughter is."

"I can't get you in there. Markey don't want to see me."

Though Little Moon was out of sight, Blessed Be, and Big Moon was swimming huge and yellow over their heads, bound by the bargain she'd made to give her anything she needed, she was taut with a fear she couldn't let Voelks notice—fear of the powersink eddying beside them, a fluid, fluctuating emptiness that sent chills through her body. There was one small glimmer of hope; the pressure from the full moon flattened it out so it oozed along the ground and left the top of the building free. If she could make it past the lower floors. . . .

The doorman stepped out to intercept them. She snapped thumb against finger, flashed light in his face and with it she blew a nada spell.

He stared dully past them, seeing nothing, thinking nothing.

She shoved Voelks forward. "Get his keys and get that door open."

The minute she stepped inside, her hands and feet went numb and her eyes blurred until she could barely distinguish between light and dark.

Voelks scuttled toward the elevators. She followed, using the sound of his feet to guide her, willing him not to notice her distress.

When she heard the muted swish of the door, she walked in, hand a little ahead of her, turned when she touched the back wall. "Let's get going," she said. She didn't trust her voice with anything more difficult.

"We can't get to the penthouses this way. You need a special key and you have to come in through the parking garage in the basement." When she didn't say anything, he swore and jabbed at a button. "You'll see," he said. "Nineteenth floor is as high as this goes."

Up and up the car went, muck swirling about her, draining strength from her body until she was afraid her bones would melt. When they rose into clean air, she nearly vomited with relief. She glanced at Voelks to see if he'd picked up on what had happened to her.

He was rubbing at his nose, a tic was jumping by one eye and his blinking had increased. He was in no shape to notice anything.

Nineteenth floor.

She closed her hand on his arm. "There's an empty apartment along there. I want you to open the door for me."

* * *

Ashfar looked around. No furniture, no shades on the windows, a faded carpet on the floor. "This'll do just fine."

"Huh?"

"Never mind." She swung around and blew sleep into his face. He collapsed to the carpet and started snoring.

She went into the largest of the empty rooms, the one that looked out through long windows onto a narrow terrace. Moonlight poured in, painting her hair and skin silver, stripping away the blood and muck, turning the yellow silk dress to molten gold.

She danced the dance, clapping her hands and chanting the summons.

The pull was fierce and immediate.

Voelks hadn't lied. Her daughter was here.

She changed the dance and changed the chant, walked the spiral into another Gate.

And appeared in the room above where her daughter crouched in a ring of white fire that kept two men away from her.

Sygny's face was bruised, her smock ripped and filthy, her feet bare, but she laughed aloud when she saw her mother.

The man who shot at Ashfar before shot again, but she was *changing* as the bullet passed through her so she didn't even feel it. She was a yellow tiger, on them before they could move. She bit the face off one and disemboweled the other.

"Mum, watch out."

Ashfar *changed* as she wheeled, was herself again in her yellow dress as the man in the doorway pointed a funnel at her and blew stinking, strangling foam at her face. She stumbled, coughed.

Sygny's fire tore past her, hit the man.

He started a scream but didn't have time to finish it. In seconds he was hard cinder and calcined bone.

Ashfar scraped the foam from her face and caught Sygny in her arms. They stood there hugging each other, laughing and crying at once. Finally, Ashfar freed herself, tapped her daughter on her face. "I said I'd come. I promised."

Signy gave her a wobbly smile, looked past her at the burned man, gulped and looked hastily away. "He wazs the bossz," she said, her voice very small and shaky, her esses whistling. "He hit me."

"It's all right, sweetie. Anyone else here?"

"No, Mum. Juszt them."

"Good. Let's go home. Your Daddy's there. He's going to be all right." She lifted Sygny into her arms, carried her over the burnt man and out onto the terrace, set her down on the small patch of grass. "Round the spiral Ashfar goes, step by step young Sygny follows."

Harlach lay sleeping, his wounds closed over, not even a scar left. The fly imps were still circling above him, but their buzzing had a plaintive, weary note.

"Go inside, Sygny, get yourself washed up so you'll look nice for your dad."

"Mum, the Due I owe . . . I killed him."

"It won't be bad, just sad, sweetie. You did it to save another person, not yourself. That counts in the Balance."

Sygny managed a small smile and went trudging off.

Ashfar unwove the spell from Harlach, let the fly imps drink moonlight pooled in her palms. "Blessed Be," she said to them. "My house and what I have is yours."

Harlach caught Sygny in his strong, thin arms, tossed her high, hugged her tight. "Your mother says you're going to come and live a while with me."

"Mum, too?"

"No, sweetie. We're going to tell folks she's sick and has to go away a while and that's why we weren't home when the police came. If anyone asks, that's what you say."

"All right."

"Sygny, come here." Ashfar lifted a silvered finger, wrote a sign on Sygny's brow. "Tik pikir," she murmured. She wrote another that crossed her lips. "Tik perkat." Wrote two more in the palms of her daughter's hands.

"Tik jarat." She sat on her heels, looked up at Sygny. "Do you understand?"

"Yes. No spellz, no sight, no signz. No Mum."

"Until the Balance comes right."

Sygny's mouth trembled, but she said the words without flinching, even the sibilants. "Until the Balance comes right."

Ashfar watched the moonlight fade from the braided Gate. With a weary sigh, she stepped onto the sand. "Let it be."

She cried out at the pain of fitting herself into so small a form, then a bird with silky yellow feathers rose from mist and flew into the forest.

THE WITCH'S CAT

by Byron Tetrick

The witch let her arm drop to the side of the plush sofa
and blindly wiggled her thick, almost manly fingers in an
entrancing motion like the poisonous ribbons of a Portu-
guese man-of-war. Her cat moved under her hand, brushing its body along the still-moving fingers till they no
longer stroked its spine and then turned back into the
hand of its master and purred in contentment as the witch
caressed it behind its ears. Between them flowed an energy that was as ancient as the bond that all living creatures once shared, but that now belonged only to the
daughters of Diana, Queen of Witches All, and their
familiars—the beasts and animals that were the agents of
their malefic witchcraft.

Her body was unclothed, as was her wont whenever
she was alone in her chambers. She would not be disturbed. No one would dare disturb her! The witch moved
her hand from the cat, and it jumped onto the sofa and
stretched, arching its back like a bow. Then, with claws
still extended, the cat stepped onto her leg and began to
nuzzle at her body, but quit when, with a snap of her fingers, the witch showed her displeasure. Obediently, her
familiar moved to her lap and quickly began purring as
the witch rubbed the top of its head in a gentle scratching. Soon it was asleep.

The cat's claws had left tiny, red pinpricks along her
legs. She inspected the rest of her body dispassionately,
not minding the thickening waist or the sagging flesh. For
with age, came power. And it was power that nourished

her . . . fulfilled her. Power was an intoxicant without equal, the quest for it all-consuming—a hunger that could never be sated . . . not for her. Its trappings amused and pleased the witch, her lofty position magnifying the perception of power. But oh, she never had enough! Its elusiveness was taunting; its wielding, so glorious! All that day she had used her power over her minions, watching them quail at her slightest frown or shrink from her laughter as she ridiculed those who foolishly voiced an opinion against her.

She felt her cat stir as, even in sleep, it shared the power-spell that linked them in age-old symbiosis. The witch massaged along its shoulders and felt its feline muscles ripple with untapped strength. Her familiar was no longer the kitten, awkward and shy, but now a graceful creature, a worthy conspirator. The witch, now breathing in almost a rhythmic synchronicity with her cat, closed her eyes and remembered the coven stories of how the witches and the beasts came together. The stories of how it once was, in a time of great change. In a time when witches had great power. . . .

* * *

"Will the boy-king do your bidding, Elynia?" The witch speaking was Hecate, namesake of the moon goddess, and queen of their coven. Her wizened body glistened with sweat, her breathing still labored from the exertion of their ring dances. All the witches stood around the great circle, their ceremony complete, their power now concentrated and pulsing.

Elynia stepped forward and thrust out her hips in a vulgar movement, squeezing her pink-tipped breasts with her hands. Her beauty was surely entrancing to all who beheld her—all, that is, except the witches. They saw only a young witch, immature in the ways of darkness, and more importantly, weak in power. But she spoke with confidence. "Oh, young Richard will do all that I ask . . . and more, as long as I give him this!" And she laughed in a girlish fashion that clashed with the crudity of her actions. Icion, an ancient-looking witch and a disciple of Baphomet, the androgynous Demon of sexual magic, turned to the witch at her left, but spoke loud enough so all could hear, "Elynia gives new meaning to the expression 'hag ridden.'"

The cave echoed with the laughter of the witches. In the fringes of the light cast by the braziers of pitch, and candles made from human fat, black dogs slunk behind rocks; other small animals, used by the witches in their craft, scurried for shelter.

"Enough!" shouted Hecate. "Upon the axis of the Plantagenet pivots our own survival. Though our power has never been greater, so it is also with the Church. Since the time of the Black Death, the Church has grown in size and power, and now I fear it seeks to root out and destroy all the rival religions."

"But, Hecate," interrupted Sabaoth, a coarse, big-boned witch whose magic was second only to Hecate's, "all across eastern England the peasants and serfs are rebelling against the clerics. Simon of Sudbury, the Archbishop of Canterbury, has been beheaded; the Prior of Bury has been taken from his monastery, and his head will soon join the chancellor's. Are not events in our favor?"

Hecate did not answer. Instead she lifted the magic sword from its place at her feet and drew a Name of Power within the circle and chanted in the ancient language of the *Stregas*—the witches of Italia. The flames from the fire at the center of the circle flared. A cloud of opalescent smoke billowed forth in swirling shades of purple and green. Upon and throughout the smoke, a vision appeared of a great battle being fought.

"What you see," said Hecate, "is the Warrior Bishop, Paul. Even now he is putting down the revolt, and while the rebels march on London, he defeats their rear echelons." Hecate raised the sword and brought it down forcefully, stabbing it into the floor of the cave. "Use your witchcraft and destroy the bishop. Now! All of you! Invoke your darkest Demon; cast your strongest spells; kill him!" Hecate's visage was distorted with hatred.

The witches looked at each other, confused, bewildered. No one chanted, not one drew a hex within the circle.

Hecate glared at each one of them, her fury now directed at her witches. Angrily, she took the sword and slashed it through the anagram, causing the fire to contract and the images to disappear. "You can't, can you? We lack the power! Our magic is pitiful in the fullness of events that sway the future. Power is the path to unfolding the future as we wish. Power is the key to the prophecy." Once more she looked down the length of her bristly, warty nose at the witches of the coven.

Singly, as Hecate's scathing gaze scrutinized them, each witch lowered her eyes in shame. Those who had never before fully experienced Hecate's anger stood on visibly shaking legs, fearing more was to follow. Truly (at least in the witch Hecate) they saw power for what power is—forcing one's will on others.

"I ask you again, Elynia. Will King Richard do your bidding?"

This time, Elynia spoke with hesitancy and obvious trepidation as she answered, "Yes, Hecate. He is enraptured. Even now I sense his pole hardening for me. But I know that I cannot hold sway over him forever."

"Good," answered Hecate. "You're learning. A man's lust never lasts for long. But use it and twist it to your purposes—our purposes." She turned toward Icion. "Teach her your wisdom. Share your potions."

Icion smiled. "Elynia will be an eager student. I will instruct her well, Mistress."

Hecate left the circle, calling Adonai—the youngest and still a novice witch—to aid her in passing out the cakes made of whole meal, salt, honey, and blood. While Adonai passed the cakes, Hecate drank ale from an ancient goblet and passed it to Sabaoth. She wiped the heavily-foamed ale from her hairy, upper lip and spoke, "While we feast, I will explain why Elynia's task is crucial."

The witches turned toward their ruler, understanding now that this was not an ordinary *esabat,* but a meeting that might determine the future of their coven, if not of all witchery.

"The Church of the Christians is facing its gravest danger since the days of the Romans," began Hecate. "Until now they have let the other religions coexist, but only because we have posed no threat. With the peasant uprising, that has all ended. The feudal system has lasted because of the Church, and the lords will fight to keep it. And if they win ... the Church will crush all who opposed it."

Hecate stuck out a bony arm from which folds of loose skin hung like melted tallow; she pointed a finger. "Aglonia, who was father to Richard?"

Aglonia, who was even older than Hecate, and who was once a very powerful—and evil—witch, answered, "Why, Edward, the Black Prince."

"And was he with us or against us?"

"More us than the Church! He was a lusty man and played the Horned God at many *sabbats*. He coupled with many of us. Why, I remember once—"

"Yes, yes," Hecate cackled. "I, too, remember." She paused and looked around the circle before continuing, "For two hundred years the Plantagenet family has worshiped Diana, but played the politic with the Church. Edward III held reign for fifty years, and we, through his mistress, shared in that power and benefited from his protection. If the witches are to survive, we will do it in two ways: the first being to ally and ingratiate ourselves further with the reins of power. You all saw how helpless our witchcraft was to destroy one soldier, much less sway a battle. But with a king doing our bidding ... we can field armies and rule nations."

Hecate directed Adonai to refill the chalice from the cauldron and carried it to Elynia, where she held the cup for her as she drank deeply of the potion-laced ale. "The boy-king, Richard, must be ours, Elynia. Use your womanhood. Use your witchcraft. Use whatever it takes!"

Again the chalice was handed around the circle, being refilled many times, as the witches planned and schemed. Their eyes became glazed with drugs and wantonness, and they began to move sensuously in anticipation of the final dance and the climax into debauchery. Sabaoth was sent to bring in the drugged peasant men.

Aradia, a witch of middle years who was once very beautiful, asked Hecate, "And what of the second way; how else can we assure our survival?"

"Ah-h-ch-ch-ch," came the reply like a hiss. "I have a plan. For a thousand years witchcraft has changed little. Our power has grown through the centuries, but oh, so slowly. It is time that changed. I have made an alliance with the king's wizard."

Stunned, the witches stood motionless. Finally one said, "I knew not that Richard had a wizard. I thought the wizards, like the druids, were gone."

Hecate smiled. "It is a well-kept secret. All the Plantagenets have had a wizard. It may well be that it has been the *same* wizard for all these years. The wizard may even be . . . Merlin, for wizards traverse worlds and time the way we mortals walk a path in a meadow.

"I have made a pact with the wizard, promising our support and that of the peasants we control and influence. In return, he will show us a new pathway to power. The wizard will attend our next *sabbat*. It portends great things for our coven.

"But come, *tonight* is a time for witches. The moon is full and power throbs within us." Hecate grabbed the chalice and lifted it high, tipping it so that the ale poured into her mouth like a phallus, the reddish ale overflowing her pointed chin and dripping onto her shrunken breasts.

The naked men were led within the circle and their bodies rubbed with the herbal juices of the belladonna. The witches once more danced, the circle closed, the sound of their ancient orgiastic rituals reverberated throughout the cave as the flickering braziers cast shadows on unspeakable acts and unholy deeds.

The wizard—who in fact *was* Merlin—walked the narrow, tree-lined path using his staff to avoid the larger obstacles, but still he stumbled and tripped often as he labored the final quarter league to the agreed rendezvous. The full moon, though it lit the path well, aided not his aged eyes. A thousand years, even if much of it was spent in a sleep-trance, was a long time to gaze upon the machinations and intrigues of mankind—to say nothing of viewing the evils of the witches. But young Richard was a worthy successor to the throne; he loved England, as did Merlin.

Thinking of the witches, his innards roiled with loathing for the task ahead but he had made the bargain, and forces more powerful than he would be invoked if the contract was not kept. Besides—and here he had to smile to himself—if the witches accepted his power-spell, though it would increase their power, the end result would be to place a limit on their witchcraft that would forever be in place once the spell was cast. He had served the English kings for a millennium, but even *their* quest for power paled next to that of the witches.

And the bargain *had* worked out well. The witches were still revered by many of the peasants. The witches had done much to convince the paganist rebel leaders that Richard was their monarch and would represent them well. The young king had valiantly faced the rebels at the gates of London and won them over as easily as young Arthur had united the warring factions so many years ago. The boy-king was now gathering the support of the Church, and had even brought many of the rival nobles into his camp. Perhaps England might find peace again, and maybe the religions would let each other exist side-by-side as in the old days.

Yes, the bargain made was worth the price. His one remaining concern—and it was very troubling—was the influence that the young witch was gaining over King Richard. Already he had left Queen Isabella's chambers and now openly bedded Elynia within the castle. Merlin had seen more than one kingdom fall, lured by lace and snared by flesh!

An owl hooted a warning. Merlin walked a few steps farther along the path. A lone figure, her naked body luminous in the moonlight, greeted him. "Wizard," she said. "I'm to take you to our *sabbat.*"

* * *

Hecate's face was flushed with purply-shaded splotches, her breathing a wheezing, death-rattle staccato. A vile-smelling sweat dripped from her body as she cavorted around the circle of power.

From the entrance of the cave came a yell, "Adonia approaches with the wizard!"

Hecate stopped her dancing. Struggling for breath, she ordered, "Bring me ale!"

The chalice placed in her hands, she threw her head back and drank lustily. "Tonight we complete the circle." She raised the goblet in a salute. "Power awaits us!"

The witches took their places around the circle.

Hecate motioned to Elynia. "Come to me." She held the chalice up to Elynia's lips until the remainder of the potion was gone. "You have done well," she crooned. "We have fastened onto a brightly burning comet whose fires will protect us from our enemies and emblazon us with reflected power. And when the comet fizzles and burns out, we will be left to rule in the darkness that follows."

Adonia entered the flickering arc of the torchlights; the witches turned toward the wizard.

He appeared not to notice their nakedness as he approached. "I have come to keep my part of the bargain," said the ancient-looking wizard in a surprisingly commanding voice. "Let us be done with it."

Hecate was not intimidated. "First explain to us your magical spell," she commanded in return.

The wizard entered the ring without invitation. Oblivious to the dangers within the circle of power, he began, "You witches once worshiped at the altar of the animistic world from which you drew upon the powers of nature and the beasts of the world. In your insatiable thirst for more power, you forsook the natural powers that are all around you, and instead called upon demons and created potions with incantations of evil and alchemic distortions of those gifts that nature gave you freely."

"Cease!" shrieked Hecate, her arms extended and nails clawing the air as if ready to tear into the wizard. "If we wanted a sermon, we could go to the church of the nobles!"

The wizard smiled, unfazed. Only a slight shifting of his hand on his staff showed that he was prepared to ward off any attack. He pointed to a shadowed corner of the cave where several animals shivered in fright. "You use these creatures like tools to be discarded when they are no longer of use.

"There!" He pointed again. "They are your new source of power." The wizard raised his staff above his head and spoke in a language unknown to the witches. From the shadows and crevices of the cave came all manner of animals: cats of all sizes and colors; dogs, mostly curs and mongrels; a wolf; a fox; two fat groundhogs; dozens of rats, many larger than most of the scraggly cats; other brutes, bizarre and mundane. The animals showed neither fear nor curiosity, but came unhesitatingly to the witches' circle and gathered on one side away from the fire.

The wizard spoke again, "Once, all the world's creatures, including humans, were linked to the forces of nature and the Great Mother; now only the lesser creatures are in harmony with the energy of the land, the sea, and the sky. I can give you a spell and a potion that will link you forever with the beasts so that with them you can draw from this energy. Your power will not only be stronger acting together as a coven, but each of you, linked with your own animal, will be able to evoke power that once took all of you together to conjure."

The witches looked at each other, at the wizard, and at the animals crouched within the ring, each imagining such power and what they could do with it. Hecate's greed showed visibly upon her cragged features, but so did her skepticism. "Give us proof of this power before we commit, for you say this linkage will bind us forever to the beasts."

Once again, the wizard raised his staff and whispered an incantation. The animals within the circle shifted and paced, their fur hackled, claws unsheathed. The fire swelled and flames rose high into the air. A power, grander than the witches had ever experienced, coursed around the circle, to the beasts and back again, growing vibrant, almost uncontrollable. "Use it," the wizard coaxed. "Taste the power and see if it is not to your liking!"

Each witch stepped forward into the circle and called upon a demon or cast a spell and felt this strange new force amplify her power. Each was satisfied that the wizard spoke the truth; Hecate had made a rich bargain. Convinced, they all shared the potion that the wizard mixed with their ale, and together they chanted the sorcerer's spell that sealed the pact.

"My word has been kept. The bargain may not be all you hoped, but you will have more power; that is what you wanted and what you received. I want only to leave this evil and foul-smelling lair." Thus speaking, the wizard pulled his robes tightly about him and left the circle.

The witches, now done with him, ignored his leaving and passed the chalice around the circle, becoming intoxicated both with ale and power. Icion couldn't resist taunting the old wizard as he slowly walked into the shadows, toward the cave's exit. "Don't leave, old man. Our fun is just beginning. I have philters that can even stiffen your old noodle. You can have all of us!"

The cave rocked with raucous cackling.

"The sheep in the fields look better than the twisted flesh I see before me," retorted the wizard and turned his back on the hideous hags.

Hecate, for a moment, thought about trying her new-found power on the old wizard, but thought it better to accept the insult than misjudge a sorcerer. It was soon forgotten, as the coven reveled in their new, augmented power.

Yes, thought Hecate, it was a masterful bargain she had made. This newfound alliance between the beasts and the witches would, like any new spell or unrefined potion, only become more powerful with use. She looked over at the beasts still gathered within the power-ring and noticed a sleek, black cat with white markings staring back at her with glowing, amber eyes. "Are you to be my consort?" she said as she walked over to the cat and lifted it gently into her arms. She held the cat lovingly to her naked body, and deep within her own breast she felt a vibratory quiver resonate between them—as if she herself was purring. A wave of raw power pulsed through her body like an orgasm.

"Oh, yes, my precious," she laughed. "You are mine . . . for always and always."

* * *

The witch looked down at her own cat and stroked it gently. Like it or not, she thought, we are linked forever to our familiars—for the wizard had *tricked Hecate.*

The witches saw their power dramatically increase. Through their familiars, they could channel forces that they hadn't even known existed. And through Elynia, they controlled Richard, who protected them from the Church as it sought to regain its power over the peasants.

The wizard's duplicity become evident only after many years had passed and Hecate's familiar died of old age. They should have foreseen that the symbiotic relationship could not outlive either mortal participant. Hecate lost much of her power and soon died herself. In turn, the other familiars died off, further weakinging the coven, so that eventually control was lost over Richard. Though a witch could take a new familiar, the spell doomed the witches—and all witches from that time on—to be continuously starting over just as both would reach the pinnacle of shared power. Sixteen years after assuming the crown, Richard II was usurped by Henry and died in prison.

Without his protection, what followed was the beginning of 400 years of persecution and witch-hunts as Hecate's prediction came to pass, and the Church began its systematic eradication of the old religions—especially witchcraft.

But the witch knew she must live with what fate had ordained. Her power grew every day, as did her familiar's. Soon her power would be unstoppable, and she had an agenda before her that would require every bit of it.

The witch lifted her cat and placed it on the thick oriental rug. She walked across the room and called after her, "Here kitty, kitty. Come along, Socks. It's dinner time and we want you to grow to be strong and healthy. We have much work to do." And thinking of that and of what power she did *have, she began to laugh and laugh. And the laugh became a cackle that echoed through the upper rooms of the mansion and carried down the stairs where a man of great power blanched in fear. Outside his office, two uniformed men, both veterans of battle, looked at each other, and they, too, feared what lay ahead.*

THE SWINEHERD

by Lois Tilton

"**H**einrich the Simple! Heinrich the Swineherd!" My brothers would always mock me when we lived together on our father's farm.

Well, I may have been simple, but I loved every one of those swine. I had seen them farrowed, and I even had names for them—Fat Otto, Old Tusker, Bristles. I knew what they liked: a cool mud-wallow, and a good scratching along the ridge of their backs with a stick. And I cared for them so well, they were the finest, fattest beasts in the village. I used to scrub each one before I drove them to market, and I was proud to see them trotting down the road, sleek and clean, and so fat they could hardly walk.

I was a farmer's son, and I was content with my lot. If my brothers had been as simple, we would have all been spared much grief and trouble.

But Arnulf and Gerhard were a pair of idle fellows who cared for nothing but their own pleasures. Their clothes were too fine to spoil in the mud of the pig yard, they were always too weary after long nights spent drinking and wenching in the village taproom to rise at dawn to milk cows and muck out the barn and the pigsty. I did those jobs without complaint and without reward, but our father could grudge his eldest sons nothing, no matter what it cost.

Alas, when the old man died and the death-duties were paid, there was not enough left to pay the debts accumulated by my wastrel brothers. The farm had to be sold. I wept when the bailiffs came to drive away the swine, the herd I raised and cared for, the herd I had expected would one day be mine. But there was no help for it, if we were all to escape prison for debt.

When it was all gone, there was nothing left but a few pennies for each of us three sons, and so we divided them among us and each went his separate way, to find his own fortune in the world.

After a long, weary journey my coins were finally gone, and I found myself wandering deep into a forest. The road was dark and overgrown, and near sunset I was beginning to fear that I might be set upon by wolves or outlaws, when I came to an unexpected clearing and there, rooting amongst the trunks of the old oaks, was the finest, sleekest herd of swine I had ever seen, more noble even than the animals I had raised on my father's farm.

"If I could only be the swineherd here, then I could be content again," I told myself.

As I stood in admiration of them, the pigs suddenly lifted up their heads all together and began to trot, squealing, off through the trees. I followed, and saw the herd file into a well-built pen beside a low stone house.

But then I stopped and lost myself in staring, for on a stool in the front courtyard a woman was seated, combing out her long black hair and singing to herself. She wore a simple garment of white wool which left her arms bare. It was bound at the waist with a girdle, and a silver ring was coiled around one arm. And as long as she sat there combing, as long as I listened to the words of her song, I was unable to move, or take my eyes away.

But then her song stopped. She stood to bind up her hair and then, picking up a long white wand of wood, she looked in my direction. "Well come, traveler. You look like a fine fellow. Why don't you come inside and share my supper with me?" And her smile promised that she might share even more.

Well, I might have been a simple lad just off the farm with manure still caked on my boots, but I could tell that the woman who stood before me was no simple matter at all and she could have no good reason to be interested in the likes of me. So I only bowed my head and said, "Mistress, I am hungry, but all I ask is to be able to earn my keep as your swineherd. I have never seen beasts as fine and fat as yours."

At that, she laughed and said, "Now, that is one answer I've never heard before in more years than you would believe! A swineherd? Very well! If that is your wish, then you shall have it!"

She led me back to the pigsty. Leaning over the edge of the pen, she scratched the nearest beast behind the ears, while the animal grunted with pleasure at her touch. "Yes, these are my swine, and I am very proud of them. If you are to be my swineherd, every morning you may open their pen and let them run free to forage in the woods, but at sunset I will come to call them back again, and they will return, whether they will it or not."

Now, I thought this was a strange thing to say, but she was my mistress, so I said nothing about it. Then she gave me a supper of lentils boiled with ham, telling me with pride that she had cured the meat herself in her own smokehouse. I made myself a bed in the back of the pigsty and settled into my new situation, as content as I might be.

Every morning I released the swine to forage in the woods, and every night at sunset my mistress came to call them back again. When winter came, I did the butchering and hung the meat in the smokehouse to cure. It was honest work, and my mistress was pleased with me.

I still had no notion that she might be a witch until one day in the spring I found her seated again on her stool in the courtyard, combing out her long black hair and singing her spell aloud. Once more I was unable to move or take my eyes from her. But this time another traveler came out of the forest toward her house, wearing torn and road-stained garments that had once cost our father good silver coin, for with a shock I recognized my eldest brother Arnulf!

He stood as enspelled as I until she finished binding up her hair, and then she turned to him with the same beckoning smile she had once shown me. "Well come, traveler. You look like a fine fellow. Why don't you come inside and share my supper with me?"

Now, Arnulf had always been one to think well of himself, and at her invitation he swaggered and strutted and followed her into the house. In the morning, when I rose from my bed behind the pigsty, there was a new young brindled boar in the pen, snorting and trotting frantically around the pen with a wild look in his eyes.

When the beast saw me, it ran to me and squealed piteously, but it was time to let the herd out to forage for the day, and so I opened the gate to let them out into the woods. In the evening, when my mistress called them back again, once more the new young pig ran squealing after me, rubbing against my leg in distress.

But in all that time I had not seen my brother Arnulf, so I asked, "Mistress, what of the traveler who came here last night? Has he gone?"

She replied, "Yes, he rose at dawn and returned to his journey."

I wondered at that, for Arnulf had never willingly risen earlier than noon. And after several days the new pig grew quieter, as if resigned to its place in the herd. Soon under my care it became as fat and sleek as the rest.

Another season passed, and I had almost forgotten about Arnulf, when once again I found my mistress seated on her stool, combing out her black hair and singing her spell. This time the hapless traveler she had lured into her snare was my second brother, Gerhard. As before, she invited him into her house to share her supper, and just as Arnulf had done, Gerhard preened and followed her inside, for he had always considered himself a handsome fellow.

But this time I recalled how Arnulf had disappeared, and so I crept up to the window of my mistress' house and watched as she brought my second brother hot water to wash with and seated him at her table. Then, leaning low as she poured, she gave him a large cup of dark red wine. But as soon as he had taken a single draught, he fell onto the table in a deep sleep.

At that, the witch—for my mistress was in fact a

witch—took her wand and tapped him on the head, and in an instant my brother Gerhard had been changed into a handsome young white boar. Then the witch drove him with the wand out of her house and into the pigsty, where he snorted and squealed in terror at finding himself transformed into a beast.

Long I sat awake that night and pondered what I had just seen. I could not escape the conclusions that my mistress was a witch who changed men into swine. All the beasts in her herd must once have been travelers, lured here and transformed by her wicked spells, just as my brothers had been.

If I had been a hero or a clever fellow, like they tell about in tales, doubtless I would have sprung up and found a weapon to slay the witch, or learned some spell to change her hapless victims back into the men they once had been. But I was only a simple swineherd. And these swine of my mistress', no matter what they once had been, were now the finest beasts I had ever seen, including the herd I had tended when I was a boy. If I was content here, why should not they be, with all the forest to root in, full of mast and acorns, and even the savory truffles that made their flesh so sweet? And how sleek they all were, with the fat in rolls around their shoulders and hams! Who was to say they were not better off now as swine than when they had been men?

So I continued as swineherd, counting Arnulf and Gerhard among the rest of the herd, releasing them from their pen in the morning and seeing them come trotting back at night. I would sometimes make a special effort to scratch their ears or the ridge of their backs with my stick, or save them a little extra from the scrapings of my plate, for they were, after all, my brothers, and they were good swine. Indeed, I think I loved them better as pigs than I had as men, for I still recalled how they had mocked me when we lived together on our father's farm. Arnulf in particular had grown so fat that I think he would have been the envy of any swineherd in the wide world.

But as the seasons passed again and winter came near,

my mistress one day came to look at the swine and choose which ones would be slaughtered for the winter. Seeing Arnulf, it was clear that he was in prime condition to provide the best hams and bacon and sausages for her table. "That one," she said, pointing him out, "that one is grown as fat as he can be."

Arnulf, hearing her proclaim his doom, squealed mournfully, and the next morning he refused to leave the pen to forage until I beat him vigorously with my stick and drove him out into the woods. For what kind of swineherd would I be if my beasts wasted away in my care?

Now, no swineherd who really cares for his animals is happy when the time comes to hang them head-down by their hocks and put a knife to their throats. But we all know that this is the universal fate of swine.

Yet I was troubled, for Arnulf, even with his brindled hide and his tusks and snout, was still my brother. How could I do it? How could I hang his quarters in the smokehouse, no matter how thick and white his fat had grown?

At last I decided I must face the witch, for the sake of my brothers, no matter how they had mocked me when they had been men. So I scraped the dung from my boots, and came to her front door.

"Mistress," I told her, "for many years I've been content in your service, but now I wish to leave and find my own place in the world, and so I've come to ask for my wages."

"Well, my Heinrich," she said, "you have been a good swineherd, and I'll be very sorry to see you leave me. But you must come into the house first and drink a glass of wine with me, before you depart."

Now, this was what I had hoped, that she would attempt to change me into a swine, as she had changed all the other men she'd lured here over the years. So I let her lead me into the house and seat me at her table, and I showed no suspicion when she poured me out a glass of dark red wine.

But instead of drinking, I let the wine run down my

sleeve, knowing that she wouldn't notice it among all the other stains. And then I let my head fall to the table, as if I had fallen asleep.

"Poor simple Heinrich," she said with a sigh. "But from swineherd to swine is no great change, is it? Indeed, I hope you'll be happy in my pen for many years."

But when she approached with her wand to tap me on the head and turn me from man to swine, I leaped up and seized it from her. One blow with it, and instead of me, there stood my mistress, transformed into a young black sow, as fine a creature as any swineherd has ever seen. She squealed terribly, but I picked up my stick and struck her smartly across her fat rump to drive her from the house into the pen.

Of course, since then I have changed no men into pigs. What need is there? Swine can live for a very long time if they are well cared for, almost as long as a man. And my sow has proved to be an excellent beast who farrows twice a year, so my herd increases yearly.

Being a simple fellow, I am well-content.

MIRACLE AT DEVIL'S CRICK

by Jeffry Dwight

Callia lay in her dead-dark room, wove her web, spun her spells, and pulled the whole farm inside herself.

When she used the magic, nothing hid from her. No brick wall could block her, no bedroom door could shut her out, no secret was safe from her prying eyes. She knew everybody's darkest secrets. She saw her ma downstairs making breakfast, still in her thin cotton robe, her hair all pulled back and mussed from sleeping. Callia heard the bacon sizzle, smelled the coffee dripping into the pot, saw her pa getting the morning paper off the porch. She saw twelve-year-old Charlie in the bathroom, lips drenched in foam as he brushed his teeth, pajama top unbuttoned down to his belly so he could see in the mirror how strong and manly and tanned his chest was getting to be.

And outside, why the sun was up already, leaping over the rooftops like a yellow-gold beacon, calling the children to another day's play, and the adults to their work. She smelled the early summer air, and it stirred her the way a woman stirs a simmering pot. All without moving, Callia whirled in the scents of young pine from up over the hill, moist earth and sweet basil from her ma's garden, old man Peterson's wheezy truck starting up down the road, and faint as ever faint can be, the buds of wild roses growing in the lee of the shed.

Charlie stuck his head in the door to her room, switched on the light. "You gonna get up today, Cally?"

Callia's magic web of seeing and smelling ripped into

tatters at the interruption, and she turned her head toward the door. "Ain't you supposed to knock? I'm getting powerful tired of you just barging in. Maybe I should turn you into a toad to learn you some manners."

"Aw, you ain't no witch, Cally. 'Sides, I bet you need me just now. You gotta pee?"

Callia made a face. "Yeah."

"Well, come on, then." Charlie pulled back the covers and swung her legs over the edge of the bed, put his shoulder under her arm and helped her slide into her chair, just as smoothly as if he'd done it a thousand times. But it wasn't no thousand times yet; it was only two hundred and twelve. Callia knew because she'd been counting right along, ever since the accident.

She could push herself well enough once she got into the wheelchair, but Charlie followed along and made sure the towels and toothpaste and whatnot were all down on the counter in the bathroom where she could reach. Pa'd put in special railings, and once she'd built up the strength in her arms, she didn't need no help with the toilet. Good thing, too. A fourteen-year-old girl wanted her privacy sometimes.

"Call me when you wanna come downstairs," said Charlie, "less'n you're gonna fly down today on your broomstick."

Callia aimed a hairbrush at his head and let fly, but he ducked, laughing, and bounded down the stairs. She grinned, too, then wheeled over, leaned down, and scooped up the brush. It only took her a couple dozen minutes to finish her morning routine, but she didn't call Charlie back right away. Instead she wheeled down the hall to her room. Getting dressed by herself was right difficult, but by leaning and rolling and pulling she got her useless legs out of the pajamas and into a skirt. It didn't hurt too much if she was careful and went slow. She pulled on a blouse, squirmed back up into her chair, and got ready to do a summoning.

She plucked a thread from the hem of her skirt and tied a knot near the end, all the while thinking Charlie's name. Then she tied another knot at the other end while filling her mind with images of herself, sitting just so, right here in her room, a-tying the knot while the forces of magic whipped and whirled around her like heat waves in the air. Then she held the two ends together, so the knot for Charlie touched the knot for herself, and she twisted the thread into a come-hither, twisted it with her mind and her fingers all at once so the binding would hold.

It was a good come-hither; she felt proud of herself. Less than five minutes later, she heard Charlie's feet pound up the stairs, pause at the bathroom, then pad down the hall to her door.

"Where you been, Cally?" said Charlie. "Ma saved you breakfast, but she's gonna be right sore if you ain't down before they leave. Why didn't you call me?"

"I did," she said, holding out her palm with the come-hither thread curled on it. "Now who says I ain't a witch? Why else did you come to my hexing?"

"Couldn't be 'cause Ma said to fetch you, huh?" Charlie shook his head. "You turned weird with all that witch stuff, Cally." He grabbed the handles on the back of her chair and started wheeling her toward the ramp at the head of the stairs.

"You're just too young to understand, that's all," she said over her shoulder. "Is Ma all ready to go to Aunt Gertie's?"

"Champin' at the door. Pa, too, don't forget. He's powerful eager to get going."

Aunt Gertie in Indiana had broken her hip, and Ma was going to nurse her. She'd be gone for weeks, but there weren't nobody else to do it. Pa'd have to drive her down there, near four hundred miles away, and that'd take all day long, so of course he wouldn't come back till tomorrow.

"You just don't forget who's in charge today. You gotta mind me, Charlie."

"Grab the brake and shut up," he said. "I reckon you're in charge of me, all right, but I gotta take care of you while Pa's gone. Don't start thinking you can run things just 'cause you're older. You got that brake tight? Here we go."

Charlie tilted her chair back a bit and set her front wheels onto the edge of the ramp. She stared down at the landing, only six steps down, but looking like forever away and just as steep. Her hand pulled up on the brake lever all by itself, pulled it tight, hung on so hard her knuckles turned white and her arm ached. Charlie went around in front, like Pa always said to do, leaned forward, grabbed the arms of her chair, and nodded. "I'm ready. Let's go."

Callia took a deep breath and released the brake just a little. The chair creaked and jerked a couple of inches down the ramp. "You holding tight?"

"I got you, Cally. C'mon."

Little by little, she eased the chair down the ramp, Charlie bracing her the whole way. She didn't breathe easy until she was level again and had wheeled into the warmth and safety of the kitchen. "I purely hate those stairs," she said, hoping for some sympathy from her ma. She wouldn't get none from Charlie. He borrowed her chair sometimes and shot down the ramp on it like he was driving a race car. 'Sides, he'd already run back up the stairs. But her ma didn't have time for no idle chat today; she was already dressed and a-standing by the door ready to go, and it was plain she was thinking about her trip and all the little details she might have forgot, and how it was too late now to attend to them, so she'd just have to pray to the Good Lord and keep her fingers crossed, too.

Callia endured the usual lecture about watching her little brother, making sure he stayed out of trouble, took his bath, didn't sass, and went to bed on time, then she kissed her ma and pa good-bye and watched while they drove away.

Charlie, now wearing only red shorts and his tan, blew past her and banged out the door right after they left, his bare feet popping on the cement driveway as he ran off. "You stay 'round here!" Callia yelled after him, but she didn't worry much, 'cause he was mostly a good boy, even if he was only twelve still and full of rambunction and high spirits. She heard him shout "Yaaaaaa!" once, then he was gone, swallowed up by the summer morning.

She ate the breakfast her ma'd left out for her, and even tasted the leftover coffee in the pot before she cleaned everything up. She didn't like coffee too terrible much, but it made her feel grown up to drink it, and she figured she'd have to learn to like it someday, so she might as well practice a bit.

Long about noon, Charlie came back from his playing, fair blowed from running so much, and so dirty she knew he must have been down by Devil's Crick again, scratching for tadpoles and crawdads in the mud. She fixed some sandwiches and milk for lunch, and made him wash his hands before he ate.

"It's gonna rain," she said. "I got a weather-sense."

Charlie nodded over his sandwich. "There's clouds something fierce out west."

"You stay away from Devil's Crick, then," she said. "You can play out back the house instead, where I can watch you."

"Rain never hurt no one."

"If you wash away in the crick, ma'd be sore, so you just do what I say, Charlie."

He shrugged, finished his sandwich, and drained his glass of milk. "You need anything from upstairs?"

Callia shook her head. "I'm all set. You go on and play, but stay in the yard."

"Okay." One second he was there, a-grinning at her with his white teeth and dirty face, and the next second he was gone, the door banging behind him and his battle-cry "Yaaaaaa!" floating back on the breeze.

She spent the afternoon daydreaming by the big front window and reading, then she dozed off in her chair, listening to the distant thunder and the cicadas and birds and wind.

What woke her was the silence. It came all of a sudden, and it wasn't until the birds started up again that she realized they'd been quiet. She didn't need no weather-sense to know something unnatural was going on. The sky was purely dark outside the window, 'cept where it was a kind of yellow-green away out to the west. And now the wind picked up, real strong for a second, so that the treetops bent way over, then went still again. There was a big clap of thunder that shook the window glass and made her heart thump, and all the birds and crickets shut up for a minute, only gradually a-starting in to make noise again.

Callia wheeled her chair across to the back door, pulled it open, and rolled out onto the wooden porch. A few drops of cold rain sprinkled across her legs, and the wind lifted her skirt and hair. "Charlie! You get inside now!" She made her voice as loud as it could go, 'cause she didn't see him in the yard where he belonged. "Charlie!"

It weren't no good calling him, but she did it anyway, all the while knowing in her brain that he was too far off to hear. There wasn't but one place he'd be, and that was wherever she'd told him not to go. "Why didn't I tell him to stay away from his room?" she demanded of the sky, like it could hear and maybe answer. But the sky didn't care; it just got on with its business, and soon the rain was coming down steady. "Charlie!" she called. "Charlie, if you catch pneumonia and die, Pa will whip you! Charlie!"

Callia swung the chair around and headed back inside. The clock on the kitchen wall said it was only six, though it was dark enough outside for midnight. She switched on the porch light, thinking maybe that would help Charlie find his way, and then settled herself down to wait in the kitchen. Then she got to thinking that he'd need hot food when he got back, so she started fixing dinner. The thunder crashed, and the rain didn't let up. If anything, it came down harder. Callia heard the trees whipping back and forth in the wind, though she couldn't see anything outside 'cept when there was lightning.

By seven o'clock, all the food she'd made was sitting cold on the table, and still the rain came down. She figured that Charlie was a-sitting out the storm somewheres, and she hoped he had sense to stay out from under the trees what with all the lightning banging around out there. Long about eight o'clock, with the rain coming down as hard as ever, she started thinking maybe he was lost. She

closed her eyes, wove her web, spun her spells, and tried
to see where he might be.

It was hard to concentrate with the thunder booming
and crashing every few seconds, and she couldn't tell
from one moment to the next what she was looking at
'cause everything was black, and nowhere did she see the
spark of a twelve-year-old boy lost in the storm. Well, if
she couldn't find him, maybe he could find her. She
pulled a thread from her skirt and made the knots for a
come-hither, binding it with the image of her and Charlie
meeting right there in the kitchen, him all wet but safe.
But even as she tied it, she knew the summoning
wouldn't work, 'cause she couldn't picture him right. Every time she tried to see him clearly in her mind, she
didn't see him smiling and safe the way he'd have to be
for the summoning to work. Instead, she saw him a-lying
on the ground, not moving, hair plastered down, his face
all peaceful despite the rain and thunder and mud.

The room got hot and prickly suddenly, and she knew
she was seeing a maybe—something that might really
happen, something that *would* happen if she didn't do
something about it. But what could she do? She didn't
recognize where he was, and even if she did, how could
she get there?

There was a tremendous flash, and a clap of thunder
right on top of it, and all the lights went out. Callia shivered, even though it wasn't cold, 'cause as sudden as a
lightning hit, she knew what she had to do. She had to go
get Charlie. And she knew where he was, too—she'd
known it all along. He was down by Devil's Crick, right
where she told him not to be.

She made herself stop and think out the route. The
shortest way was out the back, up over the hill with the
pine trees, and down the other side right into the crick.
But she couldn't go that way. There wasn't no path for
wheelchairs through the trees. She'd have to go the long
way, down along the road until it crossed the crick, then
somehow she'd have to get off the bridge and down to the
water. From there, she could follow the bank until she
found Charlie. But how would she get back? There

weren't no way she could go uphill, not unless she had something to pull on. . . . A rope! She could take a rope, and pull them back up!

There wasn't any more time to think, 'cause she suddenly remembered that Devil's Crick always flooded real easy, and it had been raining for hours already. She pictured the black water swirling and rising, with Charlie caught on a log or knocked unconscious, the water up to his knees, then his waist, then his chest, then—

No! She was moving before she knew it. Out the door, across the porch, down the ramp, and back to the shed. The wind and rain lashed her like whips and the thunder was so loud it hurt her ears. The rope came to her hand, right where it was supposed to be, and then she rolled onto the driveway, her arms pumping in a steady rhythm on the wheels. "I'm coming, Charlie!" Her wheels skidded on wet pavement, but she dug in, got traction, and sped down the road toward the bridge.

It was a long way, near half a mile she reckoned, and uphill the last hundred feet where the road went over the crick. Her arms were powerful tired by the time she got there, and she was wet clear through her clothes. The rain slacked off somewhat, but it didn't matter if the clouds broke up and moved off—the storm'd done its work already. She saw quick glimpses when the lightning flashed. Devil's Crick rushed and roared below her in the dark like it'd gone mad. The water was mighty fast and high, all aroil with tree branches and swirling debris.

She'd be insane to go down into that, not even knowing if Charlie was out there. She shouldn't have come. She knew that now. She should have gone for old man Peterson. He'd have brought his truck, and he had two strong legs for climbing, two strong arms for carrying. Even if Charlie was down there, what could she do? All she had was a rope and a wheelchair. There wasn't even a path down from beside the bridge, or if there was one, it was washed away by now.

She turned away and let the wheelchair start rolling down the bridge. It wasn't too late to fetch old man Peterson. He'd come right quick, but she'd have to go back down the road, past her house, find him in the dark and convince him that—

"Help!"

Callia jerked up on the wheelchair's brake. She froze in place, listening. It'd been awful faint, probably she'd just imagined—

"Help!"

She heard it for sure that time. It was off to the left, Charlie's voice and no mistake—even so faint and distant, there wasn't no way she'd not know her own brother's voice. "Charlie!" she yelled. "I'm here, and I'm a-coming!"

But how? She wheeled over to the guardrail and looked down. It wasn't too deep here, maybe three feet to the ground, but there was nowhere for her chair to go even if she could get it over the edge. The ground was all mud, sliding straight down into the water . . . what was that? Something bobbing in the crick, something white. . . . Another flash of lightning, and she saw him, clear as day, water up to his armpits, out near the base of the bridge, where a tangle of branches had caught on a piling.

She didn't stop to think. She tried one end of the rope to the guardrail on the bridge, the other end 'round her waist, and fell forward out of her chair, over the rail, down to land with a thump in the mud. A stone gouged her left knee, but she ignored the pain and slithered down the bank on her belly. His face was a pale blob against the dark water, only a dozen feet out from the edge. He looked to be treading water. Why didn't he swim in?

On one elbow and hip, her useless legs trailing through the mud behind her as if they belonged to someone else, she lurched forward, flung her other hand out, grabbed at the thickest branch within reach, and hauled herself into the water.

All at once she was in over her head. The current slapped at her like a giant hand, pulled her instantly downstream. She breached the surface, windmilling her arms, grateful for the muscles she'd built up by pushing her chair. In the water, her legs didn't matter so much. They didn't help, but they didn't hurt none either. She shook the hair out of her eyes, angled against the current, and swam over to Charlie with only a couple dozen powerful strokes.

She wanted to laugh and cry, hug him and strangle him, all at once. "Charlie," she said when she was near enough she didn't have to shout. "What are you doing out here?"

"I'm hurt, Cally," he said. "Maybe bad. My foot's caught. I think it's broke."

While he was talking, the current swept her downstream. She wasn't worried too much, 'cause she was still tied to the rope, but that wouldn't do Charlie much good. She swam back to him against the insistent tug of the water.

"I'm awful tired, Cally," he said. "I been swimming a long time."

She didn't say what she was thinking—that the water was already up to his shoulders, and still rising fast. She just nodded and said, "Well, hold on, I'll take a look."

She took a deep breath and pushed herself under the water. She followed his leg down and down while the crick tried to swirl her away. She couldn't see anything, but she could feel the branches, anchored deep in the muck. She explored them with her hands, ignoring the way her lungs were aching. Charlie's ankle was trapped in the crook of one branch, another log pressed against it, holding it tight. She worried at it until she couldn't hold her breath no more, then pushed up off the bottom and exploded into the air, gasping and blowing. The water was up to Charlie's neck now, and he looked mighty scared. "You just keep treading water, Charlie," she said, then sucked in as much air as she could hold and dove again.

This time she hauled herself down, hand over hand. She used his leg like a rope ladder, and went right to the tangle. She pushed and tugged at his foot, turning it this way and that, but the branches held it firm. She dribbled air out of her mouth as slowly as possible, trying to extend her time underwater. Her lungs burned and her head felt like it was going to explode. There was no way his ankle was coming loose. She finally surfaced. For a moment, she was so glad to be breathing again, and so tired, that she let the current drag her downstream. It would be so easy, so restful, to just float. But Charlie needed her. She shook her head and struck out against the flow. The water was still rising. Charlie's face was tipped back now, and the water lapped his chin and ears. "I can't swim no more, Cally," he said.

She grabbed one of his arms and shook it hard, then had to let go again to keep herself afloat. "Charlie, Charlie, you got to listen now. Pa said to mind me, so you just keep swimming, hear? That's an order, Charlie! You hear me?"

He didn't answer. His eyes were shut, and his arms weren't moving no more. The water closed over his mouth and nose, and he drifted quietly down, away from her.

"Charlie!" Callia screamed so loud she thought her lungs would come up her throat. She grabbed after him, caught one hand, and used it to pull herself down again. She found his leg, then his ankle, then the tree trunk that was pinning it. This time, instead of trying to pull his foot out, she swam along the length of the log until she reached its free end. She wrapped both arms under it, like carrying firewood, but that was no good. She didn't have any leverage 'cause she couldn't push with her legs. So she got all the way under it, her shoulders against the bottom of the crick, and pushed up and over as hard as she could. She thought her heart would burst before the log moved, but then suddenly it came free. It slid ponderously to one side, and almost landed on her legs. But she pushed against it as it was falling, got her legs out, and shot to the surface.

For a second, she couldn't find him. Then the lightning flashed. He was drifting free, not three feet away, head down, being pushed by the current. She lunged through the water, grabbed his hair with one hand, turned over on her side, and pulled him in close. She got his head up high, her right arm under his chest, and just held on. The current swirled them downstream until they hit the length of the rope, then swung them over to the bank.

Somehow she got them both up out of the water, digging with her elbows in the mud, yanking on Charlie's arms to pull him after her. She rolled him onto his back and pushed on his chest until water spurted out his nose and mouth. "Charlie! Charlie, don't you dare die!" She pushed on his chest again, then breathed into his mouth until she felt his lungs inflate. "Charlie! Oh, Charlie, baby, come on, you can't die, you can't. I won't let you!" She was crying now, her tears mingling with the rain that fell on his peaceful, upturned face. It was the maybe-picture she'd seen, him lying on the ground, body still, so still, too still. Dead. He was dead. She knew it all of a sudden.

"Wake up!" she shouted, banging on his bare chest with her fists. "Come on, Charlie, come back to me, come back. I love you, Charlie! I love you. You can't be dead. Breathe, Charlie, breathe!" She put her mouth over his again and blew into his lungs. Again. And again. And again. Then she pushed on his chest. "Come on, Charlie!" Suddenly he coughed weakly, then gasped and coughed again.

"Oh, Charlie!" She was laughing and crying at the same time now, but she didn't even know it. She cradled his head against her chest and held him tight, rocked him like a baby, held him while he coughed. He finally got his breathing under control, and she smoothed back his hair and looked down at him.

"You okay now?" she asked.

"I'm sore all over, and my foot hurts something wicked. I reckon I had my bath for tonight."

His voice was hoarse, and he looked awful young. Callia wiped her nose with the back of her hand and started crying again for no reason she could see. "You'll be okay," she said. "We'll both be okay now."

He started coughing again, and it was a couple of minutes before he could talk. "Cally, I couldn't swim no more. That's all I recollect. What happened after that?"

"Magic," she said. "Powerful strong magic. A come-hither like you never seen."

"Aw, Cally, you ain't no witch."

"You shut up," she said, and hugged him for all she was worth.

GIANT TROUBLE

by Katharine Kerr

At the top of a hill in southeastern San Francisco stood a two-story wooden house that had survived the Great Quake of 1906, as well as the Not-so-Great Quake of 1989, and looked it. The roof leaned one way; the ground floor, another; the porch hung somewhere in between. Forty-five brick steps led up from the street not quite to the rusty front gate of the postage-stamp garden. Every afternoon at about three o'clock, when she went outside to water her herbs, Ginnie would look for cracks in the concrete foundation near the hose connection. As soon as she found any, she promised herself, she would see about getting the old place propped up.

While she rationed out water to the rows of garlic, sage, basil, and dittany, Ginnie could see the entire street below and keep watch for her niece and nephew, whose elementary school stood about two blocks away. If her brother's day care person had let him down again, she could count on the kids turning up at her place. Thus, one particularly hot afternoon, she wasn't in the least surprised to see Adele and Jason trudging up the sidewalk. What did surprise her, once the kids arrived, puffing and sweating, at the gate, was seeing tear streaks all down Jason's face.

"Oh, good grief, honey, what's wrong?"

Ginnie swung the gate wide and herded the children in, but they were too out of breath to answer until she had them sitting in the cool living room on their favorite wicker sofa. Ginnie brought cold orange soda and sat

down in the armchair opposite. Her two cats, the ginger
Salamander and the black Gnome, ambled out of the bedroom to flop down near her feet.

"Now," Ginnie said. "Why the tears?"

"They're leaving," Jason burst out. "He sold them."

When he began to cry, Adele handed him a crumpled
tissue. She was nine years old to her brother's six.

"We heard at lunch," Adele said. "He's been crying
ever since."

"Heard what, honey? Who's leaving?"

"The Giants." Adele's voice shook a little. "That mean
old man sold them to some place in Florida."

Ginnie's first impulse was to call the team's owner
something worse than mean, but reason and the need to
present an adult front prevailed.

"Now, here, you shouldn't call him that. He's a perfectly decent man, and he does own the team. It's his to
sell, and he can't be expected to go on losing money. The
mayor certainly didn't do anything to keep the Giants
here."

"That's what the teacher said, too, when Jason
wouldn't stop snotting."

"I wasn't snotting."

"Were, too."

Jason raised a fist in her direction, caught his aunt's
glance, and lowered it again. Adele had a dainty sip of
her soda, then went on.

"But LaToya said her dad said that no one else can
even try to buy the team and keep it here. There was this
contract or something."

"Well, if it's all legally sewn up, honey, then I guess
we'll just have to be As fans from now on. It'll be a little
harder to get to the games, but—"

"Oh, come on, Aunt Ginnie! They got a DH. How can
I root for anyone who's got a DH?"

"Well, let's see, we can pick another team and watch
them on TV."

"Dodgers? Yuck!" Jason stuck out an orange tongue.
"Atlanta? Double yuck!"

Ginnie sighed. She was running out of comforting

things to say and fast. Adele set her glass of soda down on the floor and leaned forward, opening her eyes wide and attempting "wistful."

"Cut it out," Ginnie said. "Get to the point."

Adele grinned and sat back.

"I do love you, Aunt Ginnie. Well, we were thinking, you see, that maybe you could like do something."

"Do something?"

"Sure. You know."

"I do not know."

"You know. Like, get them to change their minds."

"I'm not in the class of people who can just call up the mayor or owners of baseball teams and say, 'Listen, Frank, listen, Bob, what's this I hear about the Giants leaving town?' "

"Oh, well, someone like you wouldn't have to talk to them or anything anyway."

Both children were watching her now with their eyes sincerely wide, their mouths half-parted in innocent hope. Ginnie sighed again, louder.

"You've been listening to those dumb things your dad says about me, haven't you?"

"Are they really dumb, Aunt Ginnie?"

"Of course they are. There is no such thing as witches."

"Oh, yeah, sure," Jason said, but sotto voce.

"Your dad only makes those remarks when he's mad at me."

"So?" Adele said. "He only calls me a brat when he's mad at me, but I'm always being a brat when he says it."

Ginnie had the brief thought of turning her brother into a toad one dark night, but then, of course, she would either have to raise the kids herself or turn them over to her ex-sister-in-law, the Jehovah's Witness. Neither choice appealed.

"Now look." Ginnie paused for a smile of sweet reason. "Let's suppose, by some really weird long shot, that there was such a thing as witchcraft, and just suppose, just for the sake of argument, that witches could work spells. Do you guys think that casting a spell like this would be easy or something? Do you think our let's-pretend witch could just throw a few herbs around her garden and mutter a few charms and poof! the team's owner would change his mind?"

"Oh," Adele said. "Oh, well, gee, yeah, I guess I did think that. Uh, it would be hard to do, huh, I mean just supposing there were witches?"

"Real hard. Why, in books you read about witches killing themselves or taking years off their lives to work a particularly powerful spell."

"Oh. Oh, well, I wouldn't want you to get sick or something."

"Yeah, kid? Gee, thanks. But there's nothing harder to change on this earth than a rich man's mind."

Fresh tears rolled down Jason's streaked cheeks. Adele pulled another tissue out of her shirt pocket and handed it over.

"But, Aunt Ginnie, you're our last chance."

"I'm afraid, honey, that I'm no chance at all."

Adele began to cry, and quite sincerely. Ginnie got up and fetched a new box of tissues from the bathroom.

Later that evening, once the kids had been picked up and her brother told off, Ginnie put on an orange and black Giants parka and sat in her rocker on the front porch. The fog was oozing over the western hills and down across the red and yellow pool of city lights, turning the air damp and frigid. Somewhere out there in expensive condos or carpeted offices, sitting in leather chairs round polished tables, powerful men reached decisions that made small children cry and women like herself quite cross. She found herself thinking about inertia, one of the major principles ruling her craft as, indeed, it ruled the physical world. Strong forces continued in a straight line, unless they met an obstacle equally strong to stop or deflect them. She doubted if she could summon enough force to do the job, not when the American version of the philosopher's stone, cold cash, was so actively working against her. There was simply no safe way to—

Safe way. The words seemed to ring in her mind. She

rose, paced to the edge of the porch, and looked out into the billowing mists.

"Safe way."

The cold she felt down her spine had nothing to do with the fog. Magic hung round those words, powerful magic, and she could think of no reason why.

"Safe way."

Again her frisson told her that the Powers were answering her wonderings in the only way they ever answered—cryptically. At times the Powers made her quite cross, too, but at least they had deigned to tell her that some possible but harmless method existed of reversing the team owner's decision. Or would she have to actually reverse it? Perhaps she could merely summon into manifestation a counterforce. At the moment, the river of inertia was carrying the team away. What she needed to do was set up a countereddy in the astral plane that would float it back again.

"Oh, yeah, sure," she said aloud. "Real easy. Just like that. Just wander out onto the planes and stir up an equally stubborn resistance."

Like another rich man? All at once she smiled, thanking the Powers in her heart. An idea had just come clear.

Since working subtle magic in the empires of the mind takes a good deal of time, it was some weeks before Adele called. Ginnie was just washing some ritual implements in the bathroom sink late one afternoon when the phone rang. Answered, it spoke with her niece's voice.

"Aunt Ginnie Aunt Ginnie did you see the paper did you did you?"

"Slow down, please. What paper?"

"The newspaper. Dad read it to us in the morning. We just got home from school, right now, I mean, but we talked about it at lunch, too. They're gonna stay, the Giants, I mean. Someone else bought them."

Ginnie deciphered in her mind.

"Wait a minute, you mean someone local, not the people from Florida?"

"That's right."

"But what about that contract? The one the owner signed, saying no one could buy the team but the Florida group?"

"Well, this new guy says he's sure he can fight it and break it. LaToya's dad says he'll go right to the commissioner if he has to. The new owner I mean, not LaToya's dad."

Ah, the stubbornness of the very rich!

"He looks real nice, and he's not bald, either." Adele went on. "The new owner, I mean. This guy who owns the big grocery stores."

In the background Jason's voice mumbled.

"Well, he doesn't own them exactly," Adele corrected herself. "He's the head of them, the president or whatever they call that. The Safeway stores, where Dad goes. You know."

"Well, yeah, honey, I do know. That's great, it really really is. I'll watch the news tonight and get all the details."

"Okay. But I wanted to call you and say thank you."

"Thank you? I didn't do anything."

"Oh, yeah, sure."

"I am not in the class of people who can just call up the head of a major chain of retail stores and say, 'Listen Peter, why don't you buy the Giants?' "

" 'Course you're not. Who said you called him up?"

In spite of herself, Ginnie had to smile. And from the wicker sofa the two cats seemed to smile in return.

SPELL CHECK

by Terry McGarry

I was distraught, I was bouncing off walls, I was on the brink. I wondered how 462 (badly photocopied nine-pin dot-matrix) manuscript pages would scatter if hurled from a sixth-story suburban condo. I imagined them floating gently down to earth, a love scene nestling in the bushes, the dedication sticking to the suntan-lotioned chest of the sunbather on the patio, the epilogue swept away by a passing bus.

I was, in the prevailing lingo, a copy editor who had gone splaa.

One more fiesty attendent, one more side-affect, one more acomodate or supercede, and I would throw my career out the window. It seemed wisest to put some distance between myself and *Ardwyn in Shadow*.

Not to mention that my alternate fantasy entailed all 462 pages landing in a pile on the head of my husband, Len the electrical engineer, with whom things were not going well.

So I took a stroll into town and, with the serendipity of fiction, came across a shop that might offer just what I needed.

The faded sign read STATIONERY—SPELLS—OFFICE SUPPLIES. I had noticed it before, in passing—although copy editors work myopically, they also learn to take note of odd details for general reference—but I'd never gone in; I bought office staples in bulk from the discount chain store.

A little bell on the door jingled old-fashionedly as I en-

tered, and the back-to-school scents of plastic notebooks
and rubber erasers soothed me. The kind-faced proprietor
straightened up from behind the glass counter. She had
been arranging gold and silver pens in the vitrine, and
they gleamed in the fluorescent light.

"Can I help you?" she asked.

For a moment I just blinked. Her face was a fascinating
webwork of lines, and I wondered randomly if anyone
had ever developed a facial version of palmistry or phre-
nology. It seemed to me that there was quite a lifetime inscribed there.

Then I explained my problem, finishing with, "I don't
know if you can help me . . . I mean, it is my *job* to fix
typos, but I'd rather put the energy into smoothing out
grammar, keeping track of logistics. . . ."

The woman was already nodding. "You need a utensil.
Something to fix things. What sort would you prefer?"

Taken aback by her ready understanding, I said, "Well,
uh, I use green FaberCastell pencils, usually. . . ."

She held up a thin, pale finger for me to wait, and
ducked through a door behind her. I caught a glimpse of
a cramped storeroom, and then my view was restricted to
a vertical section of shelving as the door swung almost
closed. I could hear her rummaging; then a grunt, and a
very long pause; and then an odd murmuring sound. A
funny smell drifted out—first sulfur, as from a match, and
then something akin to incense.

I guess the sign wasn't kidding about the spells, I
thought, trying for wryness and failing.

She emerged with a perfectly ordinary-looking box of pencils. "Will that be all?" she said, approaching the cash register. Her eyes, a gray so light they looked silver, glowed with
secret delight. I answered her with a nod, paid for the
merchandise—the usual price, I noticed, nothing extra for the
mumbles or incense—and went home feeling that if nothing
else I had at least brightened her day, and dispelled (as it
were) my own bad mood.

I was pleased when the first pencil I tried shorted out
the electric pencil sharpener. I had to dig up the old man-
ual one and reattach its loose rubber-suction base. That a

modern device had been zapped by the bespelled object—
that only metal cranked by flesh could sharpen it—
seemed evidence of its magic. I sat down in my ergo-
nomic chair, amid piles of dictionaries and reference
books.

Back to the land of Ardwyn, the distressed Lady
Karryl, and the search for the moonstone ring. Karryl was
having trouble with her lover, too, but at least her problems would be solved in another two hundred pages.

I read slowly at first, my eyes readjusting to the faint
letters; I marked the chapter head for the compositor,
added a few serial commas, corrected a dangling partici-
ple and a past-tense transitive "lay," and then, as my pencil hovered over the next line, saw that neat green
marks—in my own handwriting—had appeared on all the
misspelled words in that line. It was a pleasant, reasonable solution: I still had to do my job, correcting grammar, checking facts, flagging inconsistencies . . . but no
more would I be plagued with the endless stream of
typos!

Which didn't rinse from my mouth the bad taste of my
latest argument with Len—but hey, the distraction didn't
hurt.

After a while I got used to finding work predone as I
went along. Karryl, supposedly confined to her tower in
Castle Tirna, had just been told by Mirren, one of her elf
friends, that the ring was hidden at the neighboring Castle
Cor. The elves were helping her escape to the stables,
where her trusted young groom would have her horse
waiting. I saw her pale form dart out of the recessed
doorway and heard the sucking of her slippered feet in
the mud as she made her way toward me. I could smell
hay, and manure, and horse sweat, but it was only when
I heard the groom, Willam, murmuring to the horse next
to me that I understood that I wasn't at my desk anymore.
I was there, standing just outside the sphere of lamplight
at the stable door.

I tried to speak but found that I could not; all I could
seem to do, as Karryl came stumbling up in her wet
cloak, was observe as she took the reins and got a leg up

into the saddle from Willam. "I tell you, it's me should be going," the boy said in a low but urgent voice. She shook her head, glancing at the ethereal-looking Mirren. "No, the ring will respond only to me. It's the only wow."

I thought that sounded strange, but my rising panic overwhelmed it. This was crazy! I was freezing, getting soaked! I wanted to slap myself but couldn't move my arm. I must have fallen asleep at the desk, I thought; I was having one of those lucid dreams where you know you're dreaming but can't break out of it. Yet I watched with reluctant fascination as Karryl nudged the horse into a trot and disappeared into the black, rain-drenched night.

Then there was a flash of blinding white space, and I was somewhere else. It was a courtyard in another castle—and here came Karryl out of the darkness into the torchlight of the main gate, where Willam reached out to take the mare's reins—

"Wait a minute!" I heard myself say, and was dry and safe back in my den. What, did Willam teleport from castle to castle? I was peeling a Post-it Note to flag my query when it hit me. I'd been *there*. I had not been asleep.

I wasn't sure whether to crow with delight or melt in terror. Magical typo-fixing was one thing, but this . . .

I went back over Karryl's dialogue and found the typo. She had said, "It's the only wau"—a common slip of the index finger, and already fixed, although it hadn't been when I was in there.

I wrote my query about Willam. As I was folding the flag over from the back of the page to the front, I saw that the pencil I had used on the Post-it was one of the old, short ones; I had dropped the new pencil on the floor. Good thing, too: I didn't want to know what existence was like inside a query flag.

This was all a little more than I had bargained for. I got up and headed for the door.

"Ah, it's you," the woman said, and smiled. "I was about to close up, but please, enter."

Her wise, otherworldly expression reminded me of

Mirren's. *Are you a good which, or a bad which?* I wanted to ask, stressing the *h*s, but all that came out of my mouth was "I bought these pencils from you earlier, and they aren't really what I expected. . . ."

She looked at the box I held out. "You don't like them?"

"I think they work a little too well," I said carefully.

She shrugged. "They fix things. Just what you asked for. You don't want them, your money back, no problem."

"Well, I do like them. . . ." I was at a total loss. When I didn't go on, she drew another box of green FaberCastells from her pocket, as if she'd been expecting me. "You take these. Nothing special about these. Put the others aside until needed. Okay? No charge."

I tried to decline, saying that I had plenty of normal pencils, but she leaned over the immaculate glass counter and pressed them into my hand. She was so reassuring and confident, and her hand felt so cool and compelling, that I accepted the box, thanked her, and left.

On the way home, I kept thinking about her wrinkled face, which had the complexity of one of Len's circuit diagrams. I wondered what kind of story my face told, or Len's.

But that night, and the next, and the next—as our spats became a daily, then a twice-daily, occurrence—he was just Len, face hardened by debate or smoothed by the sleep he could instantly and effortlessly find in the midst of tension that kept me awake till all hours, aching.

I started on the next project, a cyberpunk novel, and found it unusually tough going. I just could not seem to get involved in the characters' lives. I had put the magic pencils in the back of a bottom drawer. Was it their influence I lacked? Had one taste of truly being *in* a novel ruined normal reading for me?

One night after dinner, as Len turned away when I declined to watch one of his interminable investment videos, I felt a sudden wave of utter helplessness, of total inability to communicate. How could I be so good with words on paper and so desperately unable to tell my husband what I really felt?

"I'm going to go inside and get a few more pages done," I said at last, failing to recognize the dozen healing statements I could have made. I knew he was trying to tell me we didn't spend enough time together anymore. It was true. But work had always been my refuge. I went back to my office.

Then, angry at the intractable world, I fished the magic pencils out of the drawer. "Okay," I told them, pulling my chair up to the desk, "do your worst, you bloody things."

For ten pages there was no whammy, no out-of-body experience; just the neat, magical corrections. Perhaps, I thought, my being aware of the spell would preclude its working again. But the plot was thickening, as poor ingenuous Lalley realized that she had gotten in over her head with the multiconglomerate. And suddenly I was following her down a back alley off the Strip.

She was looking for Gage, the ex-bodyguard of the conglomerate's top dog. Gage had gone underground, knowing too much about the operation. Lally's only hope for staying alive, now that she'd been framed as a corporate spy, was Gage. And I was able to move; the paralysis of my first experience was gone.

The sky was filled with giant ad lightboards that seemed to press down on my head, press me deeper into this crevice of a passage between buildings. Lalley, in her high black boots, picked her way gingerly among the reeking piles of refuse and drugged or dying humans. I could barely breathe, and an awful thought came to me as I struggled along after her: What if I got stuck here and never came out?

Terror filled me, and my legs almost buckled. I had never been this frightened, not even when I fell asleep on the Lexington Avenue IRT and ended up in the East Bronx. I wanted to curl up in a ball and beg this place not to hurt me; I wondered how anyone lived with this feeling, people in the real world who weren't protected by their protagonist status. Everyone's the protagonist in her own life story; but people die in places like this. It could happen to me.

I moaned, pathetically, amazed by my own wimpishness—and this time a sound came out. To my utter shock, Lalley whirled, and I heard the snick of her blade before the sky lights gleamed on it. "Who's there?" she demanded in a rough voice, and I knew now that it had been foolish of me to deride her innocence. Easy for me to talk, an armchair adventurer, sick now with fear. *You* try to survive for a night in a cyberpunk scenario.

"I don't mean you any harm," I said. "No, I'm sorry, that's stupid. I—"

"*Who?*" she hissed again, her face blank as the mouth of a cannon.

I couldn't help it; it was too impossible, there was nothing else to say. "I'm your copy editor."

They hit the pavement around us before I heard a sound—four teens clad in razor-studded black leather. They circled us slowly, growling and slavering like rabid animals, their eyes gleaming from Caucasian faces smeared with grease till they were jet black.

I'm going to die now, I thought. I had lived in Manhattan for thirty years, and now I was going to be killed by a street gang in a cyberpunk novel.

But they ignored me; Lalley was their prey. Without benefit of the narrative, I didn't know what *she* was thinking, but to her credit she kept calm and held the knife low as they moved closer. Then I realized, as Lally's eyes scanned past me without focusing, that she had reacted only to my voice moments before. I was as invisible here as I had been in Ardwyn.

The boys were grinning; the chilling rictuses showed metal teeth. One nodded to another and a third laughed, although nothing had been said. I took a breath and slipped out of the circle, and from behind them saw that they all had small boxes set into the bases of their skulls. Were they linked by chips?

They pounced in unison. Lalley managed to slash one's arm down to the bone and sink the knife into the side of another, but the leather seemed to take most of it. They shoved her up against the dripping cement wall, ripped her skirt and blouse open. My first impulse was to grab one of them, to pry him away from her, but the razors looked too sharp; instead I searched the ground for a weapon and came up with an old two-by-four with nails sticking out of one end.

I hauled off and took a good swing at a shaven head. I couldn't help but close my eyes as it connected, the impact jarring my arms. But it had no effect; the boy didn't feel it, the nails drew no blood. So much for me to the rescue. God, I didn't want to watch this. Lalley screamed.

Then there were four sharp pops, and the boys dropped in quick succession. I threw myself to the ground, and my face ended up inches from the blackened face of one of the boys. There was a small hole in his forehead. Blood suddenly gushed out of it.

And I was gasping and clutching my desk, squinting in the blast of bright light from my reading lamp, doing my best not to deposit my dinner on the pages in front of me.

When my eyes—and brain—adjusted, I scanned the page. There was Lalley, counting doors, desperately hoping that Gage would be behind the one she'd been told about. She heard a sound behind her and whirled, slipping out her vibroblade. There was a paragraph in which she hissed "Who's there?," but it had been excised by the editor's blue Flair. Had it been there before I went in? Did my entrance affect the narrative? I checked the last page of the manuscript; it was still 417. Going back, I made sure that, as I suspected, it was Gage who had saved her. Then I put the pencil aside. My hands were shaking too hard for me to work any more tonight.

Later on, listening to Len's breathing next to me, I realized he wasn't asleep. For him to lie awake at night was almost unheard of. He was on his side, facing the windows, probably watching the leaf pattern cast by the moonlight; the wasted romantic atmosphere made me sad. When we were first married, I would fall asleep to the comforting sound of his soft snores. Now he just sounded very far away, and although I was frightened about what was happening to me, and to us, and although I knew he was probably just waiting for me to whisper his name, I couldn't bring myself to do it. I was too afraid he wouldn't hear.

I finished the project without the intervention of magic office supplies; I would be more careful from now on about what I used them on. The next project was a light fantasy. But before I started work, I decided to try an experiment. I took a magic pencil, sharpened it carefully, and, on a legal pad, began to write down a history of my relationship with Len. Maybe this thing could be put to some decent use.

What was it about Len that had first attracted me to him? It had to be there still, hidden underneath the nine-to-five commuting engineer whose evenings were spent in front of the television and whose conversation centered mainly on finances. He had been so happy-go-lucky, so entranced by risk; he had jarred me from my sedentary life.

I wrote about our first date, when he had taken me horseback riding. Horses are big and unpredictable, and I didn't relish being that far above terra firma, but I had a crush on him, and he had taken it into his head to save me from my bookishness. "Where's first gear on this thing?" I had asked, discovering for the first time how gratifying it was to make him smile. I survived a bone-jarring trot and a canter that rattled my dental work, but I had to admit that it was uplifting, feeling the wind on my face, feeling as if I were flying. We were just turning to go back, letting the horses walk to cool off, when mine stopped and began to move in a very puzzling way. "Jump off!" Len suddenly shouted, and repeated it urgently when I stared at him dumbfounded. I bailed out just as the beast was going down for a roll. The wind was knocked out of me, but when I was able to breathe again and Len had my horse's reins, I saw his face—he was trying his best not to laugh—and cracked up. It was one of the most exhilarating laughs I had had in a long time, tears streaming down my face, and at that point I was in love.

But I was still at my desk. I'd gone back in memory, but not in body. It just didn't make any sense.

I spent a lot of time in Carthon. It was a land of lavender skies and blue-black mountains and fields of pastel flowers, and the magic there was done by wordsmiths instead of wizards, who worked their spells with elaborate illuminated manuscripts. I got behind on copyediting the project, because being in it was so much more satisfying.

My box of magic pencils was running low. I went to Mrs. Moslar at the stationery store and asked for some more, but she said she was out of stock, and though I didn't believe her there wasn't much I could do. Still, I kept erasing my marks and making them over again on the best scenes. That I was here with these mages because there was a real witch in my town never struck me as ironic. I took it all for granted now.

The day before the book was due, knowing that Len would be home in a couple of hours but wanting one last jaunt in Carthon, I sat down at my desk, a magic pencil in my hand. I noticed for the first time that the page I had written about our courtship was still sitting by the lamp, and I idly picked it up and read through it, thinking to throw it away.

But as I read, things began to occur to me. After all, I had shed my granny glasses for contacts but had not lost that bookishness; I had, rather, grown stubborn about it, refusing to compromise and spend any time with Len at all. He must feel abandoned, I thought, and must resent my work that much more. And here I was using it as an escape from confrontation, exacerbating everything. I made a note of this at the bottom of the page; perhaps tonight, when he got home, we could finally talk things out.

And there I was, standing in a clearing, watching two riders come loping along the bridle path out of the woods.

Len was young, gawky, bright-eyed, and the sight of him made my heart swell; it seemed incredible that six years had gone by since that first date. I looked pretty silly myself: I'd had an unflattering bob then, and my makeup was all wrong for the sunny day. As they passed me, they slowed to a walk. I turned and followed them, listening to their excited, awkward bantering. That was a part of courtship I wouldn't miss, although Len and I had lost the comfortable companionship that the early foot-in-mouth days had mellowed into. Maybe we weren't so different from this couple after all.

They came to a wide meadow and turned around, ready to go back. Now, of course, I knew that the horse was going to roll, and just as Len opened his mouth to yell "Jump!" the real Len, the now Len, was next to me.

"What the—" he began.

I shushed him, putting aside my own surprise to point to the couple in the field. "Just watch."

My younger body hit the grass with a flabby thud. Len slipped off his dun horse and got hold of the reins of my bay as it finished rolling and got up. He didn't ask me if I was all right, the way I remembered now that he had in reality; I'd been too breathless to answer, and could only nod wordlessly, but I'd forgotten to include that part in the memoir we now inhabited. My younger self rolled over, covered with wet autumn leaves, sat doubled up over her midriff, and then took in a huge gulp of air and began to laugh.

I looked at my Len, next to me; his face, rounder now, its angular youthfulness gone, had the queerest, softest expression on it, of awe and nostalgia and regret. He turned, feeling my gaze. "That was us?"

"Yeah."

We stood there in silence for another moment, and then he took my hand, hesitantly. "I came home early," he said. "I didn't want to interrupt you, but I thought we should talk. I looked for you upstairs and saw the thing you wrote about us, and then I really felt like a jerk, so I started to leave a message across the top, that I'd gone looking for you, in case you came back first and missed me . . . and now I'm—here."

"At least you found me."

The young riders had mounted up again. I remembered

the electric thrill that ran through my body as Len's hands touched me to give me a leg up. I turned to explain to the real Len what had been happening, and where we were.

"I hoped we could start over," he said, and moved me out of the horses' way as the couple rode back toward the stables. "But I didn't expect to be taken literally."

I smiled, and so did he, and then we were kissing each other in a way we hadn't kissed in a long time, and I was feeling a little electric thrill I hadn't felt in a long time, and we were back in my den. "I love you," Len said.

We didn't stay in that room very long.

"Only one spell per customer," Mrs. Moslar said. "You asked for a utensil to fix things, and things were fixed, yes?"

"Yes," I said, smiling. I didn't ask how she knew. Maybe it was written on my face, the way the wrinkles were written on hers, clear as day for the person who knew how to read that sort of thing. I hadn't really expected her to replenish my supply of magic pencils; I guess I just wanted an excuse to thank her. I bought an armful of more mundane supplies instead. Mrs. Moslar had guaranteed herself a long-term customer.

I didn't mind the typos anymore, now that my love life had been corrected. Words—what *I* knew how to read— were a pleasure in themselves, and my ability to fix them was a craft I didn't want usurped by magic after all.

But I didn't grind *every* bespelled FaberCastell down to the nub. And now that I've finished writing this, I really should check it over for mistakes.

Hand me that last green pencil over there, will you? And I'll see you when I come out.

BIRDS OF A FEATHER

by Charles Von Rospach

"Kevin, why do you want to be a witch? Why not be something nice, like a fireman?"

"It's my costume, and I don't wanna be a fireman! I wanna be a witch!"

"Boys can't be witches, son. Only girls can be witches."

"That's not what they said on the TV."

I stared at my son, trying to decide how to respond. That familiar little burn started up in my stomach, reminding me that in a little while, I was going to be miserable.

The phone rang, effectively ending the debate. I reached for it. "Go talk to your mother about the costume. If she says it's okay, then I won't argue about it."

"You're not going to be home for trick or treat tonight, are you?"

"I don't know yet, Kevin."

"You always leave when that phone rings. We never have fun any more. You're always gone." He looked at me, then turned and stomped out of the room.

Dammit, he's right, too. But someone's got to pay the bills, and when you work for yourself, your life isn't always under your control.

Ah, the joys of being your own boss. I'm forty-two years old, and I make a pretty good living, if I do say so myself. Worked the rat race for fifteen years until I got tired of it and got out. Now I only need to do those jobs I want to do, except for the ones I need to do to keep the creditors happy. Consulting is just another rat race, which is something none of the books tell you. It's not always fun. I might need to lose ten or fifteen pounds, and I may be working on an ulcer, but for all the headaches and uncertainties of consulting, it's better than the alternative. Seven years ago, on my last "real" job, it was fifty pounds and two ulcers, plus a marriage on the rocks, and ultimately, therapy to get it all straightened out. Life could be worse, but I wish it didn't seem like I was always having to run out on Kevin on special nights. I probably ought to get better at saying no.

I thought about it, but in the end I answered the phone before the machine grabbed it. "Jason Chilson, computer consultant." With my other hand, I reached into my pocket for my antacids. Life might not be perfect, but it could be a lot worse, too.

"Mr. Chilson?" My name is Andrew Barnheart. I'm afraid I have need of your skills tonight. I've lost some data that I need back tonight, and I've been told you're the one for the job."

I took two more antacids, just on general principles. "Okay, Mr. Barnheart. Give me the details and I'll see what I can do."

"Call me Andy. It's a Macintosh, a FileMaker database. I have some data I need to complete a project that has to be done immediately, and about an hour ago, the system crashed. Now I can't open the database, because it says the indexes are corrupt. My backups are in a safety deposit box at the bank, and I can't get to them until Monday. That's too late for this project. I've tried everything I know, but I'm afraid I'm just making it worse. I need an expert, and I've been told you're it. Frankly, I'm desperate. Can I convince you to help?"

I relaxed a little. In general, Mac projects aren't bad, and they can even be fun. It's amazing the number of ways people can play with that machine. If it was just index corruption, I could get it done and be back in time to take Kevin out trick or treating.

"I think I can help you, Andy. By the way, who gave you my name?"

"That's a little difficult to explain."

I rolled my eyes. He must have had contact with one of my special customers. You see, a while back Santa Claus's system crashed on Christmas Eve. The elves were so happy with my work they told their friends the brownies, and they told the leprechauns, who told the Tooth Fairy, who told. . . .

Well, you get the point. I work with a lot of unusual clients. They pay well, and on time (except for the Tooth Fairy, and the reward I got for helping convict her made up for it), but their jobs are never routine.

But hope springs eternal. Maybe this job would be different. I took another antacid, though.

Andy met me at the door to his house. He lived in the kind of neighborhood I only see when I make house calls. Looked the part, too, that polished lawyer-doctor look, every hair in perfect position, silver metal-rimmed glasses perched on a nose with just a hint of too much tennis combined with too little sunscreen, jeans with freshly pressed creases in them. One of those people who is clearly well-off, but without being ostentatious.

He ushered me to his office which was down in the basement. Office wasn't exactly the proper word for it, though. Sitting in the middle of the room was a large wooden desk with an office chair. On top of the desk was the Macintosh. That part was normal. The desk, however, was surrounded by a pentagram with unlit candles at each point of the star. To my left was a recliner chair surrounded by another pentagram, and in the far corner of the room was a large bird cage with a large, white bird inside. The bird stared at me for a second, then pointed a foot at me and cackled.

I sneezed.

Andy pointed at the bird. "Morgana, cut that out!" He turned back and faced me. "I'm sorry, Jason, that's Morgana le Fay, my familiar. She has, unfortunately, picked up a few minor spells of her own, and she thinks it's quite funny to pull her little tricks on strangers." Morgana cackled again. I sneezed.

Something told me this was going to be a long night.

"I know this all looks very strange, but let me try to explain what's going on. I'm a witch, and Morgana is my familiar."

"Andy, excuse the stupid question, but how can you be a witch? I thought women were witches."

He laughed. "Witchcraft has nothing to do with the X or Y chromosomes. Different types of magic—witchcraft, sorcery, whatever—are defined by the style of the spells used. It's true that in the Olden Days, the Guilds tended to be a bit, shall we say, exclusive, though, and that perception has persisted. Things are a lot more progressive today." He turned and walked over to the desk.

"In my own case, I've been doing a lot of research into the mechanics of witchcraft and spell-casting, and have found that it's all technique. If you have the right physical components, make the proper movements, and speak the proper phrases, the spell will work every time. The problem is trying to keep all three pieces of each spell straight and not screwing one of them up. If you get part of it wrong, usually nothing happens. Sometimes, though, something happens that you don't want, which can get interesting, so it's important to try to minimize potential problems.

"One of the things I've done is prerecord the spoken component of each spell and store it as a sound file on the Macintosh. These are stored in a database along with descriptions of the physical component and the necessary movements. All I have to do is bring up the proper spell in the database, bring out the items I need, and push a button. The computer speaks the spell, and I wave my hands at the proper time. Less chance of getting it wrong that way."

"As long as the computer doesn't crash."

"Yes. That was how Morgana learned that sneezing cantrip. I did all my testing with very simple spells. Unfortunately, I forgot that cockatoos are good mimics. Worse, they're intelligent animals, and she quickly figured out that if I waved my hands like this," he made a swift gesture, "and said the magic words," his mouth spit out something between a gargle and a cackle. From the corner of the room came a sudden sneeze and a disgusted gurgle. "She'd sneeze. She soon worked out how to return the favor." He looked at me. "Just be glad she never figured out the one that makes people burp. I chose a cockatoo for a familiar over a more common animal because I hoped she might be of more use in my spellcasting, with her grasping ability and her speech. What I ended up with was a three-year-old." There was a cackle, and he sneezed. "A spoiled three-year-old with a bad sense of humor."

He stared at the bird. "She's my problem, too. Once a year, on Halloween, witches have to renew the binding spell on their familiars or lose control over them. The spell has to be cast before dawn, or I lose her and have to wait a year before I can get another one, and then I'd have to start training it from scratch. If we don't get that spell out of the computer tonight, I'm screwed."

"You can't be a witch without a familiar?"

"No, not that bad. Almost. Familiars are not only necessary partners for more powerful spells, they help make all spells stronger. Think of them as an auxiliary battery, giving the system a little more boost."

"That's terrible, Andy. Let's see what I can do for you. Mac databases are generally pretty straightforward."

"Great!" He looked happy for the first time since I'd gotten there. "Before you go to work, I'm going to set up a few precautions. There shouldn't be any real problem since you aren't trained in magic, but this way, if something does go wrong you shouldn't get in trouble. It is, after all, Halloween, when the power is highest and the natives, shall we say, restless. Better safe than eternal damnation, you know."

Having come this close to going to hell with a demon whose computer I'd messed with, I knew better than he thought. "Do whatever you think is right, Andy." Hell, do it twice, Andy. I won't mind.

Andy sneezed. "Morgana, cut that out! Damned bird. Okay, you go sit down near the Mac. Take whatever tools you think you might need, because once the protective barriers are up you can't leave the circle. Don't touch the

computer yet. I'm going to set up a spell of protection
around the pentagram. That'll keep everything out until
the spell is broken. Whatever you do, don't knock over
one of the candles or scuff out the chalk lines, and if
something asks for permission to enter, whatever you do,
don't say yes. And while you're in there, don't eat or
drink anything, or you might accidentally set off a physical component of some spell. And please don't interrupt
me in the middle of a spell."

He got to work, lighting candles, waving his hands
around erratically and making noises that made me wonder whether he kept a throat specialist on retainer. The
only thing computer folks have to worry about is carpal
tunnel. It sounded like he was attempting to dismember
his vocal cords from the inside. Every so often, Morgana
would chuckle and I'd sneeze. I was quickly learning to
hate that bird. Visions of fried chicken started wandering
through my head, making my stomach grumble.

That started the burn. I reached for an antacid. Then I
put it back down. Eventually Andy wound down and
looked at me again. "There. That should protect you from
everything short of a nuclear blast."

"A *what?*"

"It's a figure of speech, Jason. We've never had anything that nasty happen. Honest. Don't worry."

"If you say so. By the way, are antacids considered
eating?"

He looked at me blankly for a second, then his eyebrows scrunched together. "You know what? I have no
idea. It's never come up before."

"Do you think they'd be okay?"

"How interested are you in being a test case?"

"No, thanks. I think I'll survive without them."

He laughed. "Smart boy. Now I'm going to go protect
my chair, and then I'll shut up and let you get to work."
He repeated the protection rituals around the recliner, this
time from the inside of the pentagram. When he was
done, he picked up a book, sat down, and said, "We're all
set. Let me know if you need me." Then he started reading.

I noticed that he was reading *Macbeth*. That figured. I sat down and got to work on the database. Since he had backups and only wanted that one piece of data, I didn't try to get fancy. After verifying that the disk structure was okay, I opened up the database with one of my editing tools and started looking for sound resources. The "hack and slash" school of data recovery, but it'd get me out of the house before my stomach imploded, and home in time for some quality time with Kevin.

Computer work seems glamorous to those on the outside, but it's really about twenty percent knowledge, seventy-five percent sweat and gruntwork, and about five percent fear and stress. I spent the next twenty minutes finding the pieces of data that looked like sound. Each one got pulled out of the file, and then I'd get Andy's attention and play it back on the Macintosh. Andy would listen, and when he was sure it wasn't the right one, I'd stop it, throw it in the trash and move on. Andy would then growl something that must have been the witch's equivalent of "reset state," and go back to *Macbeth*.

Other than that, the only other sounds were the occasional sound of Andy's pages rustling or his chuckling at some part of *Macbeth* or other, and the continuing attack on my nose by Morgana, the bird from hell.

Rustle. Chuckle. Achoo. "Morgana, cut that out!" Andy was right. She was a three-year-old. Tell a kid "No!", and he'll go ask mom. Tell a kid "No!" when you can't make him, and he'll do it twenty times just to spite you. They haven't figured out the linearity of time, or that parents have memories and might punish them later. Now is all that matters.

I wanted to kill that bird. She was the only one in the room enjoying life, and I resented it. The bitch of it was, she knew it, too. And that made it even more fun for her.

I had to go to the bathroom. Why me?

I hit paydirt on the eighteenth try. I played the resource back to Andy, and instead of hearing, "Nope. Kill it," I got silence for about forty-five seconds, followed by an excited Andy saying, "That's it!" I killed the voice.

"Great! Let me package things up so you can set it off

when you're ready, and we'll be all set. Why don't you pull down all these damn invisible walls so I can take a quick break first, though."

Andy spent a couple of minutes reversing whatever spells he'd set up, blew out the candles, and then walked over. "You can have your antacid now, too."

I gratefully reached for a couple, then walked over to my tormentor's cage.

"Morgana, do you know how close you are to being lunch right now?"

She looked at me through the bars with her big, brown eyes, and said, "Morgana loves you!" with all sincerity.

Just like a child. People without kids wonder how they survive without being drowned by their parents. It's that kids have an ability for a well-placed guilt trip. I turned my back on the bird and started walking back to the Mac. Behind me, Morgana chuckled. I sneezed. Bastard.

I went back to the computer and packaged up the sound resources so they could be used easily, which only took a minute. That's one of the things I like about the computer. When it works, it's really simple and powerful.

"Okay, Andy, we're all set over here. I'm going to try the entire sound once, just to make sure there isn't any corruption. Do me a favor and don't make any false moves, okay?"

"Great!" He came over and stood next to me. I fired off the sound, and the Macintosh started making noises like a hive of angry honeybees attacking a rabid beaver. I was amazed that humans could do that to their voices and survive.

The chant went on for a good two minutes. Toward the end, I heard a familiar rustling from the far side of the room. I prepared to sneeze. Suddenly, Andy looked over at the bird. "Morgana! Stop that!"

Too late. The spell ended, and there was a small explosion down at my feet. I jumped back and looked down.

Lying on the floor next to the desk was a large black cat. A very large, very black cat. It opened its eyes and stared at me with very yellow eyes.

Andy couldn't decide who to look at. His gaze kept

shifting from me to the cat to the computer to Morgana. Morgana chose this moment to turn her back on us and start preening. The cat stood up and walked over to me, rubbed against my legs twice, lay down on my right foot, and promptly went back to sleep.

"Well, I'll be. I didn't know she could do that." He shook his head in disbelief and turned back to me. "Jason, we have a bit of a problem. Morgana seems to have conjured you up a familiar."

"A what? I'm not a witch!

"I know that. You know that. Morgana knows that, too. But nevertheless, you have a familiar for the next year, and if you want him beyond that, as long as you continue to bind him to yourself."

"But I don't want a familiar! Can't you send him back?"

"Sorry, it doesn't work that way. He's stuck with you for the next year, and you're stuck back. It's not a real cat, after all, any more than Morgana is a real cockatoo. That's just the physical aspect they use to present themselves. If you try to leave him behind, he'll find you again. And it's not a good idea to upset familiars too much." He sighed. "At least yours can't spell-cast."

Over in the corner, Morgana chuckled. The cat sneezed, woke up, and stared longingly at the bird. I was tempted to open the cage. Very tempted.

"Andy, my wife hates cats. How do I explain this to her?"

"I dunno. Look, I'm sorry. If I knew Morgana could do this, I would have taken precautions. This kind of spell-casting is unprecedented. If there was something I could do, I'd do it. Honest.

"It could be worse. He'll only be around for a year. If you don't rebind him, he'll disappear next Halloween."

"Is he box trained?"

"How should I know? Why?"

"Because our last cat, the one my wife swore would be the last one to step foot in her house, used to spray the furniture."

"So?"

"So she had him neutered. *Can* you neuter a familiar?"

Andy looked at me, puzzled for a moment, and then started laughing. "The hell if I know! If the answer is no, I wouldn't want to be the vet who tries it."

"Well, I guess I'll think of something. Andy, if you don't mind, I'm going to leave you to your binding spell and get home. I can still take my kid trick or treating if I hurry. He's going to be a witch this year, and he'll be thrilled to know he'll have a cat for a prop." I picked up the cat. It didn't wake up, but it started purring. "I think I'll call him Merlin."

Andy laughed again. "Good thought. I'll have a little talk with my fine feathered friend later tonight, after I do my own binding."

I grabbed my bag and headed toward the stairs. At the base, I turned around.

"Hey, Morgana?" The bird stopped preening for a second and looked at me, then turned her back again.

I raised a hand and made a noise somewhere between a chuckle and a gurgle. Morgana sneezed. She started to turn around, slipped, and toppled off her perch, falling to the floor of her cage with a thud.

Andy looked at me. "Quick study," he said with a grin.

I smiled back. "I had a good teacher."

LOSE WEIGHT LIKE MAGIC

by Linda J. Dunn

I feel like shouting, "Help! I'm being held prisoner in a torture chamber!" But who am I kidding? I need to be here, working out with all the other fatties.

I step up the pace on the exercycle as I see the manager approaching.

"Hi," she says. "My name's Connie Edwards. What's yours?"

"Leesa Nite."

"Enjoying your free trial workout here?"

About as much as I enjoyed having poison ivy last summer. I nod and smile, stepping up the pace on the bike a little more and trying to look like I enjoy pain and suffering.

She opens her mouth to say something and then stops. I notice she's staring at the left bike handle.

"Is something wrong?" I ask, slowing slightly.

"What?" She looks back at me. "No. I didn't mean to stare but I couldn't help noticing your unusual ring. Did your husband give it to you?"

"Gary. My boyfriend."

"Oh." She looks back at the ring and then turns to me and says, "How about joining me in the slow cooker."

"The what?"

"Our sauna."

"Oh." I've never been in one of those before and I hesitate a second, visualizing beautiful, thin people laughing at my flabby thighs and love handles.

"I'll fill you in on my weight loss secret."

I stare at her lovely, slim body for a moment. She could be a model. "Does it involve vomiting?"

"What?"

"The last time someone said that to me, they recommended Syrup of Ipecac. I wound up in the hospital."

"No," she says. "I just suspect—well, it's a long story. I'll tell you in the sauna."

I lurch off the bike and head toward the locker room. I'm not too anxious to strip down and expose my obese body next to her perfect one, but if she knows a quick and easy way to lose weight that doesn't endanger my health . . . well, I'm right behind her.

I disrobe quickly and follow Connie into the sauna. Oh, does it feel good! Not at all what I expected. My hands feel cool and the heat is seeping into my body. I'm starting to relax as I sit down and realize we're all alone.

Good! No gawkers.

"Let me see if I can guess when you started gaining weight." Connie sits down on the redwood bench, leans back against the wall, and smiles at me.

"I bet it was right after your boyfriend gave you that puzzle ring, the kind that falls apart if you take it off."

"Well, yes." I turn to stare at her. What the heck is she insinuating? "But I hardly think there's any connection—"

"And while you're fighting the battle of the bulge, your boyfriend is eating whatever he likes and isn't gaining an ounce. In fact, he may even be losing a little weight."

"Well, he was a little chubby when we met but— Hey! What is all this?"

She sighs, leans forward, and pats my knee. "Leesa, I suspect you're suffering from the same thing that happened to me. You see, I also suddenly developed a weight problem once. In fact, I gained two hundred pounds before—"

"Two hundred—!" I try to visualize a fat Connie Edwards but I can't. She's got those beautiful high cheekbones that I've always envied on models and it's impossible to imagine that oval face ever looking round. As for her body—well, I can see everything and there's not a stretch mark anywhere. Whatever she did to lose that much weight must have been damned effective.

Or else she's lying.

She takes a deep breath and settles back against the wall again. "When I married Steve, he gave me a puzzle ring similar to yours; the kind that falls apart into a half-dozen interlocked rings if you take it off. He said it was a Middle Eastern wedding ring and joked that men give this to their wives so they'll know if their wives ever remove it."

She looks over at me and winks. "Bet you can't take yours off."

How did she know?

"I started gaining weight immediately," she says.

"At first, I attributed it to all the traveling I was doing with my new job. Hotel food isn't very good, but it is fairly fattening. I switched to salads.

"Six months later, I bought my first big woman outfit and let me tell you it was really difficult to find an attractive business suit that large.

"Of course I tried all the diet plans I could find and drove my doctor mad with constant questions about why I was gaining weight. I was sure I had some kind of disease."

She laughs nervously and stares down at her feet. "He said I was gaining weight because I was cheating on my diet.

"I was so humiliated," she says. "Humiliated and confused. But I was determined to prove him wrong. I would lose twice as much weight as he wanted me to lose by the next visit.

She looks over at me and takes a deep breath.

"I gained another five pounds by the end of the week." Our eyes meet for a moment; she blushes and turns away. "I canceled my next appointment.

"It just didn't make any sense. I was starving myself and gaining weight while Steve was shoveling down more food every night than I ate all week."

Boy, does this sound familiar.

"Then I started thinking about all the other mismatched

couples I'd seen and I began to wonder if there was something that, crazy as it sounds, transfers excess fat from one person to another.

"So I started searching through the house." She shakes her head and almost smiles. "I found some pretty weird stuff when I picked the lock on the door to his workshop. So I decided to tail Steve when he left for his next Lion's Club meeting."

She looks back at me and our eyes meet. "He was a lion all right. Spelled l-y-i-n-g. I found out I'd married a warlock and the club meetings were just a cover for secret coven get-togethers."

I gasp and reflexively pull back. Is she nuts?

"Oh, relax. Witches have been around since time began," she says. "They were the first healers and the first chemists. They only reason we didn't call them scientists is because they attributed everything to magic instead of looking for logical cause-and-effect relationships."

She's got a point. My mother grew up in the Smoky Mountains and she still uses an old book of home remedies she got from *her* mother.

She shakes her head slowly. "Some witches take a more scientific approach. But none of us have figured out how the ring works—yet."

Us? The ring?

Connie takes a deep breath and glances at me before staring off into space. "I was desperate."

She slowly raises her arm and drops the towel from her left hand. I try not to stare at the place where her ring finger should be.

"I lost ten pounds in a week after chopping it off."

"What—? Why—?"

"Because it was the ring. It wouldn't come off. Even the jeweler couldn't cut it off. But I lost fifty pounds by the time the hospital released me, and I was back to my normal weight when the divorce became final."

I stand up and move toward the doorway, but Connie gestures me back. "What's the matter? Afraid it's contagious? Or am I just hitting a little too close to home?"

I want to run like hell, but something forces me to sit.

Perhaps because some similarities bother me. The first thing Gary did after moving in with me was to start an herb garden. And although he doesn't belong to the Lion's Club, he's out all night quite frequently with members of the Elks Lodge. My head throbs as I start remembering all the other little oddities I'd dismissed in the last few months.

No. This is just too strange to believe—or is it?

I speak slowly and hesitantly, hoping I'm wrong. "Are you suggesting that my boyfriend is some kind of a master warlock and I need to chop off my finger to break his evil spell?"

"No." Connie shakes her head and smiles faintly. "There are other ways. The easiest way is to move. A witch's spell can't follow you across a body of water, you know."

So that's why I lost weight while visiting my parents in Key West!

"But he can always follow you, recast the spell, and then you're right back where you started."

She folds her arms across her chest and stares at me. "There's more, but I don't want to push you too far and too fast. You're probably already upset and confused."

Boy, that's an understatement.

"In the meantime, you're going to need to exercise for two. We're having a special this month—"

I almost laugh out loud. What a scam. She really had me going there for a while—and to think I almost fell for it. I play along with the game, pretending to consider the deal, and then head to the locker room to change.

She follows me to the door and adds, "The special's only good through next Saturday." What a great act!

I'm still giggling inside as I start to leave the clinic and see Connie blocking my exit.

"You don't really believe me, do you?" She's almost whispering.

I've never had a good poker face.

She shakes her head. "You'll learn." Connie sighs and stares at me for a full minute while I'm trying to figure out how to get around her and out the door. "Oh, hell. All right, I'll go ahead and tell you. After I moved here, I found a better way. Check out Vonda's in the mall."

She steps aside and I bolt out the door. Freedom! I walk past the food court, ignoring all temptations until I pass the candy store. I love chocolate.

I can't resist pausing to savor the aroma, and that's when I notice an odd little shop wedged in the corner of the food court. A place called "Vonda's."

They must be working together. There's no way in hell I'm going to be taken in by whatever racket it is these folks are running, but curiosity is my middle name. I decide to check out the shop—just so I can laugh about it later.

When I tell the clerk I'm just looking, she glances at my ring and smiles. The next thing I know I'm being told a fascinating history about my ring, and how it contracts with the application of certain chemicals pretty much the way heat shrinkable tubing works. The whole thing sounds plausible.

I have my doubts about the package she hands me after ringing up the sale on my charge card. But what have I lost besides four months' salary?

She smiles and waves good-bye as I leave and head toward my car. Yes, I've been scammed again—big time!

When am I going to learn? I've got three years' worth of vitamins in the closet and a coupon for a free trip to Las Vegas that I couldn't take because it didn't include transportation or hotel accommodations.

I must be wearing a sign that says "Sucker."

Gary has dinner waiting for me and smiles as I walk in the door. Always before, I told myself how lucky I was to find a perfect guy like him; but when I look at the brownie in his hand and smell the aroma of fresh-baked chocolate. . . . Well, suddenly I'm not so sure anymore.

He falls asleep in front of the TV shortly after dinner; I tiptoe over to his side and slide the ring I bought onto his finger. It dangles loosely, threatening to fall off at any moment. I pull out the instruction sheet and a package of powder and start reading aloud.

Okay, so maybe I am a first-class idiot and maybe I

have been scammed. But I'm not going to admit defeat until I carry this joke out to the bitter end. After all—

I nearly fall backward as I sprinkle the contents of the package over the ring and sparks fly. Uncertain if I really want to know, I reach out slowly and try to pull the ring off Gary's finger.

It's stuck. The ring has changed to match the size of his finger exactly. He'll never be able to get it off.

Now let me think a minute. If we've both got rings then one of two things could happen: Either we each gain weight based upon what the other person eats, or (and this is the one I really like) Gary ships all his unneeded calories to me and the ring he's wearing draws them back to him with my extra calories piggybacked on top.

I find myself giggling insanely and clasp my hands over my mouth to avoid waking him. Not just yet!

I get up and rummage around in the freezer for a minute, and then scoop up a plateful of brownies from the kitchen table. I walk back into the room as Gary sits up and starts to rub his eyes. Grinning madly, I drop a container of chocolate ice cream onto the coffee table.

He jumps and shakes his head as I flip open the top and scoop ice cream on top of a brownie, place another brownie on top, and flatten it. Opening my mouth, I cram it inside and munch loudly.

His mouth drops open and he stares for a minute before realizing something's different. He glances down at his hand and frantically tries to pull the ring off. It holds.

He's really panicking now; and I think we'll be able to reach an agreement. I wonder if we should have a simple ceremony or spring the big bucks for a formal wedding? And should we both agree to eat sensibly or should he be the one to exercise for two?

I giggle madly as I wonder if rings have been Elizabeth Taylor's problem all along. She does have a passion for jewelry.

I choke for a moment, stop laughing, and swallow. Oh, this tastes so good! I make another brownie and ice cream sandwich while Gary looks at me with pleading eyes.

I'd almost forgotten how good chocolate tastes.

WITCH DOCTOR

by Kate Daniel

The light stayed green for a shorter time each year, or so it seemed. The old woman was less than halfway across when it changed, stranding her on the concrete island in the middle of the street. Traffic rushed past on both sides, too close and too fast. When the light changed again, she carefully looked each way, then set out for the far curb. She hadn't taken more than a dozen steps when a horn blasted right behind her.

A red sports car squealed to a stop inches away from her and the driver stuck his head out the window. He was probably older than he looked; all the young men looked like little boys to her these days. But this one was old enough to be driving. And, evidently, to be drinking, judging by the slurred voice.

"Watch it, you old witch. Get the hell out of my way."

"Oh, yes, I *am* an old witch." She smiled sweetly at him. "But it's very rude of you to say so. You need to learn some manners, young man." She blinked in the glare from the strong headlights, then walked on, muttering under her breath.

The driver revved his engine and, as soon as she moved, took off with another squeal of tires. He made an obscene gesture at her back as he did, and yelled one last insult. *"Ribbet ribbet!"*

The car swerved wildly, almost sideswiping a parked car. The old lady gained the safety of the sidewalk and walked on without a backward glance.

Served the young fool right, Hazel thought tartly. Not

that she could, or would, turn anyone into a frog. The glamour would wear off before he'd gone a block. But the shock of hearing a croak come out of his mouth should sober him up enough so he wouldn't run over anyone. The clinic didn't need extra business.

A block later, she reached her destination. The plateglass window still said LAUNDRY, but the window had been blocked from inside with plywood. Neat stenciling on the door said "La Merced Clinic." A cardboard sign added *"Para mujeres y niños. Se habla español."* In Hazel Cradwell's case, saying she spoke Spanish was an exaggeration, but the patients always understood her.

It was eight o'clock at night, but the cheap plastic chairs in the front room were still filled. In one corner, a small group of children watched a rerun of *Sesame Street* in silent fascination. Many of them knew no English, but they loved Big Bird. Their mothers ignored the set, chattering as they nursed babies and waited for their turn. Several nodded at Hazel as she crossed the room and let herself in through the door marked *Private—Privado.*

The middle-aged woman who greeted her was almost as short as Hazel herself. "Full house tonight, Hazel. Luz Montoya came back, by the way; I think she's been beaten again."

"I saw her out in the waiting room. I'll take her first. Has Susan been in tonight?"

The younger woman shook her head. "I haven't seen her."

"I hoped—" Hazel broke off. If her greatgranddaughter didn't want to help at the clinic any longer, there wasn't much Hazel could do about it.

"Felicia's death upset her. She's young; she'll be back."

"I hope so." Hazel shook her head and went on back to the cramped office where she counseled patients on birth control and drug abuse. Felicia's death had hit the girl hard, no doubt, but that was only part of the problem. There was no way to tell Doctor Anna, but what had really scared Susan off was facing her own limitations for the first time.

The clinic did a lot of good, but it was only a drop in the bucket of need that was the barrio. Anna Casteñeda had started it twenty years before, with no more than a fresh medical degree and a dream. Over the years, the need had grown faster than the clinic, which had never had enough funding and survived mainly through donations and volunteer help. Hazel had discovered it after a newspaper write-up eight years before. At the time, it had looked as though La Merced was finally going to have to close its doors. Hazel hadn't been able to help with money, but she had her own way of doing things. A short time later, a wealthy businessman gave the clinic a donation large enough to let them stay open. He'd been the angel of La Merced ever since.

The door opened, and Luz came into the room. *"Buenas noches, Abuelita."* Hazel's uneven Spanish had no trouble with that: "Good evening, little grandmother." Half the patients called her that. Since she was an inch under five feet tall and several years past seventy, she never argued with the name. She had never quite figured out why a few of the older women called her *Brujita,* though. It meant "little witch," and it was as accurate as the other. But she didn't know how they knew.

"Hello, Luz. Do you need to see Doctor Anna tonight, or do you just want to talk?" Hazel's skill at keeping her thoughts off her face had been sharpened by her experiences at the clinic. Now she assessed Luz clinically while keeping a concerned smile in place. The bruises around the left eye were fresh, as was the swelling under her jaw. And there was another bruise visible under the edge of her sleeve. But this time the young woman kept her head up, instead of hiding in shame. And she wore makeup, but she hadn't tried to cover the marks with a thick layer of foundation and powder, as she had the first time Hazel had seen her. So maybe the magic was starting to take effect.

"Not Doctor Anna. This—" Luz fingered the lump on her jaw. "Is nothing. But talk . . ." Hazel gave an encouraging nod, and Luz burst into a flood of Spanish. Much of it went past Hazel, as it always did, but she got the gist. This time Luz had left when her boyfriend hit her. She wanted to know more about the school *La Abuelita* had told her about. Instead of going back to be hit again, she wanted to go to school and get a job.

"That's wonderful! You'll have to call them tomorrow morning and make an appointment, but I'm sure they'll accept you. Let me write a recommendation for you."

Hazel picked up the silver pen lying on the desk. As she scrawled out a hasty recommendation, she chanted silently, her tongue moving inside her mouth. Long practice let her keep her face almost still as she chanted. She preferred to speak aloud; doing it this way always made her feel like a ventriloquist. But the words of the spell would help Luz keep her confidence long enough to follow through, letting her see herself as an independent woman seeking an education. And the simple words of the character reference carried the glamour of conviction that Hazel had crafted into the silver pen years before.

That was all most magic was, glamours and appearances, but it was amazing what could be done with such limited power. It could convince an alcoholic he had the strength to kick booze. Or make a selfish man see himself as the generous angel keeping a clinic afloat. Or shock a reckless driver back to sobriety by making him think he had been turned into a frog. Luz would be accepted at the alternative school.

The volunteer counselors at the clinic were supposed to teach the patients about birth control and prenatal care, how to avoid AIDS and venereal disease, the dangers of drug and alcohol abuse. A lot of the job was just listening. Hazel added magic, glamours to help patients see themselves the way they wanted to be. It was a delicate balancing act, encouraging them without creating false expectations. Doctor Anna had the only full medical degree at the clinic, but Hazel considered herself a doctor as well. A witch doctor. It was her private joke.

But sometimes magic wasn't enough. As she wished Luz good luck in her badly-accented Spanish, Hazel wondered if Susan would ever speak to her again. Her great-granddaughter was the only one in the family to share her

Gift. When Susan asked to join her at the clinic, Hazel had been delighted. She should have realized the girl was too young to accept the fact that magic couldn't do everything. It hadn't been able to cure Felicia or her baby.

Luz was the high point of the evening. The rest of the time was spent endlessly repeating the lectures the volunteers all knew in their sleep. Occasionally a patient had to be referred to Doctor Anna herself, added to the next day's overlong list. La Merced stayed open three nights a week, since it was hard for some patients to come during the day. A new volunteer, a nurse-midwife, was holding a Lamaze class in the next room; Hazel could hear her through the wall. "*In*-hale, two three four, *ex*-hale. . . ."

Always more need than time. But Susan's need was just as deep as the patients', and Hazel didn't know what to do about it.

Hazel waited all week, but Susan didn't come back to the clinic. When the weekend arrived without any word, Hazel gave up. She would have to confront the girl. That Saturday she drove out to her granddaughter's suburban home.

"Grandmother Hazel! This is a surprise." From the expression on Sherry's face, it wasn't a pleasant one.

Hazel ignored it. "Is Susan home? I need to see her." She was tempted to use a small glamour. It would have made things easier, but it didn't feel right, using magic against her family.

Sherry turned up the ice. "I'm sorry, Grandmother, but she's out shopping with some friends. Acting like a normal teenager for once," she added. Sherry had made it plain long before that she considered Hazel a bad influence on her daughter.

"That's nice." Hazel ignored all of the undertones and smiled blandly. "I'm in no rush anyway. I'll wait."

She hated to do this to Sherry, but she had to see Susan. Muttering under her breath, she cast herself as an unopposable matriarch. The expected offer of tea came. Hazel accepted, careful not to see Sherry's obvious resentment. Sherry was the only child of her hidebound son, and if it hadn't been for Susan, she would have been happy to leave her granddaughter alone. They chatted, desperately polite. At last the front door opened and Susan came in. She froze when she saw Hazel, then came on into the room.

"Hello, Nanners." To unGifted eyes, she looked like a normal, somewhat sullen girl of fourteen. But Hazel saw beyond the glamour the child had cast instinctively. Susan was defiant, and guilt-ridden, and very, very unhappy.

"Did you have fun shopping, dear?" Hazel asked.

Susan had bought quite a bit. As she displayed her purchases, the level of tension in the room dropped. After a few minutes, Hazel gently nudged Sherry into leaving them alone.

"I saw that, Nanners." The chill was back in Susan's voice. "You made Mom go away, but that doesn't mean I have to listen to you. And I'm not going to."

"Susan, you can't just ignore your Gift—"

"Yes, I can. And I am, so just go away and leave me alone."

"You couldn't even walk into this room without a glamour!" Hazel let the truth of that sink in, then went on less emphatically. "It's part of you, pet. But without training, you won't be able to use it effectively."

"I don't want to use it! What good is it? Felicia *died,* can't you understand, she's dead. And so's her baby. So what difference did it make if I made her think she was important?"

Hazel wanted to put her arms around her, but she didn't dare. Give pain an excuse to turn into anger, and she'd never reach the girl. Instead, she said gently, "Felicia had AIDS, Susan. She was in bad health to begin with, and the pregnancy didn't help. There wasn't anything anyone could do."

"So why bother casting glamours when they don't mean anything? I wish I'd never met her. And I wish I'd never met you!" Without waiting for a reply, she fled.

Hazel was still sitting there, numb, when Sherry came back. "Susan's locked herself in her room, and she won't answer me. What did you say to her?"

"We were talking about Felicia—the young woman who died."

"I know who she was, and I'm sick of hearing about her!" Sherry snatched up the empty teacup that was still sitting in front of Hazel and started rinsing it automatically. "You had no business taking a child as young as Susan down to that horrible place. Exposing her to the likes of that tramp. . . ."

"She was almost the same age as Susan. Sixteen, that was all. That's why they became friends; they were alike in a lot of ways. You're going to wash the pattern off that cup if you don't stop."

"How dare you say Susan is like her! She was a *prostitute!*" The thin china shattered as Sherry gripped it too hard. Blood welled from her cut hand.

"Let me see." Hazel took a step toward her, but Sherry waved her back.

"I'm all right. Just go away."

"Are you sure? That may need stitches."

"I said go away. And from now on, leave my daughter alone, you old witch!"

Old witch. Calling herself a witch had always been a joke to Hazel, born as much of her name as the small Gift she had for casting a glamour. It wasn't witchcraft in the storybook sense; just the ability to change appearances, make people believe what she wanted them to. It only worked if she had some sort of contact with the person, and even then it didn't work against a determined mind. But she'd always been amused at the idea of being a witch. It no longer seemed at all funny.

Sherry meant it this time. Hazel tried calling, but as soon as she said hello, the connection cut off with a click. Repeated calls ended the same way, even when Susan answered. They had cut her off. Hazel kept trying, though. After a long mental debate, she called her son, Sherry's father. Roger had written her off as "eccentric" years before, and he was no help.

"Sherry told me. I don't blame her for being upset. Mother, what did you expect? It's bad enough, you spend-

ing all your time down at that place, but exposing a child
to it. . . ."

"Susan is not a child." Hazel felt a twinge as she said
that, since she called Susan "child" often enough herself.
"She's a compassionate young woman, and it won't hurt
her to learn something about the rest of the world."

There was silence at the other end of the phone. Then
Roger said, "Maybe you're right. I worry about you going down in that part of town at all hours, yet I know the
clinic does good work. But dammit, Mother, Susan is
only fourteen!"

And too young to handle the emotional load, was the
unspoken corollary. She couldn't argue, since it was what
she thought herself. And neither Roger nor Sherry knew
about the additional burden of ineffectual magic.

She started missing sessions at La Merced. *Witch doctor.* Her joke had turned to mockery. *Try healing thyself,
doc. Or thy child.* In time Susan would get over Felicia's
death. What worried Hazel was whether or not she would
accept her magic.

Doctor Anna was understanding. "Everyone needs a
break once in a while. Make your peace with your grand-
child, *Abuelita.* The clinic will still be here when you return."

But there was no way to make peace when she couldn't
talk to the girl. In desperation, she started haunting Susan's favorite places, collecting stares from the teenagers
who crawled the malls and hung out at fast food joints
until she cast a glamour to make herself unnoticeable.
Sometimes Susan was there with friends, but she always
turned away. Hazel could feel a glamour pushing her
away. It wasn't strong enough to actually repel her, but
she honored the intent. All she could do was wait and be
there if Susan ever changed her mind.

But after more than a week of tagging along after a girl
who never acknowledged her presence, Hazel was about
ready to give up. She sat in the sidewalk café and sipped
moodily at an iced tea she hadn't wanted. Susan and her
friends were less than a dozen steps away. None of the
others had spotted the old woman watching them, but Su-

san ignored her as well. She might as well have saved herself the trouble of casting the glamour.

"Abuelita!"

The nickname caught her off-guard, and she looked around. Luz Montoya was across the street, waving frantically. Beyond the range of the glamour, she had seen Hazel. Susan heard her as well; she turned and glared at her great-grandmother.

Luz yelled something else, but Hazel shrugged her shoulders. Her Spanish couldn't cope with the traffic noise of a busy street masking half the words. Then she jumped up shouting "No!" as Luz started across the street, without seeing the car that came around the corner too fast on the last glimmer of yellow. Far too fast. Screeching brakes drowned both traffic and screams as the car struck Luz, skidded, then roared away without stopping.

By the time Hazel reached Luz, Susan was on her knees beside her. Hazel reached for Luz's hand. "Susan, get back. Please, I don't want you hurt." She wasn't sure if Susan heard her, but she knew Luz didn't. The barrio girl's eyes were unfocused and she was babbling in Spanish. Shock. Hazel wasn't a nurse, but she could tell the girl was badly injured. "Please, Susan."

Susan shook her head without looking at her great-grandmother. Her lips were moving. The child must be trying a glamour, and it couldn't help now, any more than it had helped Felicia. Felicia's death had been in a hospital, away from Susan. Luz would die here, almost in Susan's arms. And it would destroy the girl.

But Luz didn't die. The ambulance arrived, and she was still conscious, still talking incomprehensible rapid-fire Spanish, holding Hazel's hand. As the paramedics carefully eased her onto a stretcher, her eyes focused for a moment on Hazel.

"Abuelita," she whispered. "I am in the school."

"I know, Luz. I know." Hazel gave her hand one final squeeze, then stood back as the paramedics loaded the stretcher onto the ambulance. As they pulled away from the curb, sirens howling, she became aware for the first time that Susan's arms were around her. She felt absurdly grateful. No matter what happened now, at least Susan wouldn't feel the full impact.

"She won't die, Nanners."

Almost as if Susan had read her mind. Hazel turned to stare at her, but Susan's eyes were following the ambulance as it wove through the traffic.

"Glamours? We can't heal people."

"Yes, we can! When I saw Luz there—she was still talking about the school. Lying there bleeding all over the sidewalk, and all she could think about was that school you got her into. And it came to me, that was what was important to her, and it would keep her alive and fighting long enough for the ambulance to get here. So I helped her have faith that she could live—and—*that's* what I can do for people, what we can do. What magic can do."

"Faith." It made sense; that was why faith healing worked despite all the charlatans. The mind could work its own magic over the body. And it was so close to what she'd been doing for years, giving the patients at the clinic faith in themselves. She'd just never taken the final step.

"I want to come back to La Merced, Nanners."

Hazel hugged her. "It won't be easy, love. We won't always be able to help. Felicia. . . ."

"After the baby died, Felicia didn't care anymore." Susan spoke quietly, grief finally accepted. "She gave up. But Luz didn't."

"I can imagine what your mother will say." The thought of what her son and granddaughter would say made Hazel quail even as she rejoiced. *For this my greatgranddaughter that was lost. . . .* Susan wasn't lost to her anymore. But Sherry would raise hell.

"I can handle Mom." Susan grinned suddenly. "I'll tell her it's good practice. I'm going to go to med school."

"You never said—when did you decide that?"

"About ten minutes ago." Susan turned serious again. "But it's not just an impulse. I can use magic to help people believe in themselves, but it takes more for people like Felicia. And not just AIDS patients. You were right, magic can't do much. But our magic *and* medicine. . . ."

It could work. As they walked back to the café arm in arm, Hazel laughed out loud.

"I just realized. You know, if you go through with this, you really *will* be a witch doctor."

Keeping family traditions alive was always worthwhile.

THE TROUBLE WITH BIG BROTHERS

by Nina Kiriki Hoffman

Ever since Halloween night Mary's brother Edmund had been acting weird.

Of course, he had changed before. When she was four and he was ten, he helped her build towers out of blocks and ran through sprinklers on hot summer days with her. When she was six and he was twelve, he sat with her after supper and helped her learn to read. When she was eight and he was fourteen, he suddenly had a bunch of friends and wasn't home as much, but he was always glad to see her when he was. She had realized then that she was losing him. She stayed close to him when she could.

Now she was ten and he was sixteen, and something strange was happening.

His voice had changed, silkened until the simplest sentence, like, "Please pass the milk," sounded like music—not like an advertisement, but like a bird singing. His eyes had new silver in their green. When he snapped his fingers, Mary heard a sound like the scritch of a match head, and something happened. Once he did it during dinner and all the lights in the house turned off. Once a window jumped open and let in a blast of wind.

This time, Edmund was studying for a math test at the table in the living room, and Mary was lying on the Persian rug watching cartoons with the sound turned down so she wouldn't bother him. The rug smelled like dust and dog. Beyond the tootling cartoon music, she heard the scratchings of Edmund's pencil, the flip of his textbook's pages. It made her feel safe to know he was in the room with her, even though she didn't know what was happening to him. Ma and Pa were in the kitchen, their voices a quiet murmur. Mary popped the tip of a Watermelon Stix in her mouth and licked it, an explosion of sweet on her tongue. It was the only candy she had left from two-weeks distant Halloween.

"Damn!" said Edmund. Even that sounded pretty. Mary glanced back at him. He slammed the book shut, then lifted both hands and snapped his fingers. Purple fire whooshed up from the textbook, muttering as it devoured the paper and filled the room with snakes of smoke.

Edmund yelled and leaped to his feet. Wide-eyed, he searched the room. He grabbed a big squashy pillow off the sofa and shoved it down on the purple fire, but the purple fire just ate at the pillow and made burned feather smells. Edmund jerked his hands back. "Ouch ouch ouch!"

Mary jumped up and opened a window to let the smoke out. "Snap your fingers," she said.

"What?" He was shaking his hands.

"That's how you started it. Snap them and stop it."

"What?"

"Just do it!" she said.

He snapped the fingers of his right hand. Nothing happened. The fire kept munching on the pillow and the book and even the top of the table—the plastic smell of the smoldering tablecloth added *ick* to the air.

"Both hands!" Mary yelled.

Edmund snapped, and the fire stopped. So did the murmuring from the kitchen. Pa came through the swinging door. "What's going on out here?" he said. "What's that awful smell?"

Edmund was staring at his fingers. Mary bit her lip, wanting to go over and ease what was left of the pillow down over the damage to the table and book, but she was too far away, and Pa would notice, for sure.

"Who's been playing with matches?" Pa asked.

"It was an accident," Mary said. Her voice came out tiny.

"What did you do?"

"I don't know." She wandered over to the table and peeked under the pillow. The book was a slick of greasy ash, the pillow almost eaten, only a few feather-spines fluttering, and she could see through the table to the floor below. "I spilled something and it started burning, and Edmund tried to put it out with a pillow, and it . . ." She covered her mouth with her hand. While the fire was alive, she had been too excited to be scared, but now she thought, *What if he hadn't stopped it? The whole house might have gone up. What if we tried water and that didn't work? What if it could burn through people?* "I'm sorry," she whispered.

"What did you spill?" Pa murmured, the edge gone from his voice, fear in its place.

"It was . . . it was . . ." Invention failed her.

She heard that match head scritch, and turned.

Edmund held a jar half full of glowing purple liquid. He screwed the cap down tight.

"What is it?" Pa asked.

Mary took the jar from Edmund and handed it to Pa. "I made it in science class," she said.

"Oh, boy," said Pa. "I need to talk to your teacher. I'm going to put this someplace safe now, Mary. Don't ever touch it again, understand me?"

"I won't," she said. "Promise."

"Good." He kissed her hair. He studied the table, poking at the ashes with his finger. "Next time something like this happens, call us right away. Glad you got it put out. Clean this up." He went to the kitchen.

Mary stared at Edmund, and Edmund stared back. "How did you know?" he whispered after a moment.

"About the snapping? I saw you do it."

"You did?" He glanced at his fingers again, then at her. His face crumpled. "I don't know what I'm doing. Things keep happening around me and I don't know why. People stare at me when I talk. Things fall down. Yesterday I took one bite of a sandwich and then it disappeared. . . ."

She couldn't remember seeing him scared before. When the monsters in the movies jumped out and she screeched, she had always grabbed *his* hand. Looking into his silvery eyes, she felt a strange warmth in her stomach. She took his hand. "Halloween," she said. "Something happened on Halloween."

"A friend put a curse on me," he whispered. "I thought it was a joke."

"Your friends curse you?" she said.

"Well, I was bothering him."

"And the curse worked?"

"He's a ghost."

"What?" She shook her head. She thought about ghosts from TV. She couldn't remember a ghost cursing anybody. She blinked, and looked at the table, which still had a hole through it, and the burnt remains of book and pillow.

"He said these words in some other language, and I felt sick, and ever since—" He frowned.

"You made that jar of purple stuff," she said after a moment. "On purpose."

He swallowed. "Yeah."

She gripped his hand and let go. "Make something else."

For a long moment he just stared at her, but at last he smiled. His eyes turned silver. He snapped his fingers and handed her a pink rose. She dipped her nose into its heavy spicy scent, and smiled back at him. She remembered watching a movie with him a week before. *If it's really scary, we can turn it off,* he had said.

"If it's really scary, we can turn it off," she said.

He knelt and hugged her hard.

WITCH-HORSE

by Josepha Sherman

Now, I'll tell you from the start, I'm hardly an expert on the old tribes here in the Northwest, even if I do have a tiny amount of their blood in me. But I've heard some of their tales about a creature so evil it's known only as the Terrible Beast: a shape-shifting being of animal cunning and sentient hatred, a being that exists only to cause harm. But something so bizarre belongs only to the days of myth, right? The Terrible Beast shouldn't have any place in the modern world, most certainly not in the very down-to-earth world of horse racing and Thoroughbred farms.

Right.

I own what is charitably called a small-scale racing and breeding stable here in Washington State (no horses in training just then, five broodmares at pasture and next to no hired help), and was at a yearling sale contemplating adding some new blood if I could find a youngster with a less than astronomical asking price.

And that was where I first saw Moonlight Lady. While all the other youngsters were squealing and carrying on like the frightened babies they were, she stood quietly watching me like a cleanly carved jet black statue of a filly. Her eyes were almost as dark as her coat, and calm as two deep, still pools. And I swear she told me, silently:

Buy me.

I did. Not because of any "equine telepathy," but because I took a good look at her listing in the sales catalog. She was described as a Washington-bred by Dancer's

Moon out of Lady's Tryst: nice, solid bloodlines if nothing spectacular. There's a racing prejudice against black horses, claiming they're unsound—that's why all those euphemistic "dark bay or brown" on racing programs—and so she went for a reasonably low price.

Well now, Moonlight Lady, as I named her, turned out to be the most composed Thoroughbred I've met. Acting like a veteran rather than the youngster she was, she underwent training without commotion, made her first start at late, lamented Longacres Racetrack without commotion, won her second start without commotion. Around the barn, Moonlight Lady was known as a "kind" horse, meaning she didn't give her trainer or handler any trouble, ate and exercised without fuss, and never bit or kicked a soul.

But there wasn't anything kind about it. It's difficult to warm to a horse who seems polite (no other word for it) but uninterested in humans, who acts forever ... abstracted.

"Almost as though she's *waiting* for something," I said once, then felt like a fool. But the only one who'd overheard me—other than Moonlight Lady—was one of the handlers, a slight, dark refugee from one of those beleaguered countries that end in "-istan."

"She wait," he assured me in a nervous undertone. "Why, you see. One day you see."

"Uh, sure." They have some weird people working at racetracks, folks who can't get jobs at more ordinary places, so I thought nothing more about it.

Moonlight Lady raced into the start of her four-year-old season, a nice, unexceptional mare earning her keep, her only quirk, if it could be called that, being a flat refusal to be hit during a race and a quiet determination to win her own way. Until the day she told us all quite plainly she'd had enough of the whole business by bolting to the outside rail during a race and pulling herself up.

"Well," her trainer (who had, after all, a lot bigger clients than me) said by way of casual apology, "she'll make you a nice broodmare."

But my "-istan" refugee pal told me as I prepared to load Moonlight Lady on the van that would take her to a new life on my farm, "Never get no foal. Not from her. No foal."

Did he know something about her health I didn't? "Why not?"

His dark eyes narrowed. Coming so close I could smell the odd mixture of horse and exotic spices clinging to his clothes, he whispered, "Witch-Horse."

"What?"

"Not true horse, she, no. Witch-Horse. A—a Power Beast, understand? Guardian against Darkness. You know? Got them, my country, all kinds, horse, dog, bird. First time see one here, me, but Witch-Horse, yes. She waiting."

"Right. A Witch-Horse who runs races. Waiting for what?"

"Who knows? You learn." He pressed what turned out to be a packet of "magical" herbs into my hand, whispered one last, "Witch-Horse, she, you see," and scurried off.

I'd see. Sure I would.

Moonlight Lady made it to the farm without, predictably, turning a hair on her black coat. Most horses coming down off the track need a long time to unwind and a good deal of attention, everything from trimming their hoofs to the quick so they can't go hysterical over their new freedom to giving them mild tranquilizers.

Not Moonlight Lady. She stepped out onto the grass of her new home with the self-possessed dignity of a queen. Or maybe a warrior. One of the most unsociable equines I'd ever seen, she refused to make friends with the other mares, spending her time alone.

Waiting.

Dammit, no, you're getting as bad as that handler. She's a horse, that's all, born of nice, normal horsey parents. She's not "waiting" for anything. Except maybe a mating come Spring.

Too late for it this year. Nothing to do but let her relax and grow sleek. And wait.

One brightly moonlit night I couldn't sleep. Finally giving it up as hopeless, I threw on my clothes and went down to hang on a paddock fence and maybe let the sight of peacefully grazing mares—who were left out all night on these warm summer nights whenever it wasn't raining—lull me.

But the only mare in plain view, starkly outlined against the sky, was Moonlight Lady. She was standing rigidly alert, ignoring me, staring into the night. My first thought was, *Bear?* Every now and then one of them wanders down from the Cascades. But if there'd been a bear or any other kind of predator, my dogs would have been barking. There wasn't a sound, not even from Dave, my nighttime guard, who more or less prowls regularly. Besides, Moonlight Lady didn't look like a frightened horse, more like one waiting—

Oh, hell, I'm not going to start that again! She's a horse, she can't *be waiting for—*

For what? This being the Northwest, clouds were rapidly rolling in across the sky, hiding the moon, confusing my vision. But suddenly I saw it, or thought I saw it: a strange, shapeless darkness against the darkness of the night. I *felt* it, like the chill that rises from a forest at nightfall. And I recognized it. As I've said, I have only a few drops of tribal blood—but I knew what was there, I knew it for the Terrible Beast.

Moonlight Lady knew it, too. Her dark eyes blazed with sudden cold light and her ears went flat back. She screamed challenge and stood so that to reach the rest of the mares, the Darkness would have to pass her first. And I felt, as clearly as words:

You shall not pass.

I heard the Darkness hiss, a sound so full of primal hate I froze in atavistic terror, thinking wildly, *A gun, I should get the rifle,* even as I knew nothing as simple as a bullet could harm it.

It lunged. She met the lunge, going up on her hind legs, striking out like a stallion. I heard the dull sound of hoofs hitting whatever passed for flesh on It, saw amazing bright, blue-white flashes where she'd struck, heard It roar in rage. Then the two rushed together, and the night pretty much hid what was going on, save for those eerie, blue-white flashes that meant the mare had gotten in a blow. The magical mare. The Witch-Horse.

God, I didn't want to believe this, I wanted to fool myself into thinking it was only two horses fighting over status the way they sometimes do. But how could I possibly not feel the fury washing over me, the pure evil hatred of the Beast, the pure animal magic of the mare? She was not a mannered, by-the-word spell-caster the way I guess some human witch might be; she was all raw, equine Power, strong, vital, alive. And the Beast, ah, the Beast was red, savage Death, the killing force of the predator gone so terribly wrong. If It won, I knew, the attack would ignore me—for the moment—and sweep over my horse herd. They would die for no other reason than that they lived.

And the mare was giving way. Step by angry step, her eyes still blazing with that incredible fire, she was being forced back. She would die, and my horses would die, that small, innocent herd that hurt no one. I smelled the clean horsey smell of them, I remembered the sweet warmth of their hay-scented breath, the delicate, awkward, charming foals skittering along beside them.

And suddenly I agreed with the Witch-Horse, my oddly well-named Moonlight Lady. This was no great battle for the world, like in those ridiculous movies, this was nothing vast at all, just one human and one ... Witch-Horse deciding that this particular evil should go no further.

I don't clearly remember what happened next. I think I grabbed whatever I could reach and threw it: rocks, a fence rail that under ordinary circumstances I probably couldn't have lifted, let alone hurled. The Darkness was far too swift to be hit by a mere clumsy human, but my sheer determination that It not hurt the innocent animals seemed to confuse it. It drew back, snarling, the sound horrifying in its mix of animal and sentient hate, but It did draw back.

And in the next moment Moonlight Lady was upon It, teeth and eyes and hoofs all flashing that incredible, magical fire. She beat It to the ground, she tore at It with her teeth, radiating pure Will, pure Guardianship—

And It was gone, just as quickly as that, vanished into the air or the earth or wherever the unkillable Terrible Beast flees when It has, so to speak, bitten off more than it can chew. We were alone in the night, Moonlight Lady and I, and for a moment, her Power still surrounding us, I was half afraid to look her way.

But look I did. Her eyes were their usual cool selves, but I could have sworn I felt quiet approval radiating from her. And I asked, not quite sure if I was being foolish, "It won't be back?"

No. Once defeated, the Beast will not return to a site.

"You ... knew this was going to happen, didn't you? You planned all this: the training, the racing."

Yes. I was born to this.

"You knew the Terrible Beast was going to break through into here and now just at this moment, just at this spot. You planned the whole thing, right from my buying you, so you'd be here to stop It."

Yes. It was my duty.

I swallowed dryly. "You're not really interested in what happens to humans, are you? You were here to protect the horses."

I am a horse. A Witch-Horse. A Guardian against one part of the Darkness.

"My God," I said vaguely, and then again, "my God."

I was sitting, without any memory of having collapsed onto the grass. Moonlight Lady chuckled, deep in her throat, the sound horses make that seems so much like a true laugh. Her muzzle brushed the side of my face in a quick, soft caress, then she was at the far end of the paddock without having seemed to move. "You're leaving, aren't you?" I asked foolishly.

I am a Witch-Horse. The Beast has been banished. There is no room for Its evil in this spot any longer. There is, elsewhere.

With that, Moonlight Lady seemed to quietly fade into the night, and I knew that the fading wasn't illusion. But she left behind her one gentle message to me that made me, confused and overwhelmed though I was, smile:

Fare well, Horse-friend.

"Fare well," I murmured to the quiet night.

GLAMOUR PROFESSION

by Beth Meacham

Agatha sat like a stone in one of the straight plastic chairs lining the walls of the conference room, toying with the carved amethyst ring on her right hand. She could see over Meg's shoulder to the surface of the big table and read the notes her boss had jotted on the pad in front of her. *"J says no—bounce RC proposal. A?"* Meg was going to wimp out again, and tell Agatha to make the phone call to Robert's agent, rejecting the book. It was no wonder that Agatha was Meg's third editorial assistant in two years.

These Tuesday morning editorial meetings were torture. Jackie, the polished blonde Editor in Chief, would hold forth on her theories of publishing and literature, then fire rapid questions at the ten editors seated around the table about the manuscripts they'd been given to read the week before. The books were always romances or sagas or self-help diet books. In the last fifteen minutes of the meeting, editors could propose acquisitions. Jackie would never say a simple yes or no; she would instead invite the rest of the department to comment. There were many discussions over lunch about how to judge Jackie's take on a proposal by the way she asked for comments. The trick was to ridicule the ones she didn't like, and praise the ones she did. The meeting would end just before noon with Jackie's assistant passing out manuscripts for next week's performance.

Agatha was growing very tired of Jackie's arbitrary abuse, and of her boss's spineless sucking up. She hadn't come to New York for this kind of crap. She'd come for

the romance of publishing, the joy of scholarship. All her
life she'd loved books, especially the big leather-bound
ones in her grandmother's library, with the ancient vellum
pages covered in spidery handwritten entries and spells.
She'd never forget the thrill she'd felt the first time she
read off the names of the minor demons, from safe within
a circle Granny had drawn. Agatha knew, more than most
people did, how a book could change someone's life. But
instead of bringing important works of natural philosophy
before the public, here she was in a flunky's job, working
for a woman who edited thinly disguised pornography
while pretending to a life of refined literary sensibility.

Having to call Meg's current lover's agent to reject his
latest book proposal was the last straw. Something would
have to be done.

Agatha leaned back in her chair and rubbed her eyes.
It was nearly 8:30 *p.m.*, but she was finally done with the
memo. She pulled it gently out of her typewriter. She had
adapted the ritual for a charm of persuasion, and used it
to make a memo; it was an interesting working, but it had
taken a lot out of her. She'd leave it on Meg's desk before
she left, in an envelope so that her boss would be the first
to touch it. If Meg thought it was a resignation before she
opened it, so much the better. Agatha patted the huge
manuscript on her desk with pleasure. If everything
worked, Meg would champion *Ars Naturalis, A Treatise
by Mistress Cleopatra Greengage,* at next week's editorial meeting.

Jackie shot down the idea. Meg argued with passion,
Agatha had to give her that, but to no avail. The meeting
ended with Jackie delicately suggesting that perhaps Meg
should take some of her accrued vacation time.

Meg had been away for a week when Agatha felt ready
to make an appointment to talk with Jackie about *Ars
Naturalis*. She had planned her approach carefully. She
had calculated the positions of the stars to a fine degree,
selected her scents and clothing and jewels with preci-

sion. A wandering imp had given Jackie a cold, and the discarded tissues had provided Agatha with stuffing for the mannequin she'd used to weave the spell-net on— much better than using stray hairs gathered in the ladies room.

Agatha entered Jackie's dimly lit office timidly, clutching the manuscript of *Ars Naturalis* to her chest. Jackie smiled reassuringly, and waved her to the comfortable chair. Agatha began with a confession:

"I . . . I wanted you to know that the book, the nonfiction book that Meg was talking about last week—it's something I wanted to do. She was trying to help me." Agatha took a loud breath, then stumbled on. "I don't think you should . . ."

Jackie interrupted. "Aren't you the loyal little thing. How long have you been working here?"

"Six months, ma'am."

"Call me Jackie, honey. Everyone does." She paused. "So what's this book that's so important to you?"

"I brought a copy . . . I thought maybe if you looked at it you might . . . here it is." Agatha pushed the manuscript into Jackie's hands, and wished she could blush. The light levels in here, though, were so low that Jackie couldn't have seen it anyway. The manuscript wasn't the original—oh, no. This copy had been made on very special paper, then linked to the mannequin that was Jackie. Agatha fingered the sapphire pendant at her neck as she subvocalized the words that would activate the linkage between the manuscript and Jackie herself.

Jackie leafed through the first dozen pages, stopping at one of Mistress Greengage's delicate watercolors. "Art? Well, it is beautiful, isn't it. Expensive to produce, though." She kept turning over leaves, reading a paragraph here and there. "Nice. Nicely written." She looked up at Agatha. "This is sort of like that book Abrams did years ago, isn't it? What was it . . . *Gnomes? Fairies?* That was a best-seller, wasn't it?"

Agatha didn't trust herself to answer that. She nodded agreeably. Like *Fairies* indeed! Comparing this work of genius, this magnificent treatise on the Art to a bit of imaginary fluff like that. She said nothing. One of the first rules of Glamour was to let the victim rationalize the compulsion herself. As Jackie settled herself into the spell, Agatha was able to relax a little.

"Well, dear," Jackie finally said, "I'll take this home tonight and give it a read myself. I think you may be on to something after all."

Meg was back for the next editorial meeting. Agatha hadn't happened to mention that she'd given the manuscript of *Ars Naturalis* to Jackie, so Meg was rather surprised when Jackie suggested that they all move down and make room for Agatha at the table. The room went very still as Agatha apologetically moved her chair away from the wall and the other assistants, and in between Meg and the men's action editor. Jackie announced that the house would publish *Ars Naturalis,* and that Agatha would be the editor of record. "Meg, dear," Jackie said, "I hope you'll give Agatha all the support she needs on this. It's her first book, after all. You've hired a fine assistant there; she's going to go far." Meg produced a convincing smile, put her arm around Agatha's shoulders and squeezed—perhaps a little harder than strictly necessary to convey approval.

Agatha worked longer hours than ever for the next few months, keeping up with Meg's submissions and paperwork and filing, while making sure *Ars Naturalis* stayed on track. She got a great deal of practice at charms of persuasion—when she started, she hadn't realized that acquiring a book was only the beginning of her headaches. There were a thousand pitfalls on the way to press—dozens of people who had to be dealt with. She had to make the art director put the right cover on the book. She had to make the marketing director budget for ads in the right places. She had to convince the sub rights people of the book's overseas audience. She had to make the head of sales believe that his reps could sell an art book.

She had to work a very difficult spell to give Meg the

gift of tongues for her sales conference presentation of *Ars Naturalis*. That worked out very nicely, in the end. Meg was applauded by the reps, reinforcing everyone's commitment to the book. At that point, the spells could have given out and the house would still have been committed to push *Ars Naturalis* up the best-seller lists.

Six months after that, the book hit the *New York Times* nonfiction list one week before official publication date. Agatha raised her celebratory glass of champagne—a gift from Jackie—in a silent toast to her Granny. Granny always had had a special way with bookstore clerks, and she and her friends had been waiting a long time for this particular book to be published.

The other editorial assistants cheered Agatha as they downed their wine, while the associate editors looked on more quietly. "What I want to know," said one, "is how you convinced Jackie to let you buy the thing in the first place."

Agatha shrugged self-deprecatingly. "Magic," she said.

Everyone laughed.

WITCH WAR

by L. Emerson Wolfe

Patricia's head tingled with the sensation, perceiving the presence of another of her kind. She squinted against the bright October sun, searching the busy downtown street. Shadow, her husky, yelped excitedly as she, too, felt the presence.

"There," she said as her eyes met those of a child across the street. "A girl, perhaps thirteen. I have no vibration from the amulet. A good omen." She glanced around for signs of a trap. The enemy was cunning and the territory was unfamiliar. "I sense it's safe. Yes, she may be what drew us here." Here was in the heart of the Bible Belt in eastern Tennessee, an ideal place for evil to do its work.

An older woman hustled the girl and two others into a shoe store. Patricia crossed the street and loosely tied Shadow to a parking meter. "Wait here. I won't be long," she said.

The group was inspecting shoes when Patricia entered. "I know they're stylish, but we need more durability for school," the woman told the children. "No, Emily. Not those. They're too expensive."

Patricia noted the girl's name and her features. She was thin, with long brown hair, olive skin and deep brown eyes, nothing like the two fair-skinned girls.

Patricia waited until the salesman brought out shoes for the girls to try on, before approaching the older woman. "Hello, I'm Patricia Astarte," she said with a kind smile and her best Southern accent. "I just moved here from Atlanta and I'm not all that familiar with the stores around here. Is this a good place?" Though Patricia looked to be around fifty, she was much older. Her motherly look made people open up to her and within minutes, Mrs. Irene Jones was jabbering off a list of her most and least favorite stores, schools, churches, and other places.

"I must say, you have a fine-looking family," Patricia said.

"Why, thank you. This is Ellen, Sue, and Emily. Emily is our foster child. She was found abandoned in the mountains."

At the mention of her name, the girl gave Patricia a mischievous smile. The salesman stumbled and dropped the shoe boxes he was carrying. Patricia smiled back and made a display of shoe polish a customer was inspecting crash to the floor.

"I must be going," Patricia said. "Perhaps I'll come to your church service tomorrow."

She retrieved Shadow and headed home to her small new house, a short distance from the center of town. "The child's name is Emily," she told Shadow. "She's uninitiated. I must begin setting up shop immediately."

Once home, she located the church on a city map, then fed Shadow and fixed some chicken and her special rejuvenation potion for herself. After eating, she retired to her basement where she finished unpacking her apothecary. She spent the rest of the evening meticulously drawing her magical circle on the floor. It was almost midnight before she finished. She went upstairs to find her familiar sleeping in her favorite corner. "I must sleep, too. Church comes early."

Patricia arrived at the First Baptist Church at ten to ten. She stood just inside the door of the vestibule watching as Sunday School let out and children joined their parents for the worship service. She spotted Irene Jones with a heavyset, balding man, who was probably her husband. One by one the children arrived. They entered the sanctuary and sat halfway up the center section. Patricia followed and sat three pews back. Emily glanced back and nodded slightly to acknowledge her presence.

Just as the organ began to play, Patricia sensed another presence. The amulet vibrated strongly under her dress. She suppressed the urge to look around, but felt a gaze burn the back of her neck. Evil was near. Taking a pen and a small piece of paper from her purse, she wrote her address, then sat patiently, listening to the minister extol the virtues of being a good Christian.

After the service, Patricia caught up with the Jones family in the receiving line. "Mrs. Jones, I want to thank you for all your help yesterday. This is such a fine church. My, your girls look pretty in those outfits." Patricia gently picked up Emily's hands as though to inspect the dress, and slipped her the paper. "This is absolutely darling."

"I'm so glad you enjoyed the service," Irene said, beaming. "The Women's Club meets on Tuesday evenings. Perhaps you can join us?"

"I'm still settling in. Perhaps in a week or two."

Patricia felt the increase of the amulet's vibration and noticed a sultry, scarlet-haired woman in her mid-thirties approach.

"Miss Veronica Blake," Irene said. "I'd like you to meet ... is it Miss or Mrs. Astarte?"

"Mrs. Astarte. My husband passed away a year ago," Patricia lied.

"Mrs. Astarte, you remind me of someone I met in Massachusetts," Veronica said. She gave Patricia a sinister smile.

"It's possible. I've traveled a lot over the years."

"I'm having a Halloween party next Saturday on Roan Mountain. Perhaps you'd like to come. I'm sure Emily would find it fascinating."

"Roan Mountain! On Halloween!" Irene exclaimed. "That's where devil worshipers go. Wild horses couldn't drag me there."

"That's nonsense, Irene," Veronica said, almost laughing. "I promise to take good care of Emily."

"I don't think so," Emily said timidly.

"Another time, then. I must be going. Nice meeting you, Mrs. Astarte." Veronica strolled away to the lustful gazes of the surrounding men.

"I have things to attend to myself," Patricia said and left in the opposite direction.

"Shadow," she called as she entered her house. "We were drawn here by more than the girl. A devil's servant lurks here, one I've met before. She invited me to the All Hallow's Eve Sabbat. She's playing some game and she means to initiate Emily. After I change, we're going to look at this Roan Mountain. We must prepare ourselves for combat."

The drive took under an hour. Patricia and Shadow sensed its evil nature, even amid its stunning beauty. She followed her instincts as she drove, turning down a dirt path off the main road, then taking a more hidden track a few minutes later. She parked where the track ended and let Shadow take the lead. The animal sniffed out both physical and magical booby traps, making Patricia's job much easier. After a fifteen-minute walk through the dense forest, they came to a clearing. An ornately designed magical circle was inscribed on the ground in the center.

"I won't disturb it," she told Shadow. "It's well protected by magic. Note the intricacy of the inscriptions. This goes beyond anything I've ever dealt with before." She took out a small pad of paper and a pencil and meticulously copied it, then they explored the surrounding territory. Patricia made notes along the way. "She'll have others with her for the Sabbat, possibly even a familiar." Shadow growled at the mention of an evil animal. "Let's go home. We don't have much time to prepare."

Over the next two days Patricia researched the circle and its designs in her books, then began making a list of spells which would help her counter the circle's magic. She also started designing her own magical circle to focus her powers and protect her from the evil forces that might present themselves.

Just after dark that evening, she felt the tingle of Emily and opened the door before the girl knocked. "Come in. I'm glad you came. Have a seat."

"Mom went to her church meeting and Dad went over to screw Miss Blake," Emily said as she looked suspiciously around the house. "I'm not sure if I should've come."

Shadow strolled into the room to inspect the guest. She stopped by the door for an instant, then began wagging her bushy tail. She bounded for Emily as the girl sat on the couch. Shadow whimpered excitedly and licked Emily in the face.

Patricia, stunned by Shadow's behavior, shouted, "Shadow! Behave!" The dog retreated from the couch and sat on the floor. "Strange, she's never acted that way before."

"Nice dog," Emily said. "Most animals adore me. Except for Miss Blake's black cat."

"Shadow likes you. That's a good sign."

"A good sign for what? Miss Blake shows up in town a couple of months ago. I sensed her, just like I sense you. Both of you are bugging me. Miss Blake told Mom I'm a gifted child and offered to tutor me. I didn't want it."

"We're here because of you," Patricia said. "Only a handful of us are born a generation. Some never know their potential. Others are killed by forces you don't as yet understand. Others live to fight another day."

"What do you mean?" Emily snapped. "I know I'm different. I can make some things happen." The girl's anger turned to sadness. "Sometimes I don't mean for them to."

Patricia knew all too well how Emily felt. "We were born with the Talent. You can learn to control it. I have. It can also destroy you." She took a deep breath. "We're witches."

"I'm no witch," Emily shouted.

"We're not what society and history has portrayed us to be . . . at least not all of us."

"Miss Blake said you'd call me a witch." Emily shot

up from the couch and ran to the door, but Patricia's spell sealed the house before she reached it.

"Listen to me," Patricia growled. "I'm running out of time. There's a war going on and your very soul's at stake. You must hear both sides."

Emily swung around and gave Patricia a fierce stare.

"I'll let you go when I'm finished. I mean you no harm."

She saw much of herself in the girl and she gave her a sincere smile. It was enough for Emily and she reluctantly went back to the couch.

"My real name is Marie Dubois. I was born in Orleans, France in 1412, not a good time to be born a witch. In 1430, Orleans was under siege by the English. A great woman named Joan of Arc broke the siege. Have you heard of her?"

Emily nodded.

"Joan was drawn to the city by the witches there, myself included, only most of them were evil. One night, I came upon her outside the city. She was talking with the Archangel Michael. Together they explained my potential. Joan only appeared to be a young girl, but she was actually a thousand years old. She vowed to teach me the craft and we became close.

"One night on a holiday called Candlemas, the evil witches gathered to confront us and try to sway me. I was paralyzed with fear. Joan gave me this." Patricia pulled the amulet out from under her blouse. The object was an ornately carved teardrop-shaped piece of amber with the inscription

SATOR
AREPO
TENET
OPERA
ROTAS

The amber was marred by a void in the center and a small crack running through the inscription.

"The amulet protects the wearer from evil. When she

put it on me, my fear fled and together we drove the witches from Orleans.

"Soon afterward, Joan returned to war and was captured by the English. She was tried as a witch, but wasn't convicted. She was burned at the stake for heresy. They say her heart was untouched by the flames.

"She gave me her spell book to guard before she left and I've added to it over the years."

As Patricia tucked the amulet away, she noticed the charm attached to Emily's necklace. "Your charm's interesting. I've never seen anything like it."

Emily held it out for Patricia to see. "I was found with it," she said. The charm was a gold bow and a quiver of arrows.

"When we have some time, I'd like to examine it more closely. It may provide clues to who your parents are."

"I'd like that. How do you know Miss Blake?"

Patricia's expression turned grim. "I was drawn to a coven of witches, good ones, in 1692. Miss Blake shapeshifted into a child and used her magic to create havoc, then blamed us. My name then was Mary Bradbury. I was the only one to escape and barely did that. I caught a fever in the wild, but Shadow appeared and brought an old Iroquois medicine woman to me. The familiar's been with me ever since."

"No husbands or children?" Emily asked.

Patricia chuckled. "I only wish. Evil uses every leverage. Look at your father. I can never let my guard down. I'll never know a normal life." She paused, sensing this was enough for now. "Give me a chance to prove myself. Don't go near Roan Mountain or Miss Blake for the next week. She means to turn you."

Emily thought for a moment, then said, "Okay, but I have to be going now."

Patricia released her spell and sent the girl on her way.

Patricia rose to meet the Saturday morning sun. She and Shadow drove to Roan Mountain amid the bright, beautiful autumn foliage. Her mood was far from cheerful. This was a day of grim purpose. She parked well away from the evil clearing and hiked three miles to reach it. She prepared her traps in the surrounding woods, then set to the task of constructing her magical circle. She worked steadily, carefully making the intricate designs, until the sun faded and the moon rose. She drank her potion, fed Shadow, and donned her mystic robe, then stepped into the circle. From there she began weaving her spell of protection and spells to prevent Veronica from reaching the evil circle.

Patricia spoke the ancient incantation, summoning the Archangel Michael. To her surprise, she received no answer. She tried again several times, growing more concerned with each attempt. Finally she heard a distant voice.

"The battle is fierce. They've captured Anthony on the sixth plane. Satan's hordes bar my way to you. You must stand alone today. Have faith, my child, and all will be well." The voice faded away, not a good omen.

A half hour later, Shadow gave a low growl. In the distance, Patricia heard the first of her traps go off. The vibration of the amulet told her evil was approaching. She released the first of her terror spells and heard howling. As the procession drew nearer, she released more spells. With each release, she aged slightly, the more powerful the spell, the older she grew.

Veronica was a powerful and cunning adversary. She had set up a preplanned path and protected it well. The witch countered most of Patricia's spells effectively. By the time the procession reached the edge of the clearing, Patricia had lost three years.

She readied a fireball spell, when she noticed a black cat prance to the evil circle, followed by two strong females dragging a naked girl. "Emily!" she shouted.

Veronica appeared behind Emily and displayed an ornate silver dagger. "Cease or I'll cut her throat."

Patricia stopped her incantation, and allowed Veronica to enter her circle. Veronica cast her own protection spell around her, then shouted, "Let the Sabbat begin."

Patricia watched helplessly as twenty of Veronica's remaining followers, mostly female, danced and performed perverse sexual acts. She felt the evil power building and knew the best she could hope for was a stalemate.

Veronica took in the power, adding it to her own, and began her conjuring spell. When the moon reached its zenith, Veronica shouted, "Master of Darkness, I command you to appear."

The moonlight darkened as a thick black haze appeared. The haze funneled down between the circles and coalesced. Patricia tried to counter the conjuring, but it was too powerful. The amulet vibrated until it sang and Patricia watched in horror as the haze solidified into the hideous beauty of Satan himself.

"Master," Veronica said proudly. "I bring you an initiate for you to mold, as well as a virgin for your pleasure."

Shadow sat growling by her mistress' circle. "I can't drive him away without Michael's help," Patricia whispered. "With him trapped on another plane, there's only one thing I can do to save Emily, but it may well cost me my life. Be ready."

Satan's red eyes turned to Patricia. "I'll deal with you later, Wiccan, but first I'll take my pleasure with the child."

His gaze focused on Emily, as all outside the circles but the familiars were mesmerized by Satan's power. "Come here, child. You'll know unbridled lust tonight and I promise you eternal beauty, wealth, and power, if you serve me. Give me the Kiss of Shame and sign in Veronica's book with your blood."

Emily, totally entranced by Satan's power stepped forward. While Satan spoke, Patricia whispered several potent spells. As Emily took her third slow step, Patricia quickly took off the amulet and threw it to Shadow. "Place the amulet around Emily's neck," she commanded, then unleashed her barrage of spells. A massive wind rushed through the trees and clouds formed overhead. Lightning flashed down at Satan and fireballs rained from the sky.

Shadow raced to Emily, knocked her down, and threw the amulet over her head.

"No," Satan screamed angrily. He threw a deadly bolt

of his own at the dog, but because she still held the amulet's chain in her mouth, the lightning reflected back. The Devil howled in pain at feeling his own sinister magic.

"Get her away from here," Patricia yelled with a haggard voice. The release of the spells took another fifteen years off her life. Undaunted, she recited more spells and released them.

Satan easily repelled the attack and swung around to face Patricia. His furious eyes glared at her. "You'll suffer unimaginable pain for this," he snarled, and began ripping away Patricia's magical defenses like tissue paper. Try as she might, Patricia stood defenseless against the Dark Master within minutes.

She saw Shadow and Emily reach the edge of the woods away from the fray. The dog transformed into a magnificent white wolf.

"My cat will feast upon you," Satan said and the evil familiar changed into a large black panther.

Patricia froze, not at the sight of the vicious cat, but at the change in Emily. The small plain girl was now a tall blonde beauty and the bow and arrow charm grew. The cat sprang hungrily for her, but Shadow leaped and caught the animal in midair. Her powerful jaws wrapped around the cat's neck and she shook it like an old rag until the body went limp. Satan's eyes widened, but before he could react, a gold arrow pierced his black heart.

His cry of anguish knocked Patricia from her feet, then Satan fell to the ground. She watched the blonde dash to the Devil and place the amulet on Satan's forehead.

"Sator, arepo, tenet, opera, rotas, I command thee and all thy kind to return to thy prison and restore those valiant souls who stood against you through time, but were lost in battle."

The amulet began to glow as Satan turned into a black haze. It was sucked into the amulet, then Blake's followers were transformed and pulled in. Veronica turned to flee, but she, too, was caught in the vacuum, which started to bend the trees with its force.

Shadow lay gently across Patricia's old dying body to

protect her from the force, as the amulet sucked the evil from all the planes.

As the winds diminished, Michael appeared and brought up his fiery sword. He placed the tip to the crack in the amber, sealing it. Shadow stood and howled loudly as Michael and the woman approached Patricia.

With one touch, Michael restored Patricia to the girl she had been so long ago. "Arise, Marie Dubois. Your long, faithful struggle has ended."

"To sacrifice your life to save another is the greatest gift one can give," the woman said. "I'm Diana. I was at Satan's mercy when I was in human form. You saved my life with the amulet. We weren't sure. The choice was totally yours."

"The plan would never have succeeded without your help, Diana," Michael said.

"I've avenged my followers by placing the vile abomination back in his domain."

She held up the amulet. A large black fly was encased where the void once was. "I sent my devoted wolf to you when we almost lost you at Salem. She's protected you well. I had to control her at your house when she recognized me. Otherwise, the plan might have failed. It took centuries to set up."

"Now," Michael said. "Your place in heaven awaits you."

"One moment," Diana said. "I want to grant this heroic woman her greatest wish. Heaven can wait."

Michael nodded and with a wave of Diana's hand Patricia/Marie changed into Emily. "Now you can lead a normal life, know the love of a man and the joy of children. Live a long and wonderful life, then take your place in heaven."

Michael smiled. "You still have some of your powers, but they're reduced. Only natural evil exists, as it should be. The great threat is gone.

"Come, Emily, I'll take you home."

TILL DEATH DO US PART

by Sandra Rector and P. M. F. Johnson

The village looked even more rickety in the afternoon sunlight than in Victor Salem's dream. Viewing these few shacks piled one behind the other up the mountainside, he felt a jolt of hope, to have dreamed something and now see it become real.

Oh, he must have watched some show years ago, some documentary about the Southwest, and the memory of this place had wriggled into his psyche. He should quit this foolishness, the effort was tiring him.

Still, why this particular village? This seemed more a place of poverty than miracles.

Victor halted his truck before a tumbledown general store. Before the sound of the engine faded, children raced up from every direction. One scrambled onto the hood of the truck. "See how clean I make your machine. Only a dollar." The urchin swept a dirty rag across the windshield.

Instinctively, Victor opened his thoughts, but received nothing. Not surprising, he could read specific thoughts only from other telepaths, though stray phrases from everyone else bombarded him constantly.

In his dream, someone he'd never quite visualized waited for him. Here in the real world, only the noisy kids of the village thronged around his vehicle, the smallest pressed up against the doors and fenders, the older youths hanging back.

Were they begging? If he gave any kid money, he

would have to give everyone some, and he didn't have much anymore. Illness was expensive.

He stepped down from his truck, passed through the circle of children. He stopped to enter the store. Inside, several dusty cans resided on the sparse, rickety shelves, but the real business of the store obviously lay in cold soda pop and cigarettes. To one side an old woman and man sat together, staring at this tall, homely invader in hostile silence.

Victor felt so alien and clumsy, invading their village, that he nearly turned around and departed. Was Claire right? Should he accept what was happening and try to enjoy the time they had left together? But finding his dream place miraculously become reality bolstered his resolve despite these sullen faces.

"I'm looking for someone," he said. They made no response. Embarrassed, he pointed to the ragged remnants of his hair. "I'm ill."

"No *curandera* lives here," the woman said.

Curandera. A healer, of course!

"The doctors say I need help," he explained quickly.

"It's illegal for anyone to practice medicine but a doctor," she said. "There's a clinic in Española. No one heals here."

She lied—she knew of a healer, that much he could sense. He felt rising frustration; how he wished his talent extended to reading their closed minds, but only general feelings and occasional idle thoughts were readily perceivable.

They glared until he purchased a large bag of groceries from whatever stood on the shelves. He departed, relieved to be away from them.

Outside he hesitated, unsure what to try next, unwilling to give up. Small whirlwinds sped down the rutted street. He felt nauseous. He stood motionless until the queasiness faded.

He needed to keep a hold on things, but lately his control over events, even over his own body, was slipping. His condition was growing worse, as the doctors had predicted. They had warned him to avoid the mountains, for fear the thin air might set off a stroke. For an instant panic overwhelmed him.

No. Their prognosis was wrong. He would win this struggle. The irony of his situation made him smile briefly; he thought of himself as levelheaded, honest, tough enough to confront anything, but here he was, chasing a miracle. The insidious strangeness of this town disturbed him. What was he doing here?

The dream had started to haunt him right after his test results indicated the cancer was spreading. When his boss learned the prognosis, he laid Victor off. Victor was too sick to look for another job, so, with nothing more constructive to do, he battled his constant exhaustion to research the most likely location of the village, based on the buildings and vegetation he recalled. To his surprise, he'd located a likely area in northern New Mexico.

Soon afterward, his doctor recommended he enter a hospice. Instead, he began his search in person.

Claire didn't travel along. Someone had to keep a job, she said, to pay for the health insurance and the bills. They kept in touch every morning and night, opening their minds to each other as always, sharing the honesty and love that made his life worth living.

His persistence paid off. After two weeks of wandering, he found the mountain, and followed the only road up its flank to this village.

When Victor returned to his truck, the children had departed in disgust, except the urchin who had so industriously dirtied his windshield. The boy was around eleven years old, with a serious face that belied his youth. He wriggled and hopped by the driver's door, unable to contain himself. "I know where the *bruja* lives."

Bruja? Victor couldn't remember his Spanish. Was that another word for healer? The boy must have listened at the door of the grocery store.

"Where?" he asked the child.

"I guide you for money."

Victor hesitated. "How much?"

"All that you have," the urchin said, and laughed.

* * *

The boy's name was Chito. He showed Victor where to park the truck in a stand of aspen several miles up the road, near the start of a trail.

The mountain rose to the east. A cloud passed over and the mountain darkened from deep blue to black. Ominous.

Victor placed the bag of groceries in his backpack and hefted it onto his shoulders. Chito didn't offer to help carry, and Victor didn't ask him. The respite that allowed Victor to make this trip was ending—he was suffering another headache. The pain grew progressively worse.

Victor and the boy began their climb, traveling on hardscrabble trails surrounded by wild purple asters, Indian paintbrush, yellow chamisa, and pinons. Paths constantly interested with, then diverged from each other. Chito didn't say much, nor did Victor. His headache throbbed constantly, and catching his breath was difficult in the thin air. Would the exertion of the hike overwhelm him? He considered going back, but if he did, where else would he find hope? He forced himself to continue.

When the headaches struck at home, he blocked his mind so Claire would not suffer, too. She came to him anyway, knowing he was having a bad time. She put him to bed, fed him soup, cleaned up when he was too ill to keep down food. He was humiliated by his own illness, that he should make her suffer. He told her he loved her, again and again, and begged her to forgive his weakness. She answered teasingly that he was the only man she had loved so far, wasn't he? He should not worry so.

As the altitude increased, they passed more ponderosa pines. He staggered several times, and had to call frequent rests. At each one the boy sat silently, his eyes never wavering from Victor's face. *Like some animal waiting for me to drop,* Victor thought. The thought goaded him to his feet once more.

Near sundown they crested a ridge. On the other side stood a shabby hut made of adobe, surrounded by patches of weeds and a few ponderosas. To the south of the hut grew an herb garden. Beyond lay a spectacular mountain range.

Chito pointed, but said nothing. For once, the boy acted cowed.

They marched up to the door. Victor knocked.

A hoarse, harsh voice spoke. "I don't wish to see anyone."

He was surprised. Why would a healer turn away a client?

"My name is Victor Salem," he said. "I've traveled a great distance to find you."

"I don't care," she said.

"Please, I have an illness," he said, rallying his energy for the argument. "The doctors say they can't cure me."

"Why should I help? You're a man, are you not? An Anglo, even worse."

"I brought groceries." He felt foolish, offering so little.

"Go away."

Chito boldly stepped forward and spoke through the door. "You say you're a great healer. Prove it to us."

"Did you not hear me, *niño?* Go back to your village or I'll put the *mal ojo* on you."

Victor's heart thudded erratically. He remembered now what *bruja* meant in Spanish. Witch.

"He won't pay me, if you don't meet with him," Chito admitted. "I beg of you, open the door."

Still nothing.

"A recurring dream led me here," Victor said.

When she did not respond, gloom overtook him.

"If you help him," Chito said, "I'll tell the people in our village of your greatness."

"Hmmph," she said, but opened the door.

She was nearly as tall as Victor himself, and slender, though full figured. Her face was proud, her clothes, although poor, seemed chosen to taunt men with her beauty. Her black blouse was so sheer that even in the fading light the amber skin beneath remained visible; her raven hair held two clusters of purple asters.

She waggled her finger at Chito. "Who are you to bring a stranger to my door? You don't even believe."

She turned to Victor, her voice filled with bitterness. "Nor does his family. His village refuses the evidence they've seen all their lives."

"You're beautiful," Chito said, never daring to look at her.

She shook her head sadly. "You disgust me. You care nothing about what is important or what will be passed on. All you think about is television and money. Where can you spend money in the mountains, Chito? I have gifts, but your family doesn't appreciate them, they pretend I don't exist. You will all cry for me when I'm gone. You will wish to know the things I can teach."

Nervously, Victor cleared his throat, unslung his backpack, pulled out the bag of groceries and handed it to her. "These are for you."

She took the bag without looking inside and placed it on the ground. "What is your sickness?" she asked, finally.

"They say I have tumors. In my brain."

"And?"

He felt a growing nausea. "And I'm sick."

"You won't admit that they've said you are about to die." She made it a statement.

"I don't believe ..." he started to protest, but a large lump of fear in his throat made it hard for him to continue.

"Where are these tumors?"

"On the right side." He pointed to the place behind his temple.

"You know what others think," she declared.

He was astonished. As far as he knew, no telepaths ever admitted their skill to mundanes. Telepaths would be freaks if common folk knew of them, targets of fear and hate.

"Why do you say that?" he asked cautiously.

"The location of your illness explains much," she answered. "Have you misused your talent?"

She reached out to touch his head, right where the tumors were located. Her hands felt hot.

After a moment, she nodded. "If I am to protect you,

I must seal away that part of your brain which you have damaged, so the danger won't spread."

Something queer lurched inside him. "You mean to seal off my tumors?"

She shrugged. "That may halt the progress of your illness." She gazed at him steadily. "This may work, or it may not. I make no guarantees to one foolish enough to misuse his skills."

He wasn't sure he heard right. "You'll take away my telepathy, and it might not even cure me?"

"Otherwise you die in a year, maybe less." Her eyes glittered, mockingly. "The choice is not easy?"

"My . . ." Abruptly, he shut his mouth. It was no concern of this stranger that Claire was also telepathic.

The *bruja* eyed him up and down. "Tell me tomorrow what you wish to do. In the meantime, you may sleep in my yard. We'll discuss further payment if you decide to proceed."

She took the bag of groceries inside and shut the door.

He lay shivering and hungry under the thin blanket that she gave him. Chito had fallen asleep instantly.

Why did the dream come to him? Perhaps his strange ability to know the thoughts of others led him to this woman. Maybe she'd called him magically, for her own reasons. He stirred uncomfortably. Probably he read somewhere, long ago, about *brujas* in this part of the country, and now that he was in need his mind had led him here.

Was the witch any good?

When he'd been more certain of himself, and sure of his world, he would have laughed at the thought. No more.

He could read a little from the minds of almost anyone, which had made him useful to his company's negotiating team, in finding their competitors' weaknesses and exploiting any frailties.

Was that the misuse the *bruja* meant?

At any rate, with his telepathy he read in this witch an utter confidence. *She* believed in herself. The truth was he, too, believed she could heal him. So why wasn't he feeling a flood of relief? A rush of hope?

Didn't he *want* her to heal him?

As he wrestled a log onto the fire, then moved closer to its warmth, he thought of the day he and Claire first met. He was walking down Newbury Street in Boston, when suddenly he was sharing complete intimacy with a stranger at rush hour. It took them an hour to find each other. They became lovers that day, and married within six months. With each passing year, they grew more in love, sharing that closeness where trust was complete, where every quirk and hope was shared by each, where a true communion of souls was a way of life.

How would Claire take the loss of his ability? He could not expect her to accept such isolation. She'd said many times that to share thoughts and intimacies as they did was more precious to her than life itself.

Over time, they'd met other telepaths—not many, but their numbers seemed to be growing. If he lost his ability, would she leave him? The thought filled him with dread.

He'd always made decisions quickly, and never looked back. He made mistakes that way, some he'd been very sorry for, but he was who he was. In his dream, he'd been so sure of the right action. Why did such doubts fill him now?

Because he could die. And he wanted to live. Oh, God, how he wanted to live.

Nausea struck without warning. He crawled out of his blanket, staggered to the edge of the firelight, dropped to his knees and vomited, feeling his strength drain out with each contraction. Finally the bout was over. He put his head in his hands. He was filled with impotent rage and fear. What was happening to him? The chilly air cut through his clothes. He crawled back to his blankets.

Exhaustion overwhelmed him. He slept.

When Victor awoke, Chito was gone. Victor didn't need to look over at the boy's bed of leaves and pine boughs to realize that. He knew as soon as his eyes opened and he saw his wallet lying on the ground nearby.

Cursing, he rose. The fire was out. He picked up his wallet. Empty.

The *bruja* emerged from her cabin, carrying an old mason jar half filled with a gray-green liquid. The morning light revealed faint lines at the corners of her eyes.

"Where is Chito?" she asked.

"He took off with my money."

A sad look appeared in her eyes. "He would do so for his family," she said. "They have little. If he has stolen from you, what he took shall be your fee to me." Tenderness softened her harsh voice for the first time. "You must forgive him. His life gives him no hope."

He gazed around at the little plot on which she lived. Nothing seemed permanent. This far up on the mountain, even the herbs had a straggly, temporary air.

"I thought you hated the villagers," he said. "Isn't that why you retreated up here?"

"I love my people, even though I'm angry with them," she said. "I only wish they'd stop breaking my heart."

"Is that why you agreed to help me, for Chito's sake?"

She shrugged. "If one would be a healer, one must occasionally heal."

She was silent, while bees buzzed in the garden. "I did it so he would remember me," she said softly, "and remind my people that I'm here, waiting for an apprentice."

The wind stirred. She made an abrupt dismissing motion with her hand. "Shall we begin your treatments?"

He took the jar from her. The concoction inside stank evilly, like old spinach and skunk cabbage. It looked murky in the morning light, with a skim of oil on top. Here was his chance to live.

He raised the jar, hesitated. Drinking the potion would separate his thoughts from Claire's forever. For fifteen years, love had meant sharing every emotion and idea. What could love mean without that intimacy?

Without such closeness, the *bruja* still loved the boy, no matter what. Victor recognized that. He loved Claire the same way, but with a pang of certainty, he knew that giving up intimacy forever was too much to ask of her.

The harsh truth was, he wasn't strong enough to chance

having to live without her. That was love in the real world, in his world.

Victor handed the jar back to thc *bruja.* "I'm sorry," he said. "A life of silence is too high a cost."

As he spoke, a tension he had not known he felt slowly slipped away. This was right. He'd made his choice, now he would accept what that meant.

"Good-bye," he said to the *bruja.* "I hope your people soon realize how much you care for them."

With that, he turned to the downward path, back to Claire.

THREEFOLD TO YOU

by Deborah Millitello

Koleesa first learned about the invasion of Visali when a handful of soldiers slammed open her cottage door. Startled, she dropped her willow wand into the bubbling potion, then cursed.

"Silence, witch!" said an officer wearing the green and gold of Visali. "Bind her," he told two soldiers, then turned to Koleesa. "Our lord king wishes to speak with you."

Soldiers tied her wrists with thongs.

"K–king?" She was unused to speaking Visalian; she hadn't spoken to anyone but Magda her cat in years. Magda! She sent a warning thought, hoping the cat was close enough to hear. "King?" She narrowed her midnight eyes. "Why?"

The officer hesitated, his thick brown brows pulling together over his crooked nose, then said, "Reff and the Maleze horde have invaded our land."

"Ah." Her voice crackled like fur.

"You must stop them," the officer said.

She shrugged back her tangled mess of gray hair. "One king, other king, all same. No help."

The officer leaned over her until they were nearly nose to nose. "You will help my lord," he said, steel soft. "Gag her."

The officer turned and walked outside. Two soldiers gripped her arms, another tied a cloth around her mouth, then the two pulled Koleesa from her cottage.

They walked through briars, brush, trees, and vines the

vibrant green of the early spring morning. Koleesa shivered as fingers of chilly air crept through her often-patched robe; the damp cold crept into her bones, aching worse than in winter. Even her anger didn't warm her. She couldn't escape; the soldiers were too strong, and she was too old.

Nearly an hour later the woods ahead thinned out, became brighter, golden. The officer called like a bobwhite, listened for the reply, then walked out of the woods to a green-brown plain covered by a tent city.

The king's green and gold tent was pitched beside the road that led to the pass through the southern mountains. Scores of other tents stood on both sides of the road. Soldiers barely glanced up as Koleesa and her captors passed them. They were too intent on huddling beside fires, rubbing hands to keep warm, and blowing steamy breath on them.

The officer strode to the king's tent, saluted the door wards who swept back the heavy flap, and entered. Koleesa hesitated, but her guards dragged her inside.

King Athelain loomed like a black bear behind a heavy table spread with a map. He stared steadily at his officer and soldiers, but Athelain's face was statue calm. "Remove her gag."

One of her guards untied the cloth.

"This is the witch?" Athelain asked.

"Yes, my lord," the officer said as he clapped his fist to his chest, then snapped his fingers. A soldier entered the tent, carrying a large bag that yowled and hissed and danced. "And her familiar."

"Magda!" Terror twisted in Koleesa's throat; she'd hoped Magda had escaped. She strained toward the sack, but two soldiers held her back. Sending a calming thought to Magda, she asked if the cat were unharmed. The cat sent back images of anger and claws scratching legs and arms.

"The cat's your familiar, isn't it," the officer said; it wasn't a question. "Your power."

"No hurt Magda! No hurt, no hurt!" Her shoulders drooped, and she whispered, "What king want?"

Athelain shifted his gaze to the rough sack that pitched back and forth as the cat tried to claw free. The soldier tied the sack to a tripod of spears set beside the table, to the king's right. Athelain looked back at Koleesa. "The Maleze have invaded Visali. I need your power to stop them."

His voice surprised Koleesa. It was mellow, almost musical, and seemed powerful enough to project for miles. But the tone—that surprised her most of all. It had authority, but no demand, no threat, a simple statement of fact.

"How?" she asked.

"Come." He motioned toward the table.

She glanced at the officer, who ordered the soldiers to release her arms. Pausing only a moment, she shuffled forward and gazed at the crinkled yellow map. Visali was outlined in black. Cities were circles; villages, dots. Rivers and the vast Lake Erlyn in the north were blue.

"Here," Athelain said, pointing at the southern pass, "here is where Reff is, according to last reports. You must stop him before he enters Visali."

Koleesa frowned, puzzled. "Big army, many men. You fight, you win."

"No," Athelain said. "We cannot reach him before he enters Visali, not even if all my soldiers were mounted. You must stop him while he is still in the pass or he will spill over my kingdom like a killing flood. You must use your power to save my kingdom and my people."

Koleesa creaked her head from side to side. "Too many men. Not enough me. No spell big enough."

His eyes fixed on her like a snake mesmerizing a bird. "Find one."

There was still no threat in his tone, but Koleesa shuddered, her throat dry, her heart fluttering wildly in her bony chest. She'd had known other kings, other lords, when she was young and had traveled the lands. Petty tyrants who'd threatened, powerful men who'd tried to frighten, but she'd never feared them. She feared Athelain because he didn't threaten. He didn't need to. He had Magda, her cat, her familiar, her very life.

"How?" she cried. "How?"

"Trap them, bury them, destroy them any way you can."

"Bury?" She thought for a few moments. "Rock?"

"No, that would block the road. We need the trade it brings."

"Bury," she repeated, her pinched face looking even more gaunt as she searched her memory for possibilities.

"There must be something you can do." For the first time, Koleesa heard a hint of desperation in his voice.

" 'S no spell."

"There is no spell?" he asked, as if uncertain what she'd said.

" 'S no spell."

Suddenly, his eyes widened. "Snow spell? Can you conjure snow? A snowstorm? One as great as an entire winter's snow in one huge storm?"

"No!" Koleesa shrank back. "No ask. Not understand."

His voice hardened. "Can you conjure a snowstorm?"

"No. Can't. Threefold . . . threefold."

"Threefold? What do you mean?"

"Big rule. Learn magic, learn rule."

"What rule?" Anger joined Athelain's desperation.

She swallowed hard and tried to stop shaking. "Rule rhyme." Closing her eyes, she said the catechism she'd learned from her teacher.

> "Good or evil that you do,
> Will come threefold back to you."

She opened her eyes. "Understand? You do. Something happen."

"You mean consequences. There are consequences for what you do."

"Yes!" She nodded vigorously. "Consequences. Big consequences for big spell. No do."

"Everything has consequences." He pointed to the pass. "If you do not stop Reff here, he will march across Visali, killing, burning, raping, destroying my people and my land. My army might be able to hold him back for a while, but he has five times as many men and stronger weapons." He leaned forward and gazed at her with eyes deep as a well and just as dark. "Whatever the consequences, I'll pay them. I, myself." He touched his chest. "I'll pay the price. I have sons to rule after me; I do not fear death. My people, my lands, are worth the risk."

"No, no," Koleesa said, dismay bubbling in her throat. "Consequences. Consequences!"

"What consequences?" he shouted.

She couldn't tell him; she didn't know. There was only dread in her heart. Then the answer came to her, like a voice in her ear, whispering in Visali the words of a riddle.

> "Land to sky to land below
> Cold death to defeat the foe.
> Gone, gone, it then will be
> Until the threefold time you see."

Koleesa gazed at Athelain, waiting, hoping he could decipher it.

Athelain frowned. "What does it mean?"

"Meaning for you to find."

"Tell me!"

"Can't tell, can't tell! Spell no work if tell." She shook her head sadly. "Poor king," she whispered. "Not understand. Not understand."

"And *you* do not understand that I will do anything, everything I can to protect my people." His voice became cold as snow. "And know this, witch: if you fail, your blood will be the second to spill on the ground." He glanced at the struggling sack. "Do you understand?"

"Yes," she hissed. "Understand."

"Then make the snowstorm."

"Magic borrow, not make." She paused, but when Athelain said nothing, she continued. "Snow is cold water. Can make water cold, but not make water. Must borrow water, much water for much snow." She paused again, then pleaded, "Think, think. Understand?"

"Yes," he said, impatient. "I want the snowstorm."

She closed her eyes and moaned softly. "Need things."

"Whatever you need, you will have."

Opening her eyes, she said, "Kettle, fresh water, fire for heating water, salt, clean sand. Willow wand, silver ring, bat dung, knife. Cup and cloth and blood—fresh blood, your blood, king."

"How dare you, witch!" The officer drew back his hand as if to slap her.

"Hold!" Athelain said. "She will have all that she needs, even my blood, if it saves my people. Gather all she has asked for."

The officer stiffened, then saluted. Glaring at Koleesa, he turned sharply and left the tent.

"A chair for her," Athelain said. A servant stepped from the shadows, startling Koleesa, and set a chair facing Athelain. "Sit. If you wish."

Koleesa sank into the wooden chair. Her knees protested as she bent them, but her feet were grateful for the rest. She closed her eyes, sent a reassuring image to Magda, and though she tried to stay awake, fell asleep.

Athelain touched her shoulder. "Awaken. All is ready."

A blanket had been wrapped around her, and her wrists were untied. She groaned as her back popped, and she rubbed the kinks out of her neck. "Please," she whispered as she looked up at Athelain, "no do. Please. Threefold to you."

"It must be done. Come."

He offered her his hand. Everyone else in the tent gasped. Koleesa was surprised by his courtesy. Slowly, she wrapped her gnarled fingers around his large but gentle hand. He eased her to her feet, released her hand, and walked out of the tent. She followed him, still surprised.

The sun shone nearly overhead as Koleesa stepped outside. The bright light made her squint and shade her eyes. A large black kettle—her kettle—hung by a chain from an iron tripod. A crackling fire had heated the water in the kettle to boiling.

The officer handed her the willow wand she'd dropped when the soldiers had taken her. "We have everything you asked for." He waved at two soldiers holding bags, a bottle, and a silver cup. He drew a dagger from his belt. "And here is the knife, but I will hold it, I will draw the king's blood."

"No." She pointed at herself. "Me draw blood. Only me or spell no good."

The officer's hand tightened around the hilt. "Never."

Athelain turned on him. "*She* will take my blood. I will do what she asks. As will you."

The officer clenched his jaw but said no more.

Koleesa turned to the soldiers holding the ingredients for the spell. "Give what ask for. Quick. Understand?"

They nodded.

"Salt." She took the bag from the soldier, grabbed a handful of salt, and sprinkled it into the kettle. "For salt draws water."

"Sand, for sand hides water." She scattered the sparkling grains in the kettle.

"Silver ring." She looked at the soldiers, but Athelain took a silver ring from his finger and handed it to her. "For silver freezes water."

"Bat dung." A soldier handed her a bottle from her cottage. "For bat dung causes water to fall."

She turned to the officer and held out her hand. "Knife."

Anger darkened his face, fear flickered in his eyes, but he handed the hilt to her.

She took it and turned to Athelain. "Sword arm." He held out his right. "Other," she said. He held out his left. "Bare wrist."

He unlaced the sleeve and gazed steadily at her.

"Cup," she said. A soldier offered her the silver cup, but she shook her head. "Hold under wrist. Catch blood."

The soldier's hand shook so much, he had to grip the cup with both hands to hold it beneath Athelain's wrist.

Koleesa looked up at Athelain. He nodded, his face calm, his eyes full of trust. She gripped his forearm, pressed the tip of the knife to his wrist, and made a shallow cut across the skin. Blood welled from the wound, oozing down its length and into the cup—ten crimson drops.

"Bind cut, stop bleeding," she told the officer as she handed him the knife. Relief had replaced part of the fear she'd read in his eyes.

She took the cup and held it over her head. "Fresh blood, king's blood, given, not taken. Blood that is life, hot and red." She poured the steaming red liquid into the kettle and stirred it with the wand. "Blood, to bring death."

She closed her eyes, felt for Magda's presence, and joined their minds. In the magic tongue she'd learned so long ago, she chanted, "Salt and sand, ring and dung, blood for death, be it now done. Water and clouds, now snow become. Let it be done, let it be done."

Power flowed into her lungs, out of her heart, coursing through her to Magda and back again, building like fire, hardening like steel. Hands tingled; skin prickled. Light bloomed behind her eyes until all she could see was dazzling white, like sunlight on snow. Suddenly, the power fled, taking the white light with it.

Her eyes snapped open and stared at the kettle. Over the potion hovered a tiny whirlwind, white and glittering, swirling, swirling. It rose into the air, growing, widening, building until Koleesa could barely see the top. The force of the wind knocked everyone to the ground, flattened the tents. The whirlwind roared like a wild beast and charged northward. In moments it had vanished.

"What happened?" the officer sputtered as he sat up and wiped dirt from his mouth. "Did it work?"

"Yes," Koleesa gasped, too drained to move.

"How soon?" Athelain asked.

She looked up at him and whispered, "Before supper."

Athelain smiled, yet there was more sadness than joy in his smile. "Help her," he told his servants. "Let her rest in my tent. Give her whatever she asks for." He knelt and took her hand. "She has saved us all. All will be well now."

A tear trickled down beside her stubby nose. "Listen.

Listen. Good or evil that you do, will come threefold back to you. Understand?"

He nodded and smiled and patted her hand. "Rest now. We will talk later."

Koleesa hobbled through the woods, away from her cottage. Magda prowled beside her. The sack tied to Koleesa's back held all her possessions—an ancient book, a few bottles and vials, a dish and cup, and five gold coins which Athelain had given her. She hadn't wanted to travel again, but she had no choice. She couldn't stay now.

The snow had come with racing black clouds. Such a storm even the oldest campaigners had never seen. Snow had begun falling just before supper, all through the night, and all the next day. Even the king's camp had received a dusting of snow, but the pass through the southern mountains was so deep that the lower peaks nearly disappeared.

The Maleze army was buried beneath the snow. The handful who escaped were quickly tracked down by Visalian soldiers. Athelain's kingdom was safe from invasion. He was deeply grateful. He'd released Magda, offered Koleesa a place at his court, and given her gold when she'd refused. As she walked east, Koleesa gazed at the green plains of Visali and mourned for them. "King not understand," she whispered to herself. But he would bear the consequences—he and all Visali. She'd borrowed water from Lake Erlyn for the spell, the great lake that fed the Visali rivers, that irrigated fields, provided water for cities, for animals, and the Visalians. Precious water, more precious than they knew. Three years without rain, three years of the lake shrinking to little more than a pond, three years of dry riverbeds, of empty fields, of death—she shuddered. She'd tried to warn Athelain; he'd been too desperate to hear her, to understand the riddle. "Threefold to you," she whispered as tears clouded her eyes. "Threefold to you."

TAKING BACK THE NIGHT

by ElizaBeth Gilligan

We gathered in the common room of the miller's large house as we had every night since the coming of the evil. My father and I were the final villagers to arrive as the last streaks of the sun faded beyond the hills. Father helped Miller Jakub bar the door. I took my place in a far corner away from the coldest of the night drafts where I could watch the others gather round the blazing fire.

I dozed, with my face pressed against the cool wall, my shawl as my blanket, listening to the men argue while their wives stirred restlessly, gathering their children close. A figure drifted into my dreams, cloaked in shadow and power with the moon shining overhead. Then a darkness that seemed to engulf even the moon stole into my vision, emanating evil, and then it turned—its red, hellish eyes ripping into my soul. I woke, muffling my scream, and gulped for air. The sting of the evil gaze made me feel tainted and I could not rest with it on me. I rose quietly, bobbing a curtsy to the men who fell silent and stared at me.

Water on my hands and face felt good, despite the cold; I was able to breathe again. I poured more water into the bowl and washed again, mindful of the men as they began to talk once more.

The wind rose outside, buffeting the house with such fury that the shutters rattled and jangled the bell charms used to ward our sanctuary. The miller's house creaked and groaned and was silent again. Mothers sighed and pulled their children closer to them. Father beckoned me to join him with the men near the fire. I started forward, careful of my neighbors sleeping on the dirt floor.

I don't know what made me stop or turn, but the urge to obey was both comforting and thrilling ... more compelling than even Father's voice.

I felt possessed by a fever that I somehow knew would not harm me as I lifted the heavy bar that braced the door. The men shouted and leaped toward me, cursing as they stumbled over their families. The fever within me burned hot and bright and then cooled suddenly as the heavy wooden door swung wide.

Frigid wind swept around the figure in the doorway, flapping the great indigo folds of the homespun cloak and making the charms and bells which hung by satin cords from the stranger's staff dance. An air of freshness, like spring rain and new grass, filled the room. A dark, slim hand—each finger adorned by rings—reached up and shifted the cowl back. The stranger's hair—loose black locks and dozens of thin braids beaded and strung with silk ribbons—flowed out.

I glanced at my father and the miller standing beside me now. Their fear stank as the silence of the villagers and our visitor enveloped us. Was I the only one who could see that this stranger meant us no harm? When no one else moved, I stepped forward. My father put out a cautioning hand, but I slipped away and curtsied awkwardly. "I'm called Valeska—"

The stranger's ringed hand touched my lips softly, then she handed me the staff. She slowly wound her way past Father, the miller, and the villagers to the fire and chair abandoned by the miller, divesting herself of the great cloak as she did so. All eyes watched her. She shook out the dew-stained cloak and laid it at her feet.

The woman was dark from the sun and the boots on her feet were travel-worn. She wasn't dressed like the village women. Her blouson and skirts were of a rich blue even our best dyes could not approach. Instead of the traditional blackwork, her clothes were covered with silver and gold floss needlework. I recognized some of the symbols on her skirts as parts of the simple wards my grand-

mother had given me. Tiny leather pouches and bundles
of herbs dangled from the silver-encrusted girdle around
her waist and, for just a moment, I thought I spied a one-
eyed tabby peering at me from beneath her skirts. All in
all, I could not say if the woman were pretty or no, but
there was a magnetism about her that drew me to her.

Jealousy flickered in my breast when she pointed to the
miller. "You will tell me about the evil."

The miller sputtered, his florid cheeks glistened with
sweat. He stuffed his smoldering pipe thoughtlessly into
his waistcoat. "Who are you? How do we know you
aren't the evil that hunts us?"

The stranger looked vaguely perturbed and then turned,
seeking something in the sea of faces watching her. At
last her blue-black eyes settled on me. Something inside,
buried deep and long years asleep, stirred as I met her
gaze.

"Tell me, child, am I in league with the demon?" she
asked. Her voice was strong and silken.

"No, my lady," I said, unable to resist.

"The girl is clearly bewitched!" the miller said and
pinched me hard.

Tears blurred my eyes and I stepped toward the safety
of my father, but Father moved away.

"She is under no spell of my casting . . . not now. Tell
them, child, how do you know that I'm not part of the
evil?"

My breath caught in my throat, afraid—not because I
didn't know the answer, but because I *did* and I had no
idea how I'd come by the knowledge. I edged away from
the miller and Father, closer to the woman, as I spoke.
"No evil may enter a home uninvited." I scurried the last
half-dozen steps so that I stood within the woman's
shadow.

The miller made a choking noise.

"Do you think I welcomed the beast that did this to my
son?" Belousha cried, lifting her limp toddler so that the
stranger might better see him.

I looked away, unable to see once more the vacant, lifeless eyes of the boy who had played in my gardens. Belousha's had been the first child soul-struck.

The stranger nodded. "No, you're a good mother who would never knowingly permit such an evil thing, but, tell me, that night ... did anyone call on you?"

Belousha snugged her half-dead child close, weeping. "There was the traveler—but he was a shy old man and kind—"

"Did he touch your son? Gift him in any way?"

Belousha only sobbed. Her husband answered, "He just stroked the boy's head as he left ... but he never crossed our threshold."

Arranging her skirts very precisely and without looking at anyone, the woman said, "This old man—you met him in the fields where you tend your flock? Perhaps you spent the day talking to him and, in Christian kindness, you sent him on his way with food from your own table?"

Belousha wailed, her husband only nodded. Around the room, parents of soul-struck children shared frightened looks.

"The demon comes in many forms ... all seem innocent to those inclined toward kindness," the woman said. She turned to the villagers. "He can take the guise of your herd dog or even the face of a loved one if he is powerful enough."

"Then what can we do if we cannot even recognize him?" the miller demanded. He looked anxiously at his neighbors. "The demon could be among us even now!"

"Tomorrow is the moonless night, the powers of evil will be strongest then."

"And how do you know this? Why should we trust you? We don't even know you!" Father said.

"What payment will you demand to free us of this demon?" the miller asked.

She smiled, turning so that her face was in shadow. "I ask no payment that will not be paid freely ... and you must decide for yourselves whether to trust me."

"And your name?" Father said.

"The demon knows each of you now ... by name and by hearth; he has no such power over me." She reached out and took my hand, drawing me around to face her. Her eyes seemed to glitter as though speckled with stars . . . and nothing else existed. That thing within me which had stirred moments before began to burn, fueled by the woman's presence. I felt as if I were growing and that nothing and no one could confine me. I yearned for the promised freedom, but abruptly the dizzying surge ended when she tapped my forehead. I blinked and tried to focus. "Sleep, child. There will be much work to do in the morning." And so I slept.

I had not been mistaken the night before about the cat. We followed him as he wound through the dewy forest, mrowing at his mistress as though in constant conversation. The woman had said nothing to me when she woke and beckoned me to follow her at dawn. My stomach growled as the smells of breakfast wafted from the houses of my friends who now, freed from their night-fears, began their day.

The cat stopped abruptly, arching his back and hissing. The woman clucked and moved forward, circling the small clearing around something I could not see. Not knowing what else to do, I did as she did. Only as I made the circle the second time did the stink of death strike me. I was glad now I had not eaten because even with an empty stomach, my gorge rose. The newly awakened inner fire shrank and I felt once more the filth of the red eyes. I looked to the witch and saw that she was studying me hard. She nodded in approval and stalked back toward the village, leaving me to follow.

Father stood by the door of our home. I recognized the anger in his eyes and bowed my head, waiting for the reprimand, but he said nothing. Uncertainly, I looked up to see he had gone into the house. He left the door open for us.

"He will come tonight," she said to no one in particular. As we sat down to the table to eat the morning coddle, she continued. "Your daughter will help me, so you must go alone to the miller's house."

"Will Valeska be safe?"

The woman looked at me, pushing back the long fall of her dark hair and braids. "Our fate has yet to be determined."

I swallowed hard, but bravely met Father's gaze. She watched us both.

"Tell me, Valeska, what happened in that clearing to wake the demon," the witch said. She picked up her cat and fed him gruel from her bowl.

"When the well dried last autumn, the men tried to dig a new one there."

Father's frown deepened. "We found only rock no matter how deep we dug—"

"So you simply filled the hole?"

We nodded.

She let the cat leap from her lap. "The demon must have been waiting for a long time. Are you ready, child?"

"What do you want us to do?" Father asked.

The witch shook her head. "Nothing. I need only your daughter."

We worked through the day. The lengths of homespun wool I had hoped would one day become my wedding dress was taken, unfinished, from the loom. The cat twined between our legs as we sewed strange lines and swirls with undyed silken floss and strands of our own hair. The lines never met, the witch made sure of this; once pulling out nearly an hour's work. She spoke only to give me directions.

The strange fire within me burned through my fingers, making me light-headed. I longed to set aside the needle, to ask questions, but the urgency was clear and I worked steadily on. My heart stopped when the door opened and only began to beat again as Father entered. He scowled at us ... at me when he saw that dinner was not prepared, but I barely noticed because I saw what my teacher saw—darkness was gathering and we were not ready.

Father didn't stay long, though I did not remember him actually leaving. I noticed the cheese and sausage left for us on the table when the witch sent me to draw water for the kettle. It seemed an odd request considering that we had not stopped to eat since breakfast. Now that the confrontation neared, she apparently wanted to cook. I did as I had done all day and simply obeyed.

The cat bumped along beside me, not talking to me as he had done with his mistress in the morning, but there . . . and in the fading gloom of early nightfall, his familiar presence was a comfort.

I hurried about my work. My neighbors urged me to hurry as they made their nightly trek to the miller's house. I waved them on and scurried back to my house.

The witch had been busy while I was gone. The lanterns were lit throughout the house, a welcoming beacon shining in the twilight. In the fireplace, she had set a fire which even now blossomed into a fine blaze. She took the bucket from me and filled the kettle.

I looked around the familiar cottage, filled with the belongings of my mother and her mother before her and the little things that were my father's . . . the pipe on the mantle, the half-mended boots. This home of my birth was the witch's chosen battleground . . . this home and I would never be the same after tonight. Sadness filled me as I said a silent farewell to my childhood.

"Why did you come?"

The witch stroked hair from my eyes. "Because you were ready. The magic within you called me."

"And the demon?"

"I felt the evil as I came closer. He's not my doing."

I felt ashamed for asking and started to speak, but she turned stern. "This is your home and only you may invite the evil inside. You can show no fear and you must invite him no farther than the matting." She pointed to the floor as she spoke, to the beautiful linen I had woven so carefully these past months. Already it was soiled by my own feet.

"How will—?"

The witch sank into the rocker by the fire and said simply, "You will know."

For the first hour, I stalked about the room listening to the crickets chirping and the rocker creaking. As the evening pressed and the day's frenzied work began to wear on me, I sank onto the hearth at the witch's feet. The cat curled into my lap and began purring.

I'm not sure when I fell asleep, but I started awake at the sound of Father bellowing my name. I was on my feet and halfway to the door when the witch softly called me back. I hesitated, "But my father—"

She looked at me with her dark, knowing eyes. The fire inside me burned and I noticed the stink of sulfur and rot. "Do what you must," she said as she rose.

"Valeska!" my father's voice bellowed once more from the darkness. "It isn't safe for you here, child. Leave this foolishness and come to the miller's house."

I stopped and looked at the witch. "It *is* my father!" I flung open the door. "Father? Father?" I started to step out into the night.

"Mind my warnings, Valeska!" the witch hissed, catching me by the sleeve.

Torn, I called out, "You should be where it's safe, Father! The night is cold."

"I came for you. I want you with me where it is safe," he said, stepping into the light shining from the house.

To save my own life, I would have sworn the man standing before me was my own father, but the fire inside shrank and I felt dirty. I reached uncertainly for the fire within me . . . for courage. As the inner fire spread, I saw the shroud of darkness around my father's image and his eyes changed from the kindly gray that I had known these sixteen years to the red, evil glow from my vision.

As I saw the demon more clearly, a hunger seemed to come over him and he stepped closer. He sniffed, like an animal uncertain of its food. "There is the taste of magic about you, Valeska."

My name on his lips chilled the inner fire. The witch, standing behind the door, touched my arm. I shook myself and moved back. "Come in from the cold."

He seemed to hesitate, then lunged for me. Claws grazed my cheek and tangled in my golden hair, drawing me toward the door. His shape twisted into a half-beast and his snarling face loomed over mine. His teeth sought my throat as claws rent my dress.

Suddenly, the witch was there pouring the boiling water onto the woolen mat and the demon's feet.

The beast's howl strangled my soul. He shrieked and cried out as he released me to turn in a circle, tearing at his hair. The house groaned, timbers cracked overhead. The matting shrank beneath the demon's feet and the uncompleted lines joined as the wool shriveled. The pentagram grew clearer and the demon grew smaller, cursing us and clawing at us.

I took the pouch from Father and kissed his cheek. I had been the witch's price. The cat mrowed as I lingered. The witch, Zorya, waited on the road ahead . . . as did my future.

I turned from my father, my home, my village, and my childhood. The inner fire burned bright, like a morning song, as I fell into step with the witch.

WITCH GARDEN

by James D. Macdonald and Debra Doyle

"**D**amned queer," Henry Thatcher said. "Right in the middle of my tomatoes."

"What's that?"

"Bunch of bumps in the ground."

"Don't sound too queer to me." Ben took a long pull on his beer, a Miller in a can.

"Six, eight inches out of the ground, where I'd run the rototiller over it not sixteen days ago? And my tomatoes growing right on top. Hard enough to grow tomatoes without this."

"Always something funny in your garden, Henry."

"Ayup. Not bad enough that last frost was in May."

"Last frost is always in May."

"Not so late in May. First freeze in September, I bet. Green tomato relish again."

"Nothing wrong with green tomato relish," Ben said.

"I like a good green tomato relish as much as the next man. Like to see a good red one, too."

Ben finished his beer and popped open another. "You had red tomatoes last year. Showed 'em at Lancaster Fair, as I recall."

"Ayup. Blue ribbon tomatoes those were. But not this year, no sir, not with the frost and those lumps in my garden."

"Suppose you'll show me your lumps?"

"Ain't any there right now," said Henry. "Spaded 'em to bits and raked 'em out."

"Don't think it's moles, do you? If it's moles, you can

get some smoke bombs down to Hicks' Brothers that'll chase 'em right out."

"Don't think it's moles. Leastways, no moles I've ever seen leave lumps like this."

Next morning there was another lump, a little one this time, four or five inches long by three wide. Most folks wouldn't have noticed it, since it didn't raise itself more than a quarter inch above the soil.

But Henry noticed things in his garden; he was there every day pulling weeds when they were no more than two little seed-leaves poking out of the dirt. Besides, he was looking out for lumps these days, since his friend Ben hadn't believed in 'em—or didn't think they were serious, anyway. But most noticeable of all, this lump had straight edges.

"And straight edges plain aren't natural in anything that people don't build," Henry said to Ben that day at noon, while they were having doughnuts and coffee.

"Sometimes not even then," Ben said. "Just look at Jensen's barn."

Henry decided to let the dirt in his garden alone this time, and see if the lump would grow big enough for Ben to see it. By late afternoon it was already looking bigger. The edges of the mound were still straight, though, even where a red-lettuce plant was growing half on, half off one side. None of the lettuce roots had been disturbed, for all the world like the lump had been there forever with the lettuce growing on it.

The whole thing, Henry figured, was maybe two feet long by now, and close to half an inch high. If it was growing that fast he should be able to see it change. But no matter how long he looked at it, nothing happened. It wasn't quite a rectangle any more, either. The two long sides bent out a little. But the edges were still pretty straight.

"God damn," Henry said, and called Ben on the telephone. "You want to see one of them lumps?" he said. "Come on over and I'll show you one."

"I'll be over after supper. I'll bring the beer this time."

This far north in summer the sun didn't set until way

past eight, near nine. The two men had plenty of time to sit on the porch after supper and drink a few beers before looking at the garden.

When they went back to the garden, the lump was there, all right: near five feet long now, two wide and an inch above the ground, with the top flat and the sides plumb.

"Look at that."

"Damn," said Ben. "Know what that looks like, Henry?"

"Ayup. Don't make me like it better."

"Looks like a coffin."

"Ayup."

"Lumps look like this before?"

"Yep."

"It's a coffin," said Ben. "Sure as anything."

"Looks that way in this light."

"Henry, I think you ought to dig down there, see what's under that lump of yours."

"Ruin two rows of lettuce, a row of radishes and a row of squash if I do."

"You can replant."

"With what? Zucchini?"

"Leastways this one isn't near your tomatoes."

"I'll fetch a shovel," Henry said. "If we're gonna dig, might as well get started."

"How deep do you figure to go?" Ben asked when Henry got back with his shovel. Neither one of them were young men any more, though a little work never hurt anybody.

"Six feet. Traditional, ain't it?"

So they started digging, straight down, taking turns.

"Don't you clean the rocks out of your garden?" Ben asked, bending down to remove one somewhere around the three-foot level. It was a big one, maybe a twenty-pounder.

"Back in the old days, folks thought that the devil put rocks in their fields to test their faith," Henry said. "They'd haul 'em out, and the next year there'd be more rocks back again. I figure I've been faithful. But there's still rocks."

The two of them never did get to six feet deep. They got to bedrock first, solid granite—either that or a boulder that was flat as a floorboard and wider than their hole was long.

"Ain't nothing down here," Ben said, clambering out of the pit.

"I could have told you that," Henry replied. "Give me a hand filling it back in?"

The sun had set, but there was still light in the sky by the time they'd done. Any time you dig a hole and then fill it in, there's dirt left over. Henry raked it out into the other rows of vegetables, and the two men headed back to the porch. Digging's hot work, and both of them felt the need to finish off the beer that Ben had brought.

"What do you think?" Henry said, after the silence had gone on a comfortable time. The sky was getting dark, the sort of deep blue that means good weather the next day.

"Damned queer," Ben replied, rocking back in his chair. He waited a minute before speaking again. "Think you might talk to some of those university fellahs down to Concord?"

Henry took a pull on his beer. "Have a lot of flatlanders tramping heavy-footed all over my garden? Thank you, no."

"It's getting late," Ben said after a little more. "Time for me to get on home."

"Ain't no moles. That's for damn sure."

"Nope, didn't see anything looked like moles."

There weren't any lumps in the garden the next day. Henry planted marigold seeds on the new-turned place. Marigolds grow well with tomatoes, and they go in salads for a peppery taste.

Next day again there was a lump. This one was about child-sized by the time when Henry noticed it when he came around in late afternoon with his watering can. Always best to water in the late afternoon, almost sunset; that way the sun doesn't dry it all up during the day and the plants can get the benefit. Weed in the morning, water at night.

This lump was shaped kind of irregular—maybe it'd had its beginning the day before, and Henry hadn't noticed because there were no square lines—and this one didn't look like a coffin. It looked like a human body: about the right length and about the right shape, with a ball at one end like a head, and sticking up at the far end a couple of what could be feet.

Henry wondered what to do. There wasn't enough time to dig this one up; he'd only ruin more vegetables and probably find nothing underneath. He figured that he'd call Ben in the morning. Both of them were retired from the paper mill, and it wasn't like they had a lot else to do.

Next morning the lump was still there, but bigger, grown almost to adult human size. When Ben and Henry went back to the garden, the lump was so high that they could both see it as they walked up. Half of the figure was in the garden, half—the foot end—in the yard around it, pushing up the grass.

"It's a woman," Ben said. "Henry, why do you have a woman rising out of your garden?"

"What makes you say it's a woman?" Henry asked.

"Looks like one. It's got long hair and a dress."

When Henry looked closer, the face was beginning to show—a sharp jaw and a thin nose, and the arms crossed over the chest with clenched fists. There were no cracks or shovel marks in the dirt. The woman-shape lay smooth as if it had been sculpted, but with the plants growing to show it hadn't been built there that day.

"Don't know why there should be a woman here," said Henry. "Hasn't been a woman within a hundred yards of the garden since Maud died."

"Didn't reckon there had been."

"You got any ideas?"

"Nope." Ben waited a minute, thinking. "Seen something in a movie once. Putting a stake through its heart."

"I put stakes in here all the time. Got my beans on some right now."

"No, I mean right there." Ben pointed to where the wrists crossed, above what looked like a bosom.

"Sounds superstitious-like."

"This thing here isn't hardly what I'd call Christian."

"Suppose not."

Henry went up to the woodpile and fetched out a piece of kindling. He found the sledgehammer he used for splitting firewood in the toolshed and brought it along.

"Here," he said. "You think this is the right spot?"

"Looks right."

Henry pushed one end of the stick into the ground, backed off, and pounded it on in.

"Let's go back up to the house," he said after he was done. "I'd like a drink of water."

Henry didn't finish weeding that day, or go out to water the garden that evening.

Next morning the lump was gone, but the plants where it had been were wilted or turning brown, even the grass. "Damn," he said, and turned over that part of his vegetable garden with his spading fork. He replanted with cabbage, but without much hope of getting a head before frost. Still, better to have something growing than nothing.

There were no more lumps for two days. On the third morning, the body-shaped lump was back. This time Henry decided to let the lump alone and watch what happened. Besides, the lump was right underneath his tomatoes, and he didn't want to see them all wither like they'd been attacked by cutworms or some such.

He looked at the garden from time to time during the next day. The mound grew and grew, until it was a full sized woman just like before. At the last, the shape in the earth was almost fully rounded, seeming joined to the ground only by a strip along where the back would be if it was a real person.

"Think of calling the minister?" Ben asked.

"Nope." Henry hadn't needed a minister but three times so far: once when he was baptized, once when he was married, and once when Maud was buried. He expected he'd be needing one again someday, but hoped to hold that day off for a while yet.

Then next morning the lump was gone, and in its place was a hollow, as if someone had slept on the soft earth for a while before standing up and walking away. Only that couldn't have been, since the tomato plants weren't broken: they grew up straight from the bottom of the depression and their roots were untouched. If you looked at it one square inch at a time, the ground in the hollow didn't look any different from the ground anywhere else in the garden.

"Damned queer," Henry said.

By two mornings later, the depression was gone, leveled out as if nothing had happened.

A couple of weeks later Henry saw Ben again.

"Ever figure out about them lumps?" Ben asked.

"Nope. Stopped as sudden as they started. Never heard of anything like it."

"Neither have I."

" 'Spect most people get 'em in their gardens don't talk about 'em much," Henry said.

He'd been right about another thing too: frost was early that year, and he had to put up all his tomatoes as green relish.

> The earth hath bubbles, as the water has,
> And these are of them.
> —*Macbeth*, Act I, scene III

AN EYE FOR ACQUISITIONS

by Bruce Holland Rogers

Leonard Vriner felt it in his bones, that old magnetic attraction that he hadn't felt in such a very long time. At first he dismissed it. The mergers and acquisitions game as he used to play it was dead, and there just weren't any easy pickings left to be exploited in a corporate raid. But the more he talked to Moscarón, the more sure he felt of the prospect: perhaps there really was one last plum to pluck.

"I can't believe you've never heard of greenmail, Mr. Moscarón," Vriner said to the man he'd just met at the thousand-dollar-a-plate political fund-raiser. "Surely, as CEO of . . . what was it again?"

"WWW Service and Supply."

"Yes." Vriner filed the company name securely in his mind. "As CEO, surely you've thought of how you would defend against an unfriendly stock tender?"

"I don't think we'd have a problem."

"Ah," Vriner said, sensing that the plum might not be so ripe. Too bad. "You're closely held."

"Not at all," Moscarón said. "We have no majority shareholders, and our shares trade on the exchange, but our many shareholders want a board and officers who know our business. They are exceptionally loyal."

Vriner was careful not to laugh aloud. How often had he heard that from directors and CEOs? But greed was a persuader that had never failed him. Shareholders could *always* be bought.

"And what does WWW Service and Supply do, exactly?" Vriner asked.

"We are," Moscarón said with a thin smile, "diversified. And becoming more so all the time." The man's eyes were brown with a greenish tint, the color of pond scum. "But you were telling me, Mr. Vriner, how you made your fortune. You said you have an eye for acquisitions. Perhaps that's a talent my company can use down the road, when we're a bit more sophisticated."

"My talents aren't for sale," Vriner said, "and I haven't done that sort of deal for a long time."

"Still, it sounds interesting."

But Vriner changed the subject. Why let a naive target know the rules of the game?

And Vriner knew the game well. In the glory days of greenmail and the two-tier tender, in the decade of boardroom bear hugs and bootstrap offers, he had learned the art of the corporate raid. Yes, he did have an eye for acquisitions, a sixth sense for weakling companies that he could buy a taste of and then devour like a shark. Or if he didn't devour, he bit so hard that company's management bid up their own stock to make the deal too pricey, and then he'd sell his stake for a bundle. Win or lose, he made a lot of money. Win or lose, he enjoyed the game.

But the game had changed. The SEC made tougher rules, and companies fought back with self-tenders and the Pac-man counterbid. Lock-up options and the crown jewel defense kept a company's most profitable divisions out of a raider's reach. There were poison pills and blocking preferreds, staggered boards and golden parachutes, and all kinds of other shark repellents. For a while, this had only made the game more challenging, but finally the defense had the edge, and the game wasn't fun any more.

So rather than talk about mergers and acquisitions, Vriner asked Moscarón what he thought of the senator whose campaign they were supporting at this dinner.

"I've only recently begun to appreciate how useful a senator can be," Moscarón said.

"You sound as if you own him," Vriner joked. "It takes

more than a thousand-dollar dinner to buy a United States Senator."

"Oh, I know that," Moscarón said. "I know exactly what it takes." He took a small box from his vest pocket and opened it. The inside of the lid read, WWWSS. "Would you care for a chocolate?"

"A product of your company?"

"A sideline. As I said, we're diversified."

"I'm allergic to chocolate."

"Pity," said Moscarón.

In the receiving line after the dinner and speech, Vriner noticed that the senator addressed his contributors by first name, and he glanced into their eyes barely long enough to convey sincerity before he passed on to the next person. "Andy, good to see you. How's business, Leonard? Delighted to have your support. Hi, David, Sheila. Good to see you." But when Moscarón came by, the senator looked him in the eye long and hard. "Mr. Moscarón," he said soberly. "Good evening, sir. I hope every little thing is satisfactory." And Moscarón just smiled.

Maybe Moscarón *did* own the senator, and that would suggest that his company had a very healthy cash flow indeed, or else some other attractive leverage that would make the company worth owning.

Vriner called his investment banker that night. "Listen," he said, "I think I've found a Saturday Night Special."

"No way," Siegel told him. "There hasn't been an overnight takeover since dinosaurs roamed the earth. What's your supposed target?"

"WWW Service and Supply."

"Never heard of them," Siegel said. "But I'll take a look. I'll call you soon."

"Call me sooner than soon. I've got a feeling."

In the morning, Siegel paced Vriner's office and said, "Their numbers look sharp, Leonard. But they can't be as unprotected as you say."

"Wide open," Vriner said. "I have it from the head man

himself. Now tell me why someone else hasn't gone after them."

Siegel shrugged. "Couple of reasons, I guess. One, maybe no one has *seen* them. It's a low-profile stock, very thinly traded. Weeks go by and no one buys or sells a share. The other thing is that, well, even from their annual report, it's hard to tell exactly what they do. I mean, they trade commodities I can't imagine anyone would want to buy. Cactus spines and live owls. Dried roots and herbs you never heard of."

"And do they do this profitably?"

"They're healthy."

"Let me see."

Vriner flipped through Siegel's report, then passed it back to him. "I wouldn't care if they were cannibals trading in human skulls, Aaron. I like these numbers. Buy me a quiet five percent, and let's go hunting."

Siegel spread the stock trades out over several weeks. Even so, the shares weren't easy to come by. He had to bid the price up to shake loose sellers. "I don't know," he told Vriner. "This is turning into an expensive stake. Maybe they've got wind of you. Making a tender might not be worthwhile."

"I want the deal," Vriner said. "I want to play the game."

"So we go anyway?"

"We go. On Friday, we go."

"It's late, and I'm rather busy," Moscarón said irritably when Vriner called and insisted on an immediate meeting. "Can't this wait until Monday?"

"I think you'd rather talk to me now," Vriner said. "In any case, you have a fiduciary responsibility to hear what I have to say. After all, I have a five percent stake in your company. I believe that makes me one of your largest shareholders, if not *the* largest."

Moscarón sighed. "All right, all right. I'll meet you in my office. You'll have to show yourselves up. My staff is already gone for the day. Do you know how to get here?"

Vriner hung up and smiled at Siegel. "The poor stiff is so out of it that he doesn't know enough to be scared."

"Where in hell did they get these colors?" Siegel said as he rode the elevator with Vriner. From the outside, the corporate headquarters from WWW Service and Supply had been ordinary enough—blue glass and black steel. The outer lobby, too, was standard and conservative, if surprisingly empty—an open, tiled atrium with a security station absent of security guards. But beyond the public face of WWW, the carpets and wall coverings were sickly shades of green and rust, colors that made the air seem stale and thick. The inside of the elevator was the color of bread mold.

"That'll be the second thing that I get rid of," Vriner said, tapping the elevator wall.

"The first, presumably, is Moscarón."

"I'm not going to have someone so simple-minded running any company of mine."

"He does seem to have a senator in his pocket, from what you say."

"Anybody who's rich enough can do that if he cares to."

"Don't kid yourself."

Moscarón's office was on the top floor, but it was hardly what Vriner expected in an executive suite. Flames flickered in the fireplace near Moscarón's desk, and the room was stuffy with stale smoke—not wood smoke, but something more rancid, like the smoke from burnt hair. The fluorescent lights seemed ordinary enough, but they cast a dim light that didn't quite illuminate the corners of the expansive room.

"My time is short," Moscarón said. "Come, sit, and tell me what this is about."

"What this is about," said Vriner, staying on his feet as Siegel sat down, "is my holding company's offer for a controlling share of WWW Service and Supply. I told you I have an eye for acquisitions, Moscarón. I also have a pretty good idea of what constitutes an irresistible price. We're buying you out at thirty-two dollars a share."

"I see," Moscarón said. "Well, it's out of the question. The company is not for sale."

"We'll see what your shareholders have to say about that. I want you to produce, by tomorrow, a list of your owners."

"This company's shareholders," Moscarón said, "are very private people. I'm sure they don't want me passing out their names and addresses to anyone who asks. Now I have things to do tonight. You will excuse me."

Vriner laughed, and Siegel said, "You have a fiduciary responsibility to your shareholders to let us make our offer known to them. Failure to live up to that responsibility will land you in civil court."

"I'm a shareholder, too," Vriner said. "My interests are your interests. Or they had better be."

Moscarón shook his head. "I don't want a court battle just now. I haven't made arrangements for that sort of thing. But I don't think you understand who you are dealing with. You say, Mr. Vriner, that you have an eye for acquisitions. Perhaps you do. But in this case, your eye has misled you. Our shareholders . . ."

Something moved in the dark corner behind Moscarón.

"What's that?" said Siegel.

"An owl," Moscarón said, and Vriner could now see it in the shadows, a small owl on a tall perch. Its eyes glinted from the darkness.

"I don't want excuses," Vriner told Moscarón. "I want that list tomorrow."

"All right," said Moscarón. "You'll have your list." He opened a confection box and pushed it toward Siegel. "Would you care to try one of these?"

"We're taking over your company and you're offering us chocolates?" Vriner said.

"You might as well know something about what you're trying to take over."

Vriner waved off the offer, but Siegel accepted.

On their way out of the building, Vriner said, "You see what I mean about this guy? He just doesn't get it."

Siegel didn't answer. He was fishing around in his mouth with his tongue, and finally he gagged and reached in with his fingers. He drew out a long, long black hair. Tied to the end of it was a wet little bundle that looked like animal fur.

Siegel had the dry heaves there in the empty hallway.

"Was that in the chocolate?" Vriner said, looking at the glistening hair.

"Must have been," said the investment banker, getting his breath. "You might be buying yourself a huge consumer product liability suit, Leonard, if that's a standard ingredient." Siegel retched again and spit into his handkerchief.

"Maybe that's Moscarón's idea of a takeover defense," Vriner said with a smile. "Nauseate the opposition."

"You still want to buy a company that makes chocolate with hair in it?"

"I want a deal, Aaron. I'm hungry for a deal."

"No one's selling," Siegel reported over the phone a week after the offer had been tendered.

"Aaron," said Vriner, reclining behind his desk, "we're bidding five dollars above the last trade."

"Yeah, but that last trade was a week ago. There's no movement. I can't even get anyone to report an asking price. It's as if we've already bought up all the shares that are going to be sold."

"Out of ten thousand shareholders spread out all over the world, out of all these penny-ante owners, you can't squeeze even a handful of shares?"

"Can't squeeze *one* share. It's like the word is out that the stock will be worth a million a share tomorrow, you know?"

"No, I don't know. This doesn't happen. People get greedy."

"I can't figure it, either, Leonard, but I'm getting bids to buy back your stake at a little bit under what you paid for it. I think maybe it's time to cut your losses and run."

"I don't run."

"Well, maybe you do this time, if you're smart. Your own stock is trading at record volume. There may be a move afoot to cut your feet out from under you."

Vriner sat up. "Moscarón?"

"I'm having Erlich & Bahr look into it. So far, the orders are spread between a dozen street names, so if it's one buyer, he's doing a hell of a job of disguising himself."

"I didn't think the old boy had it in him," Vriner said, grinning, relishing a fight.

"Don't take this lightly," Siegel said. "You're heavily defended, but there's a lot of capital moving your shares. If this is Moscarón, he has heavy hitters backing him."

"I'm going to put Logan Edwards on this. He can do a background check on Moscarón, and I'll have him check out some of the shareholders, too."

"That's going to get into some money. Ninety percent of the shareholders are overseas."

"I don't care. I want to know who these people are. What's their compelling interest in maintaining control? With a little insight, Aaron, we can still break this open."

"You're the boss, Leonard. Listen, though. I'm going to orchestrate this from bed for a day or two. I don't feel so hot. Touch of flu, maybe."

"I need you on this, Aaron."

"Have I ever let you down?"

In wing tips, a business suit and neck tie, Logan Edwards didn't look much like a gumshoe. On the other hand, he wasn't the usual sort of private investigator.

"I've pushed it hard," Edwards said, looking from Vriner to Siegel. "I've got six of my best people digging full-time into Moscarón, and we can't get much. I can tell you that he's been in New York for ten years, has been CEO of WWWSS since incorporation, and was in Gallup, New Mexico, before that. But I've had a hell of a time finding anyone who knew him, and those who did know him won't talk at any price. They're spooked, I think." Then to Siegel, Edwards said, "You don't look so good."

"No," Siegel said, blinking his red-rimmed eyes. "I don't feel so hot, either."

Vriner wanted to stay with business. "Mob connections?"

"Could be," Edwards said, "but I doubt it. There's not enough in Gallup to get the attention of organized crime."

"What about the shareholders? You've done background checks on them as well?"

"I've run into brick walls," Edwards said. "It's the same story over and over. You wouldn't believe the places where holders of small lots live. Tiny villages in Africa and South America. On the other hand, you've got big industrialists in Germany and Spain, people of Moscarón's stature and much bigger, and all of them are as opaque as can be. If my people meet them, they won't talk, and their neighbors won't talk. I can't get squat."

"For three million dollars, that's what you give me? Less than squat?"

Edwards held up his hands in a gesture of helplessness. "I'm as frustrated as you are, Mr. Vriner."

"Not yet, you aren't, Edwards. From now on, you're off retainer. Get out of my office."

Edwards stood.

"Don't do this," Siegel said feebly. "Logan is the best in the business."

"The best investigator in the business," Vriner said, "would bring me useful information about my opponent. For that matter, the best *investment banker* in the business, which you used to be, would be finding his own ways to stop Moscarón."

"Short of a self-tender," Siegel said, "what can we do? We know this is a tidal-wave open-market assault by a whole bunch of coordinated buyers."

"Don't hand me excuses," Vriner said. "Give me results!"

But things got worse. Two loyal members of Vriner's board of directors died of sudden illnesses, and another, Greg McCarthy, moved to call an emergency meeting to rewrite the corporate charter.

"Rewrite it for *what?*" Vriner said.

"To rescind your golden parachute, Leonard. I think it's pretty much unanimous that we're a company with hardened arteries."

"You can't dump me! I'll sue your ass!" Then, more gently and reasonably, Vriner said, "I founded this company, Greg."

"Things change," McCarthy told him.

Moscarón wouldn't answer his phone. Time after time, Vriner would call WWWSS, talk to a receptionist, and then be transferred to a phone that rang forever. Vriner thought of leaving a message, but that would put the ball in Moscarón's court. He decided to see the man in person, to catch him off guard if possible, though he wasn't sure of exactly what his approach would be if he could get through to him. Negotiate a compromise? Beg for mercy?

He went in the early evening when shadows were lengthening and the streetlights were coming on. As before, the lobby of WWW Service and Supply was empty.

Vriner took the elevator up. There was no receptionist in the outer office. The door to Moscarón's inner sanctum was unlocked.

A fire crackled in the fireplace, and the room again smelled of a sickly smoke. Moscarón was nowhere to be seen.

A shadow moved in the corner—the owl on its perch. Vriner stepped toward it for a closer look. The owl turned at the sound of his approach, and Vriner squinted into the dark to see it better. There was something strange about the animal, but in the half light, it was hard to say exactly—

Vriner stepped back.

The bird had no eyes. Where its eyes should have been, there were only empty sockets.

Vriner turned away from Moscarón's repulsive pet, and when he did, he saw the yellowed orbs that sat in a dish on Moscarón's desk.

There was no mistaking them, or what they came from.

They were eyes. Human eyes the color of pond scum, turned up on the dish so that they seemed to be looking at him.

What he did next wasn't rational, and even as he did it, Vriner knew that he should probably leave the things alone. But he wanted them out of his sight, out of his *memory*. Retching, Vriner picked up the dish and carried the eyes to the fire. He threw them in and heard them pop and hiss in the flames.

Moscarón's call came the next morning. "I'd like to come by for a chat with you and your banker," he said. "Say at three?"

"Siegel's here with me now," Vriner said. "Why don't you come and get it over with."

"All right," Moscarón said. "Why not?"

Vriner hung up. "He's coming," he said.

Siegel—eyes rheumy, face pale—nodded. "At least it will be over soon, Leonard."

Vriner closed his eyes. It would, in fact, be almost a relief.

When the receptionist showed him to the office, Moscarón started to come through, but then bumped his shoulder against the doorjamb.

"Are you all right?" the receptionist said, not knowing the enemy when she saw him.

"Fine, fine." Moscarón was wearing sunglasses. "You can leave us," he said, as if she already worked for him.

The receptionist closed the door on her way out, and Moscarón approached Vriner's desk somewhat hesitantly, groping for the chair when he was still a foot away from it. Siegel got up and helped him. Moscarón sat down heavily, as though grateful to quit navigating through the office.

"Well," Moscarón said to Vriner, "I have certainly learned a lot from you." He reached into his pocket and put what looked like a silver soup spoon on Vriner's desk. The handle was engraved with WWWSS.

"What's that?" Vriner said.

"An item from our catalog."

"I didn't know there was a catalog."

"As I told you when we met," Moscarón said, smiling from behind the sunglasses, "we are a diversified company. But the catalog does not circulate widely."

"Why don't you cut the crap," Vriner said, "and tell me that you're here to tender an unfriendly offer for control of my company."

"I hardly need to do that," Moscarón told him. "My associates already hold a majority interest in Vriner Holdings, but in many small bites. We prefer to be subtle. No SEC filings and disclosures this way. My associates are very private people."

"So I've learned."

"Have you?" Moscarón said. "I still don't think you understand who we are." Then, to Siegel, Moscarón said, "Show him, Aaron."

Vriner looked at Siegel. Who was taking something out of a black case. "Aaron? You're working both sides?"

"Only temporarily," Siegel said. "After today, my services go exclusively to Mr. Moscarón."

"I'll sue your ass into kingdom come," Vriner said, sitting up straight, sensing that all might not be lost after all.

"No, you won't," Siegel said, and with a deft movement, he flicked gray powder from the case into Vriner's face.

"What the hell—" Vriner started to say, but Moscarón uttered a syllable and Vriner froze in mid-sentence. He could see, he could hear, but he could not speak or move.

"Nicely done," said Moscarón. "I thank you. My current condition has naturally done nothing for my aim."

"All right," Siegel said. "He's yours. Now help me."

"I always fulfill my obligations, but I would thank you to speak more respectfully."

Siegel lowered his head. "Yes, Mr. Moscarón. Of course, Mr. Moscarón."

"Open your mouth."

Still unable to move, or even to look away, Vriner watched as Moscarón coiled a long hair onto Siegel's tongue.

"Swallow," he said, still holding one end of the hair.

Siegel obeyed, and Moscarón uttered another syllable, then began to pull gently on the hair.

Siegel gagged. "Easy, now," Moscarón said.

A black mouse, squirming and covered with slime,

erupted from Siegel's mouth. The banker turned and vomited.

"Please!" Moscarón said. "Not on the carpet!"

Siegel stayed doubled-over, catching his breath.

"You understand," Moscarón said, "that there are others. You'll be fine for a while, but if you don't come to me as they mature, they'll fill your body. To the uninitiated, it will look like cancer."

"I understand," Siegel said, wiping his brow. Already he looked better. "You have my unquestioned loyalty, Mr. Moscarón."

Moscarón turned toward Vriner. "Ah, Mr. Vriner," he said. "How very helpful you have been to World-Wide Witchcraft Service and Supply."

He sat down again, as if the business meeting were to continue.

"You've taught us a lot, sir. You've done a great deal to show us the way. Between a good investment banker and a few hundred coordinated witches, I don't think there's a company in the world that can resist us."

He stood again and leaned toward Vriner with the mouse. Something wriggled through Vriner's lips, and then Vriner felt Moscarón's fingers push the mouse past his tongue. It squirmed down.

Moscarón took off his glasses. Black and yellow eyes no bigger than large marbles rolled in his eye sockets.

"Unfortunately, your little visit while I was out conducting some night business deprived me of an important asset."

He picked up the spoon.

"We have a lot of advantages in a corporate environment," Moscarón said. "Who, in the boardroom, believes in witches? Who knows how to mount a defense against us?"

He leaned forward, and one of the owl eyes almost rolled out of his head.

"But I can't very well do business looking like this, can I? I think suspicions might arise. Agreed?"

Deep in his stomach, Vriner felt tiny teeth beginning to

gnaw. He'd scarcely have believed that something so small could cause so much pain.

"You say you have an eye for acquisitions."

Moscarón slid the edge of the spoon beneath Vriner's eyelid. If Leonard Vriner hadn't been frozen into silence, he would have screamed.

"I wonder," Moscarón said, "which one it is?"

DIDDLING WITH GRANDMOTHER'S IRON MAIDEN

by Nicholas A. DiChario

Morgan settled quietly into the large-cushioned chair beside her grandmother's bed. She tested a deep breath, still feeling the cold New England air in her lungs. A small blaze crackled in the fireplace opposite Grandmother Amelia Genaro's bed, filling the room with the smell of burning bark. Morgan welcomed the heat. She would not interrupt her grandmother's sleep.

Her trip from Boston to Grandmother Genaro's home, in the western Massachusetts community of North Windham, had been riddled with annoyances.

Morgan's supervisor at Metropolitan had chastised her for requesting vacation time during the "hectic, year-end, claims processing season." The Avis (We Try Harder) rent-a-car agent had failed to locate some vital paperless information somewhere within the abyss of his national networking system, delaying Morgan's Ford Escort by a good thirty-five minutes. Road construction detours on Interstate 90 sent her on a bumpy excursion through Millbury, and icy pavement and reduced speeds along stretches of Highway 52 made for slow and frustrating travel.

Through it all, Morgan's thoughts of James, and what—if anything—she could do about him, added to her growing anxiety.

Morgan ran her hand along the smooth cold brass of Amelia's bed. She stroked her grandmother's delicate mantilla that hung from the bedpost like the dead sail of a Spanish galleon.

Upon a bureau near the bed, encased in a polished pewter urn, lay the ashes of Amelia's third husband, Gerard. Or was it Charles? Painted on the face of the urn in red and black, resembling Goya's *The Witches' Sabbath*, sat a goat-devil among his worshipers, a crescent moon overhead, black bats on the horizon.

Morgan's eyes followed a path from the urn to a painting on the adjacent wall. The painting depicted an elderly, gray-haired gentleman in a stark-white suit, strapped to a Mississippi riverboat wheel. Several horned children, dressed in nineteenth century garb, danced and played on deck. The piece was entitled, *Twain In Pain.*

Grandmother Genaro awoke. She did not stir; her eyes simply snapped open. She clutched Morgan's hand. "James is giving you trouble," she said in a low, grainy whisper.

"I need some insights, Grandmother."

"You want the man too much. Don't be so desperate."

"Grandmother, I want to know what James is thinking."

Amelia laughed. "Of course you do, child. You want lots of nice things. You want James. You want a promotion. You want power. There is nothing wrong with any of that. You are what you are." Grandmother tilted her head to get a better view of her.

"You look healthy," Grandmother Genaro said with a note of approval. "The pressure is making you angry, not timid." She turned over Morgan's palm and began thumbing it—slow, gentle circles at first, followed by a succession of sharp pentacles. "You're the only one to come see me."

Morgan nodded. Grandmother Genaro's three daughters, Morgan's mother in particular, not only avoided Amelia, but tried their best to keep Morgan away from North Windham.

"They hate you," Morgan said without hesitation. It was the way Grandmother Genaro wanted it. The old woman's house was intentionally intimidating: Low, vaultlike ceilings; dark-paneled walls; narrow hallways. If one did not appreciate the feel of a mausoleum, one would not find comfort in Amelia's home.

"They hate me because they are jealous of my power. I have no need for them. I have no need for any of these trappings," she waved her arm at the room. "I self-indulge. I am a witch. I am a demon. Call me what you will."

Morgan fidgeted in her chair. Pride. It had been a long time since she had felt that. Her grandmother shamed her.

"What I like best about haematic power," Amelia said, "is the vision it affords." She dug her thumbnail into Morgan's palm, drawing a thin line of blood. Morgan gritted her teeth against the pain. Grandmother then sliced her own palm. She pressed their hands together and entwined their fingers.

"I assume you have mingled your blood with James'?" Morgan nodded.

"Only the blood keeps all secrets," Grandmother said, "and only the haematic witch can keep all secrets hidden within the blood."

The fire snapped and flare. Morgan shuddered.

Amelia closed her eyes—"I see James' bloodline,"—and held them closed for a long moment before speaking again. "James' marriage is acceptable to him. He likes his wife and his children well enough. You fit in nicely. I perceive no guilt. Are you familiar with the Iron Maiden of Nuremberg?"

Morgan shook her head. "No."

"A marvelous tool of torture, really. You lock a human being inside its casing and crank it shut, allowing its steel spikes to slowly pierce the wrists and ankle joints, the knee and elbow joints, the eyes and the groin. Think of the Iron Maiden as the matrix of James' mind. As long as he can distribute equal pressure to the critical junctures in his life, James is in control, James is the torturer."

Morgan frowned. "What are you implying?"

"You are attempting to upset his applecart, my dear. James won't stand for it. If you become too large, too threatening, he will force you into juxtaposition, he will crank shut his iron maiden. You are doomed to play the part of a mistress."

"I don't believe that," said Morgan. "James loves me."

"James needs sex. If he could get it from his wife, even now, even with you in the picture, he'd take it."

"No. He's afraid of his wife. I'm sure of it. What can you tell me about her?"

"James' wife, Paulette, considers herself a sculptress. James has an analytical mind, like yours. This frustrates her. She craves creativity and interesting personal relationships. She has been having an affair with a bisexual art instructor named Sheridan for two years. The affair began innocently enough. James is out of town, Sheridan's apartment is available, all very safe. But lately, Paulette craves more excitement, and they have begun to take chances. Sheridan's office at Boston University, her studio at the gallery—"

"The *bitch*," Morgan said, nearly spitting it out.

"Oh, James knows all about it. He approves of the arrangement. The busier Paulette is with other men, the busier James can be with other women."

"No!"

Grandmother Genaro's feeble body shook with laughter. "Your hatred pleases me. You want to hurt Paulette. Very good. You may not realize it yet, but you want to hurt James, too."

"That's insane." The fire, which had been a flickering warmth when Morgan had arrived, now burned fiercely, illuminating the sharp, brass pokers in the hearth. Grandmother Genaro kept only sharp instruments.

"It's never the witches who burn, Morgan, remember that."

Morgan squirmed in her chair. She wiped the sweat from her forehead with the back of her hand. "I came here to talk about James."

"Don't plead ignorance with me. You came here to control James."

"He'll hate me—I can't—I *won't* make him hate me."

"You have no idea how exciting hate can be."

Morgan watched the fire dance in her grandmother's

azure eyes, a dizzying, hypnotic interplay of color and motion. She experienced a wave of nausea. A suggestion of vertigo came and went, coupled with an equally disconcerting sense of claustrophobia. Morgan wanted to run, but her brain no longer communicated with her body. She gripped the arm of her chair to regain her equilibrium.

Once, when Morgan was a very young girl, one of her earliest memories in fact, she had been walking with her grandmother when they discovered a nest of young birds concealed in a patchwork of wet leaves. Morgan and her grandmother took each little gray and yellow bird—the birds were no larger than her own small fingers—tied stones around their wiry necks, and tossed them one by one into the waters of Beaver Brook State Park. Grandmother Genaro then sang a Spanish song in an eerie voice, and laughed herself silly.

Morgan remembered the confusion of that day, a child's confusion, a need to please her grandmother, a need to play adult games in an adult world, wondering exactly what the rules of those games were and who had made them up.

Morgan felt as if there were stones tied to her own neck right now. She could not deny the allure of Grandmother Genaro's power. She could not shake the stones pulling her down, dragging her under. But Morgan had heard, or had she read about it somewhere? that to drown was painless, euphoric, in a way, if you let yourself go.

"*Think,* Morgan," Amelia said. "You are my only apprentice. My daughters are worthless. So, too, will your daughters be worthless. Among the Genaro women, the power skips a generation. Only you can learn what I have to offer. Accept it and set yourself free. Fight it and you will be crippled, my dear, make no mistake about it. A pretty little cat without her claws."

Trapped and crippled, Morgan thought, vulnerable, bitter, defenseless. Like her mother and her aunts.

Suddenly Morgan loathed her grandmother. Why did she depend on the old woman so much? Maybe if she could cultivate her own personal power she would not have to depend on anyone, not ever, not even Grandmother Genaro. Maybe she wouldn't always feel so helpless, so out of control.

"Ah, yes, very good," Amelia said. "You hate me. You needed to admit that."

Morgan looked down at her grandmother's hand, at their fingers wrapped together like a clump of worms. She could no longer distinguish her own hand's anatomy from her grandmother's. She felt the skin of her palm stretching, breaking, breathing, inhaling Grandmother Genaro, exhaling Morgan, her grandmother's blood mingling with her own. She felt her heart hammering inside her chest. Her mind juggled fear, anger, hatred, excitement, unwilling to grasp any one emotion, unable to set any one of them free.

"There is a ceremonial song I'm fond of," Amelia said, "by Pablo Neruda. '. . . *y ahora tenemos nuevas islas, volcanes, nuevos ríos, océano recién nacido, ahora seamos una vez más: existiremos . . .*'"

"All will be new again," Morgan said, "islands, volcanoes, new rivers, oceans recently born. Let us make ourselves new again, come into existence."

Amelia looked wistful. "Sheer poetry."

"I don't speak Spanish, Grandmother. What's happening to me? I don't understand."

"I don't understand either, my dear. Haematic power does not beg to be understood, it craves only to be spent."

Yes. Morgan understood begging and craving well enough. She thought of James again. She not only yearned to possess him, she yearned to crush him. Calm, cool, in-control-of-the-situation James. James the hopelessly pitiful coward. James the sonofabitch. Morgan looked forward to commandeering his iron maiden, closing the torturer in his own device and exerting pressure—slowly, slowly, slowly—until the steel spikes cracked him like an empty eggshell and exposed him for the hollow man he truly was. James the pest, nothing more, clinging to his wife, indecisive and spoiled. She could do better, much better. She *would* do better.

Amelia, after all, had raised the stakes, upped the ante.

Amelia, just as when Morgan was a child, had forced her to ponder more serious questions other than the immediate indiscretion. Amelia, oh so like a witch, had presented the iron maiden to Morgan and had asked her to step inside, weaving the torturous device into an object of desire, an irresistible conduit of power.

"Teach me," said Morgan, offering all of her blood to Grandmother. Every last drop.

"I have already begun," Amelia Genaro said.

And Morgan felt the jaws of Grandmother's iron maiden slam shut and lock her in.

THE THREE TEARS

by Byron Tetrick

Anne laughed as she tried to coax Skye into releasing the knotty chunk of wood that now looked more like a foamy piece of soap than the rounded piece of root the dog had found in the bushes. "If you want to play fetch, you'll have to let go. Let go-o-o-o-o, you bad dog!" The dog let the "prize" drop from its mouth, but grabbed it up again as soon as she reached for it. Laughing, Anne turned to her daughter. "Katey, see if Skye will give his ball to you?"

Katey, who had been giggling at both her dog *and* her mother, put out her hand and said with the assurance of her four years, "Skye, give it to me." And then, "Good doggie," as the big, black dog set the moist blob at her feet with its tail wagging so hard that it jerked its rear end back and forth in a comical sashay.

Anne's husband, Caleb, had found the dog the previous winter in a hollow near their stream, still trying to suckle from its dead mother. Two other pups, still huddled together for warmth, were lifeless. But this pup had fought for life; and from the time Caleb brought it home, it had thrived.

Caleb had worried at first about bringing a wild dog into the house with a small child, but it had become a sweet, gentle dog. And my, how Katey and Skye loved each other! It was Katey who had named him. When she saw how the dog had one brown eye and one blue, she had said, "Doggie eye like sky."

* * *

They continued toward home, playing as they went and laughing often as their dog—with seemingly unending energy—chased and retrieved. It felt good to laugh again, thought Anne, and to see a smile on her young daughter's face.

They were returning from placing a wreath of wild-flowers at Caleb's grave. Early that morning, the two of them had packed a small lunch, and then holding hands as they walked into the woods, they picked out a bouquet of columbine, lady's slippers, liverwort, and other flowers that flourished where the stream wound through the grove of woods that marked the north boundary of their farm. When the woodland flowers were in bloom, Caleb had always finished his workday by going into the woods, washing the day's grime from his body in the cold stream, and then gathering a garland of sweet-smelling flowers to give to her as he entered their small house. Her memory of him now was always paired with the smell of lilacs, moss and of those flowers.

She quickly wiped the tears from her eyes before Katey could see them. They had both shed enough tears at the gravesite where Caleb's small, granite marker was just beginning to lose its freshly etched sheen. "Caleb Weld 1639–1663" it read. He had been clearing some trees the previous fall and hadn't come home as the sun set. Finally she had gone out looking for Caleb, finding him pinned under a large oak that had splintered at its base, falling on him and crushing his chest. He had tried to pull himself free, but had finally weakened and lay there quietly. "I waited for you, Annie," he said. "The tree shouldn't have fallen back on me, but somehow it did. I killed myself in such a foolish way, and now I leave you all alone. I'm sorry. . . ." And then he died.

Anne unbuttoned the top two buttons of her dress to let the spring breeze cool her as they reached an open expanse, clear of the trees that had shaded most of their journey. Katey walked ahead as Skye trotted alongside still holding the knotted, wooden bolus in his mouth. The whistles and trills of myriad birds filled the air rejoicing in the warmth.

The road became a steep slant that dipped into a small dale that was called "Spooky Hollow" because of the large deciduous trees that turned the glen into a dark trellis by early June and a cavern by midsummer. From the opposite side of the vale echoed the clop-clop of a horse, and Anne whispered to herself, "Please don't let it be Eunice Colle." But she knew it was by the gait of their gelding and the distinctive squeak of their buckboard as it labored under the weight of the obese Mr. Colle. She had hoped to be home before church let out, but their dallying with Skye made them just late enough that—well, she would just tell them they had been praying at the graveyard.

"Katey, wait for me. Someone is coming."

She gathered Katey's hand in hers and walked deeper into the gloom of the valley.

Mr. Colle brought the big gelding to a stop with a gruff, "Whoa, whoa!"

"Mrs. Weld, whatever are you doing in these dark woods?" said Mrs. Colle as she brushed the road dust from her lap.

Anne tried not to think unkind thoughts, but failed. Why couldn't the woman at least greet her civilly before sticking her nose into her business. "Good day to both of you," answered Anne, trying to be cheerful. "We're on our way back from visiting Caleb's grave. It's a beautiful spring day to be about, don't you think?"

"You weren't in church today. Thy time would be better spent praying for your poor husband's soul."

Anne gritted her teeth. "We did pray . . . at his grave." She lifted Katey up in her arms. "Didn't we, Katey? Say hello to Mr. and Mrs. Colle."

"Hel—"

"Shoo! Scat! Get away from the horse, you nasty dog."

Skye, his tail wagging furiously, had not left Katey's side and was enough of a farm dog to know to stay away from the horse, but Mrs. Colle reached for the whip in her husband's hand and would have struck at the dog if Anne hadn't quickly set Katey down and pulled Skye away from the buggy.

"Mrs. Colle, put that whip away. Skye wouldn't bother your horse," said Anne, still bent over, pulling the dog away. She looked up and saw Mr. Colle's eyes fixed on her breasts. She had forgotten about the buttons. She felt bare-breasted under the gaze of his slitted eyes.

His wife, noticing his stare, jammed the whip handle into his hand and said, "Well, I don't trust any dog that big or that black. Perhaps we can visit more sometime when the dog is not around. Let us go, John." With a flick of the lash, the horse jerked into its traces, the cart lurched, and with only a quick backward glance by Mr. Colle, they departed without another word.

Anne watched for a moment and then noticed the puzzled look on her daughter's face.

"Mommy, I don't like them very much."

She gave her a hug. "Neither do I, sweetie. Neither do I."

Anne grabbed Katey's hand. "Let's race Skye to the top of the hill!"

Out of breath but back in the sunlight again, they crested the knoll and stopped at a rock outcrop to rest. Even the sight of the next bend that meant that they were almost home failed to lift Anne's mood. What is happening to the good people in the colonies that makes them so mean-spirited, she wondered? Neighbors should be helpful and friendly, not cruel and petty. Of late, it had become so vicious and accusatory in some hamlets, that innocent people—mostly women—had been tried and even hanged as witches. Just in the last two years, the village of Hartford had brought thirteen people up on witchcraft charges. At least four had died during questioning or they were hanged. Such foolishness ... such insanity! Anne couldn't bring herself to believe in witches. Even someone as mean as Mrs. Colle had some goodness, a kind feeling, a redeeming quality; she just couldn't think of what it might be at the moment.

* * *

"You lust for that woman like a rutting boar. Your eyes never left her bosom."

John kept his head facing forward. He feared his wife even more than he feared the damnation that awaited him on judgment day, for he had seen her ceremonies and heard her chants on the nights of the full moon. It was the only night of the month he was allowed to have her, if that truly be what occurred; it was his wife who used *him* in ways unnatural and ungodly. He wondered how long it would be before she no longer needed him, and she caused a tree to fall and crush him as well. The evening Caleb had been killed, Eunice had returned from the Weld's woods with a knowing smile, a look that told him some evil had been done. That next day when they got word of Caleb's death, her smile only broadened; and since then, whenever he crossed her, she would say, "Remember Caleb!"

He knew that he'd better say something, for in truth the sight of Anne Weld *did* excite him with bestial passion. "I lust only for her forty acres of prime field, her hundred acres of hardwoods, and mostly for the stream that moistens her land in the driest of summers," he replied, knowing that his wife openly coveted the Weld land, and he could always turn her ire in that direction.

"Aye, they say she owns it free and clear. I don't understand how a woman can keep a farm like that up. I thought surely she would sell when her husband died. I *will* have her land! She gave her husband another hard look and added scornfully, "You are a weak and lustful man, John Colle. But in your defense, Anne Weld is a brazen temptress and hath bewitched you."

And it was those final words that planted the seed in Eunice Colle's mind and suddenly offered a solution to everything ... including the taunting possibility of obtaining the Weld land.

That night, Eunice made her husband submit to her while she punctured his skin with her teeth and bled him into an earthen jar, etched with signs and markings of the evil one. To that, she mixed the sexual fluids that she drew from his body in a way that brought more pain than pleasure. Then, waiting for the dead of night, she slipped fearlessly through the dark forest to the Weld farm where she concealed the vile mixture, returning as the first rays of the sun touched the sky and lifted the veil of darkness.

A few days later, Anne was just finishing unhitching the mule when she heard Skye's barks and walked from the barn to see Mrs. Colle, Reverend Benham, and the magistrate walking purposely toward the house. She hollered to them, "I'm at the barn!" Waving her arm, a neighborly smile on her face, she added, "What brings thee here today?"

The magistrate held out a sheaf of paper as he walked up and said, "Mrs. Weld, you have formally been charged with the practice of witchcraft. You will come with us to be judged by the colony's legally appointed inquisitor and others deemed appropriate by the church."

Anne's laughter at the idiocy of the charge died in her throat as she saw no trace of a smile, only stiff, grim faces that seemed unnaturally large and looming.

The magistrate moved a step forward, and Anne moved a step back. The impossibility of what was happening was rapidly becoming reality and she considered fleeing. But she knew the charge must be answered; besides, she had nothing to hide.

A mother's fear suddenly overwhelmed her. "What of my daughter? Who will watch over her?"

Again the magistrate took another step and then lunged at her, grabbing her arm roughly and twisting it so that she fell on one knee. "Come, witch. Don't worry about thy child. It will be looked after."

Anne was taken to the prison house, a building adjacent to the Magistrate's Office. Visible from the sole window in its large, barren room was the stockade used for public humiliation and punishment. For several hours she waited, her emotions alternating between anger and fear.

Finally, a dour-faced entourage entered, taking seats facing a single chair where she had been roughly instructed to sit while being questioned. Mrs. Colle sat directly in front of her. Reverend Benham and the magistrate sat at each side. Apart from the others was the local representative of the Connecticut Colony's "Court of Assistants" who would make the initial judgment. Stationed at the door was the magistrate's dim-witted assistant, a hog-faced man with a bull-like body.

Mrs. Colle started by accusing Anne of sexual witchcraft. She accused her of being a succubus who invaded the sleep of her husband causing bizarre sexual dreams. Mr. Colle was brought in, and he told of Anne possessing and ravaging him in acts of perversion and bestiality. Vivid nightmares that lasted through the night and left him, waking in the morning, sapped of life and bearing scratches and wounds that would fester painfully for days. He showed a ragged, seeping puncture of his womanlike, flabby breast that clearly showed human teeth marks.

Speaking to the colony official, the magistrate told of searching the Weld farm and finding evidence of witchcraft. He brought forth an earthen jar covered in mysterious markings. Inside, he explained, was a bloody mixture of fluids that he presumed the witch used in her heathen rites.

Mrs. Colle, her voice as shrill as a crow's caw, accused Anne of further witchery. She told of seeing mysterious, flickering lights coming from the Weld's farmhouse after the death of Caleb Weld; she suggested that Anne was communing with the devil and using his disciples to do her farm work while everyone slept—for how else could one woman run a farm herself? Most damaging of all, she described the "Devil's Dog" that had come to live with the Welds shortly before Caleb's death, and of the beast's "evil eye," and how its "eye-biting" power had lamed their horse.

Anne shook her head in disbelief as the charges were made. When finally she was allowed to answer, she tried to speak calmly, though her fiery rage at her neighbor's lies made it impossible.

First, she denied any sexual thoughts of Mr. Colle, finding him repulsive in the extreme. Glaring at Mrs. Colle, she suggested that the cause of his perverse nightmares might lie closer to home. Of the vessel, she knew nothing, only that it was not hers, nor had she ever seen it before. The flickering lights were from the lone candle that she used to read a bedtime story to her daughter Katey before they both retired to an early bed, since Anne woke before sunrise to do her farming chores. Why a candle? She had to cut any expense she could, not wanting to use the more expensive lamp oil. She was able to keep up with the farm work because Caleb had been a masterful farmer who had left her with a well-planned and organized farm and some money that enabled her to hire out those few things for which she lacked the strength. Besides, the Porter family—her decent and kind *other* neighbors—had helped her many times.

And her gentle dog, Skye? They had found him as a pup, barely alive in their field. One brown eye and one blue? Why, probably a dozen barns in the area had a kitten with the same mix.

Her explanation was greeted by stony silence.

For a moment, Mrs. Colle looked as if she would speak more, but instead she whispered something to the colony official. He in turn whispered to the magistrate and then stood and said to Anne, "I find evidence enough to hold thee for further questioning. If thee be a witch, confess and repent now, for I can offer thee leniency only this once. Do you confess, Anne Weld, of practicing the dark arts of witchcraft?"

Anne's throat suddenly lacked moisture even to speak. A thousand thoughts raced through her mind—even that of confessing to this foolish charge, but she knew to do that might mean hanging. New England abided by the tenet: "Thou shall not suffer a witch to live." She was no witch! She was a God-fearing, honest woman who treated everyone kindly. Someone would come to her aid. And for the first time since her husband's death she thought in anger: *Caleb, why did you have to die. I need you so much . . . and I'm so afraid.*

She looked at her accusers and shook her head. She tried to look defiant, but her bravery deserted her. Helplessly, the tears flowed from her eyes.

"So be it," the official said. He turned to the magistrate and ordered: "Guard her well. Constrain her as you see fit, and be on the watch for animals that may be her familiars. I have sent for an inquisitor from Hartford. He is an expert in obtaining confessions and hath assisted in the witch trials of sixty-two and three."

They manacled one arm and attached the chain to a thick wooden support post, leaving a thin blanket to sleep on and a chamber pot within reach. Anne slept little. She awoke once with a start to find the oafish assistant reaching for her and cried out.

He grabbed her free hand and laughed. "I can do to thee what I will." His coarse features were distorted by lust, and she feared the worst as he began to paw awkwardly at her breasts.

She twisted uselessly, trapped by the manacle and his ironlike grip. Desperately, she said, "If you do not release me, I will turn thee into a toad!"

His eyes grew large and he backed away, almost tripping over his own cloddish feet in his haste. He left her alone the remainder of the night.

Not long after sunrise the same four—what? accusers, jury, judges?—entered and immediately began the proceedings. A fifth person, the Inquisitor, sat next to the colony official but initially took no part in the questioning.

Anne was allowed a few sips of water, which only served to heighten her desire for more. Her body ached from the manacle and the hard floor, and she felt filthy.

Mrs. Colle had been busy. Several of her friends testified against Anne, accusing her of all manner of witchcraft. Reverend Benham—never once looking directly at Anne—recalled how Mrs. Weld was inattentive and irreverent during church services. He judged that she was one with the devil, and one whose soul could never be saved.

The magistrate coaxed his dullish assistant to come forward, and in obvious superstitious fear, he testified that Anne had threatened to turn him into a toad.

At that point the Inquisitor spoke a few words to the colony official and then stood and said, "I have heard enough. I deem she is a witch and need be coerced into confession." Walking up to Anne, he asked her, "Do you still refuse to confess?"

The dark, almost black eyes of the Inquisitor held no hope of kindness. His pale skin was drawn so tightly over his bones that he looked like one who had just risen from his deathbed. Anne searched for something to say, anything that would make this come to an end, but all she could say was, "I am not a witch. Please let me go. I have harmed no one."

The Inquisitor ordered the magistrate: "Secure her to this post; someone bring me shears for cutting . . . and a razor and a pin."

The magistrate locked both her wrists in manacles, jerked her to her feet, and attached the shackles high onto the post so that Anne's arms were pulled tightly and uncomfortably above her head. Mrs. Colle returned with the requested items, unable to hide a sadistic smile.

"First, we will look for the devil's mark," said the Inquisitor. Then to Anne's horror, he began pulling her clothing from her body. She cried out and pleaded with him to stop, finally kicking out at him, trying to twist away from his hands. But he called the magistrate and his assistant to bind her legs and hold her while he removed the last of her clothing.

Now naked, utterly exposed to all in the room, Anne was subjected to humiliation after humiliation. They shaved off all of her hair including that on her private parts. The Inquisitor handled her body like a carcass on a hook as he explained to the room how the devil leaves his sign on his disciples. He scrutinized every inch of her, commenting at times: "One must be suspicious of even ordinary things." and "Here, this mole is probably her 'witches teat' from which she suckles her familiar." And finally, holding a breast roughly in his hand, he called them all forward to examine the sprinkle of light freckles along the top swelling of her breasts, saying, "Look upon this! The unholy number '6' hidden among the spots on her body."

The Inquisitor asked for the pin and began probing at her most delicate parts in search of what he described as "insensitive spots where the devil hath touched her."

Through it all, Anne tearfully pleaded for mercy, crying out for help that she knew now was not to be. The shame of her nakedness quickly diminished as her horror grew. It appeared once the needle started piercing her flesh. Her last thought as she slipped into unconsciousness was that nothing could get much worse.

She was wrong.

A sharp slap stirred her.

"Witch, will thee now confess?" came a voice ringing inside her head. Another stinging slap opened her eyes, and the voice had a head. "Will thee confess?" said the skeletal face of the Inquisitor.

Through parched lips she replied, "Rot in hell, you bastard!"

Dimly she heard the Inquisitor say to the magistrate, "See that she sleepeth not, and be cautious for trickery. I will question her further on the morrow."

The night passed in cycles of wakefulness and pain, followed by something other then sleep, more like a state of delirium in which she dreamed of home, and Caleb, and Katey. She knew not that the night had passed until she heard the harsh voice of the Inquisitor again asking her if she would confess.

The Inquisitor questioned her for hours. She no longer thought of her nakedness, only of her immense thirst, and the pain of her bloodied wrists where the manacles had cut deeply whenever her quivering legs had failed her.

Reality shifted and slid, fading at times to distant voices against a background of a constant hum of fatigue.

She tried to move her mind back to the refuge of her dreams.

But the Inquisitor wouldn't let her.

"Is this your beast?" he asked.

Anne heard a familiar whine, and she forced her eyes into focusing. "Skye!" she cried.

The magistrate's simpleton held a long pole with a rope attached that circled Skye's neck. In his other hand, a club.

The Inquisitor inspected the dog, and then turning to the others, said, "This dog clearly shows the mark of the devil with its strange eyes." He walked to the back of the room and pulled a small table over near the one window in the room.

Pulling a knife from his pocket, he said, "Kill the animal. I will have a look at its innards to search for further signs of the devil."

"No!" screamed Anne. "No, no, no ... no ..." her voice trailed off, and tears filled her eyes as the club fell. Skye whimpered once before the club struck again.

Anne's body convulsed with racking sobs, and she spewed forth what little remained in her stomach. Her mind shut down, blocking the sounds of the Inquisitor as he went about his grisly task.

"Will thee sign the confession?" came the familiar voice through the haze of her fatigue and pain ... and hopelessness.

Another night had passed in a timeless blur, marked only by her unremitting thirst, and the unceasing torment of the magistrate and his idiot. The oaf had lost his fear of Anne, seeing how truly powerless she really was, and increasingly had become bolder in his molestations. Anne had reached the point of no longer caring, wanting only to escape to the haven in her mind where Caleb and Katey waited.

And at times she succeeded.

But now the Inquisitor was reaching in and trying to pluck her out.

"Witch! We have your daughter here. We have Katey."

Her eyes snapped open. There, being held by the clawlike fingers of Mrs. Colle, was her darling Katey, her little waif . . . her reason for living. A whimper as mournful as Skye's last breath sounded in Anne's throat and grew in strength until it became a plea from her soul. "Please don't hurt my baby. Please, please . . . don't . . ."

Suddenly, the Inquisitor's face blotted out everything. He leaned in so close that for a second she feared his lips would touch her skin, and said, "Anne Weld, unless thee confess, and do it *now,* your daughter will be swum in the village pond to see if she, too, is a witch. If you will confess, I will allow the confession to state that thee imparted none of thy evil on thy child, and the child shall be set free. How answer thee? I must have thy answer."

She and Caleb had seen a woman "swum" in Hartford during the sixty-two outbreak. They tied her right thumb to her left big toe and left thumb to right big toe, and then threw her in the water. According to the Inquisitors, if the person floated, they were held up by the devil and thus a witch. The poor woman hadn't floated, but neither was she pulled from the pond before she drowned.

Anne tearfully looked upon her daughter for what she knew would be the last time. "I confess," she said. "I confess to being a witch."

Anne was released from the manacles and dressed in a coarse-weave shift. She was allowed to drink some water, but only enough to moisten her throat so that she might speak. Finally, she was given the paper to sign that contained her "confession" of witchcraft.

Later that day, Thomas and Alice Porter, her kindly neighbors, were allowed to visit. They told Anne how they had not been allowed to testify in her defense because "they had no evidence and thus lacked a reason to testify." Anne's heart near burst with joy when the Porters told her that the colonial officials had agreed to let them raise Katey. They promised Anne that Katey would know the truth about her mother, and that they would love her like their own.

Tom held Anne's face gently between his own rough,

farm-hewn hands and looked deeply into her eyes. "Anne,"
he said, "it may not be the right thing to tell you, and I wrestled madly with this, but you have a right to know why this
was done to you." He shook his head back and forth, as if
in disbelief himself in what he had to tell. "It was done for
greed . . . the Colles' greed. They hath laid claim to your
farm under the laws of ecclesiastical jurisprudence." Tom
shook his head again. "The judge and the accuser have the
right to the confiscated property of those condemned for
witchcraft."

The magistrate helped Anne walk the last paces from
the prison house to the gallows. She welcomed the end to
it all. English law forbade torture; and what they had
done to her, they reasoned as just. But they *had* tortured
her, body and soul, and now Anne struggled to walk the
final few feet.

Anne stopped in front of Mrs. Colle and whispered,
"Before they hang me, Eunice Colle, I am going to name
thee as a witch also, and swear it before God. I want thee
to suffer as I have."

Eunice laughed. "No one will believe you." She then
put her head close to Anne's and whispered back, "I *am*
a witch, but by accusing you, I further divert attention
away from myself. Now go die like a good girl." She
started to laugh again but stopped. Suddenly, she wanted
only for Anne to be dead, and soon! What if she had mis-
calculated and Anne succeeded in casting even a shadow
of suspicion? Her husband would break at the first question, much less any torture. A search of her farm would
reveal the cave of her coven, and the artifacts of her
witchcraft. More than once, a gallows confession had
caused tongues to wag and more necks to stretch.

Anne calmly took the final steps to the gallows.

Eunice's heart pounded in her chest. She sucked in
each breath, chanting as she exhaled, "Hang her. Hang
her. Hang her."

The colonial official opened a parchment and read:
"Anne Weld, having confessed to witchcraft and been

found guilty, under the rule of English Colonial law, you are sentenced to hang until dead. Have thee a final word?"

Anne looked down upon her townspeople. She looked at Eunice Colle and could see the fear writ upon her face. She *could* accuse her and maybe be believed, but that would only create more fear and hatred in the town. Katey would grow up here. Anne knew that she could not do it.

She said instead, "Naught, but I am innocent."

The magistrate tilted her head back and placed the rope around her neck. Anne now could see nothing but the azure sky, the deep blue reminding her of that day when Katie named Skye. She remembered what a joyous dog Skye had been from the first day they rescued him, as if he knew that every day was a gift. And then to die so cruelly. A sudden sadness squeezed her chest; and though all the cells in her body lacked even one drop of moisture, still, a single tear formed in her eye and trickled down her cheek.

The magistrate adjusted the rope and pulled it taut. Anne wondered if Katey knew about Skye. *Don't be too lonely, my darling. Oh, Katey, my beautiful, loving child, I'll miss you so!* And from somewhere within Anne's soul came another tear that gathered along her lower lid, until it, too, slid gently along the path of the first.

The magistrate made one final adjustment and stepped back. Anne's final thought was of Caleb. That big, wonderful man who taught her love and gave her pleasure, and shared her love of all living things. Suddenly, she knew. She saw with a clarity, a flash that lit the heavens, Caleb and she would soon be one! A final tear appeared. It sparkled in her eye . . . for just a moment.

"See! See! I knew she was a witch," cried Eunice Colle, hysterical in her relief that Anne was dead—and silent. "Three tears! Everyone knows that a witch can shed but three tears!" she screeched, conveniently forgetting about Anne's tears of pain as the needle had pierced her body; or Anne's tears of sorrow at the death of her loyal dog; and finally, as if they had never happened, ignoring the tears of heartbreak Anne had shed as she said good-bye to Katey for the last time.

Eunice started giggling uncontrollably.

The Reverend Mrs. Benham was one of several ladies who backed away from Mrs. Colle. What strange behavior, she thought! And that funny looking wart on the back of her neck; she'd never noticed *that* before. She wondered. . . .

THAT OLD BLACK MAGIC

by Deborah J. Wunder

"**G**od damn it! Turn that thing down!" Glenn's head poked through the open window, only to be met by laughter from the five boys sitting on the steps of his building. *It's more than a sane person can stand.*

"Whachoo gon' do 'bout it if we don', ol' man?" More laughter from below. He pulled his head back into his apartment. *A good question,* he acknowledged, shutting the window. *What can I do against five of them?* He shook his head. *And what in Hell did they mean, "old man?" I'm only in my forties.*

Glenn had lived in the Village for twenty years, although he had moved to Grove Street only five years ago. Then, he'd felt the shady residential street to be a haven from the noise of the jazz and folk music clubs as they converted to rock and roll, vying with each other for the crowds of tourists and NYU students roaming the streets on any nice evening. With the onset of spring, however, it seemed as if the noise had followed him. Rock and roll, rap, and all the myriad bastardizations thereof filled the quiet places—the cafes, the parks, the street corners. Everywhere radios blared out a cacophony that Glenn felt was designed to numb nervous systems. Cars with radios weighing as much as, if not more than, their motors roamed the Village, playing at top volume, regardless of the hour, driven by wild-looking kids—mostly male.

Glenn sighed to himself, then popped a Dave Brubeck disc into his CD player. He had broken down and gotten one, although he still thought of them as bourgeois toys, when he realized that if anything happened to his record collection, it would be impossible to replace. Over the last two years, he had worked hard at duplicating his collection on CDs, which he now browsed through with an almost sexual pleasure. He followed the Brubeck with Sinatra. *Even that progressive DJ, um, Scelsa, likes Sinatra. Plays him among the rock and roll every so often, too, just to let people know what a classic is. Bet those punks downstairs never heard* this *music up close.* He moved about the apartment, getting ready for company, the back of his mind turning over the problem the kids had posed.

His haven of peace had been destroyed by them. *Hell, I bet even a Christian saint would find this hard to bear!* He sighed as a particularly loud boom box passed below his window, drowning out both his stereo and the kids on the stoop. When it had moved out of hearing range, he reprogrammed his CD player and let the mellow voice of Sinatra at his prime wash over him.

I can see I'm gonna have to do something about this. I can't stand it anymore! He concentrated, then moved toward the window. He could hear cries of consternation, as the boys flipped their station selectors, trying to find a station that wasn't doing a Sinatra retrospective. He then stood back as rocks began to batter the wall next to his window. Cries of "Hey, man, wha'd you do?" "How'd you do that?" and "Fuck you, man. We gon' git'choo!" rose from the stoop. Glenn let the stations linger on the music he liked for fifteen minutes, while he gave his living room a few final touches. He knew he couldn't sustain the change for too long, or he would drain what little ability he'd been gifted with. Meanwhile, though, the sounds from the street were, finally, music to his ears.

Glenn had learned to tolerate a lot of the music from the sixties and seventies, although some of the art-rock stuff got a bit far out (and he could have lived without the advent of heavy metal), because two of his lovers had been musicians in bands that played "classic" rock. It had been pleasant to discover that a lot of the music they played and listened to had a good, solid jazz or blues basis. Some even bore traces of derivation from classical music. *But that damned rap garbage! If those kids want to ruin their hearing, that's their problem. Why should I have to be subjected to it? I bet they'd hate it if they were forced to listen to Cleo Laine or Ella Fitzgerald.* He sorted through his collection, planning a musical seduction, humming along with Sinatra, hoping his guest would share his preference for good pop vocals and show music.

Glenn answered the door on the second knock. He knew that it was Chris because the building's security required all visitors to be buzzed in by residents.

"Hi!"

"Hi, Glenn." Chris smiled shyly.

Glenn appraised his guest, his glance taking in every detail from Chris's sun-frosted hair to his Spanish leather boots. *He looks good enough to be dinner ... well, at least dessert.* "Glad you were free tonight. Come on in." He took Chris's jacket, and draped it over the chair in the foyer. He watched as Chris looked around the room—bentwood furniture with a light finish, framed theater memorabilia, softly diffuse lighting.

"Your apartment is gorgeous," Chris sank into one of the floor cushions near the coffee table, grimacing. "Would you have some aspirin?"

"Sure. Or ibuprofen or acetominophen. Which would you prefer?"

"Plain aspirin, thanks." Glenn disappeared into the kitchen, returning with a goblet of water and a small container.

"Chris, what's wrong?"

"Nothing major. Just a headache from running that gauntlet of boom boxes between here and the train."

"Why don't you go inside and lie down for a bit? I can whip up some food while you rest."

"Well, if you're sure you don't mind. . . ."

"Why would I mind? C'mon, the bedroom's this way." Chris rose and followed, as Glenn told him about his earlier run-in with the kids on the stoop. "I swear, Chris, one day I'm going to do something. I just need to figure out what. Now you get comfortable, and I'll wake you when the food is ready. Do you prefer fish or meat?"

"Fish, thanks."

"Sleep well, Chris." He dimmed the bedroom light as he left the room.

As the potatoes boiled, he scooped some mayonnaise into a bowl. As he mixed in spices, Glenn thought again about the boom boxes. *Maybe I can swing this a bit differently. What if . . .?* He stopped what he was doing, and tried to remember his physics classes. If he remembered correctly, and concentrated on the right frequencies, he might be able to affect the soundwaves across the transmittable spectrum. He turned the small kitchen radio to the classic rock station, turned the volume down, and concentrated for several minutes. *Damn! No change at all. There's got to be a way.* He went back to preparing the fish, letting his brain play with the notion as he basted the filets with mayonnaise dressing and prepared the oven. He placed the pan with the filets just under the largest flame his broiler was capable of, and drained the potatoes. He mashed them with a generous amount of milk and butter as the fish broiled. He tried various techniques—first, for focusing his consciousness; then for isolating the correct frequencies—and, by the time dinner was ready, the radio was playing the closing chords of "The Fairy Tale." Glenn set the dinner table, then went to wake Chris.

"Shee-it, it's that old man stuff again!" Marcus spun the dial through several stations.

"I do believe we are gonna have to teach that boy to stop messing with our music."

"Now, Junie, we don' . . ."

"Naw. We don' wan' hurt him, we just wan 'im to leave us 'lone."

"Hey! Check this out! Even that asshole talk show guy is talking about this Sinatra dude." He motioned for silence.

"Jeez, that's old."

"Nah, listen. One of his callers just claimed that this

Sinatra believes in Satan." The boys crowded around the radio, not noticing other groups of their friends doing the same thing.

"This is Bob Halloran, and I'm speaking with Frank from Piscataway, who believes that the great Frank Sinatra is a worshiper of Satan. Go ahead, Frank."

"Well, it should be obvious to anyone who's listening, Bob."

"What do you mean? Masked messages? Backwards lyrics?"

"Heck, no. I'm talking about right out in the open, where our kids can be seduced by it."

"Yeah. Like we'd listen to that crap." Junie mimicked the M.C. Hammer/"Feelings" commercial, followed by high fives and back pounding by his friends.

"Can you give us some examples, Frank?"

"Check this. He's baiting the guy."

"For starters, there's 'That Old Black Magic,' and 'I've Got You Under My Skin,' not to mention 'Witchcraft,' 'Devil May Care,' and 'Bewitched, Bothered and Bewildered.' And didn't he even try singing some of the rock garbage that those spawn of Satan British kids made popular?"

"Spawn of Satan British kids?"

"You know, Bob; the ones who said they were more popular than our dear Savior."

"I believe it's time to move on to our next caller, so thank you for sharing your opinion with us, Frank." Marcus shut the radio off.

"Do you suppose he's for real, man?"

"That nut?"

"Nope. The singer-man."

"You believe that crazy guy? Next thing, you be tellin' us yo' sistah's a virgin, when we all know better."

"Maybe we should check it out?" Junie was the one who had turned them on to house and hip-hop. It was also his radio, so he commanded a bit of respect from the gang.

"Check what out?"

"That music. You remember the names?" He turned to Marcus.

"Sumpin' about black magic, was one; and one about devils, I think. Hey, man, where you be goin'?"

"I'm gon' see if that call-in guy's right."

"Chris."

"Mmm." Chris stretched. Glenn's bed was comfortable, and his headache was gone.

"Dinner's almost ready."

"There in a moment." He stopped in the bathroom, and splashed some cool water on his face, then walked into the living room.

"Hi. Sleep well?"

"Yeah. I feel a lot better. What's the music?"

"An old Sinatra song, 'It's Magic.' Do you like Sinatra?"

"Well, I don't know all that much of his stuff, but I enjoy the ones I've heard." They moved toward the table. "Can I help with anything?"

"Everything's ready. You just relax and I'll serve." Soon they were eating, and carrying on a wide-range conversation.

"Hey, Ma! You still got those ol' records o' yours?'

"William Thompson, Junior, don't you 'hey, Ma' me." She shook her head. "What do you want my records for?"

"Some guy on the radio was talkin' 'bout this Sinatra dude, an' it sounded kinda interestin'. Figured if you still had yo' records, I could listen."

"You want to listen to my old Sinatra records? You're up to something, I can tell."

"Honest, Ma, I won't hurt 'em. I just want to see if what the radio guy said is right."

"Well, I guess you can't do too much harm to 'em at this stage. Okay. But you be careful with them, you hear?"

"I promise, Ma." He took the records from her carefully, and went to his room.

After dinner, the gang met on the front steps again. The

radio was still playing Sinatra, and Junie was blasting it as loud as if it was the latest rap single. The other four looked at him for a moment, then at each other. Finally, Marcus screwed up his nerve.

"What's up, man?"

"Marcus, you gotta hear this stuff."

"Why I gotta hear some old guy sing, Junie?"

"Because he good, man. And you gotta hear the band behind him—sounds kind of . . ." He searched for a moment. "Seamless, yeah, that's it. Seamless." He nodded, satisfied with his description.

"So?"

"So. So it the kind of stuff that ladies like."

Marcus grinned. "Old ladies, like our moms." He and Tony high-fived.

"No, chump. Ladies. Uptown ones."

"Hey, I don' wan' none o' that. You got to spend too much bread on 'em."

"Also, knowin' this stuff makes us different. I mean, we sing, right?"

"We do try, we sure do try."

"Well, maybe this give us some kind of edge." He shifted on the stoop.

"Edge?"

"Yeah. We could break out some of that stuff—maybe swing it upbeat a little; we'd sure sound good."

"What?"

"Hey guys, this stuff was made to be sung like we do."

Tony looked at him for a moment. "I guess we could try working up a piece or two."

Afterward, they cleared the table, and had coffee in the living room. *Soon,* Glenn thought, *we'll head into my room.* He said nothing, just enjoyed feeling Chris' body leaning against his as they watched *The MacNeil/Lehrer Report.* "Would you care to stay the night, Chris?"

"Yes." He smiled. "I'd love to."

"Do you need anything?"

"Just a towel."

"Let me know when you want to go to bed."

"Now seems about right."

"So it does." Glenn's heart was pounding as he and Chris entered the bedroom.

Ten months later, a black limousine pulled up at Glenn's Grove Street home. A uniformed chauffeur opened the rear passenger door, and five boys spilled out. They rang the bell marked "3R," and were buzzed in.

Glenn answered the door on the second knock, as usual.

"Hi! Glad you could make it."

"Hey, ol' man, we owe you big." They had moved beyond Sinatra, and were pretty much responsible for the current revival of forties and fifties music that was sweeping the country.

"I heard you boys are playing the Garden next week."

"Yeah. When you pulled that trick on us, you ever think we'd play it out?"

"No. I'd just wanted some peace and quiet."

"So where be your fee-ahn-say?" Junie dragged out the last word.

"Almost ready."

"You nervous?"

"A bit. Of course, I was pleased when you called and offered to sing as our handfasting present."

"No sweat, man." Marcus grinned and shook Glenn's hand. "You gave us our edge. Like Junie said, we owe you big. This make us even."

"Whatever. Excuse me a moment." He wandered off to find Chris and the priest, to let them know everything was ready.

Chris was in front of the mirror, still trying to fix his tie.

"Here, love, let me." He tied a perfect four-in-hand knot. "You look so good I almost can't wait for everyone to leave."

"Who was at the door?"

"The kids from the stoop. They weren't kidding about singing for us."

"Well, Glenn, if you hadn't gotten so fed up about the noise that night. . . ." His voice trailed off.

"I know, Chris. Still, I was lucky that things worked out so well for all concerned. After all, I hadn't thought about the consequences."

"Sometimes, my love, instinct is the only way to fly." He took Glenn's hand, and they went toward the living room, where by rite of handfasting, they would marry.

THE JOURNAL OF #3 HONEYSUCKLE LANE

by Leo Hernandez

The journal of Pennyfeather Sampson, witch, and Gypsy, wrinkle-dog familiar.

Wrinkle-Dog familiar *extraordinaire*, Gypsy says to add. Huff, puff. Anyway, I start a journal for every trip and every change of address, and this is the journal of our adventures at #3 Honeysuckle Lane. Here's how Gypsy and I look right now: I am 25, my hair is red (this week), I have a tan that goes three-quarters of the way up my arms because I drove 2,000 miles wearing a short-sleeved shirt, and I should be walking more. Gypsy is three, cream-colored, and plans on staying cream-colored. I am under orders to note that her tail is curly, her ears nice and round and folded over in a most fetching way, and her face wise. She threw up for one whole day of our epic five-day journey from the flatlands, which adds considerably to the charm of fetching ears, don't you think? I mentioned the throwing up in the journal for that trip, but I think I need to keep reminding myself of it so that I don't forget why Gypsy should not ride in trucks.

Things were slow in the flatlands, *hechiceras* are thick on the ground there, so I figured it couldn't hurt to see if all those people who said things like, "You're talented, but you need to be where the work is . . ." were right.

My arm didn't have to be twisted; I was tired of the brain-baking heat in the flatlands, so now Gypsy and I are living with hills on one side of us, and water on the other, and cool weather in between.

* * *

February

In the new place. It is a curly little Victorian cottage that hunches shoulder-to-shoulder with other curly little Victorian cottages. There is a miniscule front lawn I could cut in about ten minutes with a pair of safety scissors. The backyard is plum trees and lilies. It's shady and has a good wet smell to it. There is a scraggly scrap of "yard" that runs along the south side of the house, and there is a little workshop window (which is wobbly in its frame) that looks out on it. Some view. Gypsy wants me to plant tomatoes there, but it's hard to get to. Maybe in the backyard. . . .

My neighbors are coffee merchants and dressmakers and people who work in the city and witches. Mostly witches. The woman who lives next to me (on the scrap side of the house) is a witch named Cribble. She dispenses utility spells and raises tailless cats. She also dispenses gossip; she gave me most of it as she hung over our backyard fence and smoked a green-banded cigarette. I now have the dirt on all of the people who live on Honeysuckle Lane. (Not that I wanted it.) Gypsy doesn't like "the Cribble" (that's what she calls her). She says the Cribble has ". . . chicken legs, and that is not meant to be a description to make your mouth water." She also says people who gossip are hiding something.

Gypsy asks me to note here that she really likes the coffee merchant. She (the coffee merchant) likes dogs, so she gives away chewies to them.

Busy. (No time to plant tomatoes! I buy them at the produce stand.) My handwork has never looked better. My charms have been selling well. A few people have called at the house, to have curses removed. Even though coming into my house turns almost all of them (when this happens, I've only charged for confirming that the curse is lifted), I still have to report them to Inspector Saiko in the Mystification (strange name) division of the police department. It's tedious, but I'd much rather have the tedium than have a witch selling nasties. Those sort give the rest of us a bad name, and, personally, they piss me off. I think dispensing curses is Real Work for Real Shitheads.

March

The Cribble mows lawns. Ours, and several other people's. She does this without being asked. I guess I don't care, at least it saves me the work. Strange, but harmless.

An agent (Mr. Merrriman) offered me a contract to make charms and do blessings for businesses in the city. (He says the couple who used to do the work for him were sloppy and slow.) Interesting work. I am supposed to call on him in the city in May.

Hair is black. Makes me look like a cadaver. Changing it back to red.

Rumors going around about where some of the curses I took off are coming from, but nothing worth writing down here.

April

The Cribble is still mowing our lawn. I found out from the baker that the Cribble has been doing this since before we moved here. Gypsy says she's a control freak and a "neat nut," but there's a slob in her dying to get out. Where does Gypsy get these ideas?

Got spit on by a kid at a party.

And, except for that, it was a great party. Lots of iced coffee, amusing conversation. We stood in the kitchen with the lights off and watched the sun go down: the sky went from hazy gold to pink to navy. Gorgeous.

I was standing under a second-floor balcony talking to this nice warlock named Rosas, and I was getting around to asking him out when I noticed a dripping in front of me. I stepped out to see if the ceiling was leaking and got a big gob of spit right in my hair. I usually have a sixth sense about these things. I mean, normally I would have seen something like this was about to happen and avoided it. The kid grinned over the balcony at me.

"Let's trade places!" I scowled at him. The little punk disappeared and took his goofy grin with him.

It's hard to ask for a date when you're wiping spit out of your hair. Rosas didn't seem mind. He said yes.

Went to dinner with Rosas. The rest of the evening is not for this journal. Heh.

Work has slowed down. Have had a cold for a week. I'm all snuffly, so I sound a lot like Gypsy now, which she likes.

May

The Cribble Update:

She's still mowing the lawn. She smokes while she does it. It makes her look like the Little Engine That Could.

We avoid her, though, and she seems to be avoiding us.

Obviously, the Cribble cares too much about how other folks keep their houses. Gypsy thinks that if someone took the Cribble's push mower away, she'd be squatting on her roof, picking off the baker's customers. I'm not going to let Gypsy watch any more TV news. It bothers me, too, but I don't think the Cribble is one yard away from violent insanity. I *am* beginning to think she is deeply, deeply weird.

Found out Mr. Merriman gave the work he promised me to the two witches he said he fired.

I found this out because I went and visited him at his office on the day he said to visit. I met this witch and warlock who were leaving as I was going in. Gypsy wants me to add in *her* impressions of them, since I don't want to put in *my* impressions of them.

Gypsy: "*He* is skinny and soft-looking. Smells unhappy. His familiar rides on his shoulder, so no matter where you're standing its behind is pointed at you. *She* is very, very short and smells as ugly as she looks. I want to ask her if she's had any billgoats on her bridge lately, but Pennyfeather won't let me."

Isn't Gypsy sweet?

The warlock's cat was riding butt-first, just like Gypsy described, and when he saw me he started tugging on it to get it to turn around. It responded by digging in with all four feet and yowling. I nodded politely and bit my tongue hard, so I wouldn't smile. Gypsy turned her back and laughed. Bad dog.

The witch pounced. "Are you looking for work with Mr. Merriman?" she asked.

I didn't like the way she asked, so I decided to fib. "Just a social call."

The warlock stopped fighting with his cat. "Well, I bet there's plenty of work if you're looking for it," he said helpfully.

"We just got a contract to do a lot of buildings," the witch broke in. "Entry charms, blessings, stuff like that."

Gypsy stopped laughing when she heard that. My tongue froze between my teeth. "How nice for you," I lisped. "Pardon me." Gypsy and I pushed past them. I looked over my shoulder as we continued up the hill. The warlock's cat had turned and was presenting his bottom again.

I found out when I got to Merriman's office that he had given the work to the two witches I met. They were the ones he said he wouldn't hire again. He explained, in this annoyingly apologetic way, that he *had* to give the work to these two witches because he sort of owed them, and he hadn't really meant he was giving me the work, and he was sorry I misunderstood.

"He shouldn't lie," Gypsy said. "He doesn't have a flair for it."

"Duh," I answered.

Mr. Merriman looked at us nervously because all he heard was Gypsy wuffing and me saying "Duh."

"You're not going to put a curse on me or anything?" he asked, and laughed a nervous "huh-huh-huh" kind of laugh. Gypsy and I treated him to a withering glare, said good-bye quickly, and left.

"We didn't want to work for him, anyway," I told her. "You can tell he doesn't know anything, and he's suffering from brutal cranio-facial disease. I can see why he's got curses on his mind. That witch looked like a curse, didn't she?" Gypsy laughed and said I was pretty nice, considering.

Work is realllllllly slooooooow. Using the time to learn some new handwork techniques and study.

Rosas hasn't called for weeks, and he's not returning my calls. Phooey on him, then.

June

Work is slow, slowslowslowslow again. I've been feeling too tired to even think lately, and my spells seem off. Maybe it's just me, but it looks like Gypsy's coat is falling out. My clothes look shabby. Nobody around here is talking to us much anymore. I don't understand why. I hope moving here wasn't a mistake, after all.

The Cribble Update:
Still mowing the lawn. I drew some black-eyed Susans on the front walk, so I can feel like I have some control over what's in front of the house.

Work has picked up a little.

Rained a few days ago, and washed away the drawing I made. It's not the rainy season, and it only seemed to rain on this block. Something's wrong.

I'm still feeling tired, and a little blue (make that a *lot* blue, positively *indigo*), so Gypsy is in the kitchen making me a special lunch to cheer me up. She's opening a can of tuna. I have no idea how she does this because I've never watched her do it, because I promised I never would, so I don't—

Back. Gypsy and I are heroes. We should get purple hearts, or something, we look like we've been in a fight:

I have stitches in my right forefinger and a bruise on my forehead, Gypsy has a bandage on her paw, and her coat is patchy. (I was right. Her hair *was* falling out!)

All the witches on Honeysuckle have been fussing over us both. They brought us lots of food and presents. One of them fixed my finger, which had a nasty cut on it. I am in a happy, chocolate- and cordial-induced stupor. Gypsy is lounging on a pillow, and receiving visitors as if she were a queen. If someone rubs her round ears one more time, they might fall off, if her whole head doesn't fall off first from the swelling.

The Cribble won't be our next-door neighbor anymore; she was hauled off by the police hours ago on felony charges of being a haggish TOAD. Okay, okay, so there's no such charge. (But there should be!) Gypsy says I need to back up and explain what happened after I stopped before. I was basking in the moment, I told her, but here's what happened:

(cue portentous music)

Gypsy howled from the kitchen, and it sounded like someone was tenderly twisting off her hind leg. I ran out to see what was wrong with her. She was bleeding copiously from her right front paw. There was a can of tuna on the floor next to her: it was half-open, and the edge of the lid was a ridge of nasty-looking triangles. She'd tried using the juice can opener to open the tuna.

"Why this one?" I asked her.

"I couldn't find the right one." She looked sheepish. "I'm not cut too bad, but I better go run water on my paw."

I picked up the tuna and the opener. "I'll finish this, then." Now, if I didn't know what I know now, I would have still been wondering why I didn't at least finish opening the can before I tried to drain the tuna, or why I bother to begin with. I got a fork and pushed back the lid on the can, but I didn't take it the rest of the way off and was using it to squeeze the water out of the tuna. The fork snapped suddenly, my hand slipped, and the lid bit into my finger in two places. It hurt like shit. I yelled and dropped the tuna and what was left of the fork and grabbed my hand while I bent over the kitchen sink. I bent too fast, though, and banged my head on the edge of the sink, which hurt like shit, too. (music goes waan waaan waaan waaaaaan) I felt like the fourth Stooge.

Gypsy shot out of the bathroom. Well, she shot out as fast as a four-legger shoots with a limp. She leaned against the back of my legs while I ran water over *my* cut. It wouldn't stop bleeding. Neither would Gypsy's. Her cream-colored paw was red.

"I think you need a healing on that, Gypsy."

"Nonsense," she answered. " 'Tis but a flesh wound. Did you manage to save the tuna?" Then she passed out as cold as a fish-market mackerel.

I wrapped our cuts and staggered up the street, carrying Gypsy the Dead Weight, to the closest witch (besides the Cribble, that is) to get patched up.

I never had a dog before I had Gypsy. I always had cats. I liked carrying cats; they were floppy and light, like bags of silk. Gypsy was no bag of silk. She was a bag of lead bricks.

Lucky for my back, she woke up after half a block, and could walk again. Not so luckily, the witch wasn't home. We kept going. The next one wasn't home, either. Or the next. The baker was still in his shop. He saw Gypsy and me, and taking pity on us, put us in his auto, and drove us to the vet. Gypsy protested the whole way; she had always seen witches when she needed help, she wasn't just any dog. We found out that the Honeysuckle witches (including the Cribble) had all gone on a picnic. Without us. Gypsy tried not to look hurt.

The vet's assistants made a big to-do over "poor widdle Gypsy," feeding her cookies and playing with the wrinkles on her head, which Gypsy (of course) liked. The vet turned out to be a nice woman named O'Brien. She raised an eyebrow at being brought a familiar, but she sewed up Gypsy's paw with dispatch, and gave us a shampoo for Gypsy's coat. Gypsy worships her now. (Gypsy says: "Do not. I just respect a pro.")

With Gypsy back together, I felt like I could handle my

own healing if I had to. "Let's go," I said, heaving her bulk off the vet's table. "Wub!" she answered.

"Quit kidding around, Gypsy," I said.

"Wub. Weeeerf!"

I felt a little squeeze of panic. (cue violins: long whiny hmhmmmmmm note) I grabbed Gypsy's ears and stared into her eyes. She looked scared.

"So what is Gypsy telling you?" O'Brien asked.

"Wub, werf," I said. "Which means, 'You're a goddess.' Excuse us."

(portentous music continues)

Gypsy and I rode back home with the baker (who had been nice enough to wait). We huddled close.

"I know it's kind of obvious *now*, Gypsy, but we've been cursed. We need help."

Gypsy started barking wildly. "Do you think it was the Cribble, Lassie?" Gypsy started to foam. The baker was cringing.

None of the witches were home from their picnic yet, dammit. I decided to call Inspector Saiko, even though I wasn't sure it would do any good. I thanked the baker as he pulled up to our house, promised a charm in return for the ride (even though I wasn't sure I could still make one), and apologized for the cream-colored hair all over the inside of the car. Gypsy flung herself out of the auto and barfed explosively. I guess cars are out for her, too.

We ran up the stairs two at a time. Every tread we landed on cracked in half with a sound like a gunshot. (music: the whole orchestra goes Whomp! Whomp! Whomp! with cymbal crashes as the stairs break) We made the porch—and discovered we couldn't get in. The locking charms wouldn't answer us. I started to swear, hopping around in frustration. I was going to have to break into our own house.

We walked around to the back, we didn't want any passersby who didn't know us to see us. Hell, I didn't want anyone we *did* know to see us acting as our own second-story men.

None of the windows would budge, and I didn't have a knife to try and jam into the back door. I remembered that little window that looked out on the scrap had never been fixed, and was probably weak enough to smash, if I had to.

(more whiny, nerve-grinding violins)

Gypsy and I walked around to the scrap. It was weedy and it smelled awful. Gypsy growled and squeezed past me. She zigzagged through the weeds, pointing and barking. She stopped at a spot in front of the window and started to scrape at it with her back paws, making an awful racket.

(music begins to crescendo)

I pushed her out of the way to see what she was carrying on about.

Under the weeds was a pile of chicken bones. (reet) I looked at the other spots she'd stopped at and found more chicken bones.

Foul-smelling chicken bones. (reet)

And cigarette butts. (reet)

Green-banded cigarette butts. (reet reet)

With lipstick marks on them, in the color the Cribble wore. (reet reet reet reet)

(music reaches crashing climax)

I was pissed. White-hot PISSED. I forgot about opening the window, and started flinging bones and cigarette butts over the fence, screaming words I'd rather not admit I said. The bones felt particularly nasty. As I went for the big pile, Gypsy said, "Stop!"

I didn't notice that I could hear her say something besides "werf." I kept on tossing the bones, so she butted me, and knocked me down.

"Stop it!" she said urgently. "Don't touch any more of them. They're leftovers from curses the Cribble has made." I crabbed backward out of the space, breathing hard.

"Jesu," I panted. "Now what?"

"We can probably get back in the house. Let's call the police."

The house did let us in. I was starting to feel pretty good, better than I had in a long time.

"I feel good. Great in fact. How about you?" I asked Gypsy.

"Me, too. I feel really great. Kind of invincible!"

Most of the Cribble's curses were relatively small stuff; zits, clumsiness, body odor. A few of them were not so small: accidents, money loss. And the toad threw the waste from making them in my and Gypsy's backyard, with the obvious results.

There's no such thing as felony Waste of Protein or felony Useless Sell-Out Hag (or felony Wrinkle-Dog Endangerment, adds Gypsy), so the police had to arrest the Cribble for plain old felony witchcraft. As Inspector Saiko said in the paper: "Normally, she would have only been charged for a host of misdemeanors, however, the effect of disposing of contaminated evidence in (Ms. Sampson's) yard added up to a felony." The Honeysuckle witches offered to help remove whatever residual problems the Cribble's spells caused.

Gypsy (smugly): "I told you she was hiding something."

I raised a cordial to her. "So you did (I grinned wickedly), Baldy."

July

Busy again. Not much time for journal-keeping, so here are the high points:

Having to turn work down. Rosas called. (hubba, hubba) The Hag's swarm of tailless cats were all adopted. Her house was fumigated and put up for sale. A nice french horn player bought it. I hear the round, warm notes of his music rolling up the street in the evenings.

I planted some tomatoes in the scrap. I know it's late in the year, but I thought I'd try anyway, for Baldy ... I mean Gypsy.

WOODEN CHARACTERS

by Roland J. Green

It was hot, and in that year the sewers had not reached Twomford. The streets stank the afternoon Olivia Dzun visited me.

Her blued hair and olive skin did not surprise me. Most witches take much custom from artists of one sort or another. Artists do not often go to the temples, to babble of their sins to priests.

So I had known the painter who did Olivia's best-known poster, the one of her as the Dancing Queen in *Marplots of the Margrave*. He said she was as handsome a woman offstage as on, but in quite different ways.

Her being at my door at all was a surprise. Actresses like her can have more potent witches running to their doors. This is not only because we are all fighting for what little trade is left for a proper witch, either. It is because seeing where and how our patron lives may give us useful ideas. Sometimes it is the idea of not taking the work, or even going to the police (more tolerant than priests, by and large).

But Olivia Dzun came to me that summer afternoon. When I saw her at the door, my first thought was to sneak a look into the street. If she had come by hired carriage or even hansom cab, the neighbors would know and my reputation would shine brighter.

Even witches cannot easily sneak, if they know no spells to silence rusty hinges. The shutter's hinges screamed like a marshsoul and Olivia Dzun glared. Her face was as potent as certain lesser spells for paralyzing the limbs and tongue and slowing the breath and heartbeat.

"I left the cab at Mason's Square and walked," she said. "I feed no one's custom before they prove they deserve it."

That was the way our conversation began and continued. She seemed to know the folly of needlessly keeping secrets from a witch when you seek her services, but somehow always made the truth bite. I understood then why her art was so highly praised. No one with a tongue like hers would have risen high with less.

"My lady," I said at last.

"You know quite well that I have no right to that title. The Chancellor and I were not even handfasted."

"The courtesy—"

"Courtesy and three mugs of beer will give you a full chamberpot," she said. "Pray speak plainly."

"Mistress Olivia," I said, gripping both my needlework and my temper, lest I thrust the needle into my visitor. "Both of us need to speak plainly. You have come some distance on a day unpleasing for traveling. I trust it is for some other cause than to prove the sharpness of your tongue."

At that she actually smiled, the smile of a wolf who had just sighted a particularly succulent lamb. "I was prudent enough to dress rather lightly under this respectable gown," she said. "No doubt that would add to the scandal if I were run down by a butcher's dray returning to my taxi, but *I* have more than needlework to fill my days."

That stung, as a reminder of how long it had been since I had been offered an honorable piece of witchwork. Or for that matter, *any* kind. It did not sting me to crawling.

"I could doubtless conjure up an illusion of corset and petticoats that would endure until you were in the cab," I said. "But am I right in judging that you had something more important in mind?

"I wish you to shame Roald Symban."

No witch these days can avoid reading the brassbit papers. From them, I that knew Symban was Olivia's lover: within my mind I uttered mild spells of aversion. Lovers' quarrels have both enriched and ended witches.

The price she offered promised enrichment, or at least

money to keep me in Twomford long enough to find enough honest patrons to keep me at my work until I reached thirty. A prudent witch will put aside the vials and spells then, and wed some man of broad tolerance or at least limited curiousity. Otherwise she must use illusion spells for the Great Rite, and can less easily pass as a young widow, to allay suspicion or raise sympathy.

"Shame him as a man or as an actor?"

"The two are not separated, with him."

"Something that made him give a wretched performance, for example?" I could cast at least three spells for that, skyclad and without warning.

Olivia's mouth went slack for a moment, as if in some unwholesome ecstasy. Then she said—almost sighed, indeed, "Oh, yes. In two days, the Procurator of the Royal Lands will be in the audience. If Roald ruins that night's performance of *The Climbers*—oh, yes."

I needed no more. Roald Symban was a considerable figure on the provincial theater circuit, but had yet to play a command performance in the Royal City. The theater-mad could bring that about, or make it certain that no theater in the Royal City would let Symban tread its boards.

"Why?"

"Why what?"

"What is your grievance against him?"

"What cause have you to know this?"

"The cause of any crafter who wishes to do her best work for one who pays her." I seethed within; of all times to abandon frankness for mystification!

She pondered long enough, that I was driven to pressing her, something I have found it wiser to avoid.

"Some spells can slay if misused. Is your grievance against him great enough to risk that fate for him, and for yourself the fate meted out for procuring death by witch-craft?"

"You would perish with me."

"A companion in the chamber does not ease the pain or silence your screams."

"You speak as if from experience."

"Only from that of friends, let the All be praised."

"Very well. I do not wish him slain even by chance. But he must be made to give the most abominable performance of his career. One that will keep him from the Royal City for years."

I could tell she wished to be silent. I wished otherwise. I plied my needle in a pattern I have known to subtly loosen tongues.

"If he goes to the Royal City, I will not go with him. That foolish chit Valetha will share his bed there, until he tires of her."

"Would not a spell on Valetha do as well?"

Anger crackled in Olivia's voice as she shook her head. "It was not her fault. A taste of Roald—no woman can be blamed for wanting a full banquet."

"But would not her misfortune distract—?"

"If she fell dead at his feet, he would step over her corpse, while searching the audience for his next woman."

Roald Symban was beginning to seem the sort of man whose discomfort would be a service to all women. I kept my face a mask, however. Overeagerness leads to underpayment.

We spent long enough bargaining that I offered tea. Ice was too dear this summer for my purse, but Olivia drank her steaming cup eagerly. I thought of adding silencing powder, but that is even dearer than ice. I would have to trust her discretion, and she mine.

We agreed to establish a place where we might safely leave messages. I wished it to be within the theater. She wished it at the company's hotel. We agreed on using both, which accomplished my intent: her permission to visit the theater before the night of the play.

Lovers' quarrels hold enough perils for an honest witch. She who leaps into one without studying the ground beforehand should have her wand broken over her head, or be well birched with it!

The next day I visited the theater.

The Excellency lay in a good quarter of Razhton, the next town toward the Royal City on the Great Northwest

Line. I took the train myself, although it meant a long walk from the station. Cabs not only cost silver, they have drivers who can remember whom they carried.

It did not help that it began to rain on the way from the station, so I reached a deserted theater drenched nearly to the skin. A raddled and sodden woman is even more memorable than a kempt and dry one, however, so I did not miss an audience.

I quickly rejected any spell involving fire, either in casting it or in its effects. The Excellency must have been built when a theater and a temple could not share the same quarter. As little as an overturned candle could have started a blaze ending in scores dead from burns, smoke, or trampling. I noted that the place had been fitted with gas lights, and thought of offering for honest work in spell-testing the joints of the gas pipes.

That would mean revealing both my craft and my face to an engineer, however. Engineers are no more discreet than most, and less willing to believe that a witch can do anything worth paying for.

I resolved to pass myself off as a woman searching for work in the wardrobe room. My skill with a needle will pass muster, without the aid of spells that anyone but another witch can detect.

So I went down to the dressing rooms and tried to look at one and the same time confident, needy, and skilled. I still think that took acting almost the equal of any in the company's.

It seemed a stroke of fortune that the first person to wander by and be deceived was Roald Syndam himself.

"What ho, ma'am?" he said. His jocularity seemed as much part of him as his teeth. I saw that it was not reserved for the stage. "Do you need directions or assistance?"

"Directions, if you can give them, to find who hires workers for the wardrobe. I trust that you have costumes in need of a good hand with a needle?"

Syndam smiled. "I can hire. But we have had two days since the last play closed. Our own needles have been busy, and there may not be—"

At that point I interrupted him by bursting into tears. Nor was it entirely acting; Syndam was smoking a cigar that could have quelled mutiny in a hussar regiment, had they breathed the smoke. My eyes ran, and if I had been wearing stays I would surely have fainted.

"Come, ma'am. So fine a woman should not be abroad on a day like this. Look at your gown."

I had, before leaving home. It would pass as a respectable woman's when dry. The rain had made me look like a woman of scant means or scant virtue, perhaps both.

"Forgive me, Mr. Syndam. We get along well enough, most days. But my husband has been away at sea so long, and now the baby is sick from the heat. The doctors ask so much to treat a flux and can do so little. . . ." I started crying again. This time I had to act; he had stubbed out his cigar.

"Well, I think I would be ten kinds of fool if I couldn't find a way to help you," Syndam said. His voice was gentle, confiding, even wooing. His arm across the small of my back was gentle, too, but likewise firm in urging me toward his dressing room.

The door had closed behind us before I saw what lay on the table beside the mirror. Nobody heard my pigsqueal of alarm, or if they did they doubtless guessed Syndam was "at his work," like the tinker in the song.

"That's—?" I said, or rather, stammered, as I pointed.

"Oh, you mean that," he said, picking up the antique short sword. "Well, we are doing *The Climbers* in classical costume, so I thought we should be armed accordingly."

"How long have you had it?"

"You seem very curious about our properties, ma'am," he said, then smiled. "Do you repair those as well as costumes?"

"No. I just—I never thought to see actors using a replica of the Sword of Wunscharf."

If you know nothing of magic, that name will mean little. To a witch, who must know the Eight Perils by heart, it is a name to conjure with—or rather, *not* conjure with. The Sword of Wunscharf is one of the Perils that turns back any spell cast on the wearer against the spell's caster. It has been said that it will even strengthen the spell on its return journey, if it was cast with evil intent.

"It was my grandfather's. He was the first actor in our family, but where he found it, I have no idea." Syndam flourished it so that I feared for the gas fixtures. He saw my unease, and put an arm around my shoulders.

"It's just brass, under a thin washing of silver. We have to touch it up with paint every time we use it, or it would disgrace a company of street players. I suppose I really keep it as a good-luck charm."

He handed it to me. The weight was about right for what he had described, much too light for a real sword ten centuries old. I still sensed that it had once been in the presence of magic, even if it had none itself.

As I held the sword, I also sensed Syndam behind me. Then his lips were on my neck, and his arms around my waist—or to be precise, a little higher.

"Come, ma'am. There is no need to worry about going back to the baby without something for the doctor. There's more need to worry about being sick yourself, if you don't climb out of this sodden rag and get warm."

In that stuffy dressing room, after the surprise of seeing the Sword, I was already warm enough. But clearly his rituals were as important to him as mine to me, even if aimed differently.

Much practice had made him deft at undoing women's clothes. I was swiftly out of the gown, glad I had brought nothing of my craft except what was sewn into the concealed pouches in its lining. Then I was out of more, and asked the All that Olivia or Valetha not wander by.

The spell I chose was that of the Living Statue. The name exaggerates. The worst it usually does is stiffen the joints so that the victim can only move like an aged rheumatic.

The Climbers involves much agile prancing about. Being unable to do it would make Syndam look foolish and fumbling in front of highly-placed witnesses without endangering him or anyone else.

I did not feel as ready to avenge his bedmates as I had before. One part of Roald Syndam's anatomy needed no stiffening!

I did not risk staying the night. But I contrived to do some of the work I had asked for. While mending the lining of the cloak Syndam would wear in the play, I sprinkled some sawdust from one of my pouches inside it. Rock dust or iron filings would have made the spell even more potent, but this was sawdust of keelwood, heavy and dense.

With the sawdust in the cloak lining, I would need no wand, braziers, or chanting to cast the spell. I did need to be in the theater, and that meant not only a ticket but a disguise. A ticket was easily obtained from Syndam, for the appropriate price.

A disguise was something I would have to provide myself. Asking him not only meant paying yet another price, but making him curious. Syndam's wits might not be as stout as his loins, but he was far from a fool.

In the end, I came to the theater in the garb of a yet-unsworn temple maid. They have some freedom in their garb, as long as the hood conceals the hair and the lower part of the face and the gown is long and full.

Temple maids were not common in the first-rank seats; I drew some curious looks. I could not do without the superior view from those seats, however.

None of the looks were from Syndam, when he came on. In truth, he had no mind for anything else when he was performing, just as he devoted himself wholly to pleasure in a shared bed.

The cloak danced and whipped about him so that I feared for the seams. I also feared the continued absence of the Procurator, but royal officials of his rank are seldom slaves of the clock.

This was no exception. It was ten minutes into the second act before he entered his box. I thought I could see more sweat on Syndam's face than the heat of the lights allowed. I know he would have seen more on mine than he did while we amused ourselves.

I clasped my hands over the buckle of my belt (simple

pewter, but with a vial of a certain powder built into it)
and arrayed my thoughts. Then I did the same with my
breathing, and finally my throat, so that I could form the
words of the spell without sound or movement.

> "Fix his joints, fix his bones.
> May they become like unto stones.
> Gather, hardness, gather madness,
> until he knows in stiffness, sadness—"

I continued, until in the space between one breath and
the next I felt the belt buckle grow hot. It was not spirit-
heat, either. I smelled fabric scorching.

I clawed at the buckle, and felt more than heat. It was
like touching an earth-powered wire. Magic was working
here, not all of it mine.

That was the last conclusion I reached with a clear
mind. The next moment, something flew from out the hilt
of the replica Sword of Wunscharf. It flew so high and so
violently that it struck the ceiling forty feet up and
brought down plaster.

Nobody in my rank of seats cared about plaster. Half
were scrambling to get away. The rest stared alternately
at the sword hilt, now pouring out green light, and at me.

I did not know why they were staring at me, until I
tried to rise. My legs began by obeying, then swiftly re-
belled. I sank to my knees, then held up my hands, to see
if they told me anything.

I saw that my palms were scorched pine, my fingernails some other wood, naturally dark (ebony, perhaps).
As I watched, my hands stiffened into the position of supplication. I could not move them. Then it was the fore-
arms and elbows, the upper arms and shoulders—

I suppose I should be grateful that the return of the spell
of the Living Statue was so powerful that I lost my voice,
before I could scream and call attention to myself.

My mind lives on inside the wooden remainder of me.
I suffer no hunger, thirst, or any sort of physical need.

But I can hear well enough and see dimly. I have heard and seen enough to know how I came by my fate.

Syndam indeed wore a replica of the Sword of Wunscharf, but a piece of the soulstone that was the source of the real one's power was encased in its hilt. When I began my spell-casting, a lead plug older than our reigning House blew out. The soulstone did its work as the legends of the Eight Perils foretold.

I had sought to turn Syndam's joints as stiff as wood. The spell returned upon me so powerfully that I turned into a wooden image.

It would have taken more than that to deceive Roald Syndam (Chevalier Roald, now). He recognized me, fell on his knees, embraced me, and praised in his most eloquent manner my dauntless courage, in taking on myself a spell meant for him. He would make an annual offering to any temple that took me in and prayed over me every day, that I might return to life.

The temples were eager. (After all, Roald Syndam had the Procurator's ear.) I have been kept close, within the library of the Temple da Morcan. For three years, no honest witch has been within furlongs of me.

If I ever do become flesh again, I will *be* a temple maid. I have been so fervently prayed over for so long that there is no witchcraft left in me!

THE WITCHES OF DELIGHT

by Kathe Koja and Barry N. Malzberg

THE QUEEN OF THE DEAD: In the recurring dream, assaulting him now with speed and force the sheer imminence of which made him gasp, he was present on something called the Storm Planet, a place of brown earth and strange devices, drooping foliage, sullen gardens, the cries of animals in the distance and he, Thompson, was pinned in the mud, shoulders to the ground, groaning in that dense, wet, lush entrapment. The dreams were palpable: he lay planted in the earth until she came upon him, dressed in rags and patches of the finest black, the glittering surfaces refracting the enormous dark from which she came, emergent as some new light, focusing upon him and "I," she said, "*I* am the Queen of the Storm Planet, I am the Queen of the Covenant." Her witch's face, her witch's hands reached toward him, entrapped, in thrall and he could feel those hands, cold and clamping touch upon him, on his body, on his flesh.

"*Here,*" she said, "here is that which you have always wanted and in this tossed and demented place, the place they sent the dead animals and dying children from all the planets of the commonwealth, all the living worlds." It was as if Thompson could feel himself closing upon her, as if it was not only his destiny but all of history which subsumed him. "I am the Queen of the Covenant," she said again, above him, atop him, straddling him with those long, long legs, long white thighs beneath the black. "*I* am that darkness you desire," and somehow he was freed then but freed only to turn halfway in the mud, arms reaching, half-erect and suspended in that posture of supplication and with her strange, dawning smile, the touch of disaster and history at the edges of that smile and the smooth, passionless lust which took and took and would never quit and—

It was at this point, always this point that Thompson was pulled from sleep, yanked to terrible awareness and attention in this bed, poised and seemly bed with coverlets, sheets, pillowcases, and wife, the bed in which he had lain like a ghost for all of these years, a ghost seeking substance and yanked again and again to this consciousness which was like a blow ... but now, expelled from the dream, from the Storm Planet and its covenanted Queen the bed was something encountered each time as if from the beginning, its warmth no comfort, the implacable posture of his wife—her bare back, her round pudgy shoulders angled away from him as if to underscore the difference between real life and *his* life, between storm internal and Storm Planet, between her own warm indifferent contours and those long white thighs of dream and that voice again, his memory: "I am the Queen of the Covenant." Basking in his own reluctant fire, the building heat. "And now you know," she had said, would say again. "And now you know." But this was not so; torn from the dream Thompson felt again and again that he knew *nothing,* that all the tablelands of his life had only been dumb and measureless terrain possessing meaning only insofar as they had taken him to this fundamental and disastrous state of incomprehension: bellied-up cattle on the conveyor belt, through the slaughterhouse to dismemberment.

He met her in a gallery, white walls, black and white photographs: FACES OF DESIRE, some sullen model with her tits pointed at the camera, nothing he cared for, or not much anyway. Not a big crowd, but one pleased, it seemed, with itself, its collective presence, his own presence in it less explicable than some but he knew what to say, words and smiles, knew what to do, when to nod. It was all beyond him in most ways anyway, or he was beyond it; black and white, tits and ass, you could get the same thing at any newsstand, but, of course, here it was Art. Here you could see the model herself, right there in sheath dress and pumps, linked arm in arm with the photographer and smiling like a monkey, some new kind of primate evolved past the power of speech straight into the epigrammatical. He would not stay long, would finish his drink—some bitter wine, almost black in the white light—and go.

And there she was.

The Queen of the Covenant, a woman who looked exactly like that ragged and ferocious figure of his dreams, against the wall like some cold sculpture, and she slid against that recollected figure from sleep with the interlock of synchronicity. She was not looking at the photographs, she was not looking at him. What engaged her he could not see, but she was—if not smiling—then ready to smile: at something. And then her gaze moved, long axis of attention at pivot and point, and then she *was* looking at him, directly at him, so directly that he expected her nearly-smiling mouth to open and say *I am the Queen of the Covenant,* so directly that he had to, *had* to look away—and did—and looked back to see her leaving, walking out into the downtown night.

He followed her. Why not? Why not, not hurrying, not appearing to hurry, keeping that long form in sight—why not? She walked like a woman used to walking, to covering ground, like a woman who knew where she was going, and turned at last down a corner, up half a block, into a bar.

Not a frenetic singles bar, not a neighborhood joint which his late dad had used to call a tavern—his late dad had never been assaulted by dreams, lying on his deathbed, his vast and growing surprise and "Joe," he said, "Joe listen to this, I had the most terrible dream, the dream of my life, I dreamed that I was dying." No Storm Planet for him, no glamorous witch in rags—just a nondescript place, easy listening music and distant, shadowy booths and drinks that were not too expensive—well, not for him anyway. These days nothing was too expensive for Thompson, the grind of chronology reminding that he was forty-five, he was going to die, he could feel the weight and consequence of his mortality droning through him. More behind than ahead and in his cells the knowing drift, the warm bitter hunger of decay. So have a drink. Have a lot of drinks.

In his cells. Greet the reaching and insistent hand of darkness. He was full of little sayings, little pseudo-insights like that now. Write deep, think shallow, hammer away with the short sustaining strokes, make the short long in all of the wet and necessitous places: that was what he believed. Or believed he believed; who was to say? Dream or waking life, woman or witch, what difference, what matter, where was she now in this lesser darkness, so feeble beside her own element: heat and ash—where? And his own smile, like hers in the gallery merely imminent, barely there: creature not of dream but his own projection, there was no Queen of the Covenant, Queen of the Dead. She was just a woman with some resemblance, and he could consider the coincidence later. Now, however, it was important to get down that first drink, start the motors of essentiality and when he had done that and had done it again and perhaps again, well, then was time enough to look around, measure the night's clientele, plan his own evening in his own way. Tonight he was not in a hurry, time enough to study the rolling hills and declensions of what would be his night, regardless of the impact of this contrivance; time for him and pace, too, and he wanted, if possible, to have a good time in his own way.

Was that wrong? Was there something wrong with a good time? His old man, now, had not had too many good times, he had been saving them up perhaps and then in the hospital it had occurred to him that he had waited too long to make the withdrawal. That sense of betrayal in the old man's face might have been something meant for Thompson, too, another avatar of dream. Was it too much to ask, just not to be his father and to find his possibilities where he might.

Oh, yes, grant him that, drink in hand in this little,

compact shell of time, just a little solace after the rigors and idiocies of the day and there were as always more than enough of both. He was, as he liked to tell people, especially women, a professional writer, he was a man who made his living with words and images and if at bottom, on the unforgiving cusp of the bottom line the images belonged to others, well. Well, then that was not so bad, was it? There were a million more painful and degrading ways to make a living and if he could not think of any offhand, why that was just fatigue talking, it meant and indicted nothing and most essentially and personally not him.

She was wearing a loose black dress that did not touch her knees. She had beautiful legs; she was beautiful in or out of planets or dreams. Not model-beautiful, not like a centerfold or an actress but in a way that made him sit up straighter, a way that made his smile manifest, the way a man smiles to himself before going out to attempt something he knows he can master but that on the way will take sweat and effort, perhaps more effort than he fathoms at the outset; but not more than he is willing to expend. Some nights he had his own exhaustion to battle, some nights he looked only for the easiest, cheapest, quickest thing on the menu but tonight was different. Dream or no dream he was ready for some acrobatics, ready to talk and spar a little, do the things she would want, a woman like her; just speculation, but he had his instincts. There were some things you could tell right off and she without speaking, without so much as turning her head in his direction, was telling them to him now. Instincts were almost always and in all circumstances better, and surely more dependable, than words; you need not be a professional writer to know that.

No hurry; he did not rush, there at the bar and he ordered another drink, this one to sip, not like numbers one and two which were almost purely sheer lubricant, instinct's grist. She crossed her legs again, picked up her drink, set it down on the napkin, pink napkin, pale drink the color of beach sand, white sand, the way it had looked on that island, what was it? Somewhere white and blue, that disastrous weekend with Megan, sunburn and Margaritas and screaming; on the flight home she had tried to spill hot coffee on his lap and then wept into her hands, slow sounds like a dying ox and he hidden behind some plastic-bound travel magazine wishing he were on some other flight pointed like an arrow for someplace far away. He had thought of writing a story about it, her tears and his stoicism seeming a fine ironic balance, a juxtaposition both terrible and fair until he considered that she had wept from anger and he had raised the magazine from cowardice, and silly boredom and immature rage; she had screamed at him beside the baggage carousel, he had slammed the taxi on her coat and anyway he was not in the business to write stories, fairy tales for adults and in that whole situation there had been not one salvageable image, nothing to which any other reasonably sane human being might want in any way to vicariously relate or achieve. People felt bad enough about everything as it was; they did not need any more bad news from him. Hadn't his old man made that point somewhere along the line? *People just want to be entertained,* hadn't he said that?

Distracted by these speculations, he found he had ordered another drink and when he checked again—black dress, pale glass—she was gone from the booth but a moment's reconnaissance placed her there, by the ladies' room: reemerging as calm and satisfied as an athlete, a swimmer in deep water, her dress moving around her beautiful legs and she had to pass him to get to her booth or the door, either way. What's your pleasure? And now his pleasure was to watch her, just watch and try to decide which way she would turn, her posture and direction to decide his: the booth or the door, the lady or the tiger. Long steps and then she was passing him, she was turning right—to the booth, she was sitting down again, smoothing her dress the way women did, palms in brief and ladylike sweep down her ass and without thinking he was on his feet, empty glass left behind on the bar and in two steps, three he was beside her, smiling (but not too widely) and asking if she would like some company, if she would mind if he sat down: and what would she say? *"I am the Queen of the Covenant?"* Stop it, he told himself and: "Sure," she said. "Go ahead." Her voice (was it?) not the voice of dream at all, a dark husky voice and she smiled, a slow smile as he smiled back: and as if his motions were a coin in a slot a barmaid appeared: "Scotch and water," he said, "please. And——?" looking at her, and she named a drink, some liqueur he did not recognize; and then they were alone and smiling at each other, half-wary, half-friendly, like two animals who meet on the street, two domesticated pets: wordless investigative snuffling at one another's dampness and rigor: breathe deep, get information, let the instincts flow: go. Go on.

Drinking, smiling, talking: "Did she like photography?" he asked, "did she go to the galleries much? Patron of the arts?" and she laughed, a genuine laugh he thought; and then said, "So what do you do?" as if he had just asked her the same question although he had not. "How do you earn your daily bread?"

"I'm a professional writer," he said, with what he felt was genuine modesty. His father had had his own opinions, a writer for a son, well. "Where I come from," his father had said, "stories are not a job. Where I come from, let me tell you——" and no, no, shaking his head, not all that again: "let me tell you what it is to be in exile": *no,* no more. "I don't want to hear it," Thompson would say, had said, "I know plenty about exile myself." Plenty: but not now, now he must just sip from the drink, await the next question which he felt he could anticipate correctly and answer at pleasurable leisure; but she did not have a next question, she did not speak at all, only smiled until his own smile felt somehow diminished and faintly suspect, the grin of someone who is proud for no good reason and he drank again to mitigate his confusion, asking as soon as he had swallowed, "What do *you* do?" trying and failing to skirt the emphasis which was he felt unnecessarily bellicose, but it was there and it was too late and she was still smiling, reaching for her own drink with long fingers and she said, "I'm a model. That's what I do."

"Really?" Although he did not believe her. "That's great, that's a great job. You must meet a lot of interesting people."

"No," she said, "I don't. As a matter of fact I don't think I've met one single interesting person in the last three years." Her fingers, he thought, were extraordinarily long, almost freakishly so. Maybe she was a hand model? "Although maybe I'm just too demanding," she said. "That could be it."

"That could be it," he said, agreeing, pretending to agree. "But I think in this world a person gets what he asks for. What she asks for. Don't you?"

"Depends," she said, "on what you ask for."

"Depends," he said, "on what you want."

No one said anything then for a few moments which felt long, but which he imagined in fact were not; and then he finished his drink, long lubricious swallow and she opened her purse and put some money on the table, more than necessary for their drinks. "Come on," she said, sliding out of the booth; she was a little taller than he, long legs (white thighs, a dream of closure, of expended heat). "Let's go."

"Where?" It was the wrong thing to say, stupid and unlike him not to be able to play along, not to speak the language but already she was moving too fast, brisk scissoring stride and distracted as he was by the sway of her ass, the motion of her body beneath the dress he found it easier to say nothing; outside now in the early dark, the air as warm as it had been when he entered the bar, warm and humid as a body under a dress, as a hand on another hand and her hand was in his, now, as simple as that. Every bit as simple as that although—and make no mistake, it was his hand in hers, not hers in his; he was not leading, this was her expedition—nothing, he knew, was ever as simple or certain as he, or she, or his dead father or any of them had ever hoped or planned or engineered it to be. In the stories—his, too—they always walked away hand in hand, the glances met and the clothes melted and nobody had to wear condoms or take out tampons and nobody ever laughed at the wrong time or called the wrong name; or the wrong number. And the orgasms were simultaneous, always, bucking and groaning and heaving onto the same plane at the same heart-pleasing time: and there was no wet spot, and no silence afterwards, no distance as distant as a Storm Planet, no exile in bed or out.

But this was not a movie or a book; this was her hand around his and her pace and her dress gleaming faintly green under the streetlights, and the faint damp scent of her skin, sweat and effluence, and the feel of his own body. Two animals, sniffing in the street. He said, "Where are we headed?" with what he hoped was casual interest and she turned her head, a queenly motion and "Not much longer now," she said. "Unless you mind a little walk?"

"No," he said, pressing her fingers. "No, I don't mind at all."

His father in the hospital bed, a vigorous man, wasted now and wasted was the word: so much time left, Thompson thought, seen from the vantage point of his own forty-five years, seventy was not that old, not that old after all, was it? Lying still, some pain medication drifting through the veins, eyes swimming in deep REM and he must have been dreaming: as his son dreamed, of a woman, dark witch in storm and covenant? or of home, his left-behind country, his long travels from there to here, then to now, health to a kind of debilitation the long-ago immigrant could surely never have imagined or dreamed; dreaming now and Thompson quiet in the bedside chair, wondering if he ought to go home, wondering if his father would wake to know him gone.

Wondering, half-dozing himself: and his father's voice startling him, *"Joe,"* imperious, calling his name: *"Joe,"* and—"What?" he said, rousing himself. "What is it? Do you want the nurse?"

"Shut the door," his fatter said. "Go on, shut it: she won't come unless you do."

The nurse? The door swung to, heavy hospital door and

silence now between them, silence in the room, silent in the bed and his father's thin body beneath the sheets, Thompson staring, wondering what was to happen next and: in wonder, in childlike embarrassment seeing that his father had an erection, moving eyes and hands grasping, gently grasping under the sheets, the drift of pale green cloth and

"*Oh,*" his father said, "*oh, yes—*"

And the smell of something warm, hot, hot to the touch. Thompson looked around and around the room, head back and forth like a dog smelling fire. "*Oh, yes,*" from his father again and on the bed now a presence, legs and arms, long bare torso wrapped carelessly in rags: her head back, her eyes bright and ringed with soot and sweat and darkness, her hands on his father's body, pinching and plucking through the sheets, her palms in slow circles, her hand now a loose and stroking fist and his father's groans, Thompson's stare, feeling his own heat, his own erection, staring and staring and his father's cry, guttural and foreign, past all language and the woman cloaked in imminence, the passage of time and generations, turning to Thompson now, smiling to him alone even as her hands worked mercilessly the old man's body below: "*And now you know,*" she said.

and the sheets wet, translucent stain

and his father alone in the bed, groaning, groping for the call button, crying for the nurse and Thompson's own cry almost comical in its bewilderment, rising clumsy from the chair to hurry to the door, open the door and let the nurse come in.

Her apartment was as bare as money could make it: black and white and hardwood floors, slim white gurney sofa and she made them both drinks from a tiny little bar that looked like something salvaged from a military base. Oblong shadows in differing shades of grey, her face in shadow, too, as she said "You read much history? Do you know anything about history at all?"

It was not a question he expected; hasty swallow and he coughed a little, trying to clear his throat enough for speech and she laughed, a genuine laugh of genuine amusement: "Don't worry," she said, "there's not going to be a quiz; relax." Her face, the glass in her long fingers seemed to be two parts of the same device, a disassembled instrument, technical, surgical, prepared for a particular usage that both she and time would reveal. She uncrossed her legs, let one touch his—deliberately, he thought; he could be sure of some things anyway.

"You a history buff?" he said, to say something; her question had put him off balance in ways he neither recognized nor enjoyed. "You like history?"

"I am history," she said, and stood up; she was naked under the dress, something else he had not expected, the dress itself dividing as it fell around her feet, high heels and she did not remove them, did not for a moment move at all: stood before him in pallor and moisture and gray oblongs and he felt his erection as if it were a separate part of his body, wisps of thought congealed in his flesh, some strange new grafting made of equal parts meat and lead. Bending, reaching, extracting him with those surgical fingers, crouched like a beast before him, animals in the street and she pulled his pants down to his ankles, shackles now, immobilizing him although at that moment he would not have moved if motion had been an option. "I'm Anne Boleyn," she said, with an extra finger. "I'm Sylvia Plath. I'm Catherine the Great. I'm a witch. I'm the queen of air and darkness, I'm Marie Antoinette of fucking France," she said, and her mouth closed along the length of him, her long damp fingers curled like iron in the straining muscle of his thighs, closed and rose and fell again and again and when he reached blindly for her head, the moving planes of her face he felt beneath his fingers something both pliable and strong, something harsh that was in no way bone, no human bone at all. She took him inside, then released him, then reeled backward in a speedy dancer's crouch and he plunged into her, the union that complete. "I am history," she said, "that is part of it; I am Medea in Jason's cage and his intention was to take her slowly, slowly, bring her to screaming boil against him, but she made splinters of that idea, converted his empty little plans to knives which splintered inside"; he felt himself impelled and rising, rising, he felt then the enormous grief which she must have wanted to bring to him, the grief of history doubled by the taunted helplessness of his genitals and he found himself dragged in the few desperate heaves she gave him through all of the centuries of Golgotha and torment, martyrdom and doubt, slaughter and possibility and his orgasm, yanked out of him, was a cry of assent to all the whips and blood which dangled from the eaves of retrospection she had provided. He lay atop her gasping, her small pointed breasts sending their deadly little messages against his chest, and then she heaved, he expended, she thrust back, he spilled and rolled helplessly, lay staring at the ceiling.

"And that's how it is," she said. "That's how it is to fuck history. Do you understand now? Do you know the spangled and continuous griefs of your darkness; do you? Are you ready for the future now?" He could not understand what she was saying, moved without sound like a tongueless beast, head back and forth. "That's you," she said. "One spill and coma, all of you the same. But who of you are equal to your shared history? I want you to leave now. Go. Take your history and go."

Unresisting he stood, shaken, tried to assemble his clothing while she sat with her long hands folded and looked at him. Her features were pallid and perfectly closed; they gave off neither heat nor light, like Stonehenge or the Easter Island statuary, like the earth of sleep and dreams. "When do I see you again?" he said. "Will I see you?" "Oh, you like it," she said, "you like the darkness, don't you? You like your history even if you understand none of it, you are all creatures of history, yes? Perhaps I will see you in the bar again," she said, "and then again I may not. But do not try to see me here, that would be a very bad mistake. You do not come to the Queen's quarters unbidden, is that understood?" Diminished, he stood before her, feeling the slow weight of his humiliation casting him down, down, the glaze of her shielded nudity more implacable than that of his own knowledge.

"Yes," he said, "yes, I understand." She said, "Then, go," and he left. He left her bare apartment and stumbled to the street, caught in the shyness of the college boy, the adolescent in his first brush with sex: the boy with his hand in the girl's baggy sweater, his father's hand on the window, on the latch to call him home: yes. He walked the streets to his car, feeling himself reassembling slowly, slowly; by the time he was in the car he felt almost normal, almost back to himself. *Oh, was that a weirdo tonight,* he thought. *Forget the dreams, she's crazy, crazy as dying Dad, dead Dad yelling and flopping around in the bed.*

Driving, and home, Megan in bed, the boys sleeping, everything very peaceful at midnight and why shouldn't it be, why should there be anything but peace as he undressed, sponged off in the bathroom, lay next to his sighing wife. "Fairly well today," he said, although she had not asked, "got eight pages done and then went out for dinner and drinks with Ed, guess it ran a little later than I expected." She said nothing; Megan had ceased to say anything years ago, adopting instead a doctrine of silence more telling than any speech could be. Lying beside her, musing in the night, feeling himself straddling not only the evening but all of history again as he worked himself into a tumultuous and colorless sleep, spelunker of the unconscious, moving ever deeper into the blackness of his own history, the histories of silence under the sheets.

And no dreams, tonight, no dreams at all.

In the morning he felt very calm, but the calmness went away in the rompings and sputterings of preparation for school and then after the boys' thunderous decampment he faced Megan in one of those pure and empty moments which occurred occasionally, less often than before but still once or twice a week, and as urgency rose to her eyes, as her mouth seemed to open like the orifice it was not for the question which would yank him out of all this and place him in some new unwanted connection, he said, "I've got to get going. I left off at a bad point, George came in too early, I lost a whole transitional page, I might lose a chapter." The usual bullshit; he could have been yammering sports or discussing furniture; what did it matter? Did it matter? Megan looked at him and said, "All right, then, go. Get the work done." And he thought again, *She knows, she knows everything, she's not stupid, not misled but accommodated,* accommodating to her own history of which who knew how much she shared with him. It was a strong and distasteful thought, although not enough to stop him, hardly enough to change anything at all.

He left the house thinking he would take the bus but then stopped himself in the thought, the idea of a chance, just a chance that he might look for the woman again later and if so he would stay in the city late and would need the car so he decided to drive. But once in the city, at the office, he had to come to terms with the pure lie with which he had worked himself to this point. He would see her, he must see her or at least attempt to see her or he would die and so gave up even the pretense of working and wandered around the streets a little: a bookstore, a porno movie, a call to Megan later saying that he had to work late again tonight, make up the time he had lost yesterday, the moments of history demolished although of course he did not say that to her.

The bar was crowded, but the woman was not there. He stood at one place in the bar waiting for her, waiting and trying to think of nothing at all but it was very difficult, a blank mind was not the absence of desire and by the time she came in at ten p.m. he was almost drunk and nearly incoherent, smelling like Scotch and hunger, propped against the bar. He had been afraid that she would ignore him, but she came at once to his side and said, "You look anxious, you look very anxious."

"I'm not sleeping much," he said.

She smiled at that, raised her drink, drank it as he stared at her in thrall, in astonishment. Her clothing was the same as yesterday's but new, as if she had only one idea and compiled rather than assorted her clothing. In the small, dark place which they opened up between them no one penetrated. After ten minutes of almost pure silence, she said, "All right, you know what you want to

do, so let's do it. Come on," she said, and he took her
wrist and rose, the first time in three hours to a feeling
unsteady, as he had when he stood rapidly yesterday after
their—what? lovemaking? sex? conjoinment, what? Their
dream: their shared dream of history. Her apartment and
it was the same again, she looked at him, bent her head,
stared at him in and out of that closed mask of her face
and said, "You, too, take your clothes off," and he undressed. "Do you know who I am?" she said.

"Yes," he said, "you're history, you—"

"No," she said. "That was yesterday. History was yesterday. Today I am your future. Today I judge you, today you
know the price. Do you understand that?" Her flesh was
cool, wickedly damp against him. "I am the Empress of the
Pleiades," she said, "I am the Queen of the Dead Light, of
the living and the dead. I am of the Storm Planet inciner-
ated for my love in the one hundred forty-first century, I am
the Mistress and Angel of the Third Transcendence. I am
your death," she said, "and your transfiguration and your
light and the extinction of your life," and she hauled him
over her with the slewing speed of a master landing some
great game fish, some wet beast from the sea, and in the
motion he felt penetration's instant shock and then, like
yesterday but not like yesterday at all he was all in and out
of her, the thin, gray spaces of the indefinable and mindless
future drifting around him, a future of which he was not
part; a future of which he could barely conceive and his
death-rattle began, the Cheyne-Stokes of signaled mortality
and he heaved and moaned, dying in the embrace of death
itself as she took him over, tenderly and carefully, into the
uninhabitable and eternal future.

He spilled and spilled, wet and heavy and when it was
done looked at her from his dead eyes. "Oh, yes," she
said. "Now you do understand, don't you? It is the Res-
urrection and the Life, the transfiguration and the eternal
sleep as well; now go," she said. "Go, that's all for tonight, for the Storm Planet which died the way you did."
He stumbled for his clothing, utterly in thrall, incapable
at the moment of speech of any kind; to save his life he
could not have said a word, nothing to her now. "The fu-

ture," she said, "is history, history is the future, all of
them bound. Go on; look for me but not here, in the public place."

And he reached toward her, in that brief warm flicker
of passage, he thought that they might have touched, but
that was not clear, nothing was clear. And he was out on
the street again, the thin, blank, brutalized spaces of the
stars circling in the scrim of obliterate consciousness as
he went to the car, as he found his way home: the house
quiet again at midnight but empty this time, all of the
bedroom doors open as they never were, quiet and the living room lights on like witnesses to a disaster unceasing
and he thought, *She's left me,* the thought itself like a
light flickering, *she's left me, she's been warning me and
now she's finally gone.* But then as he turned toward the
kitchen he saw the body, the long crumple of limbs and
bones, and it was his father in stricken angles on the floor
of the living room, the curtains blowing through the open
window, the outlines of blood and fluid like a puzzle on
the floor and a crack in the heart of the puzzle and he
cried out, a long shrieking cry which did not bring
Megan, Megan or the boys. *Oh, God,* he thought, *oh,
God, oh, God* and ran to their rooms, bedrooms and beds
and all of them filled with his father, his father's face
grave, composed, the exile come home at last. In one bed
he lay on his side, in the other on his back, in the third
in fetal curl and everywhere the spill, blood and what
Thompson now saw to be semen and Thompson stumbling in shock, stumbled rising from the shock, stumbled
to his car. He did not know what to do. *Oh God, oh,
God*—in the empty car, the dead house, the house of
dreams and through and past a long dreaming passage he
was again on the streets of the city, he was in the bar, the
place almost empty, the bartender mopping slops and
filled ashtrays and the clock at 2:15 and the woman at the
far stool, wearing the outfit and its colors again, talking
in her deep voice to two men.

He came toward her and she looked past them, fixed
him with a long, cool, blank gaze, then reached out her
hand, gathered him toward her, pressed his wrist. "Later,"

she said to the men, "later." To him she said, "Pay my bill." He reached and produced from his wallet a twenty-dollar bill, put it on the counter; "that's enough," she said. She led him from the bar and they walked to her apartment. He was incapable of speech. I have had a terrible tragedy, he wanted to say, but did not. Whose? Whose terrible tragedy? He would have to explain and the truth was that he simply did not know. Her gaze was sympathetic but closed, her fingers on his wrist those of a pale and inscrutable insect; he could feel jaw and mandible meet in his wrist. In the apartment she locked the door, gazed at him with insectile inexpression, then again shed her dress in that same motion. *Witch?* he thought, oh, no, it was not that, not *that,* it was—

"Undress," she said.

"Is this it?" Thompson said. "Is this where it ends?"

"Quiet," she said. "No argument. Take off your clothing right now." He heard in her voice the imperiousness of the young Queen, some elegant indication of that vulnerable presence who so many millennia ago had taken charge of the galaxies, racked the clusters and streams of those galaxies in their fixated places, had scattered the stars like semen through the cusp of their fingers. "Now," she said: and he did, and stood before her.

"Do you know who I am?" she said, gesturing with her right hand, a closed fusion of fingers, and he said, "Yes, I know who you are."

"Tell me," she said.

"You are the Queen of the Covenant," he said, could have said more: queen of all the spaces hidden between the stars, the dead winds of space, the hush of the winds between those empty places and the cries of nascent lives in the chemical swamp of their origin: time and null-time, the covenant, the promise of life to emerge from the slow and boiling spheres: you are the queen. "History," he said, "that's what you are, the future and the past all contained."

"No," she said, "I am not."

"No?" Stupidly, helplessly as a child and he felt the whine, the fall, the slow descent within that could have been the shrieking of the copper planets, torn from their orbits, dropped into the sun. "You must be that," he said. "The dreams, the promise—my father—"

"You are wrong," she said, "all of that was only to haunt you, to deny you the essential truths until I was ready to cast that full and final spell, until I was ready to draw you into the gigantic reach of time."

"History," he said, "that's what you are. History. The future. The past." All of consequence contained in her, clasped between her legs, the fire of her breasts, deep and cleaving countenance, but she shook her head, amused, her features suffused with a casting radiance which in turn suffused the room, broken spaces, bent edges.

"No, I am none of these," she said, "and you are capable of seeing so little, what you see you can glimpse only through the lenses of your own need; you see through a rathole, the smallest arc." He reached toward her, the steely surfaces of her body moist and hot and seeming to repel.

"The present," he said, "you are the terrible and inescapable present"; the present which had hammered him in place made of him—fatherless, helpless, in permanent exile—a puppet of his own inextricable darkness, she was all of the present rolling beyond him as encapsulated and yet limitless as the grief cries of his own heart.

"And no," she said, "no again. I am not that either. Come to me," she said, "come closer. Touch me, taste me." Her darkness, the garments rich with the tones of her flesh and they were her flesh, she had surrendered to her own nakedness. "Here," she said, "come closer," and ah, the tilt of her head, the smell of her flesh, why had he never noticed that smell before? The scent of his father's cancer had risen up from the sheets, had reeled from the walls, had clung riotously to the walls of his own home, this night, this death: and breathing now, breathing her in and: "I am duty," she said, "I am honor. I am not the Queen of the Covenant, not for you because for such as you there *is* no covenant, no trust. Honor and duty," she said, "virtue, custom, dignity, the decency of civilization, the *caritas* of the long-suffering; I come not from the star but from the self, I am emergent not from the Storm Planet which is only your own ruined, faithless, worthless landscape: no, I was remodeled to your ugliness by the fury of your need. I am the compact of love and compassion, that is the covenant: of perfect need and need at last fulfilled."

He came against her, wet, empty, his genitals limp as a broken limb, ineffective and, "Honor," she said, "duty, courage." His heart rested against her, helpless, finite. "Do you know?" she said, "do you know of witches, do you know that there are witches for all the worlds, each world a witch: each huddle of stars a plenitude or infinity of crones or princesses and I am the Queen of the living and dead spaces within *you*. Attend to me," she said and he lay against her, stunned as stone, graven as death.

"Do you see now?" she said.

He saw. He saw everything as the old man must have seen it in that dream of death which was not death, understood it all as he sank like wood, like prayer against her. As the Queen, as the Lady of the living and the dead took at last a perfect and irreplaceable pity and carried him, carried him all the way to that broken and terrible place which in all aspects and conditions swaddled him, bound him; suffocation, shadows, expiration, death.

Thompson lies there: beneath the witch of the worlds, queen of covenant, bitch of last and final consequence, in passage and at torment: subsumed by history, overtaken by time and content at last not to rise.

In the earth the creatures consume him: still-life: bones and stones and he hears and sees nothing, he is the Storm Planet itself and against him not only his lost and clinging father but the witch of all the worlds carrying, carrying, carrying him past the grave of desire, to the place where he had tried so terribly to be in the stilled and streaming light which falls and falls and falls forever, to the maw of forgiving witchery and the kisses of dead forgiveness in the dark.

* * *

HORST AGAPE: Breast in his hand, that rising softness, suggestion of dark beneath the tremble and then the sudden turn, arm yanked down, inner arm hard against his palm—stop it, *stop* it!—and his retreat, hand falling to waist in a paroxysm of smiling failure, embarrassment, retraction: and her hard little face turned away, catching the lights of the gallery, none of the light for him.

"What do you think you're doing, Horst? Is this the time?" No, it was not the time, obviously, time past for the splendidness of the inappropriate. A past, a history between them in which this had not been the case but Horst could not bring it to remembrance, not now or here: locked doors, the suggestion of early arrivals casting shadows against the glass, but it was not yet 7:30, the gallery never opened early and certainly not on an opening night: FACES OF DESIRE, her important new show and: "I have things to do, Horst," she said, "can't you keep yourself busy? You don't have to stay, you know"— and hopelessly he raised a hand, gestured again at her breast. "No," she said, "not that; no more. What do you think this is? Are you crazy? Don't you understand?"

Did he understand? In the old days—the pre-Margo days, there must have been such a time, a time blessed by the absence of her spell—it seemed to have been different: hand on breast anytime, anywhere, in the bedroom naked, on the streets with coats piled over, on the way to the checkout line, at the movies, hand on her breast like a key in the door and that instantaneous response, swift gasp, surprised little cry and then she would cave against him, he would feel the rising pressure of her breast, breast and hand conjoined and how many times, even in public, it seemed that they were virtually ready to screw right then, in the gallery, white walls and long windows, in the supermarket backed against cereal boxes or the threatened tumble of apples, in the bookstore, in the theater; oh, they had been crazy in those days, crazy in a different way than Anne's question now: are you crazy?—Are *you*, Anne?—and maybe it was all the same, open up, close down, the retraction or offering of self the same sussurating gasp, draw in, draw out. Happy times, then, Horst and Anne in those days, before Margo, Margo the model, the big M, Margo the feathery construct of a woman with the small eyes and large mouth, the delicate, limpid, pallid breasts, no invitation there and Anne had gone crazy for Margo from the very first, first shoot, first session, had barely retained any control, had kept her on the floor, backed against the wall for hours.

"I've never seen anything like this," Anne had said. This was before she had stopped talking to Horst about any of it, before the freeze, the death of shared history. "She opens up for the camera," Anne had said, animated, warm, her hand on his forearm, "she opens up the way men open up in pain and need for a woman. She breathes, she inhales, she takes it *all* in. I've never done work like this. There has never been anything like this."

Had there? How could he know? Horst had come to Anne only a few years ago, difficult time, strange time, his odd bankrupt emigre's life seemingly—as he now regarded it—only a protracted and unpleasant preparation for this culminating affair, photographer's affair—was even his name part of it? did she know?—photographer and art director meeting in the late afternoon in the office, heads together over her portfolio and then later the standard requests, the shrugged acknowledgments, the concealed but unhidden conjoinment in the back booth of this place or that until so easily that it had been impossible to define transition Horst had slid into it, slid into this new posture, this new lover as Horst the emigre had, deficient in language, irony and all bedrock sense of self slid into the United States a dozen years before on borrowed credentials and continued to skulk, modestly but with a hunger impenetrable on the surface of this privileged and concrete place, like a man at a party to which he has not been properly invited; and beneath that surface (which was his surface) at last to feel the hard edges of the *shtetl*, the barley soup and incomprehensible consonants of the grey regime slide from him and he had become if not native then better than native, aware to the tips of his fingers and never more so as when he had at last found and plowed this troubled photographer, midwestern emigre herself, all of the continent cleaving to him, clambering, Anne clambering up to and over him as the rotten paupers of the dead regime had crawled over the scraps and rags of history itself, less abstraction to them perhaps than he with his assimilated English and mild instinct for design, after immigration, after Anne, before Margo had come from the agency and sauntered, then spread, then careened into their lives with an enormity which now seemed to Horst as inevitable as his own lies to the office of immigration: expensive suit, lifted hands. "Am I curious to know the nature of these forms?" he had said to the agent, "or do I sign to my contribution? I do not know"; and that uncertain, contrived English amusing the agent even as Margo at the beginning had amused Horst: he had been let through. And so had she.

And now the Margo prints, silver witchery of nudes and half-draped studies, shadows and hard lines, that stare everywhere through all the spaces of the gallery, the prints unframed, unmatted, pinned heavy to the walls as if they were broadsides, posters announcing some cold new insurrection. Murmur and shuffle through the windows, Anne had always had a certain audience; "they would come for you at any rate," he wanted to tell Anne, "this Margo has no real hold on you, it is you who has imbued her with substance and with mystery." But to say this, of course, would do Horst no good at all. Deficient yet in language and in full relation to circumstance, but still he was alert enough to know that.

And Margo herself now emergent in sheath dress and pumps, glancing at Horst, glancing away—hating him as always, the competition of their relationship defined Anneward from the outset—then her gaze onto Anne, her center and home: *his* home first although of course she did not care about that and: slow radiance casting its own lights, looking at Anne as Anne looked at her, as the two women leaned toward one another, yearned toward one another; and stricken, useless, loveless Horst in his own stippled posture of attention, gazing at them both as if they were one person until Anne broke the spell by turning from Margo, turning to walk to the door.

"Time for the hordes," Anne said, to Margo, to the prints of Margo; Margo said nothing. Horst remembered

the hordes; he had been among them, stamping and
coughing in a million lines, later in the immigration center as their collective presence, his presence among them
worked to dismantle that drooping elegance which he had
tried so stringently to cultivate, turned him in his own
gaze, as he waited for the interview, into some harsh,
evicted peasant, landless, friendless, homeless, the stain
of his dispossession like Cain's kiss on his forehead: as if
with one swift look all could tell there was no true place
on earth for him.

And see Margo now, her smug silence, her expensive
dress (purchased with Anne's money despite her own ex-
orbitant agency paychecks): leaning against the wall like
a spoiled adolescent, an indulged and bilious pet, waiting
as if she had always belonged in this place, this gallery,
this coveted spot beside Anne her creator, Anne who had
constructed of her gawky, reedy, sullen non-appeal something fierce in its mystery, fathomless and profane in the
mysteries of its desire: Anne who had made her and in
the making unmade Horst in turn, Horst in the corner
now, hands in his serviceable working-class leather jacket
regarding the opening doors, the twos and threes hand in
hand like a hand on a breast, the touch denied, Anne's
touch on Margo's arm.

And later, in the darkness, the bedroom, that head in
profile against the fat-folded pillow, his own body lumpy
and cold and hairy and: afraid to touch her, afraid to
reach for the place not there: "Anne," he said, careful to
speak without inflection, "Anne, it was a good show."

A long pause. He knew she was not sleeping. At last:
"Yes," and her hand very warm and reaching backward,
behind her back to press briefly against his chest; "yes,"
she said, "I think it was."

Without invitation, afraid of eviction he began to touch
her, stroke the bones and muscles of shoulders and back,
the small razored strip of hairless skin at the nape of her
long neck, skin and body the landscape of more than desire, the desire for more than sex: touching of her for a
long, long time, until he knew she would not turn to

move into his arms, until he realized that with her own small hand she was already touching herself.

"Anne? Is she there?" Margo on the phone, bare of all affect, making sure, he thought, that he knew she asked for nothing, not even information, from him. Anne's apartment silent around him, Anne's books and photography magazines, Anne's phone in his hand. Sun through the farthest window, long dusty line of light theatrical, unreal, as if it contained no warmth at all.

"No," he said pleasantly. "She is not."

Her pause: cat's breath, fast and scentless. "Then where is she?" Margo said.

At the movies, at the grocery, in the park; in bed with a lover muzzling between her legs, biting her thighs the way you do, I know how things are between you, I know what goes on, do you think for one moment I don't know what goes on? As if he could smell that sour passion of hers, Margo's hunger, Margo's lust for more than fucking, more than slippery fingers and rolling eyes, the way one dog smells another; he knew *exactly* what was going on and the more it had to do with hunger the less it had to do with sex, although paradoxically it was in its own way pornographic, the true pornography that has to do with the stripping down of substance, the bold flat nakedness of all affect that makes of desire less than a reflex and passion no factor at all.

"I don't know," he said. "Perhaps you can call the gallery."

Her disconnect abrupt but not unanticipated, Horst conscious then of a sudden warm impulse to call the gallery himself, see if Anne was there: he had no idea where she was, had assumed she was with Margo. Whose image now confronted him, perpetual, matted in white, framed in black, black and white nude in a posture of crucifixion: long arms draped over warping boards, long legs splayed open as in the most clinical pornography yet the image itself gave no heat, was not sexual, was not designed to arouse in him or any viewer the urge to possess except in a fashion more shattered and warped than the boards upon which she hung; what was remarkable about this photograph, about Margo herself, was her seeming ability to represent, clothed or unclothed, with props or alone, that kind of cluttered, inward-facing, outward-repelling aspect which he had seen in less exquisite and brutal form in much American photography; that intimacy, that fury of juxtaposition, the people and the goods (although his was not a phenomenon confined to advertising photography, even through his thick immigrant's skull Horst knew that; unless all photography could be considered as advertisement and why not?), the people and the people, all of it too *close:* huddled, stricken, merging or more properly yearning to merge—as Anne yearned for Margo, as Margo yearned for Anne—in a way which Horst supposed could be understood as the essence of consumption in this riotously consuming society; but below that or above, deeper, blacker, to be viewed and understood as an extravaganza of need, cornucopia of loss, a cry for the kind of closeness bare proximity cannot give, the penultimate cry of the heart for succor and for home.

See that crucifixion again in the moving band of sunlight, in the spangle of moving dust and see the other pictures, too: dressed like a slattern and a housewife, masked in hideous carnival drag, folded like sculpture into a space too small: Margo naked, hands against breasts, mouth an O of mock concern, legs torturously extended toward the camera, the viewer, offering not closure but an apex of further need, that dry pudenda like the hole in the heart which cries for more: too much: yes. Margo again, grasping a wall, palms flat to the wall, tapered fingers demanding the carved and stony secrets of that wall; Margo in robes and a crown of pearls absently looped through her hair, one strand cupping an ear as Horst imagined Anne might have herself reached toward Margo one positioning hand and all of it—robes, pearls, ears, hands, yearning lips and empty eyes forming a community of necessity, cramped and hammered like seeking, yearning, empty Horst himself, wanting the place of rest from the vantage of postures which seemed to deny its very possibility, which drained time from history and history from time and left nothing, nothing, nothing in its place ... oh, it was subtle, all too subtle for him, but he knew need when he saw it, knew Margo's eldritch hunger as surely as he knew his own, knew, too, Anne's isolating denial of that hunger, her refusal to countenance or feed what was so obvious, so painful, so painfully present and real.

And where was Anne, if not with Margo?

Where was Margo, if not with Anne?

Horst alone in the apartment, looking at the pictures, seeing the pictures; the afternoon gone in vision and in light, dissolving into darkness, into vodka, into the tears and trackless plans of the exile, into sleep with his head on the tiled kitchen table, like a peasant in a way station worn by the journey yet to come.

"I want to be in the pictures," Horst said.

Anne in sullen and unnecessary overheads, false fluorescence and daylight on her face making of her someone different, older; secretive and weary of secrets: turning toward but not to him, then firmly away. Encumbered by mail, a jumble of magazines, postcards announcing gallery openings, ugly bright images in her pale hands all tumbling now atop the kitchen table, last night's vodka bottle still empty, still there.

"What does it take to be part of your pictures? What does it take to make Margo of me? I want to be Margo if that is what is necessary. Instruct me," he said; she would not look at him. "I am instructible, is that your word?" He went to her, touched her shoulder, her face, saw the sudden congealment of her features, that rising defense and said: "No, no, not that, I will not touch, I am not here to touch. What do you want me to do?" he said, His head ached from the drinking, he had scoured his body, scraped at his teeth, tried to become clean but still felt porous, in pain, a peasant with muddy feet: lost in the anteroom, come for help but given nothing, not even direction, not even the first idea of where he might go to find the place where he must be. "What do you want me to do?" he said again. "Do you want me to alter myself, cut off my balls to be part of your pictures? How do I join you, in this sorority, is that it? I will do whatever you say," he said to her, "I will make whatever you will."

She said nothing.

"Tell me what there is to be done," he said, "and I will do it. Do you think I am, what, playacting? No: see this." And he pulled at his trousers, brown corduroy, gold zipper, pulling both down to show her hairless genitals, the skin of his crotch and thighs scraped pink and sore. "In your bathroom I did this," he said. "While you were away."

"I was on a shoot," she said, staring, staring. At last he had all of her attention. "I didn't—I thought I told you, that you knew—"

"With Margo?"

"She was there."

The phone began to ring; she let it ring; the machine answered, recorded the call, they could hear the tinny buzz of the voice which Horst thought might belong to Margo; where was Margo now?

"Where is Margo?" he asked.

At first she did not answer, then: "It isn't Margo you're worried about, not really." Said like a counselor, a psychiatrist, the professionally compassionate but with an undertow, a depth just glimpsed: something there in her eyes. Not really Margo, is it? Her hands, free of mail, magazines, encumbrances, moved in a brief circling gesture, an encompassing motion, something a guide might do. You must go all the way, a guide might tell the lost one, you must go all the way in to come all the way out and she spoke, said something, Horst did not hear or hearing did not understand and so that she would understand spoke his position once again. "Tell me what is to be done and I will do it because I must, you see, Anne? Because I must." Looking at her he could sense her opening, not her cunt as in those lost times, but her brains, the sizzling and heated portions of the brain which fused with the lenses and he thought: *I am ready, I am ready to hear this: I am ready to accept the conditions. I accept plight*

*like a troth, I enter into this because it is where I have to
go.* Standing there in peace, his mind as open and bleak
as a cannon's mouth he looked at Anne feeling the ancient and terrible weight of his history, rootless, graspless,
devolve upon and past him, past her, past clinging and
saturation, past negative and light: felt his genitals begin
to stir but not with passion: felt her hand upon his wrist,
tugging him, leading him to the space he must now oc-
cupy, the square of light which would from now on be his
home.

"Do you see now?" she said to him.

Still-life: bones and stones, he hears and sees nothing,
he is vision itself and against him not only his lost and
clinging history but the history of her sight as well, the
power and grave satiety of the witch of all the worlds
carrying, carrying, carrying him past the grave of desire
to the home which he had tried so terribly to find, to
keep, to be; in the stilled and streaming light which falls
and falls and falls forever, to the gaze eternal of forgiving
witchery and the dead forgiveness of kisses in the dark.

STOCK ANSWER

by Leah A. Zeldes

A loud buzzer rang.

Hegewisch Pulaski started, spilling some of the contents of the heavy cauldron she had been lifting from the big commercial range.

"Damnation! Not again!" she said as she set the pot back down. She waved her short arms excitedly, muttering a few words under her breath, and stomped heavily out through the double doors into the dining room. Behind her, the mess began to clean itself up.

Like hundreds of other diners on suburban highways throughout North America, the Castlescape Restaurant, on U.S. Route 27 a few miles north of Bennington, Illinois, serves an uninspired range of breakfasts, burgers, and dinner fare, plus ice cream and "fountain creations." A nondescript building at the edge of a strip mall, it holds a couple dozen shabby, wooden booths, a worn Formica counter lined with red-vinyl-covered stools and one of those revolving pastry displays filled with cakes that look better than they taste. To all appearances, the Castlescape is a completely unremarkable establishment.

But there really is a castle, crenellations and all. It stands on the hillside opposite, overlooking the restaurant—the replica, in all but size, of Vianden Castle in Luxembourg. Built in the 1930s by a maniacal fellow named Ted Bettendorf, this edifice is a private residence, not open to the public, and has little to do with our story, other than occasioning the name of the restaurant.

In summer, once the trees leaf out, you can barely even see the castle from the Castlescape. So it's not exactly a trendy, tourist eatery.

And that entirely suited its owner and chief cook, Hegewisch, who'd bought the place knowing its business was not brisk. Except on Friday nights, during the all-you-can-eat fish fry, and at lunchtime, when the Big Castle, a half-pound beef patty on a kaiser roll, was a favorite with a few neighborhood businessmen, things were pretty quiet at the Castlescape.

But the modest trade provided Hegewisch with an income adequate to her needs and, in the slow periods between mealtimes, the large commercial kitchen was the ideal site for what she thought of as her "real" work. For Hegewisch envisioned herself an author, and was engaged in researching a book of recipes.

Recently, however, the restaurant's business had been picking up—to the point where it was entirely too busy to suit Hegewisch. Through no effort of hers, the place had acquired a certain local notoriety, and the kitchen buzzer interrupted her constantly as people dropped in at all hours of the day.

Where once Hegewisch could count on at least three good hours of working time between lunch and dinner, now she was lucky to get in half an hour without interruption. And today somebody was coming along every fifteen minutes, at least. Sighing, she shook her frizzy brown curls and returned to the kitchen after serving the latest between-meals customer his coffee and cheesecake.

"Now, where was I? Oh, yes." She lugged the big pot from the stove to her work table, stirred it, and began ladling the murky contents out into plastic freezer containers.

"Nothing like a good supply of basic stock," she said, as she dipped a tasting spoon into the greasy liquid. "*Hmm.* I must note down the addition of the fenugreek."

Hegewisch reached a plump hand for a thick, well-spotted notebook and thumbed rapidly through it until she came to a page headed, *Basic Brown Stock—used as a base for many other recipes, especially those involving transference, such as potions for transformations, for imbuing one person with the characteristics of another, for transmutations of metals, for various metamorphoses, for reversing love potions made with White Stock....*

As she picked up her pencil, the buzzer sounded. "Damn!"

Two teenagers were wanting ice cream sundaes. She checked her watch and scowled. "Shouldn't you still be in school?"

"We have last period off," one of them said.

Hegewisch sighed and dished out the sundaes, then hurried back to her work table. Nearly three o'clock! Her night cook would be arriving shortly to begin preparing for the Friday night fish dinner trade—people dine early in the suburbs—and she had to get everything out of sight before he got there. And she hadn't even had a chance to test her new recipe yet.

She had not finished stowing the stock in her special corner of the big, walk-in freezer when the buzzer sounded once more. "Oh, no. Why me?" she muttered, and left the containers to continue putting themselves away while she went back out into the dining room.

The teenagers were ready to leave, and she stopped to take their money at the register before bringing a menu to the new customer, who had seated himself in the back booth—the one that afforded the best view of the castle. Another tourist, Hegewisch thought grimly.

Coming closer, though, she recognized the scrawny, middle-aged man who sat in the booth. The window's light shone on a long, narrow face and wire-rimmed glasses, a monkish fringe of sandy hair circling a bald pate. He looked up from the dictionary he was reading as Hegewisch approached.

"I know you," she said. "You're that sci-fi writer."

The man winced. "I do write science fiction," he said.

"You wrote that book, *Castlescape Chronicles.*"

He looked gratified. "Why, yes—I did."

"Pretty popular, isn't it?"

"It had a certain modest success."

"Lots of the people coming in *here* lately seem to have read it," Hegewisch said bitterly.

She glowered. "Isn't there some kind of law against taking the names of people's businesses and using them as the titles of books without permission?" she demanded. "Shouldn't you have to pay me royalties or something?"

"My dear lady," said the writer, taken aback, "surely you can't claim to own the *word*."

"I can't, can I?" She pointed to the Webster's he held. "You're not going to tell me you found it in there? Tell me it wasn't *this* place that gave you the idea!"

"Writers don't pay royalties for their ideas. Ideas are free."

"Free, huh? Even if the people you steal them from suffer by it?"

"I'm afraid I don't understand. How could you possibly suffer by it? Even if someone connected my book with your restaurant, it would only give you free publicity."

All the day's frustrations burst out of Hegewisch. "Free publicity, *hah!*" she shouted. "Suppose I don't want free publicity? Especially *your* kind. Damn weirdos coming in here all the time—and it's all your fault."

"My dear lady, I—"

"I'm not your dear lady!" Hegewisch snapped. "What do you want to eat?"

"Eat? I...." He looked at the menu as if it were a snake. "Oh, just coffee."

"*Hmmph!* Well, you'll have to wait. I have to make a fresh pot." She stomped back into the kitchen.

"Coffee ... *I'll* give him coffee," she muttered, snagging the last plastic container from the air as it made its way toward the freezer. She busied herself at the Bunn-O-Matic.

When she emerged from the kitchen a few minutes later, coffeepot in hand, the writer still sat in the booth looking stunned. She brought him a cup and poured. He looked a little dubiously at the dark, greasy fluid and then glanced at Hegewisch's grim expression. Hastily he took up the cup and sipped.

He grimaced. "Excellent coffee," he sputtered, "excel . . . *ribbet!*"

Hegewisch looked down. Where the writer had been sat a large, fat frog.

"Well," she said, "*that* recipe works OK."

She picked up the frog and carried him into the kitchen just as Julio, the night cook, came in the back door.

"What you got there?" he asked.

She showed him. "I found it in the dining room."

"You want me to put it outside?"

She considered a moment. "No, there were a couple of kids in here earlier. Perhaps it's a pet and they'll be back for it."

Hegewisch set the frog carefully into the large terrarium in which she grew her special herbs. "It'll be okay here for awhile.

"Oh, by the way, Julio," she said, as she headed back toward the dining room to clear the last booth, "the coffeemaker needs cleaning again."

The frog was not a very happy frog. It spent its days crouching listlessly in the far corner of the terrarium, refusing to eat the fresh flies Hegewisch caught for it.

"What am I going to do with you?" she said. "I suppose I shouldn't be so quick-tempered, but it's your own fault anyway.

"And I can't very well change you back now. Even if nobody believed you—and who would?—it would focus too much attention on this place. I'm too soft-hearted—I ought just to put you out in the road."

Julio came in then, and regarded the frog skeptically. "That one sad frog," he said. "He don't croak, he don't do nothing, just sit there by his lonesome. Maybe he need him a friend."

"Maybe," said Hegewisch, putting on her coat. "I'll see you tomorrow."

The next day was a bad one. The buzzer sent Hegewisch scurrying from the kitchen every ten minutes, and she was so busy flipping burgers and dishing ice cream that she could not begin any of her work. She looked sadly at the stock container she'd set out to thaw, and then glared at the frog.

"This is all your fault," she growled, and went out in answer to the summons of the buzzer.

A tall man was sliding into the last booth as she came out. His high forehead, bushy black eyebrows and thick mustache gave him a saturnine expression. He wore a light jacket with the words "Galactic Way" stenciled on the right side.

"Nice view," he said, as Hegewisch handed him the menu.

"Yes."

"Friend of mine based a book on it."

"Really?"

"Yes, perhaps you know him? A sad thing—he disappeared about a week ago. Just vanished. I came up to see his wife, poor woman."

"Yes ... I remember reading about it in the paper. A real shame. But perhaps he's just off on a toot. You know how those writers are."

He drew himself up. "I know exactly how writers are," he said stiffly. "Not all of us go off on ... toots."

"Oh," Hegewisch said, "another writer. I might have known. He was a good friend of yours, you say? Do you write sci-fi, too?"

"I've written a few books," he said dryly. "You know, my friend's wife just remembered he had said something about stopping here the day he disappeared. Did you see him?"

"Oh, no. He hasn't been in here in a long time."

"Are you sure?"

"Of course I'm sure. What do you want to eat?"

"Eat?" he said. He looked down at the menu. "Oh, let me have the Big Castle and coffee."

As Hegewisch headed back to the kitchen she heard the man say to himself, "I *still* think somebody ought to tell the police he might have come in here."

A short time later there were two frogs in Hegewisch's terrarium.

* * *

"I don't know why I bother," Hegewisch said crossly, as neither frog deigned to show any interest in the fine selection of flying insects she'd brought them for breakfast. They sat at opposite ends of the terrarium, silent and unmoving, except for the pulsing of their yellow throats and the occasional blink of their sad, bulbous eyes.

"I'm going to have to get rid of you anyway. But what good is it, I'd like to know, turning people into frogs if they don't croak, and don't hop or eat flies or do anything froggy?

"Maybe," she mused, "there was something wrong with that recipe. Maybe I ought to try it without the fenugreek." She busied herself at the range.

The morning went well, but the afternoon proved to be another busy one, and by three o'clock Hegewisch was hot, tired and extremely aggravated. The place had emptied out for the first time in hours, and she was standing by the register when an intense-looking, dark-haired man came in, carrying a stack of magazines and a notebook.

She sighed and reached for a menu. "Sit anywhere," she said.

He headed toward the last booth. She started toward him with the menu but he waved it away. "Just coffee," he said, and began leafing through the magazines and jotting down notes.

Hegewisch was chagrined, but not surprised, when she saw the cover of one of the magazines.

"Another science fiction writer," she said.

"Why, yes." He fished out a business card and handed it to her: *SF magazines edited, fine stories written, future writers trained,* it read. "I'm on my way up to Lake Grenada to run a writer's workshop and I thought I'd stop."

He gestured out the window. "I've heard so much about this place. And of course, I couldn't go past Bennington without stopping to see poor—"

He looked up. "Say! What did you mean by *another* science fiction writer?"

"Oh, nothing," Hegewisch said. "I'll get your coffee."

* * *

The three frogs sat morosely in the terrarium. Hands on her broad hips, Hegewisch regarded them in frustration. "There's nothing wrong with the recipe," she said. "Maybe science fiction writers just don't make very *good* frogs.

"But I must do something about you today. Julio is beginning to wonder. You know, that's always the trouble with writing recipes—getting rid of the results of the testing."

But beyond this one irritation, the day was going swimmingly. The restaurant had been quiet as a tomb all day, with only a handful of lunchers coming in promptly at noon and leaving just as promptly before the hour struck 1:00. Hegewisch had had a very productive day, and by late afternoon she felt so cheerful that even the sound of the buzzer failed to bother her.

She came out of the kitchen in time to see a short, rather pudgy woman slide awkwardly into the last booth. Stringy red hair hung in limp corkscrews around her chubby face. The woman gazed out at the castle, her expression sorrowful.

Hegewisch, bringing the menu, eyed the newcomer curiously, wondering what troubled her. Then she got close enough to read the woman's T shirt, which read, "Hoover College Science Fiction Club." An involuntary groan escaped her.

"Coffee?" she offered.

"No, thanks," the woman said. "I don't drink coffee." She took the menu but did not open it.

"You're not a science fiction writer, are you?" Hegewisch asked.

"Well, yes," the woman said, "I am." She turned an unhappy look back out at the castle. "At least, I used to be. Maybe now I'm just a science fiction teacher.

"In fact, I'm on my way to teach a writers' workshop. Another writer was supposed to do it, but he never turned up, so they asked me to fill in. As long as I was coming this way, I stopped here in hopes of a little inspiration."

"Just for inspiration?" Hegewisch said, cautiously.

The woman pointed out the window. "I used to write about exotic worlds and magical castles and mysterious wizards. Now I only teach other people to write about them. I thought maybe looking at that would help."

"Wizards?" Hegewisch said. "You didn't write that book about the wizard of West Chicago?"

The woman nodded.

"I read that," Hegewisch exclaimed. "I thought it was very good. Maybe not quite right on how magic works, but very nice reading, and quite original, too. Not like *some* people's. . . . But you haven't had anything new out in a long time, have you?"

"No," the woman said sadly. "I just can't seem to get anywhere. Every time I try to sit at the keyboard, I find myself distracted by a million other things. Maybe I don't have the right stuff in me anymore."

Hegewisch thought of her own book, and all her interruptions and frustrations, and she was moved. "Aw, don't worry, sister," she said. "You'll get there. Cheer up and have something to eat. I've got just the thing to fix you right up."

She reached back somewhere into the air behind her and brought forth a menu card. "Today's special," it read. "Frogs' legs."

THE HIDDEN GROVE

by Michelle Sagara

The children had been crying for centuries.

Here, in the willow groves that had defied farmers, and then developers, for centuries, the sounds of their voices had softened with time—but they had never disappeared, and they never would. Just beyond the edge of the grove, grass gave way to concrete, concrete to pitted asphalt. People came and went, crossing the unnoticed boundary and leaving empty cartons, plastic bags, and echoes of lunchtime gossip in their wake. They didn't hear the crying; the attenuated whisper of ancient voices sounded like wind.

Then she came, and the heart of the grove stirred as if it remembered her loneliness in its sleep.

The willow grove was a sinister anachronism, surrounded by office buildings and a restaurant that had seen better days. That wasn't why Alia hated it. She had chosen her desk with a view in mind, but the view was now permanently shuttered to close out the grove.

What it didn't alleviate was the sound: Alia could hear, faint but unmistakable, the voices of weeping children. Sometimes they were gentle, almost rhythmic—a child's cry before sleep overtakes it; sometimes they were the sobs of resignation and unending pain.

The first time she heard them, she ran to the grove's edge. There, on the border between cement and grass, she stopped abruptly. Wary, she stared into the shade and the shadows, looking for children beneath the long, supple fingers of the willow trees. Instead, she found employees of Goodman, Lovich & Thompson, eating lunch, reading magazines, and generally enjoying the sunny weather.

She knew, without asking, that no one else could hear the weeping. And she knew better than to ask; she knew how laughter could cut. But she would not join her colleagues in what they called the park.

It started that way, with the crying. It ended a different way, and in between, Alia Stevens found herself driven to seek out the history of the willow grove. She had no idea where to start, but the insistent voices of dead children would not let her rest. Rest was all that she wanted; that and silence.

She began by asking her colleagues if they knew anything about the park. They didn't, but one of the clerks suggested, in a rather condescending way, that she might want to try the Department of Parks and Recreation. She ground her teeth, smiled politely, thanked him—and followed his suggestion.

"I'm sorry, ma'am, but that property isn't under City jurisdiction. Those trees aren't ours, and if they've caused any damage to drains, pipes or power lines, you'll have to take that up with the owner." The young man was brisk and efficient—an unusual sight amid so much bureaucracy.

"Do you have any idea who owns the grove?"

"The what?"

"Park. The park."

"No, ma'am, not personally. But it's not that hard to look up in the municipal listings."

By five o'clock, Alia Stevens held a pad of paper that contained a day's worth of scribbles, scratches and sketches. Two words stood out: Magdalena Rawlings. The name of the woman who had owned the grove for the last twenty-nine years. There were other names that came before it, but no owner—save one—had held the land for less than twenty-six years; no owner, save one, had held it for more than twenty-seven. Magdalena was the latter, and the former was the titled original owner; the only male name in the bunch.

Alia's fingers traced the letters that were all she knew of the owner of the willow grove.

"Alia!"
She started, and suddenly turned her face away from the sun. "Yes?"
"I said, it's nice to see that you've finally decided to let a little light in. Especially since you've got the second best window in the office."

The words took a moment to penetrate, and when they did, the person who had spoken them was gone. Alia barely noticed. She spun in her seat and stared, not at the outside world, but at the window itself. The blinds that she had painstakingly installed were gone; the window, instead of being a barrier against the outside world, now let too much of it in. She could see the heart of the grove: willows weeping like children in the wind.

She wondered how long she had been staring at it without really seeing it. She wondered who had removed her venetian blinds, but she was almost afraid to ask.

There was only one name in the phone book that was even close: Madga Rawlings at 333 Hazelton Crt. There was a regular seven digit phone number as well; Alia copied it down. Then she curled it up and tossed it aside.

You're just being crazy, she told herself. Forget about it.

But she could hear the children crying, as if for justice, throughout the night—and when she did finally sleep, she dreamed of uprooting the great old willows and exhuming hundreds of decayed little corpses from beneath them.

She wanted to hurry through work, but four emergencies came up, and three of them required her immediate attention. Overtime had never been so unwelcome, and Alia struggled to concentrate on it as the sun set and the shadows cast by the grove grew longer. One by one her coworkers' desks emptied; the office became, by degrees, a hushed and quiet place.

Except for the children's voices, there was no noise; Alia's fingers had long since become rigid and frozen as they hovered over her keyboard. She was not, she told herself, as she grabbed her purse and jacket and left her office in disorder, frightened. She did not expect to see the ghosts of feral children crawl up through the pores of the earth's surface to confront her.

But in the streetlamps, the grove's shadows twitched against the wind as if struggling to escape. She walked on the opposite side of the street, as quickly as she could without drawing the attention of anyone—anything—that might be watching.

Hazelton Court wasn't within easy walking distance; in different circumstances, Alia would have taken either a cab or public transit to reach it. But she didn't know she was going there until she saw the smudged street sign at the corner of Hazelton and Cross Road. She knew she had been walking; her feet ached, and the moon had shifted its position, lowering itself gently toward the horizon.

She stopped walking and stared up at the signs. Since she first heard the cries of the grove's children, reality had eroded, and this strange waking dream had shifted gradually to take its place. Why else would she be on this dark road, beneath that moon, at this place?

She drew breath, noticing as if for the first time the faint traces of traffic and industry that settled into her lungs. House number 333 was not that far away, and she had come here to talk of the willow grove, although she hadn't done so deliberately.

The street was empty; the lights seemed dim. Houses in the city had very little frontage, and what there was of it was usually expensive. But the two- and three-story homes had receded into shadows; they were obvious if she squinted hard to read their numbers. Soon, she stopped taking care to do even that.

There was one house, on the left hand side of the street, that seemed well-lit and well tended. It was a small, brick Cape Cod cottage, with roses on trellises at either side of an elaborate door. Ivy covered brick like a shadow. In the darkness, Alia could hear the tinkle of water in a fountain, although the fountain remained hidden from her vision.

She turned up the walk to this house; it had no brass numbers, no plaque, but it was the right one. She walked up to the door, stopped, and inhaled deeply, for strength. The smell of roses wiped clear the hint of city pollution. With a lighter hand, she reached up and gripped the big, brass doorknocker; there was no bell, nothing that looked electronic. In fact, the lights at the house's front looked almost like kerosene lamps.

The door opened with the friendly creak of joints that need just a little oil. Alia had thought to see shadows, darkness—but the woman who stood framed by carved, Victorian lintels stood in front of a well lit, cozy vestibule.

"Hello?"

Alia had the grace to blush. "Hello." She paused, because she suddenly didn't know what to say to the middle-aged woman in the clean, but unpretentious clothing. "You—you've never met me."

The woman's lips curved in a friendly, if somewhat confused smile. "No, I don't believe I have."

"My name's Alia Stevens. I'm terribly sorry to intrude on you, but I was hoping that you could—" could what? She turned self-consciously to look out into Hazelton Court.

It wasn't there. Grass and fields stretched out for miles as far as her night-eyes could see. Her mouth went dry; her eyes lost their ability to blink for a few minutes; her hair, just like that of any story's frightened victim, stood on end. She turned back to the older woman, as if forced to it.

The woman's expression hadn't changed. "Yes? Ms. Stevens, are you all right?"

"I—" she spun again, and this time in the fields of night, she could see the dark shapes of rustling willows. "C–could I borrow your phone?"

"Yes, of course. Has your car broken down? Has something happened?"

"I—no. Yes." Alia shook her head and lifted her hands to her cheeks. She wanted to be out of the fresh, country air; wanted to be confined behind four safe walls, with light and warmth for company.

"Maybe you should come in and sit down for a moment. You look rather pale." The woman extended a hand, and as Alia shook it, she said, "My name is Magda Rawlings. I'm pleased to meet you."

The vestibule gave way to a parlor—for want of a better word—with a love seat, two wing chairs, a low, rosewood coffee table, a fireplace, and a rather ornate writing desk. On either side of the fireplace were bookshelves with leaded, beveled glass panes enclosing antiquarian volumes.

"Do you like books?" Magda Rawlings asked, noting the direction of her unusual visitor's stare. "Most people don't these days." She shook her head; a strand of graying hair fell loose from her bun and lay across her forehead.

"I like them," Alia said softly.

"The phone is over there. It's inside the upper right drawer of the desk. I have a phone, but I don't like the look of it in this room, so I do my best to hide it."

"Phone? Oh—the phone." Alia swallowed. "I—thank you." She walked over to the desk and gingerly pulled open the delicate drawer. Light flared up like solar fire; Alia screamed and pulled her hand back, clutching it tightly to her chest. Openmouthed, she turned to stare at Magda Rawlings.

Magda Rawlings was staring back at her, only this time there was no confusion in her gaze. Instead there was something that resembled compassion—or worse, pity. "My name," she said, in a voice that was subtly altered, "is Magdalena Rawlings. I own the witch's grove." She began to move toward Alia, and Alia scrabbled away. "Look at your hand, Alia. Look at it carefully, and tell me what you see." Her words had deepened and strengthened so much it sounded as if they should had been spoken by many people, not one.

Trembling, Alia did as ordered. In the flesh of her palm, tip touching the base of her middle finger, was a slender willow leaf. She could not name it. Instead, she raised a shaking hand and turned it, palm out, fingers spread, to face Magdalena Rawlings.

"As I thought," Magdalena said. "It's the witch-mark." She shook her head slowly, deliberately, and as she did, her hair slowly came down in a widening spiral at her back. "The parlor isn't the place for you, Alia; not yet. Come out to the farm with me." She held out a hand.

Alia stared at it, and after a moment, it was withdrawn. "Come," Magdalena said again, her voice softer. "I'm well past my time, but there are things that you have to understand."

Alia didn't want to understand anything; she wanted to leave. More than that, she wanted to eradicate all trace of the mark from her left hand. She was surprised to find herself following Magdalena Rawlings as the older woman led her through the parlor, the hall, the kitchen, and a small mudroom. It was as if she was under a spell.

A spell. The witch's grove.

"What do you see, Alia?" Magdalena's voice was quiet, almost subdued, as she opened the mudroom door into the night. "I had a garage built fifteen years ago. My neighbours have a grape arbor in full bloom near my fence; it surrounds a pool."

Alia shook her head; she heard the words as if they were uttered in a language she could not speak but knew enough of to identify. She had never seen stars so clear or the moon so bright. There was no light pollution hovering across the horizon like a white coccoon; there were fields, and beyond them, forest.

Then, as her eyes readjusted to the night, she saw a tall rectangular shadow that loomed above the fences and cattle-runs in one pasture. Light flickered in the cracks between two boards that had seen better days.

"Barn," she whispered.

"Yes."

Just beyond the barn, but visible from the house, was the willow grove.

"You're twenty-seven; you are of the age. You came to ask me about the witch's grove. Return when I call you."

Alia turned to speak to the woman beside her. There wasn't one. And there was no house, no lights, no warmth. There was a chill breeze through the tall grass and the sounds of sleepy crickets in place of the city sounds that were so much a part of her life she didn't know what made them anymore.

I don't want the answer. Her mouth mimed speech. She tried to vocalize the words, but none came; the corn stalks bending in wind had a stronger voice, a greater presence, than she. She looked down and saw grass, weeds, the scuttle of something nocturnal. Minutes passed before she realized why this felt wrong.

She had no feet, no legs, no physical presence; the moon caused her to cast no shadow, but rather, to be one. The chill she felt had nothing to do with the weather, and everything to do with the darkness.

But light came from one place on the field: the barn. She searched the shadows that enfolded her, seeking what remained of Hazelton Court. Then, squaring her shoulders and changing the fall of linen against her skin, she began to walk in a straight line toward the flickering light.

The light came out to greet her, leaving a tail like a meteor's in its wake. She raised her hand and in it an old lantern began to creak and sway with the night wind. The ground was treacherous in the darkness; she had to be careful of the well and the sudden little precipice that jutted out just before the barn.

She wiped her hands in her skirts and felt her lower lip as her canines bit through it. No, no—she couldn't do this. She had to go back, had to go home; he would see her soon and then she'd be in for it.

Where is home? Who is he?

She stood, frozen, and the lights continued to flicker in the barn. There were no screams; whatever work was left was silent work. She wanted to run, but whether forward or back she could not say.

Mary was not in her bed. Not in any room of the house. Neither was he. They had both vanished without a sound, and like as not, only one of them would return come dawn. It'd happened three times before. Once, when she was nineteen, pregnant again with her third child. Once, when she was twenty-one. The third time when she was twenty-three. This was the last time, the last one. She'd sworn it. She isn't young anymore, not at twenty-seven, and she'd lost all but one of the children; all her daughters. She'd given him no sons.

Then get moving, get moving, you weak-willed fool; it's late, time's pressing. But he'd hurt her, she knew it. If he found her, he'd hurt her. And what had she thought she'd do here? How had she thought to stop him? She swallowed; the sides of her throat clung together like frightened children. Fear kept her here, halfway between action and flight. Fear held her in its deceptive arms as time passed. She told herself that she heard nothing, that nothing but light was amiss in the barn. She didn't believe it.

Maybe if she'd left, she could have.

The barn doors blew open; the light of a single lamp glowed at his side like an inferno. He held his night's work by the hair. It followed him limply; there was no life in it to put up any resistance.

She dropped at once to the ground, using the hill's shelf to hide her lamp and her expression; using it to try to protect herself from the truth: her failure. Her throat moved; her stomach twisted. In their wake, a sour smell. Too late. Always too late.

Now was the time to run home; he'd catch her here, and it would all be for nothing. Mary was beyond her.

No, it won't be for nothing. They've been buried like heathens. I'll find out where; I'll find out that much. At least then they wouldn't be trapped for an eternity.

Oh, but she would be. Because she'd seen him, with Mary behind him like any farm animal chosen for festivities. She wouldn't forget it, or what it meant. Not even in heaven, if heaven was open for women who failed all of their earthly charges, could she ever stop seeing it.

[Alia. Alia Stevens. Return now.]

She rose, catching the lamp in a shaking hand; Alia
Stevens did not. On a cedar deck, she finished throwing
up and then sat rocking back and forth, her arms wrapped
tightly around her shoulders.

"Did you see the grove, Alia?"

Alia shook her head, trying to take in air and reality at
the same time.

Magda Rawlings looked up at the waxing moon, the
hint of a frown across her forehead. "That's bad," she
said softly. "You've not much time, and the moon might
well be too strong." Then she shook her graying head.
"Come in, Alia. Come in and I'll try to tell you what
you've seen."

Alia knew what was buried in the willow grove. She
knew whose voices she heard when she worked at Goodman, Lovich & Thompson. She knew who she dreamed
of, and what their deaths had been. She even knew why
the cries were quiet; terror does that.

She gazed down at her hand; the willow leaf trembled
there as if in wind. "What is a witch mark?"

"The moon will tell you," Magdalena answered. The
older woman seemed tired, even apprehensive, as the
hours dragged by. "You've been long in coming, Alia."
She glanced out of her windows, seeing what Alia could
not: city streets, city lights. "And you've the hardest
stretch to walk yet. Ah. There. It's time." She rose, although what clock told her to gain her feet, Alia couldn't
say. "Come."

This time, Alia followed with greater reluctance and
less fear. The moon was low and full and waiting; she
could see the sorrow and anger in its ancient face. Almost, the expression there began to deepen and
strengthen as Alia watched.

"This is important, Alia: Return when I call you."

The barn was dark; the light had been leeched from it
by the center of the willow grove. It flickered, giving the
shadows a life of their own. The shadows had voices;
those voices called Alia.

She was walking, quietly, in the moonlight. She and

Alia were not the same woman, but they walked, step for step, the same road this night. They found the same path through the tall grass and goldenrod, trod in it with the same care, lit by the moon's white light, cool heat.

And when the grove opened its doors and revealed its heart, they were both struck silent at the sight of her husband, digging by lamplight. His sallow skin was filmed with sweat and darkly stained.

He was singing.

His song was a wild croon, a savage keening; as they came closer they could see that not all of the water that gleamed on his cheeks was sweat. Tears ran, dark and dirt-mired; he shuttered his eyes every time his hands crossed his extremely narrow field of vision.

Alia stood frozen with lack of comprehension. The other woman slipped away from her, drawing closer and closer to husband and daughter. *"What have you done to my Mary?"*

He turned, his shovel spraying dirt at her feet. In the lamplight other bones could be seen, jutting above their disturbed earth coffin. His singing stopped. "You shouldn't have come here, Eleanor. You're too old for the willows."

"The willows?" Her voice was almost plaintive.

"Can't you hear them? They're magnificent, Eleanor— and they're mine. I do—" he swallowed and closed his eyes, "what I have to for them."

Alia looked down at her hand, at its mark. It shimmered in the moonlight with its own life. She listened; she could almost hear its voice. It spoke as he did.

"They say, *give me children*." He stepped forward, his arms raised, his shovel just above the line of his shoulders. His wife took a step back, raising her own to defend her face, her head.

"They were not speaking to you, James Barnow." Both husband and wife turned at the sound of Alia's voice. She should have been surprised that they could see her, but she wasn't; the willow trees were glowing faintly over the open grave.

Oh, the waste, the waste of it. Some part of her wanted

to weep. She was no longer afraid. The moon above her head was a tiara; the trees at her side were her honor guards. She forgot that she had ever feared them.

"I own them," the man shouted back, wife forgotten. "Who else would they speak to?"

"Me." Alia spoke with the moon's voice. "They were never meant to be left to anyone but us; their voice is too strong." She lifted her hand to catch a spill of moonlight; the willow leaf sat in her palm like the tip of a spear.

"James Barnow," her voice was cold, "the only life you had to give to the grove was your own." Moonlight became lightning, an act of wild magic. The man's face wore his outrage, his fear, his longing—but he had no time to express them. His shovel hit the ground with a thud, and Alia turned to Eleanor Barnow. The third of his wives.

She raised her hand again as Eleanor stared, speechless. "The groves are your responsibility. They must never be given to anyone who does not bear this mark."

Eleanor Barnow nodded, speechless, and then bolted like a rabbit, severing all ties, all the hidden links, between them.

[*Alia. Alia Stevens. Return now.*]

Alia heard the call; felt the pull of a witch's voice. But the willows exerted a call of their own, their voices soft and sinuous, their fingers a gentle rustle in the night. Hushed, expectant, they whispered their joy and their desire to Alia Stevens, and she listened because she had never been spoken to in such a way by anyone.

Magda Rawlings sat in her kitchen, her hands warming a cold cup of coffee. Her brow was creased with worry and concentration as she called a second time. And a third.

The moon was strong. Magda feared a return to the farm, but what else could she do? Alia Stevens had not returned—and it was imperative that she not remain in the grove at that time.

Magda went out the mudroom doors, lifted her left hand, and began to speak, when Alia Stevens, surrounded by a lambent silver, walked onto the deck. Before she could stop herself, Magdalena Rawlings dropped to one knee and smiled with relief. "You've returned."

"Yes," Alia said slowly. "I've seen what the grove holds. I know why we're charged with its keeping. I will guard the grove to the twenty-seventh year; I will find a new keeper when I tire." She held out her left hand; Magdalena grasped it peacefully. When they parted, Magdalena's left hand was unmarked.

"Thank you, Alia."

But Alia was no longer listening to Magda.

The children were still crying; she could hear them, would hear them forever.

But above them, she could hear the purr of the willows. She placed a hand gently over her stomach. In three times three months she would return to the grove with a mystery, and the voice that she added to its circle might one day be raised in joy.

AN UN-FAMILIAR MAGIC

by Mel. White

Vidalia McGuzela lifted the lid of the stewpot hanging on a hook over the fire and cautiously tasted the bubbling broth. Supper was almost ready; she could hear the thumping of her grandmother's walking stick coming up the flagstones of the path to the cottage. She reached into the vegetable bin and pulled out an onion, sighing as she did so. Keeping house for her grandmother wasn't a pleasant job, but it was the only thing available for a spinster of twenty-two. The walking stick sounded louder now, rapping noisily on the porch. It required no magical powers to figure out that her scrappy grandmother was mad at someone again.

"I'm gonna put the FIX on that woman!" Ouachita McGuzela announced as she stormed into the room, slamming the front door open like a crack of thunder. Vidalia barely looked up from the onion she was peeling. It wasn't hard to guess the subject of her grandmother's wrath.

"What's Sibley Choudrant done now?" she asked.

"She's tryin' to put the hex on Ruston DuBach so he'll marry her, and she'll end up with him an' ol Cato d'Lo's fortune, too—that's what!"

Vidalia slid the onion onto the wooden tabletop and began carefully slicing it. "Sibley isn't the only one who wants him. Ruston DuBach's a handsome and educated young man," she observed, "and Talulah said that Cato d'Lo left him nearly a million dollars for his inheritance. They may not have thought much of him and his family when they left Lumbago Creek twenty years ago, but everyone who's got an unmarried daughter was downright eager to greet Ruston DuBach when he came in on the morning coach. That's what Talulah says."

"Talulah wouldn't know a million squirrels if they climbed up her leg," her grandmother sniffed. "Fact is, his late and unlamented uncle willed thirty thousand dollars an' his land to Ruston. That's not as rich as the kings of Croesus, but it's not hayseed an' moonshine, neither."

"Talulah said that folks are so eager to have Ruston become their son-in-law that they've been buying up love charms from everywhere and paying lots of money for them. She says that Naill's getting rich selling love charms made by his great-granny," Vidalia said.

"Your sister's entirely too nosy for her own good," Ouachita mumbled as she leaned her walking stick beside the door. "And Naill's great-granny didn't know a hex from a spotted cow. Those things he's selling are just old junk jewelry that she had bought. Some folks'll buy darn near anything."

Vidalia wiped her nose on her sleeve and sniffed loudly. "Talulah also said that competition is so fierce that Friendship Clamrock actually paid to have a love spell put on Ruston," she added. Ouachita sat up, her eyes narrowing ominously.

"Oh, really? Did she say who Friendship went to?" Ouachita queried in a too-casual tone. Her eyes glittered with jealousy. Though Ouachita had retired from formal spellcasting twenty years ago, her days as a self-styled commentator on magical events were not over. Vidalia picked up the second half of the onion and began slicing again.

"Talulah says that Friendship's getting the spell from Pendora Fishbinder."

"Pendora Fishbinder? She don't know nothin," her grandmother sniffed. "She only does two spells because they balance each other. The good luck that comes from doing the pox spell balances out the bad luck that comes from doing that 'love at first glance' spell. And if one of them goes wrong, all she has to put up with is a bout of heat rash."

Her grandmother's attitude was typical of the older generation of spellcasters, who'd devoted their lives to their art. They were often contemptuous of the younger generation, who preferred to avoid the arcane contortions of logic and devoted themselves to quick spells and fast love charms. Vidalia didn't blame them. Hexing was a complex skill and the laws of magic were similar to Newton's laws. For every magical action there was an equal and opposite reaction. Every spell for the benefit of someone also brought a balancing stroke of misfortune. The spell that brought a man the girl of his dreams also brought with it the mother-in-law of his nightmares; a situation that few were eager to have land in their metaphoric laps. And few people were willing to have a spell cast on them to turn them into a human gargoyle with body odor that would drop a fly at sixty paces in exchange for having a small fortune land in their laps.

"Why'd she go to Pendora Fishbinder?" her grandmother prodded.

"I think Friendship Clamrock really wanted to go to Quality Pushfeather. But Quality's raised her prices ever since she started using familiars. Friendship couldn't buy a potion from her now."

"Quality Pushfeather? Hah. That one don't know nothin', neither," Ouachita snorted, dismissing the oldest practicing hexenmacher in Lumbago Creek with a wave of her blue-veined hand. "Quality just hexes and lets the good luck come to her and the bad luck fall on her familiars. And the critters hereabouts know it. There ain't a cat in all of Lumbago Creek who'll come to her for love nor liver. She's paying Froggy Clamrock to catch frogs and bugs for her hexing, since there ain't much that bad luck can do to a frog or a bug except make it explode. Exploding bug gets all over the walls and floors, you know. Can't hardly get bug out of the wood when it's exploded like that."

Vidalia nodded mechanically in time with her grandmother's tirade. She was familiar with Ouachita's opinions about the younger generation of spellcasters in Lumbago Creek. The matriarch of the McGuzela clan was known far and wide for inflicting her opinions on anyone or anything who'd stand still for fifteen seconds.

Hexing was the traditional way of settling problems in Lumbago Creek, and a powerful hexenmacher could name his or her own price for any spell. Whoever had the most money could buy the best hexenmacher, and often the appearance of the party of the first part with the spellcaster of the second part was enough to force a prompt resolution to most social issues. Ouachita maintained that the new generation of spellcasters had little taste for the risky business of developing new spells—and perhaps they *were* incompetent when it came to magic. But she didn't like the way her grandmother's eyes glittered as she fished among the odds and ends over the fireplace.

"Granny, you're not going to do anything rash, are you?"

"Good heavens, child! You worry too much," she answered as she tucked a packet of dried leaves into a pocket of her apron. "You just tend to that stew. I think I'll go upstairs and have a lie-down for a bit."

"Being that Sibley's the strongest hexenmacher around, I suppose that she'll end up with Mr. DuBach," Vidalia said mildly as she slid the slices of onion into the bubbling stewpot, wondering if she could bait her scrappy grandmother into revealing her plans.

"She will over my dead body!" Ouachita snorted indignantly. "It's time she learned that she ain't queen. Having Ruston and the money end up in someone else's hands would be a good lesson for her and it's high time I showed her who was what."

Vidalia probed carefully. "You got someone in mind, Granny?"

"I got a client in mind, if that's what you mean," her grandmother declared, poking a spoon into the stew. "And just because I retired don't mean I'm dead yet. Now where's my books? I need to get to work. Ruston DuBach's gonna get himself a bride."

Vidalia's heart thudded painfully. She had been in the crowd of gawkers when Ruston DuBach, dark and elegant, had emerged from the coach. His years of schooling at the Noodle Dome public college had done wonders for him. While Cato had been a hunched and soured old miser with a voice like a squeaky pump handle, his nephew Ruston was as tall and elegant as one of the statues of the old gods she saw in the Temple at Far Littlehaven—and just as approachable. Vidalia had watched him from the safety of the Lonely Petunia's side porch and made a small wish for herself that somehow Ruston DuBach would fall madly in love with her.

You and every other woman in Lumbago Creek, she reminded herself.

Ouachita pottered around the parlor for a few minutes, digging out old packets of herbs and other spellcasting tools. "I'll just go find my reading glasses now," she announced brightly as she tucked a blob of red wax in another apron pocket and turned toward the staircase at the back of the house. "And don't you worry none, child. I won't do anything rash. I'm just going upstairs for a bit of reading right now."

Vidalia set the knife down and wiped her hands. Ouachita wasn't fooling either of them. While she couldn't stop her headstrong grandmother from going to the Lonely Petunia, Vidalia knew there was a chance that she and her sister could come up with a quick plan to get Ouachita out of the inn before the other spellcasters tangled in a major hex war. If Ouachita's spells were as bad as Talulah said they were, the results would be disastrous. Having your poor old grandmother turned into a frog would make things terribly awkward at family reunions.

"Granny, I'll be back in a few minutes," she yelled as she tossed the towel down on the table and sprinted for the door. With any luck she might get a half-hour start over her grandmother.

The Lonely Petunia was the best place in Lumbago Creek to get all the gossip. It was also the ONLY place in Lumbago Creek; an all-purpose establishment serving as post office, general store, pub, hotel, stable, and tourist trap. Vidalia sprinted down the long hill toward the Petunia. It was later than she'd expected; high water in the creek had forced her to take a detour and she could only hope that nightfall would slow her grandmother down. With any luck, all the spell-brawling would be over by the time Ouachita got there.

Ruston DuBach sat at a table beside the window, staring longingly at his reflection. Vidalia slid into a chair at a small empty table and waved to her sister, Talulah, who was serving customers at the bar counter. Talulah ducked a pinch from a traveler, slapped a plate in front of a tired-looking woman, and hurried over to Vidalia's table.

"Oooh, have YOU been missing things!" Talulah announced, setting the silverware in front of Vidalia.

"What's been going on?"

"You missed some of the wildest hexing round these parts since the Great Kudzu Wars," Talulah grinned.

Like most of Ouachita's descendants, Talulah could see spells, though she didn't have enough hexenpower to actually cast them. This made her a fairly good reporter on all the magical gossip of the area.

"Tell me about it," Vidalia demanded.

"Well, it's been going on for hours. It started when the lovely and elegant Ruston poked his nose out of his room and came down for tea. He said he was meeting Summerall here so they could go out to look at the estate."

"I hope someone warned him about the way Summerall drives," Vidalia countered. Lumbago Creek's sole lawyer, Summerall F. Theeabov, had always dreamed of being a racing jockey and insisted on showing his clients how thrilling it was to speed across the landscape in a light buggy. It usually only took one ride with Summerall to convince clients that they would go to any lengths to avoid a repeat experience. People had been known to confess to crimes that hadn't been invented yet after a trip in Summerall's buggy.

"I don't know if he was warned. If he was, he's still riding with Summerall. Anyways, while he was staring at the stuff Naill claims is poached eggs, Magray Maggingsly came storming in and said that Cinnamon Clamrock had cornered Summerall over at the post office and was asking him questions about a will and waving around some of her money. Meanwhile, her daughter and Quality Pushfeather came over here to work on Ruston."

Vidalia nodded. Summerall was easily distracted by money. No doubt he was as hypnotized by Cinnamon's waving greenbacks as a chicken was by a chalked line. "Did Quality Pushfeather have any luck?" she asked.

"Depends on what you mean by luck," Talulah grinned, twisting a lock of her blonde hair. "A complete matching set of cockroaches was done in by her love spell fallout and Naill's fair-to-steamed about trying to get exploded cockroach off the walls. You shoulda seen the way Cinnamon's daughter screamed and ran out when the bugs blew up. Then Magray Maggingsly says she don't mind exploding bugs and goes over there and offers Quality two silver dollars if she'll do just one spell on Ruston for her."

Vidalia glanced over at the oblivious target. "Doesn't look like it did much good."

"Well, while she and Magray were haggling over price, Pendora Fishbinder waltzed in with Airria Palindrome and started to work on Ruston. Pendora was using that old 'fall in love with the first person you see' spell and Airria was waving her handkerchief at Ruston, hoping to catch his eye. But just as Pendora's spell hit, Froggy tripped over Ruston's feet and then Ruston started eye-balling Froggy Clamrock in a friendly way. Froggy started threatening Quality that if she didn't take the spell off Ruston, he'd never bring her another frog no matter what she paid him! And you know how—"

"Right," Vidalia interrupted, rubbing her forehead. Trying to follow Talulah's narratives required leaps in faith and logic that would test the patience of most theologians. "One of Pendora's spells hit the wrong target. So what happened next?"

"Then Quality used her last frog to knock Pendora's spell out. That frog just bugged out its eyes and shriveled up like a rock. Quality was most upset and started eye-balling the room, looking for someone to use as a luck collector in place of a familiar. Froggy Clamrock done lit out for home when she started staring at him. . . ."

"The spells. What happened to Mr. DuBach after that?" Vidalia prompted warily. She pushed her glasses up on her nose and looked across the room. The hexenmachen stared at their target like chickens eyeing a fat June bug. Ruston, oblivious to their attention, was staring fondly at his own image in a small handheld mirror.

"Pendora Fishbinder hit him with a triple 'fall in love with the first one he sees' spell. Darn near floored me, it did. Airria must have paid her a lot because I never thought she'd go that far for a client. Or course, she's got—"

"TALULAH!"

"Okay, okay. Don't get sore. Anyways when the spell hit, he was checking his hair in the mirror, so he fell in love with himself." Talulah grinned, giving the table a quick flick with her washrag. "An then it was a competition— Quality and Pendora mutterin' spells while Magray and Airria glared at each other. In the past hour Ruston's been in love with the postal rider, Froggy Clamrock, the inn-keeper, the innkeeper's daughter, Great-granny Clamrock, two passengers on Abelian Parsestring's stage, and the pic-ture of the nude lady in the bar."

"Geez," Vidalia said, chewing on the earpiece of her glasses. "And to make things worse, Granny's on her way here. And she's determined to put a hex so that Sibley Choudrant won't marry Ruston DuBach."

"Well, things just got worse than that, sister mine."

"How could they possibly get worse?" Vidalia count-ered.

"Sibley Choudrant just walked in, and she's carrying her familiar."

"WHAT???"

"Yeah. Third table from the corner. Right rear. And— get this—her familiar's a cat!" Talulah said, pointing to a table behind Vidalia.

Vidalia turned, staring at the redheaded hexenmacher.

"Where did Sibley get a cat? There haven't been any cat familiars in Lumbago Creek since the Great Kudzu Spell Wars back in '93."

"I dunno. But that white thing that she's got is sure a cat."

Of all the familiars used by hexenmachen as all-purpose psychic "whipping boys" for spell backlash, cats were the most popular and most difficult to obtain. Hexenmachen had tried using other things such as inanimate objects, but there was little that could happen that qualified as good luck or bad luck to a rock. Rocks, instead, stored up the accumulated karma and tended to release it all at once and at the most inconvenient time of all. Thus a spellcaster might drop dead of acute halitosis on the very day that a messenger arrived to tell her that her Great Uncle Aldo had died and left her a huge baronial estate.

But there were some problems in using living creatures for earthing magical effects. One of the more common consequences of a spell going awry was that the familiar would explode. It wasn't wise to get too close to a hexenmacher's familiar—physically or emotionally.

For a while, they tried using cockroaches to earth the power, since few people minded if roaches disintegrated in a spectacular way. However this practice came to a quick end when Balmoral Beantwiddler discovered that after being at ground zero for eight or ten spells, cockroaches evolved into two-foot-long invulnerable scuttling monsters that invaded the pantry and demanded longer and messier lunch hours. Popular opinion held it that the hexenmachen needed something too fat to hide under the sofa and too stupid or independent to gang up on the hexenmacher in the middle of the night to earth their magical overflow.

Some eighty years after that, cats were declared to be the perfect familiar for hexenmachen. Generally clean and usually quiet except for the occasional bellowed MEOW that meant "feed me," a cat's idea of good times and cosmic harmony was fish kibble six times a day and a toasty spot by the fire to nap on. Disasters usually took the form of hairballs that the cat considerately coughed up in unexpected places around the hexenmacher's home, sharing the negative karma with the hexenmacher and reducing its effects. But during the Great Kudzu Spell Wars, cats of Lumbago Creek had learned to duck whenever any hexenmacher started mumbling and waving their arms and now they were rare indeed.

"I don't know where Sibley got a cat from. It's not from around here," her sister shrugged. "I think it's stolen or lost from some lady. It's got long white fluffy fur and looks like it should be sitting on a silk pillow and drinking cream."

Vidalia glanced at the corner. "Wouldn't be stolen," she said. "That'd be too much bad luck. Probably lost and she found it. Or took it as a fee for something she did for some lady in Hillshire."

"Looks scared," her sister commented sympathetically.

"It's got every right to look scared," Vidalia muttered. "It's got a short and eventful life ahead of it."

"Poor kitty," her sister murmured, watching the huddled lump of white fur. Sibley smiled and waved imperiously at her. "I'd better go see what the old bag wants," Talulah muttered, fixing a bright and very insincere smile on her face.

Some people merely sit at a table. Sibley Choudrant reigned over the whole corner of the Lonely Petunia where she sat. Patrons who were aware of the spell wars moved quickly to the edges of the room, out of line of fire. Sibley nodded and smiled at them like a queen acknowledging her subjects. Vidalia stared at her and thought sourly to herself that Sibley didn't need any love spells to attract men to her. The red-haired hexenmacher had a figure that most women only dream of (and men dream about) and warm full lips. Most of the men in Lumbago Creek had fallen in love with her at one time or another, but Sibley had never shown any interest in any of them—until now.

Sibley's demands seemed short enough, for Talulah only stayed at the table for a few seconds. Then she nodded as she left Sibley's table, then went over to the other hexenmachen in the room. After a moment, the others rose and approached Sibley's table, looking like they wanted to bite the red-haired beauty. Sibley smiled and pointed to the two chairs at the table and Vidalia strained to hear the low-toned conversation.

". . . after all, I AM the most powerful hexenmacher in Lumbago Creek," Sibley was saying to the others. "I wouldn't want you to be hurt, dears, when my spell hits the lovely Mr. DuBach and your hexes come back to you. So this is your one and only chance to remove them yourselves."

Quality Pushfeather stiffened. "I don't think . . ."

"Exactly," Sibley smiled, petting her cat. "That's why you'll be in trouble when my spell is triggered. You don't have anything to earth the backlash when it comes in." She leaned forward and cooed sweetly. "How many bugs did you lose when Pendora Fishbinder's spells hit? Five? Eight? I'm stronger than her and you're out of bugs. That means it'll all fall on you."

She paused, letting her words sink in. "Now, you might have been saving all your luck for when you ran out of frogs and bugs, but I don't think you plan that far ahead. I'm doing Wisdom Henmender's True Love Forever Spell—the one from old Patience Clamrock's book. I've got a cat to earth the leftovers in, but you don't have anything at all. I suggest you call it a day and take off your spell and go back to hexing warts."

Quality Pushfeather paused, and Sibley began mumbling. The older hexenmachen gasped and made a swift gesture as she bolted for the door. Magray Maggingsly, seeing her spellcaster and her hopes vanishing simultaneously, yelled something that no lady would ever say in public and charged out the door after her. Sibley smiled, scratched the cat under its chin, and waved imperiously at Talulah. "Bring me another cup of tea," she said, staring in triumph at Ruston DuBach. "And you can take away that other cup. Quality Pushfeather doesn't seem to be in the mood for my hospitality." She gestured and muttered and Ruston DuBach suddenly blinked in astonishment as the spell accumulation was lifted from him. He stared sheepishly around the room. Heads turned quickly and conversation resumed at an artificially bright level; the noise of people pretending that nothing had happened.

Pendora Fishbinder looked around the room. Airria Palindrome held up two more silver dollars, and after a long moment held up a third. Pendora hoisted her nose in the air, waved her fingers, and muttered the Love At First Sight spell. Sibley sneered.

"It may be old, but Boxen Wanderwood's 'Love At First Sight' is one reliable spell. And it's one you can't break without terrible things happening!" Pendora said defensively. "Or don't you read the hexendiagrams?" she asked, referring to the hexenmacher's all-purpose book of notes and spells that told how many points for good or bad each spell was worth. With careful use, you could make sure that the number of bad points and the number of good points were about the same and be relatively safe from whatever it was that enforced the laws of Karma in Lumbago Creek.

"And that spell works so WELL, dear," Sibley said, baring her teeth in something that might have been a smile. "Ruston now seems to be in love with the stuffed moose head. Was that your original customer? I know you've been hard up for patrons lately, because they've all been coming to me, but I thought you usually stuck to living clients. I didn't know you worked for the dead as well."

Pendora Fishbinder huffed up like pouter pigeon and Vidalia wondered for one moment what Naill would say if Pendora exploded all over the walls. "You should leave, dear. I'm starting my spell," Sibley said. "You know what broken spells do to you."

"I'll stay," Pendora Fishbinder said defiantly.

"It was your choice," Sibley said, sealing the action with a wave of her long-fingered hands. "If you drop dead of heat rash, it's not my fault." There was a sudden hush, as though everyone in the room suddenly stopped breathing.

"Leave be with that hex!" a cracked voice commanded. Sibley blinked and turned. "Ouachita McGuzela," she said in a voice like sweet poison. "Don't tell me that you came to make Ruston DuBach fall in love with you! I'm not sure there's enough hexenpower in the world to do that."

Ouachita drew herself up to her full height of four feet, eight inches. "I've got more'n enough hexenpower to stop you, girl!" she said regally.

Sibley sneered. "You? You retired years ago after your hexing quit working. You're ancient history—and I DO mean ancient. Go home and look after your garden, Granny, and leave the hexing to those of us who've got the powers—or do I have to prove to you that I'm the strongest hexenmachen in Lumbago Creek?"

Vidalia pawed her sister's arm "Quick!" she hissed, "Distract Sibley—drop a beer or something on her head! I'll see if I can get Granny out of here!" She rose and started toward the tableau as Sibley began casting her spell. "NO!" was all she had time to scream, and then the aura around the cat flared peacock green and blue and the lights went out. This was followed by a shriek and the sound of cloth being ripped.

Vidalia paused, panting in the darkness. It was probably dangerous to show a light, because Sibley might be in the mood to fire a spell at anything that moved. But fear for her grandmother overcame any dread of personal danger. Vidalia fumbled in her pocket for a match. She scraped it along the rough floorboards and held it high, looking around to see if any damage had been done. Then she grabbed a candle from a nearby table and lit the wick; its feeble golden glow brought an air of normalcy to the inn. The inn's furniture, at least, was intact. Naill didn't get upset about a little spellcasting on his property as long as nobody damaged the furniture.

She reached for the candleholder on the table and encountered another warm, groping hand. Startled, she looked across the surface and into the eyes of Ruston DuBach.

"Hello," he smiled. The universe seemed to stand still for a long moment.

"Hello," she managed. There was a long pause. Her heart thudded painfully against her ribs.

"I'm Ruston DuBach."

"I know," she said, and mentally kicked herself for the lame-sounding conversation.

"That was wonderful the way you lit that match after all the lights in here went out." He didn't seem to be doing much better at small talk, she noticed.

"Really?"

"Really. I don't know why the lights went out like that. There must have been a gust of wind or something."

"It gets windy in these parts," she said.

"You sound like you're someone who really knows the area well. You know, I'm supposed to go out and look over Cato's estate. They said that I shouldn't ride anywhere with Summerall F. Theeabov, but I could use the help of someone who knows Lumbago Creek," he smiled. "I have no idea where Uncle Cato lived. Maybe you could ride out with me and show me around. It strikes me that a man could get into a lot of trouble if he got into the wrong place at the wrong time."

You don't know the half of it, she thought as she smiled into his deep cornflower blue eyes. "I'd be glad to help, Mr. DuBach."

"Call me Ruston," he said softly and she blushed furiously.

Across the room, matches began to light other table candles. Naill's customers began checking themselves to see if they'd acquired any extra limbs when the lights went out. "There're certainly a lot of interesting people in Lumbago Creek," Ruston commented, still holding her hand. "Does everyone around here mutter to themselves?"

Muttering reminded her of Sibley, and she turned to look at the still dark corner where the hexenmacher had been sitting. A huge figure bulked there, whimpering softly to itself. Vidalia raised the candle a little higher, revealing a shape that looked like Hercules—if the demigod had overdosed on steroids and weight training classes. "Sibley?" she asked hesitantly.

"DON'T LOOK AT ME! DON'T LOOK AT ME!!" came the tortured scream and the bulky figure scrambled for the door of the inn. Those who could see what Sibley had become gasped and recoiled in shock. Ouachita McGuzela simply nodded with satisfaction.

"She always said she was the strongest hexenmachen in Lumbago Creek," Ouachita commented. "I guess there's no disputin' that now. She could lift carthorses if she wanted to. Last time I saw muscles like that was on the poster of the circus strong man . . . now what was his name . . . the one that came through here two summers back."

Vidalia turned in time to see Ouachita pick up Sibley's familiar. Cat and hexenmacher looked at one another and apparently came to some sort of understanding, for it bumped against Ouachita's chin and rumbled a loud purr. "What a sweetie-lovie!" Ouachita cooed to the cat. "Poor little pussums come home with Ouachita?"

"My, there are certainly some . . . unusual . . . folk around here," Ruston said as he stared at Sibley's departing form. Vidalia turned and looked back at her grandmother. "Mr. DuBach . . ." she mouthed slowly at her grandmother. Ouachita McGuzela held a skinny forefinger to her lips as her familiar slowly winked one china blue eye at Vidalia. Lumbago Creek's hexenmacher was still queen of the spellcasters.

THE SPELL

by David Gerrold

My next-door neighbors have six children. This is not enough reason to hate them, but it's a good start.

The smallest one, Tali, is ambulatory, but still preverbal. She is not a problem. She can stay. We will leave her name off the eviction notice.

Next up is Nolan. He has been retarded at the age of three for four years now. Nolan is an interesting social experiment. What do you get if you allow a child to raise himself without any parental involvement at all?

He breaks things. He takes things. He denies accountability. He starts fires. He blames other children. He screams. He goes into other people's yards, and he climbs up onto the roofs of houses—usually his own, but occasionally the roof of a neighbor as well. He throws things over the fence into my yard, oftentimes aiming for the pool. A half-eaten Taco Bell burrito must be retrieved within the first thirty minutes or you can plan on having the filter cleaned again.

Wait, there's someone at the door—

(on paper the pauses don't show)

—it was Nolan. I can't even write this down without one of the little monsters knocking on the door. They have been sent to bedevil me.

Next up are Jason and Jabed, hovering somewhere in age between eleven and juvenile hall. Jason and Jabed are the coming attractions for Nolan's adolescence. They specialize in noise and attitude. They have no manners. They

have no courtesy. They have no conception of considera-
tion for others.

My life was quiet and peaceful once. I work at home.
I take my time to think things out. I sit in my office and
think and write. I sit in my living room and read and listen to classical music; Bach, Vivaldi, occasionally a
Shostakovitch string quartet—nothing too strenuous. I
open all the doors and all the windows, and the cross
breeze keeps the house pleasant and sweet-smelling. I
would love to be able to do that again. Last year, I paid
six thousand dollars to install a 12,000 BTU air condi-
tioner on the roof so I could close all the doors and windows and still keep working. The noise from the fan
drowns out the softer strains of Debussy.

In the afternoon, they play touch football and baseball
across three lawns. Mine is in the middle. Even the judi-
cious planting of large amounts of purple Wandering Jew
has not deterred them. They leap over it . . . sometimes.
They scream, they shout, they claim the ball in midair.
"It's mine—mine!" Their voices are atonal and disso-
nant, precisely mistuned to jar with whatever music is on
the turntable.

In the evenings, they play basketball in the back yard.
I used to go to bed at eleven. But they play basketball until one in the ayem, shouting and jabbering. The basketball hoop is opposite my bedroom window. It serves as
the perfect acoustic focus aimed at my headboard. I am
not making this up. A specialist in theatrical sound systems came out to my house, took some measurements,
and ran them through the computer.

Jabed and Jason like to climb roofs, too. Last January,
they climbed up on the roof of the auto parts store behind
the alley, and plugged up its storm drains, just for the fun
of it. When the big rains came in February, the water pud-
dled on the roof. The weight of the water brought the
whole ceiling crashing in, causing over a half-million dollars worth of damage to the store. The police refused to
arrest the boys because of insufficient evidence. In Au-
gust, they were accused of stealing 120 dollars from a
neighbor's wallet and spent the night in juvenile hall. The

next day, they were swimming at the same neighbor's house. How do they get away with it? What magic are they working?

Then there's Vanessa. She's another sweetheart. I think she's eighteen. She takes care of the kids while Mom's at work. No, check that. She's *supposed* to take care of the kids while Mom's at work. What she does is have parties. One of her friends once took forty bucks from mom's purse—but Mom and Dad blamed every other child on the street for the theft, and when the truth came out, didn't bother to apologize.

I'm not the only one who feels this way. The neighbor on the other side of Hell House has developed an ulcer. The neighbors across the street have put their house up for sale. Half the parents on the block have forbidden their children to play with the demonic brood. This is validation. It's not me. It's *them*.

Mom and Dad. Lyn and Bryce. He's a former minister, she's a former cheerleader who never aspired to anything more than the right shade of blonde. She hasn't yet noticed that her tits are working their way south and her ass is spreading faster than the crabgrass on their lawn. I gave up on my lawn this year. There's no point in it while the crabgrass sod farm next door is so aggressive.

Their philosophy of childrearing is nonexistent. They daydream their way through life, drifting from one day to the next, oblivious to the fact that they are loathed by all of their neighbors. No, check that. They are loathed by all of the neighbors who live close enough to know who they are.

Oh—I almost skipped Damien. He's the one I like. He moved out and went to college four hundred miles away. We only see him on holidays. He has manners and courtesy and is obviously a changeling, not a real part of the family. He wants to major in art. Maybe he's gay. I hope so. I'd like to see the look on their faces when he comes home with a boyfriend. Idle fantasies of revenge are rapidly becoming an obsession over here.

I like to believe I'm smarter than they are; but I still haven't been able to plot the perfect crime—one that would allow me to chop their bones into fragments, burn their house down, and salt the earth into toxic uninhabitability, without anyone ever suspecting that I was the agent responsible. In some matters, anonymity is preferable to acknowledgment. Revenge is one of them.

It bothers me, because I am supposed to be a specialist in revenge. Writers, as a class, are the research-and-development team for the whole human race in the domain of revenge. We ennoble it, we glorify it; we earn our livings inventing wonderful and exotic ways to justify the delicious deed of puncturing the pompous who make our lives miserable. We create virtual daydreams for the masses in which the mighty are humiliated for their misdeeds of oppression against those who are still climbing the evolutionary ladder. It is our job to tend the flames of mythic vision, creating the cultural context in which the arrogant are accurately mirrored and drawn, so that all will know who they are. It is our job to prepare the ground so that the thieves of joy can be reduced to craven, whimpering, pitiful objects of scorn and abuse.

And . . . the fact that I remain unable to find a way to drive these people screaming from their house frustrates me beyond words, because it implies that I am not yet a master of my trade. If anyone should be able to envision a suitable revenge here, it should be me. Through a delightfully Machiavellian bit of timing, innuendo, and legal maneuvering, I once engineered the enforced exit off the Paramount lot of a particularly leechsome lawyer; studio security officers arrived with boxes, and physically escorted him off the premises—so abusing a few troublesome neighbors should be easy. Shouldn't it?

The problem is Grandma. Theirs, not mine. Grandma is a space-case. Not of this world. She exists in her own reality of hydrangeas and luncheons and Cadillacs. Life is pleasant, life is good, there are no problems. Let's all be nice to each other and everything will work out fine. She sees and hears only what she chooses to. Grandma owns the house and Mom and Dad and all the little Mansons live in it rent-free. They couldn't afford to live in this neighborhood otherwise. There is no way they're ever go-

ing to move out. Ever try to pull a tick off a dog?
Grandma is the problem—
   (narrative interrupted again)
—that one used up the rest of my evening. While I admit that it gave me no small amount of satisfaction to see
three police cars pulled up in front of *that* house, it did
not bring me any joy. I appreciate the validation, I do not
appreciate losing half a day of working time.

This time, Jason was chasing Damien with a knife,
threatening him. Damien socked him with a frying pan in
self-defense. Damien got arrested. He'll end up with a
charge of child abuse on his record. These people have a
way of getting *other* people in trouble, and coming out
unscathed themselves. It's a talent.

Part Two:
That was six months ago.
   The day after I wrote that, I ran into my friend, Sara
McNealy. Sara is a witch.
   I had stopped in at Dangerous Visions bookstore in
Sherman Oaks to deliver my monthly box of books that
I would rather not have in the house and to select a few
volumes in return that would enhance my bookshelves.
Given the fact that most publishers seem to have given up
the publication of real books in favor of the production of
commodity products, the task of reinvigorating the sleeping sense of wonder becomes harder and harder every
year. Nothing destroys a person's enjoyment of a subject
as fast as becoming obsessive about it. Never mind.
   Sara was standing at the counter, chatting with Lydia
Marano, the store owner. There were two other customers
in the back of the store, browsing through the nonreaders'
section, looking for the latest *Star Trek* novel.
   Sara doesn't look like a witch. She does not have flam-
ing red hair. She does not have green eyes. She does not
dress in flowing capes with unicorn embroidery.
   Sara is short, not quite dumpy but almost, and she has
little tight black curls framing her pie-shaped face. She is
given to flowery dresses and little round spectacles, that
look like windows into her dark gray eyes. She looks like

a yenta-in-training, but without the guilt attached. She is obscenely calm and unruffled.

Sara never talks about the goddess, she is not given to feminist rhetoric, and she rarely reads fiction. She created her own job, managing the computers for a major theatrical booking-chain. She is the first stop for technical support for a very small and very exclusive group of science-fiction, fantasy, and horror writers. She is equally conversant with nanotechnology, transhuman chickens, selfish genes, undisturbed universes, dancing Wu-Li masters, motorcycle maintenance (with or without the zen), virology (both human and silicon strains), paleontology, biblical history, and several mutant strains of Buddhist discourse. She can quote from Sun Tzu's *Art of War* as easily as from *The Watchmen*.

She does not cast spells herself. She works only as a consultant, serving as the midwife at the spellcasting sessions of others. She was telling Lydia, behind the counter, about her experiences breaking up a fannish coven, trying to grow hair on Patrick Stewart. "Finally, I just flat out told them, 'Witchcraft is potent stuff. Every spell you cast uses up part of your life force. If you assume that every spell you cast takes a year off your life expectancy, you don't do it casually. You save it for things that matter.' "

I looked up from the copy of *Locus* I was browsing through. They hadn't reviewed a book of mine in years— not since I'd requested that the reviewers read the books before writing about them. "Hey, Sara, didn't you say there were ways to rebuild your life force?"

"Oh, yes." She smiled sweetly as she said it. "Creativity. Haven't you ever noticed that a disproportionate share of conductors, writers, musicians, directors, et al, live well into their 90s? The act of creation is very powerful. When you bring something into existence out of nothing, it become a focus for energy. If you create positive energy, you get invigorated. If you create negative energy, you diminish yourself. You can't afford the luxury of nastiness."

"You're right, *I* can't—but what if you don't have a choice in the matter?"

"You *always* have a choice," she said.

"You don't know my next door neighbors."

She raised an eyebrow at me. A raised eyebrow from Sara McNealy is enough to curdle milk.

I refused to be intimidated. "My next door neighbors are destroying my life," I said. "They're noisy and intrusive. They've upset my whole life. My writing is suffering. And I can't afford to move."

Sara scratched her nose. "Negativism starts by blaming the other person. It's a way of avoiding personal responsibility."

"I'm not avoiding personal responsibility," I said. "I just don't know what to do."

"What result do you want to produce?" Sara asked.

"I want them to move away. Very far away."

She nodded. She was thinking. Lydia studied us both. Sara was turning over ideas in her mind. She said, "You could invite an evil spirit to move in with them. But that's dangerous. Sometimes the spirit decides it would rather move in with *you*."

"No, no spirits, thank you. Is there some other way?"

"Are you willing to pay the price—time off your life?"

"I'll earn it back with increased writing time. Won't I?"

Sara didn't answer that. At the same moment, we both noticed that there were suddenly other customers waiting— *and listening*. Sara put down the copy of *Chaos Theory* she had been browsing through and drew me carefully aside, leaving Lydia to ring up another large royalty for Stephen King.

"Listen to me," Sara said softly. "Witchcraft is a very specialized form of magic—you're trying to control the physical universe with experiential forces. That means that you need to create a specific context and appropriate symbology with which to control those forces. I prefer to do it with symbolic magic, rather than calling on spirits. Sometimes when no spirit responds to your call, new ones are created out of nothingness, and that can be extremely dangerous. Young spirits are . . . well, they're like kittens and puppies. They leave puddles."

"Can't I just animate the life force of their property or something?"

"It doesn't work that way." She frowned. "You're going to have to give me the whole story if you want me to advise you."

I took Sara by the arm and led her to the specialty coffee shop next door. She had hazelnut coffee with bay leaves. I had fruit tea. I can't stomach caffeine. I told her about the Partridge Family from hell; I didn't leave anything out. I even told her about Princess, the unfettered cocker spaniel who never missed a chance to run up onto my porch and bark *into* my house.

Sara listened intently to the whole story without comment. Her dark eyes looked sorrowful. I could understand why she was such a good witch. Most of it was good listening. When I finished, she said, "You have a great deal of negative energy bound up in these people. That's a very expensive burden you are carrying. It needs to be released." She made a decision. "I'll help you."

"How much will it cost?" I asked.

She shook her head. "Witches don't work for money. Prostitutes do. Witches take . . . *favors*."

"Okay, I'll read your manuscript," I said with real resignation.

"Sorry, I have no interest in writing a novel."

"Thank God."

"Don't worry," she said. "I don't want your soul. Writer's souls are usually very small anyway, and not good eating. Too much gristle." She reached over and patted my hand warmly. "We'll talk about your first-born later, all right?"

I assumed she was joking.

Part Three:

Sara showed up 7:00, carrying two shopping bags.

"Ahh," I said, thinking I was being funny. "Did you bring the right eye of a left-handed newt? The first menstrual blood of the seventh virginal daughter?"

"This is California," she said. "There are no virgins. I brought pasta, mushrooms, bell peppers, tomato sauce, olives, garlic bread, salad, and a bottle of wine. Let's eat first, then we'll plan. Did you get the Cherry Garcia like I asked?"

"Of course, I did." I took the bags from her. "But I really have to say I miss the old traditions of witchcraft."

"Do you want to dance naked around a bonfire at midnight?"

"Not particularly."

"Neither do I. Open the wine."

After dinner, we cleared the table and spread out our plans. "First of all," Sara said, "You have to decide what power you want to invoke. Who are you calling on to do the deed?" She handed me a printout. "You don't want to invoke the powers of Satan, whatever you do. Dealing with demons is also dangerous; for the most part, the demons are only facets of Satan anyway. You don't want to do anything that puts your immortal soul in danger. I'm just showing you this to give you some sense of what you're going to be dealing with.

"Lower down, you have the lesser spirits and the spirits of the dead. Also not recommended. Spirits usually have their own agendas. They're very hard to control, and almost never grant requests. Spirits are deranged."

I scanned the lists with very little interest, then passed her back the printout. "Let's stick to white magic, okay?"

'Right." She passed me another set of pages. "See, the thing is, you have to invoke *some* power to energize the spell. Otherwise, it's like a new Corvette, all shiny and beautiful, but without an engine it isn't going anywhere."

"Yeah, I just hate it when that happens."

She ignored my flippant interjection. "The problem with Western magic is that as a result of the pernicious influence of Christian theology, Westernized magic has anthropomorphized everything; we've given personalities to supernatural forces. It gives them *attitude*. It makes them impossible to deal with. But when we go back to the Eastern disciplines, we're operating in a whole other context. The truth is that the flows of paranormal influence are directly linked to the yin-yang flow of solidity and nothingness, of creation and destruction, of beingness

and nonbeing. Real magic happens when you align yourself with the flows of chaos and order. When you ride the
avalanche, you need only a nudge to steer it. If you want
to have a profound effect on the course of events in the
physical universe, without running the risk of a serious
causal backwash of energy, you have to create spells that
are in harmony with what the universe already wants to
do. From what you've been telling me, it seems to me
that the universe already *wants* to do something about
these people next door. All you need to do is give it a focus."

I wasn't sure I understood anything of what she said,
but I nodded as if I did.

Sara wasn't fooled. "Listen to me. Remember what I
said about negative energy? You can't afford it. You are
a fountain of creative power. You can't risk having your
spring contaminated. You have to act now before you are
permanently polluted. But whatever you do—you have to
make sure that you don't do *greater* harm to yourself."

"What are you recommending?" I asked. She sounded
so serious.

"Think of the peacock," she said.

"Pretty. Loud. Pretty loud." I free-associated.

"Do you know what a peacock eats?"

I shook my head.

"It eats the poisonous berries. It thrives on all the tox-
ics that other birds won't touch. And it turns them into
beautiful peacock feathers. That's the peacock—it takes
nastiness and turns it into beauty. That's your job. Find a
way to take all the stuff about your neighbors and turn it
into something useful and rewarding and enlightening."

"A nice bonfire is the first thing that comes to mind.
We could dance naked around it."

"It's time to stop being silly," Sara said. "You asked
for my help. That's why I'm here. What kind of spell do
you want to cast and what power do you want to invoke?"

"I want a spell that's quiet and unobtrusive. Inconspic-
uous. It shouldn't call attention to itself. No fireworks.
No explosions. No ectoplasm, no manifestations, no mys-

terious cold spots. Just something that makes them *go away.*"

"That's the best kind," Sara said.

I was looking at the list. "Let's invoke the power of the universe," I said.

"Huh?"

I pointed at the organization chart. "Look, all the power flows from the top. Let's go to the source. Let's call upon the universe to activate the spell."

Sara thought about it. "It might be overkill."

"There's no such thing as overkill," I said. "Dead is dead."

"How big an impact crater are you willing to live with?" she asked. "Remember, your house is well within the blast radius."

"We're going for gentleness, aren't we?"

"Gentleness is not delivered with a firehose," Sara said.

"Good point. We'll have to be careful."

"There could be side effects. You're probably going to get hit with some of them. Are you sure you want to do this?"

I nodded. A thought had been lurking at the back of my mind for three days. Ever since Sara had first begun coaching me. Now it was ready to blossom forth as a full-blown idea. I handed her my notes. 43 ideas. 42 of them had been crossed off. Only one remained.

Sara looked at it. She frowned. She narrowed her eyes. Her eyebrows squinched together. Her lips pursed. All of the separate parts of her face squinched up for a second, then relaxed, morphlike, into a big happy grin. "I think you may have a real talent in this area," she said.

She took her pen and double-underlined my note. *Love-bomb the bastards!*

Part Four:

At a quarter to midnight, we began. I went out to the backyard and flipped off every circuit breaker. There was no electrical power at all to the house. There would be no contaminating fields of magnetic resonance. The computers had all been unplugged. The batteries had been removed from every radio and flashlight.

Sara gave me a diagram, and I began to lay out a complex pattern of 39 votive candles. As I went around the room, lighting them, I recited a simple prayer of absolution. "May this light give me guidance. Help me align myself with the flows of universal power."

When I finished, I began unwinding a long yellow cord around the room, putting a loop around each candle as I strung a spiral pattern leading to an empty plate in the center. I sat down at the outside of the spiral and held the other end of the cord. I began winding it around the fingers of my left hand. The power would flow from my heart to the empty plate. And back again.

I looked to Sara. She nodded. I hadn't forgotten anything.

"Hello," I said.

I waited a moment. If the universe was listening, it hadn't given me any evidence. But then again, the universe never gives evidence of its involvement. It's just there—the ultimate in passive aggressive.

I took three deep breaths. I closed my eyes and took three more. I waited until I thought I could see the candle flames through my closed eyelids. Then I waited until I was certain we were no longer alone.

"Hello," I repeated. "Thank you. I apologize for any intrusion this action of mine might represent. I only wish to serve the flows of the universe, not to impede them. And I hope that the universe will let me be a part of its grander plans."

I waited. This time I got the feeling that some*thing* was waiting for me.

"My neighbors," I said. "The people who live in the house next door. Particularly Bryce, Lyn, Vanessa, Jabed, Jason, and Nolan. I believe that they have been impeding the natural rise toward godliness. Perhaps it is through no fault of their own. Perhaps it is because they have been seduced by the darker flows of nature. Perhaps there are reasons for which I have no language. Whatever forces are at work, I believe that they are at odds with the natural flow of universal power and goodness."

I glanced over at Sara. She was watching me intently. She nodded and smiled.

"I believe that somehow they have become separated from their own abilities to connect with others and feel compassion. I believe that they are unable to know the effects they have on the people around them. I believe that they do not see the pain they leave in their wake."

With my right hand, I placed a bowl on the empty plate in the center of the room. I poured red wine into the bowl, then I placed a single rose blossom in the wine. "I offer you this gift," I said. "I do so freely and with no thought of personal reward or gain. I ask nothing for myself, nor for anyone close to me. I ask only that you grant my neighbors an opportunity to join our larger purposes, to swim in the flow of universal spirit that heads inevitably toward enlightenment. Please help direct their energies toward goodness and joy."

I bowed my head. "Thank you," I said. "Thank you for listening. Thank you for being here. Thank you for letting me serve you tonight."

And—maybe it was the sudden breeze from the door—but every single candle in the room went out simultaneously.

"Nicely done," said Sara, after a long startled silence. "*Very* nicely done."

Epilogue:
The next morning, I felt rather silly for having gone through such a baroque ritual. But I made up my mind to wait a week. Or two. Or even six.

Nothing happened at first.

Then, one horrible weekend, *everything* happened. Lyn and Bryce were out somewhere. Vanessa had invited five hundred close friends to a backyard bash, with 600 decibels of heavy metal rock music and illegal fireworks. Jabed and Jason were sitting on the roof of the garage throwing cherry bombs into the dancers, which triggered a spate of angry gunfire between members of two rival gangs who were try-

ing to crash the party from the alley side of the yard. In the
ensuing panic, several automobiles were smashed into each
other as people tried to flee—a dead-end street does not lend
itself to an orderly evacuation. In the confusion, Nolan found
the box of fireworks and managed to light both them *and
the house* on fire. By the time the police and fire department
arrived, the structure was sending fifty-foot flames into the
air and I was hosing down my roof and praying that the
overhanging tree wouldn't catch. The fire crew couldn't get
through the mass of cars to the fire hydrant, and even if they
could have, it wouldn't have done any good because someone had crashed into it, knocking it off, sending a high-
pressure fountain spraying high into the air where it made an
impressive, but otherwise useless, display of uncontained
aquatic energy. They ended up taking one of the units
around to the alley side and backing it into my backyard so
they could pump the water out of my pool and onto the
neighbor's roof. It took them twenty minutes to knock down
the blaze, leaving the house a charred and waterlogged mess.
By the time they were through, there were over twenty police vehicles on the block, three ambulances, and four news
vans.

In the aftermath, four stolen cars were recovered from
joy-riding gang-bangers, seventeen people were arrested for
possession and dealing of illegal substances, twelve illegal
weapons were confiscated, and twenty-six of the party-goers
spent the night in jail for being drunk and disorderly. Fourteen outstanding warrants were served for offenses as varied
as unpaid parking tickets and felony armed robbery. Vanessa's friends were an assorted lot.

The following Monday, Lyn and Bryce were investi-
gated by the Department of Social Services.

And I called Sara and asked what went wrong.

She told me not to worry. Everything was fine. Just be
patient.

She was right. It took a while for everything to get
sorted out, but eventually, it did.

The judge ordered three years of family counseling for
the whole clan. Vanessa was put on probation, conditional
on her remaining in Alcoholics Anonymous. Jabed and

Jason were put into a special education program to help them recover from prolongued emotional abuse and also to prevent them from drifting into patterns of juvenile delinquency. Nolan was identified as suffering from a serious learning disability and is now in full-time therapy. Tali is in preschool. Damien is president of the local Gay Students' Union chapter. Grandma had to sell the house to help Lynn and Bryce cover the legal expenses. They all live with her now.

The insurance company leveled the remains of the house and sold the land to the city for use as a pocket park. It wasn't cost effective to rebuild.

To paraphrase my favorite moose, sometimes I don't know my own strength.

For a while, both Sara and I were concerned about the backwash from the spell. We'd love-bombed the entire family, and they were all definitely much better off than they had been before. But Sara was afraid that there would be serious side effects to the spell that might affect both of us. If there have been any, we haven't noticed them yet. But then again, we've been much too busy. Sara's planning to move in with me next month, and I've applied to adopt a little boy. And I expect to get back to my writing Real Soon Now.

Tanya Huff

VICTORY NELSON, INVESTIGATOR:
Otherworldly Crimes A Specialty

☐ **BLOOD PRICE: Book 1**   UE2471—$4.99
Can one ex-policewoman and a vampire defeat the magic-spawned evil which is devastating Toronto?

☐ **BLOOD TRAIL: Book 2**   UE2502—$4.50
Someone was out to exterminate Canada's most endangered species— the werewolf.

☐ **BLOOD LINES: Book 3**   UE2530—$4.99
Long-imprisoned by the magic of Egypt's gods, an ancient force of evil is about to be loosed on an unsuspecting Toronto.

☐ **BLOOD PACT: Book 4**   UE2582—$4.99
Someone was determined to learn the secret of life after death and they were about to make Vicki Nelson's mother part of the experiment!

THE NOVELS OF CRYSTAL

When an evil wizard attempts world domination, the Elder Gods must intervene!

☐ **CHILD OF THE GROVE: Book 1**   UE2432—$4.50
☐ **THE LAST WIZARD: Book 2**   UE2331—$3.95

OTHER NOVELS

☐ **GATE OF DARKNESS, CIRCLE OF LIGHT**   UE2386—$4.50
On Midsummer's Night the world balance would shift—but would it be toward Darkness or the Light?

☐ **THE FIRE'S STONE**   UE2445—$3.95
Thief, swordsman and wizardess—drawn together by a quest not of their own choosing, would they find their true destinies in a fight against spells, swords and betrayal?

Mercedes Lackey

The Novels of Valdemar